COCHABAMBA
CONSPIRACY

Callahan Family Saga
Book 1

Brinn Colenda

Southern Yellow Pine
Publishing

Published by:
Southern Yellow Pine (SYP) Publishing
4351 Natural Bridge Rd.
Tallahassee, FL 32305

www.syppublishing.com

This is a work of fiction. Names, characters, places, and events that occur either are the products of the author's imagination or are used fictitiously. Any resemblance to actual persons, places, or events is purely coincidental.

The contents and opinions expressed in this book do not necessarily reflect the views and opinions of Southern Yellow Pine Publishing, nor does the mention of brands or trade names constitute endorsement.

ISBN-13: 978-1-59616-057-6
ISBN-13: ePub 978-1-59616-058-3
ISBN-13: Adobe PDF eBook 978-1-59616-059-0
Library of Congress Control Number: 2017961090

Printed in the United States of America
First SYP Publishing Edition
November 2017

To Linda and Jacob

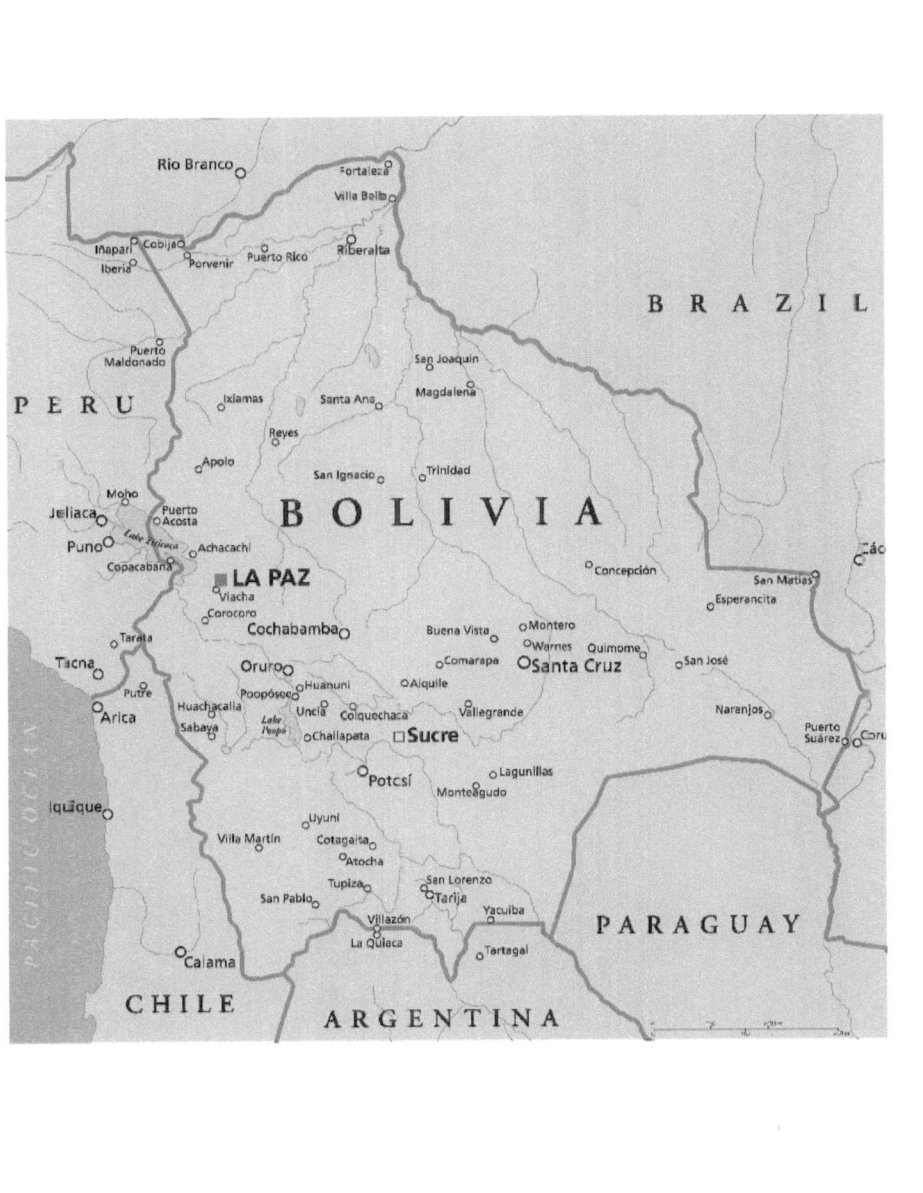

Prologue

Godhra, India, 1995

The deaths began on the ninetieth day. They were gruesome, messy, and necessary. Ninety days of over one hundred degrees. Soaring temperatures burned off the clouds, leaving bright blue skies and a heartless sun. Torrents of rats fled the parched fields for the cities. With them came their fleas. With the fleas came the bacteria, *Yersinia pestis*. The plague.

Dr. Nikolai Yazov drove through the panicked crowds, leaning on his horn. He dodged yet another loudspeaker van vainly exhorting people to stay inside and remain calm. The roads from the city were swollen arteries, sluicing the living away from the dead and dying.

At the barricades surrounding the city's main hospital, Yazov—a large, pale-skinned, fifty-two-year old—parked, then pushed through the mob that jammed the hospital doors. He flashed his identification badge and impatiently brushed aside the Indian policemen.

Inside, he was assaulted by the smell of harsh disinfectants. He tied on a surgical mask as he followed the arrows on the wall to the main administrative offices. The fresh paint and gleaming tile shouted Ministry of Health showplace. All the better. Three minutes later, a distraught senior Ministry official rushed up.

"Dr. Yazov! Thank you for coming." The Indian offered a latex-gloved hand, then snatched it back, bowing nervously instead.

Yazov smirked behind his mask and nodded. Nothing like a virulent epidemic to make the locals embrace Russian assistance.

"The patients are this way."

Yazov observed the chaos as he pulled on a gown and gloves. Medical people scurried everywhere. The Ministry doctor looked terrified. So did the nurses. No backwoods bumpkins these, but medical professionals overwhelmed by the viciousness of this disease.

Stacks of lab reports teetered on the desks of the central administration area. He knew what they said. He had spent four years of his life developing this particular strain. As First Deputy Director of *Biopreparat*, the ultra-secret Russian biological warfare agency, Yazov had supervised hordes of scientists working on biological weapons. During the twentieth century, over twelve million people had died of plague on the Indian subcontinent. Yazov attributed nearly one hundred thousand of those deaths directly to his strain. The people here served as his test subjects, sophisticated laboratory rats.

Yazov entered an open bay ward, trailed closely now by three Indian doctors. The first patient was semiconscious, his face a mass of blotches like an obscene case of acne. His chest rose and fell heavily and, despite the morphine drip, he moaned with pain.

A nurse handed Yazov the chart: pustules, headaches, nausea, exhaustion, fever, cramping. He flipped back several pages. Tetracycline, the drug of record for plague, the best drug they had, wasn't working. He knew it wouldn't. Yazov had genetically engineered this plague to both resist tetracycline and burn hot. The trick was to get it hot enough so that it ran its course rapidly, quickly killing its host, thus limiting its spread. This grotesque-looking life form before him had been a normal, healthy human being only four hours ago—and should be dead just hours from now.

With his escorts, he marched from ward to ward and reviewed case after case. The top four floors of the hospital contained only the patients with the new strain of plague—the strain the Ministry of Health officials vehemently denied existed in the country. He saw India as a country posturing as a modern, technology-based nation with a thriving modern middle class, instead of the overpopulated, backward cesspool that it was. Ordinary plague scares were bad enough to deter foreign investment. A resistant and more deadly plague was something this government simply could not admit to the world.

Yazov's engineered outbreaks had caused India to turn to Russia for covert medical help just as it had done with the old Soviet Union for its secret nuclear weapons program. It was his job to control the new plague while the Indians dealt with the "normal" plague epidemic.

Several members of his Russian research team, each one hand-picked, met him on the top floor. Yazov watched with approval as they moved through the wards, carefully taking blood samples—very carefully—samples that would not make it to the laboratories of the Indian health authorities but would be on the next flight to Moscow.

The Ministry doctor accompanied Yazov downstairs for decontamination. "What now?" His thin voice grated on Yazov.

Yazov bit back an impatient answer. "I have considerable faith in your judgment, Doctor. Your people are doing superhuman work. The rate of admissions has diminished. In my opinion, this outbreak will end quickly, just as the other sub-strain did two years ago. Continue to burn everything, including—no, especially—the bodies."

The Indian nodded. "It will be so."

***

Yazov left for his own lab on the far side of the city. The goal was near: a bioweapon to return Russia to its rightful place of dominance. Soon, Yazov's allies in the Duma would either be able to muster the votes to get rid of that drunkard Yeltsin, or manage another lead-induced "heart attack" for which Russia was so famous. Then they'd replace him with someone who had the courage, the *khrabrost*, to actually use this research. Yazov thought ahead to even more powerful weapons. The most exciting possibility was the Machupo virus recently discovered in Bolivia. It caused a particularly virulent hemorrhagic fever that seemed to melt the victim's organs. He had ten times more people working on it than the Americans, a 1990s version of the space race, a race that Russia would win.

Yazov knew that time was running out. Unless his political cronies succeeded, the glory days of Russian science were about to come to a dead halt. Gorbachev and Yeltsin had already gutted the military. Soldiers and sailors roamed the streets hungry, uniforms in tatters, unpaid, often forced to sell military equipment to survive. Downsizing the Biopreparat was their next target. Rumors had percolated throughout the Russian scientific community for months now; the newly elected, democratic politicians planned to sacrifice his programs to the Americans for trade credits and political points. In the USSR, a supposedly classless society, scientists had held remarkably high status: the best food—after the Politburo, of course—trips abroad, good schools for the children, spacious housing. The largesse had continued even after The Fall. Yazov still had his dacha in the forest outside Moscow. But now the future was clearly in the hands of the politicians and, sadly, Nikolai Yazov was no politician.

He parked and entered the wooden warehouse on the outskirts of the city. Technicians in clean white coats tended the small cages that lined the wall by his desk. Immediately the smell of dung and disinfectants enveloped him—laboratory animals mixed with medicines—like a pet store in a hospital. He loved the irony. He hurried to his desk and picked up a sheaf of messages.

"Dr. Yazov?"

Annoyed, Yazov looked up from his papers and half-turned in the direction of the speaker, a short, overweight man in the wrinkled suit of a Russian bureaucrat. Yazov vaguely remembered him as the Russian consul. His companion was taller, an arrogant-looking man whose appearance shouted KGB, or whatever it was calling itself these days. Undoubtedly a colonel. Nobody of consequence. He turned back to his work.

"Dr. Yazov, we're from the embassy. You are ordered back to Moscow, sir."

"Go away. Can't you see I'm busy? I am working on a project directed by the Politburo."

"Those orders are rescinded. Colonel Godunov will escort you home."

Yazov looked into Godunov's smirking face. This was no ordinary recall to Moscow.

The colonel straightened up, tugged on his tunic to erase an imaginary wrinkle, then took Yazov's arm. "Come along," he ordered. "We have airline reservations for you."

Yazov yanked his arm away and reached into a cage. He spun around toward Godunov, thrusting a squealing, wriggling rat into his startled face.

"Don't you touch me, you arrogant bastard!" He maneuvered the frightened colonel into the corner. "How would you like to get to know my little friend here? In no time, you'll be leaking fluids from every opening in your puffy little body."

He stepped back, a crooked smile on his face, and allowed the colonel to escape.

"Come back tomorrow evening. I'll go with you then."

Godunov shot Yazov a look of hatred as only a KGB colonel could do as the two men stalked out.

Yazov laughed out loud. It wasn't every day he could terrorize a KGB asshole by waving around a rat. He walked to his office, settled into his chair and tried to think. Now he couldn't go back to Russia, tomorrow or ever. He was a communist and a scientist in a country that no longer valued either.

But where to go? The choices were limited for offensive biological weapons scientists. Back to Iraq? Saddam Hussein had a sizeable bioweapons program, one that Yazov had helped launch. But Saddam's nerve failed and the damned Americans bombed Iraq, the cradle of civilization, back a hundred years.

No, Iraq was out. Despite the scientific opportunities, he simply did not like the place. Besides, he couldn't function under the pervasive eye of the secret police, *Al Mukharabat*.

North Korea? He shuddered. No chance.

Work for the Americans? Yazov cursed. He would rather die. He'd never defect.

One socialist country had a decent, even world class, biomedical industry—Cuba. Was leaving one socialist country for another really a defection? He paused as he considered his question, then smiled.

Yes. The Cubans could use him. They would be delighted to have someone of his stature, especially since the Soviet Union, and now Russia had left Cuba to its own fate. Fidel would welcome him. Fidel would love to stick his cigar in the eyes of both the Americans and the Russians. And Yazov had always preferred rum to vodka.

Chapter One

442 Tactical Fighter Wing, Luke Air Force Base, Arizona
Three years later

Lieutenant Colonel Thomas Callahan, Operations Officer, 442nd Fighter Squadron, sauntered into the squadron command section, still mildly euphoric from leading a training mission in the McDonnell Douglas F-15C Eagle through the hot and stormy skies over Arizona. His sweaty flight suit clung to his lithe body, causing him to fidget as he stood looking over the messages stacked neatly in his desk in-basket. Amazing how much paperwork was involved in keeping the planes flying. It sometimes seemed to Tom that only when the required paperwork exceeded the takeoff weight of the aircraft would a flight occur.

"Excuse me, Colonel Callahan."

Tom looked up into the round, smiling brown face of Senior Master Sergeant Mario Torrez, his chief of administration.

"Mario, what are you doing here? Did you find a house already?"

"No sir, I—"

"Damn it, Mario," Tom said. "Do I have to remind you that your house just burned down? Get out of here and find a place to live! Take care of your family! Do I have to make that an order?"

"Easy there, Colonel." Torrez raised his hands in surrender. "I just stopped in to show the guys a coupla things. I'm outta here now. My wife and I are gonna meet with a real estate agent this afternoon, a retired master sergeant I used to work with." He pointed to the phone. "Right now there's a Lieutenant General Walters on the horn."

Torrez waved goodbye as Tom settled back into his leather chair, plunked his feet on his desktop, and picked up the phone. "Yes, sir, I am standing at attention."

Walters laughed. "And it's a good thing too, mister. How you doing, kiddo?"

"Still slipping the surly bonds of earth in the Eagle, Uncle Harvey, and loving life."

"Boy, you really know how to rub it in—here I sit, strapped to a desk in the Pentagon." Walters sighed. "How's Colleen?"

"Great, sir." Tom absently unzipped a pocket and dug out the Saint Christopher medal he always carried in flight. Since he insisted on driving expensive sports cars too fast and expensive aircraft immeasurably faster, Colleen had asked that he always carry the medal. Like the altar boy he once was, he kissed it and slipped it back into his pocket. Life was sweet. "Colleen's passed all her exams and only has to finish her dissertation. She loves it here. You know, Uncle Harvey, you really need to get out here and fly with me."

Walters sighed again somewhat more heavily and cleared his throat. "Tom, what do you know about Bolivia?"

"I know that it's where Butch Cassidy and the Sundance Kid got killed."

"You must know more than that, son," Walters said. "Right now the President thinks South America is vital to American interests. Congress and the Secretary of Defense are all in a lather to make something substantial happen in Bolivia—like right now. So of course, the USAF guy we had in the Military Group in the embassy in La Paz screwed things up so bad it'll take a genius to straighten it out. The Ambassador fired him yesterday."

Uh-oh. This was not sounding good.

"Despite the fact that the Bolivian Air Force commander is as pro-American and competent as you'll find in South America," Walters continued, "our program is basically dead in the water. We need an exceptional Spanish-speaking lieutenant colonel pilot to be Chief of the Air Force Section in the Military Group to get things up and running properly."

Tom swallowed. "Well, sir, I feel confident that the boys and girls at the Military Personnel Center can find you dozens of likely candidates."

"That's simply not so, Tom. I had MPC run a computer check to find our man. There aren't that many qualified people and only one really good choice."

"Uncle Harvey." Tom hesitated. "Why are you telling me this?"

"Let's just say I was hoping that I could get a certain multi-lingual lieutenant colonel with two MIG kills in the Gulf War to step forward."

"Sir, with respect, I say again. I am a fighter pilot, not a paper pusher."

"Don't give me that, Colonel. You are a brilliant officer, just like your father. Earning flag rank involves a lot more than just flying jets. And you know that."

Tom cursed to himself but said nothing. He glanced at the precisely notated calendar on his immaculately arranged desk—only three more months until he assumed command of his own F-15 squadron.

Walters snapped, "I take it you're not going to make this easy, young man."

Tom clenched his teeth. Walters was not just any general. He was a former wingman for Tom's father, Brigadier General Sean Callahan. After the senior Callahan was shot down in Vietnam, leaving Tom's mother with four children, an estate valued at three and a half million dollars, and a hole in her life that she would never fill, Walters had acted as Tom's surrogate father.

"Sir, it depends on who is talking to whom," said Tom. "If it is Uncle Harvey speaking to his godson, my answer is 'Bolivia? Me? No way.' I'm a fighter pilot, not a diplomat. And I desperately hope this is one of your practical jokes."

Tom closed his eyes. His carefully constructed world could explode here: his squadron command, Colleen's doctorate, the long-planned-for baby. He drew a deep breath. "If it is Lieutenant General Walters speaking to Lieutenant Colonel Callahan, my answer is, 'When do I report for duty in Bolivia, sir?'"

"Tom, if it makes you feel better, this comes straight from the Chief of Staff. The Ambassador's pissed. The State Department's pissed. And now the SecDef is pissed. We've simply got to have you. This selection is going to be scrutinized by every asshole in the State Department." He paused. "And that's a lot of assholes!"

"For one guy to 'Oblivia'?"

"If it weren't that important, Tom, I wouldn't be taking away your command. Your combat record and Silver Star medal will play big in Bolivia. We have you scheduled for a couple of short orientation courses and a quickie check-out in the Beechcraft C-12. At least you'll fly some down there. I'll email you the details in a message later today...."

Damn! Colleen was going to freak.

"...Probably twelve months, accompanied if you want," finished Walters.

"You mean, accompanied if I can convince Colleen to drop her studies."

"Look, Tom—"

Tom's stomach knotted up. "Don't worry, General, I'm your guy."

"Good man," said Walters. "Just talk with Colleen, son. She'll come around." The phone clicked dead.

Staring into the now-dead receiver, Tom fought the urge to throw the damn thing at the wall. But thoughts of his derailed career vanished as he considered the coming confrontation with his wife. A spasm of pain lanced through him. After three years of searching, they'd finally found a fertility specialist here in Arizona who had offered them some hope of having a child. Damn.

Might as well know something about the damn place before talking with Colleen. He logged onto the Internet and ran a search on Bolivia— sixty-two thousand, eight hundred ninety-four results. The first entry was a travel writer who called Bolivia "the Tibet of the Americas, the highest and most isolated of the Latin American republics." Terrific!

Forty-five minutes later, having read through the major articles, Tom figured he'd better head down to the university, find Colleen, and get it over with. He'd rather have an appointment with a proctologist.

He maneuvered his red 1960 Jaguar XKE roadster in and out of the afternoon traffic winding southeast from Luke into Tempe. The wind flattened his hair as he worked the gearbox up and down, cursing

Walters, the Air Force, and his own overwhelming sense of duty. He darted smoothly around cars as he blasted into the city. *Whoa!* Tom cursed at himself. No point in adding to your collection of speeding tickets just because that famous Irish temper's loose again.

He wheeled into a parking space across from the entrance to Arizona State University where he expected to find Colleen. He spied her long blonde hair as she sat on her favorite park bench, engrossed, as usual, in a textbook.

Colleen looked up as he approached, her smile radiant. "Hi, Sweetheart," he said. "Surprise!"

She rose. An inch taller than her husband, the statuesque Colleen looked more like the Australian surfer girl and model that she had once been than the university economics professor that she aspired to be. "Hello, luv." She paused as she sized him up and a frown furrowed her flawless skin. "What's up, flyboy? Why aren't you at the squadron?"

They sat and Tom took a deep breath. "Harvey Walters called this afternoon. The Air Force is sending me to Bolivia for a year."

Colleen blanched. "What are you talking about? Why you?"

"Apparently the guy they had there screwed things up and they need me to unscrew them."

"Tommy, you're a brilliant officer, possibly the best fighter pilot in the Air Force. What are they thinking? It's appalling! Not rational."

Tom forced a smile. "Colleen, you're talking like an economist."

"I am an economist, Tom. We seek to allocate resources efficiently, something the Air Force apparently needs to work on." She shook her head. "When?"

"ASAP. Harvey says next week."

"Next week! And your squadron command? Tommy, you've waited all your life for that."

He shrugged. "Orders, Colleen. I get paid to obey them."

Colleen waved him silent. "We were supposed to be here for another two years. What are our chances of having a baby if we leave?" She pounded her knees. "I'm so bloody angry, I could spit."

She jumped to her feet and paced in front of the bench. Tom's heart sank.

10

Colleen glanced down at her watch. "Look, I can't talk about this now. I have a seminar to teach in fifteen minutes. Why don't you go over to the aikido dojo and work out with some of the lads. I'll meet you there after class."

"You're the one who needs to let off some steam, Colleen." He smiled. "Don't take this out on your graduate students."

"I'd be doing them a favor. If they plan on becoming economists, they need to develop thick skins."

Two hours later, Tom leaned against his Jaguar in the dimly lit parking lot outside the aikido dojo. The workout had failed to calm him. His muscles tensed as he watched Colleen drive up and skid to a halt in front of him.

He winced as she slammed the car door and stalked up the sidewalk. She stood facing him, hands on hips. "Tommy, what about the baby?"

A nervous cough rasped through the air. Tom looked to his left and saw three stocky, unkempt men standing in the dim light in front of them.

"Excuse me, folks," said the one in the middle, stocky man, mid-forties with yellowed teeth. "I hate to interrupt a tender moment, but we just rolled into town." He gestured at three large motorcycles parked at the curb. "Could you tell us if there's a good cafe nearby?"

"Sure," said Tom, relieved at the interruption. He pointed south. "Down this road about six blocks on the right. A place called Reno's. It's pretty casual. Serves good Mexican food."

The man's face broke into a crooked smile. "Thanks." Then he added sheepishly, "Look, we're tapped out. Could you front us some cash?"

Tom pulled a gold money clip from a pocket and peeled off a twenty-dollar bill. "Here," he said, "take this and have a good meal."

"Thanks, pal," the leader said, showing his yellow teeth. "We will." He paused. A crafty look came over his face. "On second thought, perhaps not just yet." He whipped out a huge Bowie knife from behind his back. "I think we'll just take the rest of that cash—and your wallet too."

Tom stared at the knife then back at Yellow Teeth. "Aren't we being a bit melodramatic? I mean, Bowie knives went out of fashion long ago."

"Don't get smart with me, asshole." He gestured with the knife. "We're taking your money." Yellow Teeth's ugly face broke into a gap-toothed grin. "Not to mention your lovely lady friend."

Tom smiled and made no move to comply. "The last guy that went after my wife with a knife ended up in the hospital."

"Oh, yeah. Now you're a tough guy. Get the bitch, Charlie!"

Charlie lunged for Colleen. She stepped right and caught the man in the ribs with a slashing kick. He fell to his knees clutching his side. Two lightning punches smashed his nose and split his lips. Blood spurted. He fell back onto the ground, covered his face and shrieked.

Tom grabbed Yellow Teeth's wrist and snapped him to the ground. With his foot in the man's armpit, Tom torqued the arm. Tendons and muscles stretched and ripped. Yellow Teeth screamed and dropped the knife. Tom pressed his foot and swiveled the arm, grinding the joint again for good measure. More screams. He locked eyes with assailant number three. "You thinking about joining in the fun, scumball? You want my wife to kick your ass too?"

Yellow Teeth screamed again. Number three stepped back, held up his hands and shook his head.

"Then get out of here while you can. Now!"

Tom watched the men stumble away to their bikes. Tom turned to Colleen. "Well done, Sweetheart! I guess I should have mentioned that it was you who put that last guy in the hospital."

She smiled and bowed. "Thank you, sensei. Again." She stroked his cheek. "Looks like I'm going to have to go to Bolivia with you, Tommy. Who'll take care of you if I'm not there to protect you?"

Colleen slid into his arms and hugged him close. "I remember when you left for Iraq. I can't bear to be apart again. We'll just have to keep trying for the baby the old-fashioned way."

He wanted to shout. Perhaps this wasn't the disaster it seemed. And just maybe they had solved Mario Torrez' housing problem.

Chapter Two

Wallerein Compound Outside Tripoli, Libya

"*Verdamnt!*" Kurt Wallerein cursed as he stepped out of the darkness into the hot afternoon wind. He hated the dry air and the smells of the desert, so unlike the cool, wet sea breeze of his childhood in Hamburg. He blinked and cursed again as the bright sunlight slammed into his watery blue eyes. He was accustomed to the dim indirect lighting of his underground bunker where he had spent the majority of the previous five years.

Hernando Cortez, the Cuban Ambassador-at-Large, sat at a table under the swaying palms, arranging and re-arranging bottles of dark Cuban rum, probably a gift from Fidel himself. Cortez had been educated at the Patrice Lumumba University in Moscow, according to his dossier, which meant he had been fully indoctrinated in socialist theory. Wallerein smiled, having penned many of the writings in the curriculum.

The Cuban ambassador stood as Wallerein approached. With a wave of his well-manicured hand, Wallerein motioned the younger man back into his chair, sat and waited for Cortez to begin.

"*Señor*, I bring you greetings and warmest regards from *El Presidente*," said Cortez in flawless English. "He thanks you for agreeing to this meeting and hopes that you are well and in good spirits." Cortez smiled, revealing his perfect teeth. "Fidel extends to you an invitation to be his guest in Cuba. He would like to discuss recent events in the socialist world. He sees opportunities in the former eastern bloc and would like to hear your opinions."

He would, indeed, Wallerein thought, carefully concealing his elation. He must be correct, calm, the total professional. He was, after all, Kurt Wallerein; feared, hated, and hunted by every intelligence and law-enforcement organization in the West.

A large armed guard popped out of the door to the bunker and peered around the yard, squinting against the sun. Spotting Wallerein, he trotted over and saluted.

"Comrade Wallerein, it is time."

Wallerein motioned Cortez to follow as the guard led them towards the doorway to the marble foyer. Another bulky, heavily armed guard stood at attention.

The guard punched a code into the control box. The whitewashed wall behind him opened with a quiet whoosh to reveal a small elevator that silently eased them down into a long, cold hallway. Dim lights cast long shadows on stark concrete walls utterly devoid of decoration or even paint. Along the hall were openings for several offices and one conference room, all jammed with computers and cluttered, over-sized desks.

In the large room at the end of the hall, a cold light emanated from a bank of massive television screens along one wall, showing broadcasts from major international cities. Placards under each screen proclaimed: London; Berlin; Washington; Cairo; Moscow; Tokyo; Paris. The dim light revealed the forms of a half-dozen men, all armed with pistols, manning Wallerein's command bunker, a gift from his Libyan benefactor, Colonel Gaddafi. The bunker was also filled with sophisticated high-tech computers and encrypted communications gear that Wallerein needed to direct his network of operatives in their assassinations, kidnappings, bombings, and hijackings. Wallerein manipulated events and controlled operations while protected by the sympathetic Libyan government.

The large screen directly in front showed a BBC film clip of the Wailing Wall in Jerusalem, interspersed with pictures of Palestinian Arabs and Israelis throwing rocks, shooting, and rioting in the streets.

Wallerein noticed Cortez' inquiring glance. Nodding, he said, "*Ja,* here we can track results of our operatives as well as collect real-time intelligence, gathered for us by our friends in the international media."

14

The monitor labeled "Washington" flashed with the CNN logo. Wallerein motioned and a technician transferred the image to a much larger screen on the far wall. The familiar sunburned face of the CNN Middle East expert appeared.

"Just last month, the Bi-Lateral Council of Jerusalem, an interim government made up of officials from Palestinian Arab and Israeli communities, was inaugurated here. Designed to bring peace to Jerusalem by internationalizing the government of the city where the rights of both Arab and Jews would be protected equally, the creation of the Council was met with much fanfare and hope. And much opposition from extremists on both sides."

Photos of six officials appeared on the screen. All were middle aged or older; one man was in traditional Arab robes, another was a rabbi with a long beard and earlocks, two were females.

"Three days ago, all six of these courageous officials were kidnapped in one of the most outrageous criminal actions in a land that has endured more than its share of crimes. The kidnapping has led to widespread rioting and looting. Dozens of people have been killed and hundreds hospitalized as Palestinian youths battle with Israeli army patrols and Palestinian police."

The image cut away to a view of more troops firing tear gas and rubber bullets as they battled a crowd that threatened to overrun the streets.

The correspondent continued, "Israeli government officials deny that the kidnappings are part of a larger effort to destroy the latest peace initiative in the Middle East. As evidence, they offer the fact that the kidnappers immediately demanded an undisclosed ransom. The families of the captured officials have issued pleas for the group or groups holding the hostages to show mercy. Unconfirmed reports indicate that the families are talking with the kidnappers. Officials from the Israeli government are quick to deny those reports because it is official government policy not to negotiate with terrorists. Nevertheless, the families are in seclusion, and our sources indicate on-going negotiations."

The light on one of the consoles flashed. A technician offered the phone to Wallerein who held it for a moment. "Turn off the sound and put this call on the speaker." The tech pushed a button, and the CNN announcer went mute.

"Comrade, the ransom demands have been met. We have the money. Our people are clear." A muted cheer broke out from the bunker's staff.

Wallerein acknowledged the cheers with a small bow then waved them into silence. He spoke into the phone. "Excellent work. Kill the hostages and get out according to plan."

"Kill them?" asked Cortez. "But I thought you said the families had paid?"

Wallerein allowed himself a smile. "Don't let sentiment cloud your judgment, comrade." He raised his voice. "Shoot them now! Make the rabbi die slowly."

Shots rang out from the speaker. Wallerein counted them: one, two, three, four, five. Then a pause. One more and a scream. Another. More screams. Then another and silence.

"It is done, comrade," said the speaker.

Wallerein glanced at Cortez, who was wiping his face with his hankerchief. "Never forget, these people were our enemies, working to accommodate the Zionists. They are counterrevolutionaries, interrupting the inevitability of socialism."

He ran his fingers through his blond hair, now streaked with gray, as he regarded the smaller man. Cortez was a leader of the young generation of socialist leaders emerging in Cuba, a member of the new socialist aristocracy, technocrats who made speeches and wrote reports but had never pulled a trigger.

"When I was with the Red Brigades, my first operation was the taking of a fat German banker, a friend of the corrupt government in Bonn and an enemy of the people. His bank paid over a million marks for his release. I shot him myself and threw his body in a sewer." His smile broadened. "He was my uncle."

VIP lounge, El Alto Airport,
La Paz, Bolivia
Six weeks later

Tom Callahan felt as if someone had sucked all of the air out of his lungs. He knew this often happened to flatlanders upon arrival in La Paz. El Alto, at 13,313 feet, was the highest international airport in the world. Yet he was still unprepared for the effects of the altitude. Tom looked anxiously at his wife, slumped next to him on the couch. Colleen gave him a wan smile.

"Here, drink this," said the embassy staffer. "It'll fix you up in no time." Neither of the Callahans resisted the cups of steaming, pale yellow liquid.

"What was that?" Tom asked after he drained his cup.

"Coca tea."

"What?" said Tom, his empty cup clattering on the table. "You gave me coca tea?"

"Relax," she said, laughing. "People in the embassy drink it all the time. Even gave some to George Schultz when he was visiting here as Secretary of State. It's great for *soroche*, the high-altitude sickness that you have and stomach aches, headaches. Whatever." She laughed again. "Yes, it's made from the same coca leaves that produce cocaine, but the tea doesn't have the narcotic alkaloids so it won't cause you to test positive."

Well, maybe. Tom bent over with nausea and the most incredible splitting headache. Okay, so he was paranoid about his health. As was every military pilot. He declined a second cup.

Commander Matthew Schmidt, U.S. Navy, and his dark-eyed wife, Olga, entered the small room. "How are our visiting dignitaries feeling now?" he asked. "They've been plying you with *mate de coca*? Good. Normally I bring a thermos to the airport. Never can tell when somebody's going to keel over from the altitude."

Olga patted Tom on the shoulder. Her husband, a tall, red-haired man with friendly eyes produced two black diplomatic passports. "I managed to convince Bolivian immigration and customs that they should accept these. Here you are, all stamped and official. You are now fully accredited members of the U.S. Embassy in Bolivia."

Tom reached for the passports. He already liked Schmidt, sensing a kindred warrior under the easygoing exterior. "Thanks, Matt."

"Oh no, Tom, it's I who should be thanking you. I'm tickled pink that we have a new Air Force weenie in the MILGROUP. Now you can take some of the flak I've been catching since the departure of your predecessor."

Colleen laughed. "Thank you all for coming to meet us. I thought at first it was unnecessary, but I'm very wobbly and appreciate the help."

Schmidt said, "You'll adjust within twenty-four to forty-eight hours if you take it easy." Then he chuckled, "Although some people never do get the hang of it and have to be flown out."

"Oh, Matthew!" Olga exclaimed, elbowing him in the chest. "That's the last thing they want to hear right now." She turned to Colleen. "Don't worry. We all felt the same crummy way you do now when we first arrived. You'll be better in the morning, which is good since we have lots of settling in to do."

Tom watched as Olga sat on the arm of the couch, took Colleen's hand, and fussed over her. The elegant Olga seemed as genuine and open as her husband.

"Your bags are all loaded," announced Matt. "Let's go. The descent into La Paz city will help you feel better."

En route, Matt gave a running commentary on the sights. The airport in La Paz was located on the high plateau called the *altiplano* that surrounded the city on three sides. La Paz was built by the Spanish conquistadores in a valley that fell away from the altiplano. He stopped at an overlook for the requisite first look down at the sparkling lights of La Paz, lighting up the incredibly black void that held the city.

"It's magnificent!" Colleen said, soroche forgotten.

"Everybody says that," Olga agreed. "From here, La Paz is one of the most beautiful cities in the world. The lights sparkle like that because there's virtually no smog here and the air is so thin."

"It looks like it was dropped into a hole," Tom said.

"Yeah," Matt laughed, "it's like somebody shoveled San Francisco into the Grand Canyon."

The rest of the drive passed quickly as Schmidt expertly maneuvered the MILGROUP Land Cruiser through the evening congestion, still heavy at ten o'clock. Headache miraculously now gone, Tom peered curiously at the crowded sidewalks. He was used to the sights and smells of Third World countries, but the aromas of La Paz were in a class of their own. His nose was assaulted by a pungent mixture of car fumes, spices, and cooking from the busy open-air markets, and aromas from the filthy public latrines. *Cholas*, or Indian women in the colorful traditional dress topped with their trademark bowler hats, mixed with western-dressed Bolivians. Four star hotels rose side-by-side with dilapidated adobe buildings with broken windows.

The caravan deposited the Callahans at an embassy apartment in a plain building near the Schmidt's house in the neighborhood of Sopocachi, known as the Georgetown of La Paz. Ignoring Tom's protests, Matt insisted on carrying the bags to the elevator and into the rooms. The furnished apartment was small but quite adequate, especially since the Schmidts had stocked the kitchen with a week's worth of interesting-looking edibles. Olga gave her personal guarantee that the vegetables had been rendered safe for consumption by a presoak in a mild iodine solution to kill the hostile local bacteria.

"Turn in early," said Schmidt. "You'll feel better tomorrow. Don't forget to meet at our house at ten o'clock for brunch. Adios."

Tom closed the door and stood at Colleen's side. Through the picture window they watched the dancing lights of their new city.
Tom finally asked, "Well, what do you think so far?"

Colleen's blue eyes were large and luminous in the reflected light. "Tommy, you silly sod, stop worrying about me." Colleen slid closer "I can see right now that it's going to be quite an adventure. The country is much different than I had imagined. I think it's going to be a fun year. Anyhow, it's going to be much better than having you gone in Desert Storm."

Tom wrapped his arms around her and kissed her gently. "But since I am here..." She nuzzled his neck.

19

He laughed. "And what about all that advice about keeping exertion levels low for the first forty-eight hours?"

She took his hand and led him through the living room to their bedroom. "No problem, flyboy. You monitor my heart rate and I'll monitor yours."

***

The Callahans strolled hand-in-hand through the narrow tree-lined cobblestone streets in the crisp morning air. They arrived at the Schmidt's ornate wrought iron gate exactly at ten o'clock. After repeated punchings of the doorbell, Matt arrived to open the gate, hair disheveled, still buttoning his shirt. "Sorry," he said with a sheepish grin. "My fault. I forgot you were fresh from the States. Nobody here ever shows up on time."

He ushered them through the large, well-appointed house, the air filled with the enticing spices of exotic cooking. Tom caught the unmistakable scent of garlic mixed with cilantro that took him back to his youth in Spain.

"Olga's in the kitchen with our cook. The MILGROUP Army section chief, Lieutenant Colonel José Hernandez, and his wife, Graciela, will be arriving soon. She's seven months pregnant with their first child. Fortunately, she's from Quito, Ecuador, which is pretty high up in the mountains as well, so she's used to the altitude. How was your first night in La Paz?"

"Terrible!" Tom replied with a wink at Colleen. "Just as you predicted. We couldn't sleep at all. We even drank the quarts of bottled water you left for us. All that did was to make us get up and go to the bathroom all night."

Matt nodded. "Yep, almost everybody has that problem in La Paz at first. The lack of humidity and the altitude really wreck your life for a few days. You'll be okay soon. Just stay away from alcohol."

Tom nodded. "Matt, how did a blue-water sailor like you get assigned down to a land-locked country like Bolivia?"

Matt motioned for them to sit on the large, living room leather couch as he poured cups of steaming hot chocolate. "Connections, my

20

boy, connections," he joked. "Actually, I volunteered. My last tour was working in special operations, especially with the SEALs and their Small Boat Units. I decided that this was a good place to come for a shore tour. Bolivia, which is almost the size of Alaska, has roughly the same miles of rivers as the U.S. has miles of coastline hence the need for a river-oriented navy. I'm supposed to help the Bolivian Navy set up a riverine patrol force."

Colleen asked, "How do you like the living here?"

"We love it!" he said, "The people are wonderful. The weather in La Paz is superb and the scenery is magnificent. I've even put in for a one-year extension on this tour."

Tom smiled at Colleen. She sighed with relief, then turned his attention to the front door where the Hernandezes and Olga had just appeared.

"I'm sorry that I wasn't at the airport last night," said Graciella in Spanish. "I was a little under the weather. Please excuse me."

"Don't worry, *Señora*," replied Tom in Spanish. "It would have been silly for you to go to the airport if you were sick. You're here now. That's what is important."

"Oh, you don't sound like a gringo at all," she said, switching to English. "Your accent is so elegant, so Spanish—and your proper use of the subjunctive, very impressive!"

"Thank you." Tom grinned. "My father had two tours of duty near Madrid when I was a boy. We had Spanish maids and I went to Spanish schools. Nothing like Jesuit priests to pound home the finer points of Spanish grammar!"

"And you, Colleen?" asked Graciela. "Do you also speak Spanish?"

Colleen shook her head. "Nobody I knew in Australia spoke Spanish. I didn't even know what a taco was until I met Tom."

Tom said, "Colleen does speak pretty good Japanese, though."

Colleen laughed. "After we got married, Tom was sent to Stanford University to get his MBA. I attended classes as well. I thought that eventually we would end up back in the Pacific so I took Japanese." She glanced at Tom. "I had my own in-house tutor. Tom also lived in Japan as a kid and is fluent."

Graciela smiled at Colleen. "If you can learn Japanese, you can certainly learn Spanish. Olga and I will teach you."

José Hernandez impressed Tom immediately. Matt had told him that José, a slightly built Puerto Rican, had an easygoing demeanor which belied a fiercely competitive spirit and acute intelligence. He had spent the early days of his Army career in the infantry, followed by two tours in the Special Forces. While training for the elite Army Delta Team counterterrorist battalion, he had been nearly killed in a parachuting accident, ending his career in the combat arms branches. Intelligence shone from behind those friendly black eyes.

Graciela Hernandez was as pleasant and easygoing as her husband, dark-eyed with high cheekbones. Her attractive features were just starting to puff from her advancing pregnancy. Fluent in English, Matt said she was busy completing requirements for an undergraduate degree in French.

The Bolivian maid motioned Matt to the telephone in the anteroom. He rejoined the group three minutes later. "Well, that didn't take long. That was the Ambassador. Tom, we've been summoned. Hope you aren't too hungry."

Tom shrugged that it didn't matter if he were hungry or not. "So tell us about this meeting with Mr. Ambassador Brent."

Matt rolled his green eyes. "Brace yourself, pal. He's still pissed off at the entire U.S. Air Force because of your predecessor."

José laughed. "That's for sure."

Olga protested. "What's the rush this morning? Surely he's not holding Tom responsible for what happened before he got here?"

Matt looked at Tom carefully and measured his words, "The Ambassador told me that he's reserving judgment on your qualifications until he meets you. He's going to drill you today to see if your Spanish is up to speed. He said that if you didn't measure up, he'd put you on tomorrow's flight back to the States, no matter what the Air Force said."

Tom felt the heat rise in his cheeks. This wasn't what he had expected this fine morning. First a summons, then a threat.

Matt laughed. "Relax, Tom. He hasn't a clue that you speak like a member of the Spanish royal family. Just give him a good burst of your ever-so-proper Castilian Spanish. He'll be thrilled. Then if you can manage to contain those fighter-pilot instincts of yours and not pee in any of his potted plants or throw food in his lap, you're a shoo-in."

Had his predecessor actually urinated in the Ambassador's plant? Tom had been to a few parties like that. This was going to be an interesting interview.

Ambassador's Residence,
La Paz, Bolivia

Schmidt and Callahan, now in uniform, walked the three blocks to the Ambassador's home very slowly.

"Tom, as you have undoubtedly noticed, the streets in La Paz have good reason to be described as either uphill or downhill rather than north or south."

Tom grunted in agreement. The cobblestone street to the Residence was distinctly uphill. Tom, panting, was painfully aware that the normally frenetic Schmidt just strolled along, casually describing the scenery.

"This park is named Plaza Abaroa after a hero of the War of the Pacific between Chile and Bolivia, which was allied with Peru. Abaroa gathered a people's army to fight a major battle along what is now the border between Chile and Bolivia. Way outnumbered, he was given the opportunity by the Chilean army commander to surrender. His message back to the Chileans was something to the effect of 'Screw you.' Sure enough, the Bolivians were slaughtered."

"Sounds like the Alamo," Tom said, puffing.

"Yeah," Schmidt laughed, "except the Bolivians also lost the war. The peace treaty gave Bolivia's coastline to Chile. And they're still pissed about it, more than a hundred years later. Bolivians are wonderful, hard-working people, but sometimes they have a tough time getting organized and pointed in the right direction. Which, of course, is why you and I are here."

***

Crossing the Plaza Abaroa put them directly in front of the Residence. Heavily armed Bolivian police guards surrounded the large, ornate, and very white southern-style mansion, mute testimony to the numerous death threats received by George Brent.

Another Bolivian ushered them through the three-story foyer, up a grand sweeping staircase straight out of *Gone with the Wind* and into the Ambassador's suite of offices. The potted palm to the right of the French doors was much taller and greener than any of the others. A victim of USAF urinary target practice? Spectacular artwork hung on the walls of the large rooms. Obviously Ambassador Brent was either a man of some taste or an aggressive advocate of American art.

Tom studied the paintings, entranced. He was examining a signed original by the renowned Kiowa artist, Robert Redbird, when Ambassador Brent entered the room.

"Gentlemen," said Brent, a tall slender man whose East Coast accent rolled off his tongue. "I apologize for the delay. I had to take a call from the undersecretary." Ambassador Brent carefully examined Tom as they shook hands. "Well, Colonel Callahan, *bienvenido*. You like the painting?" he asked in Spanish.

"Yes, sir," Tom replied, also in Spanish. "Redbird is one of my favorite Native American artists."

Brent pointed at the picture. "Tell me about this one," he commanded, still in Spanish.

Tom grinned to himself. So it begins. "Just look at these lines, Mr. Ambassador. Typical of Redbird. You can sense the spiritualism in the chief's face, and feel the uplift in the soaring of the eagle, something that always appeals to me, of course, as an Eagle pilot. And those wonderful lighting effects leap out at you, no matter where you stand. Magnificent!"

Ambassador Brent's face broke into a broad smile. "You seem to be well acquainted with art, Colonel."

Tom shrugged. "My mother is an artist. She dragged me through half the art galleries and museums in Europe while I was growing up. Learning about art was more an act of survival."

Ambassador Brent motioned toward the corner where a middle-aged man in the advanced stages of male pattern baldness waited for them. "Allow me to introduce you to our other Air Force officer here in Bolivia, the Defense Attaché and our ranking military person, Colonel Richard Adams."

Colonel Adams had found the bar on the far side of room and was helping himself to the scotch. "Welcome aboard, Callahan," he said, waving his drink. He stared at the younger man's uniform with its six rows of ribbons. "I see you spent some time in Saudi."

"Yes, sir. Nearly five months."

"Well, Colonel, you certainly made good use of your time. I haven't seen that many combat ribbons since 'Nam."

Adams lifted the liquor bottle questioningly. The Ambassador held up two well-manicured fingers indicating an inch and a half of liquor. Adams expertly splashed the liquid in a glass, added a single ice cube and handed the drink to him. Matt cheerfully ordered rum and Coke while Tom asked for a mineral water.

"Commander Schmidt told me you had a touch of soroche last night," said Ambassador Brent. "How are you feeling today?"

"Much better, thank you, Mr. Ambassador. I'll be fine in a couple of days."

"We've been pouring mate de coca into the Callahans since they arrived, Mr. Ambassador," Schmidt said.

Amused at Tom's uncomfortable expression, Brent flashed a wide smile. "Don't worry, Colonel, we all drink coca tea here. It's quite good for you. When I was in Bolivia twenty-five years ago as a Peace Corps volunteer in the mountains near Cochabamba, I drank it by the gallon. Probably kept me alive in those mud villages." Switching back to Spanish, he continued, "Colonel, how much do you know about what we're doing here and your part in it?"

Tom replied in Spanish, "Sir, I had one day of briefings at the Pentagon, a couple of hours this morning with the MILGROUP and some unclassified reports that Matt sent me. That's it."

"Good. I wanted to brief you myself in order to impress upon you just how difficult our task is." Brent settled into his comfortable leather armchair. The silver-haired ambassador picked up a report from his side table and showed it to Tom. "This is what I'm concentrating on. We are working here, believe it or not, using an extradition treaty between the United States and Bolivia signed in the early 1900s in order to prosecute Butch Cassidy. One of my biggest agenda items is to convince the Bolivian Congress to update that treaty to specifically include *narcotraficantes*." He tossed the report down and stared hard at Tom who had seen that look before. This was a serious player.

"I will deal principally with the politicians while you in the MILGROUP will deal with the military. I want you to get as close to the Bolivian Air Force general staff as possible. I cannot emphasize strongly enough the importance of direct military-to-military relations. We need to convince them to cooperate with us. Your predecessor was, shall we say..." Brent paused and stroked his prominent chin, then said with the closest thing to a real smile Tom had seen from him, "...not helpful in these discussions." The Ambassador shuddered. "I trust you will be more diplomatic."

Brent stood and extended his hand. "Glad to have you here, Colonel. Matt, make sure he makes the staff meetings. He should also meet with the Air Force commander, General Camacho, as soon as possible. One more thing, Tom. People in Washington haven't caught on to the fact that lots of things are happening down here, far too much to be handled by the number of people we have in the Embassy. It's going to be a busy year for you." Turning to Adams, Brent said, "Dick, I need to fly to Potosi tomorrow morning. Can you make the C-12 available?"

"No problem, Mr. Ambassador. We can fly you down and use the flight to give Tom his in-country check out."

"Good," said Brent. "Matt, I'd like you to go as well." He turned to Tom. "Matt just finished a project to drill a tunnel in a mountain outside Potosi and build a road into the city using a reserve U.S. Army engineering battalion." Brent grinned at Matt and clapped him on the shoulder. "Since then, the city authorities won't let me do anything without his approval."

Matt wagged a finger at him. "You've got nobody to blame but yourself, Mr. Ambassador. When you sent my wife down for that month, she charmed their socks off."

"Olga does know how to work a crowd," Brent conceded, laughing.

As Tom and Matt Schmidt departed the Residence, Matt clapped Callahan on the back. "You did great, Tom! Congrats and welcome to Bolivia. You're the right guy, in the right place, at the right time. And we're doing the right thing down here." Matt smiled his big smile, "Now, if we can get those clowns in Washington to leave us alone for awhile, we might be able to get something done."

Chapter Three

Chalupa's Restaurante,
La Paz, Bolivia

Porter Nelson studied his dinner companions as they ate. Scruffy with multiple tattoos, they looked about as tough as they come, certainly at home in this restaurant. Nelson had chosen Chalupa's, with its hard plastic tables and unmatched chairs, dirty floor, and smoky, noisy atmosphere to show them that he understood their world and could live in it as well as they could.

Nelson was used to being overshadowed physically, but not as much as he was right now. An athletic five foot eight, he looked like a steeplechase jockey next to these guys. Peter Hudnutt was a barrel-chested Australian whose size, craggy face, and thick neck could fit in with any linebacker in the National Football League. His Bolivian partner, Luis Garcia, big even by NFL standards, was positively enormous by Bolivian standards, like an Hispanic version of the giant in Steinbeck's *Of Mice and Men.*

This was Nelson's chance to convince the two men that he could help them while helping himself. So far, he wasn't having much luck with the stoic Garcia.

"Luis, I'm a freelance journalist, not a gold miner like you two. I can show you a whole sheaf of references and published articles on subjects from Thailand to Africa, if that's what you need. I'm not after your gold. I'm after my story, that's all. You two have been to the uplands area between Peru and Bolivia. I need to go there. What I'm asking is to go with you."

Garcia pulled apart a chicken wing. "Why? It's nothing but mountains and jungle—some of the roughest terrain in the country."

Porter shrugged. "That's where the story is. I've done this sort of stuff before, Luis." Nelson sipped his beer. "I've heard rumors of *Sendero Luminoso* guerrillas using this no-man's land between the two countries."

Garcia took his time to cut a chunk from his slab of nearly raw meat. He chewed slowly, frowning. "I never seen no government forces from either country up there."

"My point, exactly," replied Nelson. "Look, the Sendero is engaged in a fight to the death with the Peruvian government. Guerrilla fighters roaming around Peru are always subject to attack by government forces. Rumor has it that they slip across the border into Bolivia for a little R and R. I want to check that out, maybe get some pictures and interview some of the leaders."

"From Sendero? You are loco, hombre."

Nelson grinned. "Of course I am. That's why I'm a journalist."

Hudnutt laughed. "We've been to the area three times, Porter. The river has deposited alluvial gold downstream in the Pando region around Riberalta. Obviously, the gold has to be washed down from somewhere. We haven't found the source yet, but we've got a pretty good idea."

Hudnutt turned to his friend. "Porter can write a story about us as well as about the Sendero, amigo. If we find the source, we come back, file our claim and Nelson publishes his story in the international press."

Garcia took a swig from his beer and belched. "So? What do we get outta this?"

Hudnutt said, "The story will legitimize our position, Luis. Remember when the Bolivian government used some legal loophole to steal the claim of those American companies in Potosi?"

"Yeah."

"This would keep the government from screwing us."

"What's to keep him from publishing before we're ready and starting a gold rush?"

"My mate at the BBC said Nelson's alright," Hudnutt explained.

29

"Can you keep up with us, *Señor* Investigative Journalist?" Garcia challenged.

"If you guys can do it, so can I."

***

Two days later, Porter Nelson found himself heading north, wedged in a Toyota Land Cruiser with his miner compadres and all their gear.

The highway from La Paz zig-zagged up the hill and staggered through the neighboring city of El Alto. Nelson had gotten to know the sprawling city of more than a hundred thousand people. It reminded him of a dusty, dirty, small scale Hong Kong, completely congested, overhead electric lines crisscrossing the roads, lacing the dilapidated buildings together, innumerable people carrying enormous bundles of what seemed to be everything they owned.

The official city signposts were in Spanish though most of these people spoke only an Indian dialect or at best Spanish as a second language. The lingua franca here seemed to be Quechua. Nelson took in the scene, fascinated as always with the chaos of third-world cities. Hudnutt swore repeatedly as he swerved to dodge the dangerously overloaded multicolored buses that careened through the crowded streets. He leaned on the horn, yelled out the window to verbally bludgeon people out of the way, and finally headed the Land Cruiser out of the city.

They drove the one highway that crossed the altiplano on its way north into the mountains. The desolate brown of the enormous plain, seemingly as flat as the outfield in Yankee Stadium, stretched in all directions, its movement towards the horizon interrupted by the twenty thousand plus foot high, snow-capped mountains of the Cordillera Real. The sky was nearly always obscured by thick dreary clouds that stretched over the mountains but which never seemed to produce any rain on the almost Sahara-dry altiplano. Further on from El Alto, villages became smaller and poorer, sometimes mere collections of mud huts, some with crumbling walls, most without electricity. Markets were choked with *campesinos* in traditional garb, dark-skinned women wearing multi-colored skirts and black derbies, gorgeous small children with enormous black eyes running everywhere, older children with cheeks already starting to get the leather texture of their parents from too much wind and too much sun. In the vast fields separating the tiny villages, Nelson saw llamas herded along the road. Shepherds, almost always children, stared at them as they drove by.

The "highway" deteriorated into a dirt track, rutted and dusty. Porter shook his head. *I ought to do a story on life in the altiplano,* he thought. *Some editor somewhere would appreciate the beauty of these people and how tough it is to live here.*

On the road for over twenty back-breaking hours, twice they had blowouts which required unloading the vehicle because the weight of all the equipment was too much for the jack.

Finally entering the mountains, they climbed up into steep-sided valleys. Porter saw boulder-strewn streams plummeting down mountainsides, throwing up mists that shimmered with moving rainbows. They drove up into the rugged, vibrant greens of Bolivia's high jungle, filled with banana plants and trees and flowers he had never seen before. He kept busy snapping several rolls of film. They spent the nights on the side of the road. Nelson took his turns at guard duty, staring into the incredible blackness. The quiet was almost overpowering.

After two more days climbing up into the mountains, they entered the village of Huataguya and rested for a day. Garcia and Hudnutt bought more supplies and two pack mules to haul them into the steep valleys of the high jungles; they hired a teen-aged local *campesino* named Santiago to take care of the mules. Nelson spent his time nosing around the small village, interviewing locals and gathering background material. They unloaded the truck one last time and lashed the supplies onto the mules.

Garcia picked up his pack as if it weighed nothing, turned to the others and said, *"Vámonos."* They simply walked out of the village into the jungle.

Dark was the jungle, dark and still. Three days into the trip, an exhausted Nelson thought the plants were not nearly as interesting as they had been in the beginning. The intermittent rain and low clouds made the jungle surprisingly cold at night. Often, they saw the tracks of animals. During daylight, Nelson sweated as he trudged through the thick undergrowth, pushing away the ferns and always on the lookout for danger. Twice he thought he glimpsed something large moving through the bushes. Several times he heard the screams of jaguars, always at night and always sounding way too close. But he was more afraid of the snakes.

The fourth night, they gathered around the campfire, bone weary from all the climbing.

"Man, this country is unbelievable," said Porter, "I can see why the Sendero would like it here. No law except for the gun."

"Like your old Wild West, mate," said Hudnutt. "This is the end of the road."

"What road?" asked Nelson with a laugh. Another jaguar screamed in the distance, startling him.

"Don't like big cats, eh, Porter?"

"I'm quite comfortable being at the top of the food chain, my Australian friend."

"Well, you're not at the top here, mate."

"I know. That's what I'm having a hard time with."

"It's going to get worse," said Garcia. "What's the matter, this too remote for you?"

"Hey, I know what it's like to be in the boonies," protested Nelson. "I've worked in the mountains in Borneo and Thailand but I'm used to seeing the sky—at least once in a while. We've been in the dark so long that I feel like a hobbit."

Hudnutt handed Nelson a well-worn topographical map. They examined it by flashlight. "We're very close to the Peruvian border. Tomorrow afternoon, we should cross this last ridge and see the river. The Sendero could be anywhere around this area."

***

By late the next afternoon, Porter found himself bone weary, struggling up yet another damned ridge, Luis Garcia in the lead, as usual.

"Here it is. We've made it!" Garcia shouted back to the others.

Nelson felt a surge of exultation. Sore muscles forgotten, he sprinted to the top. He caught a glimpse of the river some two hundred feet below, twisting through the steep valley. His foot caught a root. He pitched forward. Arms flailing, he smashed down hard. His face hit a rock and he saw flashes. For an instant, he was still, flattened on the slanting surface like a tortilla, terrified to move.

Then he began to slide downward, pulled by gravity and the weight of his pack. Frantic, he dug his fingers and toes into the rough ground. The root of a scrawny shrub slowed him for an instant. He broke free with a lurch and rolled down the steep slope. Nelson willed his legs and feet to dig in harder. One foot snagged and torqued his leg back. He heard the ankle snap. He screamed in pain as he plunged over the ledge. He bounced as he smashed into the granite walls. Sky and earth whirled as he somersaulted down the steep slope.

***

Nelson felt something wet on his face and heard voices. He tried to turn his head but couldn't. Any movement made the agony worse. He had so many aches and pains that he couldn't focus. Voices slowly penetrated his mental fog, words unintelligible.

Breathing hard, Nelson fought back panic and the almost overwhelming waves of pain as he forced his eyes open.

Hudnutt was bending over him. His face broke into a grin. "Hey, mate, you had us worried there. We thought you were a goner."

Porter willed himself not to faint again as his companions gently untangled him from the branches and rocks. He felt their expert hands assessing the damage and listened through a fog as Hudnutt described his injuries.

"Both legs broken, Porter, at the very least." He opened Nelson's shirt and whistled. "Massive bruises, mate. I don't know how you survived that fall. You are one lucky lad."

Porter gasped in pain as Hudnutt moved his legs and doctored the wounds as well as could be expected using the battered first aid kit.

Garcia cut some splints from saplings he found near the water's edge while Santiago set up camp.

After the rudimentary medical attention, Nelson watched as Hudnutt, Garcia, and Santiago gathered on the other side of the camp. The conversation grew animated. Nelson's Spanish was good; he caught enough of the exchange to know they were deciding his fate. Hudnutt's voice was even and controlled, Garcia's louder; Santiago's was downright angry.

The conversation ended abruptly when Garcia grabbed Santiago by the throat with one hand and lifted him into the air. Hudnutt shouted at Garcia who dropped Santiago. The boy crumpled in the dust.

Garcia snatched up his rifle and stalked towards Nelson. "You are a pain in the ass, gringo."

"Calm down, Luis," said Hudnutt. "You said it yourself, that fall could have happened to any one of us."

Hudnutt squatted on his haunches and stared into Porter's eyes. "Listen, mate, we can't carry you out of here. You're too banged up."

Nelson felt a sudden surge of fear. Was he going to die today? He forced a smile. "What's the plan?"

The Australian suddenly reached behind him. Nelson's heart almost stopped at the flash of a knife. Then Hudnutt produced a map with his other hand and held it close to Porter's face. Using his knife as a pointer, he said. "We're right about here. We'll hike out to the east to the town of Apolo. Probably take three days or so. There's a small Bolivian Air Force base and a radio station. We'll call for help."

Nelson leaned back and tried to get his breathing under control.

"What's the matter, Porter?" asked Hudnutt. "That's the best we can do!"

"It's okay, Peter, it's okay. Sorry," Nelson managed to blurt. "I'm just glad you have a plan." He managed to reach out to Hudnett's knee. "Thanks, man." Then a thought struck him. "Don't leave me alone. Please."

"Don't worry, mate. Santiago agreed to stay to keep the fire going and take care of you."

"It didn't look like he agreed to anything to me."

34

Hudnutt chuckled. "Luis has a way of convincing people to do things they don't want to do."

"You have to leave right now? Can't you stay the night?"

"Port, you know better than that. We need to make tracks while it's still light."

Porter struggled to control his fear as he watched the miners busy themselves with preparations. They tethered and unloaded the mule, then replaced the mining equipment in their packs with food for their forced march. Garcia swung his pack onto his back, turned and disappeared into the foliage. Hudnutt followed and waved good-bye without looking back.

Gone.

Porter watched as Santiago dug a small hatchet from the packs and started cutting wood for a fire. The pile grew larger as the boy hacked and hacked, ignoring Porter. Finally, he stacked some sticks together in a crude mound.

"*Fósforo!*" he said.

"What? *Qué?*" Porter stammered.

"*Fósforo!*" said Santiago in an angry voice. He made a motion, one hand crossed the palm of the other.

Oh, shit. Matches. Of course! Porter pointed to the side pocket of his pack. Santiago grabbed the pack, yanked open the pocket, and snatched the tube of precious matches. He threw the pack down and kicked it out of Porter's reach, spilling its contents out over the dirt.

Santiago lit the fire and pocketed the matches. He continued to move supplies around, muttering all the while. It began to rain and the temperature dropped. In the semi-darkness, Santiago sat on a log in the flickering light of the campfire while he cooked, their only rifle within arm's reach. He wrapped himself in a blanket and lit a cigarette with a branch from the fire.

"*Una manta, por favor,*" said Porter, indicating Santiago's blanket. Santiago glared back and did not move.

"*Una manta,* goddamn it!" said Porter, acutely aware that the boy was also angry and had the only weapon.

Santiago threw Porter a blanket. Despite his pain, Porter struggled to make himself more comfortable. He managed to reach the strap of an empty canteen and fashioned it into a makeshift pillow. Exhausted, he slumped back into his crude bed. He would deal with the asshole in the morning.

As darkness fell, Porter again fought the rising fear. The emotion was a screaming awareness of his vulnerability and dependence on a teenager who hated him. During the night, Porter drifted in and out of a fitful sleep, his shivering body aching. Dimly, he saw the hazy image of Santiago as it moved about in the dark. He dozed again, gradually emerging from his painful night. Then he jerked fully awake, heart pounding.

Santiago, the mules, and most of the supplies had disappeared.

Chapter Four

El Alto Airport,
La Paz, Bolivia

Tom Callahan stepped out of Colonel Adams's staff car and peered around the airport. To the east and south majestic snow-capped mountains reached over twenty-one thousand feet; to the west and north lay the vast, wind-swept and barren altiplano that reached to the horizon where it was abruptly met by more high mountains. The effect of the huge panorama made the airport look almost like a model on a kid's bedroom floor.

Colonel Adams led Tom through the bustling airport lobby to a door marked "*Meteorología*—Restricted to Flight Crews Only." Once in the crowded room, Adams took a dog-eared copy of an old flight plan from his briefcase and began to laboriously transcribe the information to a clean copy. Tom asked the Bolivian meteorologists for the weather reports at Potosi and the neighboring city of Sucre, the designated alternate airfield.

Walking back to the staff car, Adams said, "I never bother to ask for the weather forecast. Those guys aren't any good. Besides, none of the bastards can speak English."

The vehicle crunched across the gravel as it made its way across the unpaved areas surrounding the C-12 parking ramp. Normally, the two pilots split the preflight inspections, with the copilot making the "walk-around" or exterior inspection and the pilot performing the interior checks. Adams wandered off, leaving Tom to handle everything.

Tom went through the pre-start checklist, visually and physically checking the position of every switch and knob. He used his extra time to set up the cockpit with his maps and to review the flight. Having taken all required charts home the previous night, he had committed to memory all takeoff, climb out, and en route procedures. Settling back into the pilot's comfortable cushioned seat, he let the familiar excitement start to fill him. A grin spread slowly across his face. Nothing else in life came close to the exhilaration of flying. He loved strapping on an aircraft, anything from crop dusters to jets.

A moving cloud of dust announced the Ambassador's caravan as it pulled up to the aircraft parking apron. Two Chevy Suburbans full of armed guards flanked the Ambassador's black Cadillac. Colonel Adams miraculously appeared as Ambassador Brent, Commander Matt Schmidt, and two Bolivian police bodyguards walked to the airplane. The bodyguards carefully eyed the small crowd of curious Bolivian Air Force, *Fuerza Aérea Boliviana* (FAB), civilian workers that had gathered at the arrival of the limousine.

Adams followed the others up the steps, shut the door behind him, checked the passengers on his way to the cockpit, and flopped into the copilot's seat. He picked up the blue plastic-covered checklist.

"Parking Brake—Set"

"Chocks—Out"

"Battery—On"

"Beacon and Nav Lights—On"

"Number 2 Propeller—Clear"

"Number 2 Engine—Start"

Tom and the colonel methodically marched through the checklist, pausing as Adams pointed out several differences in the published version taught in the USAF school at Andrews Air Force Base and the high-altitude version needed at La Paz.

"El Alto Tower, Spar Niner Niner ready to taxi."

"Spar Niner Niner, cleared to taxi runway one zero left."

Tom taxied the winding route to the main taxiway, passing the armed T-33s of the FAB *Grupo* 31 on one side and the Bolivian Army hangars on the other.

38

"Spar Niner Niner, cleared for takeoff runway one zero left, winds light and variable."

Tom maneuvered to the very end of the active runway and held his brakes as he smoothly ran up the engines. He gave a warning glance over his shoulder to the passengers and got a thumbs-up from Brent. Checking the engine settings once more, he released the brakes.

He focused on staying straight down the runway and waited for the aircraft to accelerate. Even though he had made the calculations himself, Tom was surprised at the length of time required to reach takeoff speed in La Paz. *Sure would be nice to have some afterburners now*, he thought.

Between glances down the runway, his eyes flitted across the engine instruments and the airspeed indicator. The needle of the airspeed indicator moved ever so slowly towards rotation speed as the end of the runway rushed at them. Tom eased back on the control yoke and the nose wheel lifted off, followed by the mains as the end of the runway whipped by.

The climb-out was smooth, and Colonel Adams handled the copilot duties quite ably. Leveling off at Flight Level 270, or twenty-seven thousand feet above sea level, Tom inhaled deeply, surprised at the clarity of the view from the cockpit. The white-capped mountains were knock-out beautiful; the glaciers and snowy overhangs stood out in crystalline detail. Brilliant sunshine filled the cockpit and turned the off-white wings dazzling white against the purple sky.

The route of flight led them down the western edge of the *Cordillera Occidental*, or the western ridge of the Andes, past the mining city of Oruro. The city was nestled against the mountains overlooking Lake Poopo where the drain off from Lake Titicaca ran. The run-off plain was so flat and the air so dry that the water evaporated before it went very far, leaving a huge salt flat around the large lake. The salt flats extended far off to the right into the frontier with Chile, shimmering pale white in the sunshine, like a low cloud deck. As they proceeded south, the terrain turned even more stark and rugged and reminded Tom of the desolate areas of Nevada and Arizona, except more mountainous and much higher.

While Adams chattered on, Tom, almost unconsciously, used his left thumb to trace the route of flight drawn on his chart, moving along the course as the ground features passed. Focused outside the cockpit as if still on the lookout for enemy fighters, he watched for the landmarks he had identified from the charts, eventually sighting the famous *Cerro Rico*, or Rich Peak, close to the city of Potosi. The mountain had been mined continuously for over four hundred years, leaving it considerably smaller than Tom had imagined. Its striated remains looked like a tooth stripped of its enamel in preparation for an artificial crown.

After identifying Cerro Rico, he managed to locate the city itself. The unremarkable buildings of Potosi blended into the dirty brown of the desolate countryside. The airport was squeezed into a narrow valley between two large mountains. Tom grinned as he regarded the terrain; the steep approach required for landing at Potosi, coupled with the nearly thirteen-thousand-foot altitude and short runway, made for the kind of sporty landing pattern he loved. He set up his pattern, brought the aircraft smoothly around, compensating for the tricky winds on short final, and kissed it on. Applause sounded from an appreciative Ambassador and Matt Schmidt. Adams said nothing.

Since Tom and Matt's meetings finished before the Ambassador was scheduled to return to the airport, they indulged in a brief sight-seeing trip through the old city. Tom's first impressions of Potosi from the ground matched those from the air: poverty and dust. Through the grime, the ghosts of elaborate facades and balconies bespoke of better days. Tom had spent enough time in Europe to be able to distinguish the merely old and dilapidated from the historic and dilapidated. Potosi was a historian's dream.

Matt swept his arm toward the oldest area of town, tumbledown buildings with ornate balconies threatening to collapse on pedestrians below. "I love this old place. I spent nearly three months of my life here working with the Bolivians trying to finish that engineering project. Olga came down and we stayed in this wonderfully beat-up hotel right out of a seventeenth-century travel service. It was like another honeymoon."

They arrived at a well-preserved stone building, with an elaborate carved facade and iron gates. A small plaza in front made the setting even more elegant and imposing. The presence of two national policemen who slouched by the gate indicated this was a place of some importance.

"Here's something that should delight the Spaniard in you, Tom," Matt said as they descended into the cool, dim interior of the ancient building. "This is the Royal Mint, *Casa de la Moneda*, founded in 1572, where the first coins in the New World were minted."

Tom stood in the main room, surrounded by glass-topped wood cases that contained books as well as coins. He scanned the room slowly, absorbing the quiet atmosphere. "Whoa, Matt, look at this. These are the archives of the city, the original documents from the sixteenth and seventeenth centuries!"

Matt nodded. "They're in great shape, too, because of the dryness of the air. I've seen them, but I couldn't make out the old Spanish text."

Tom carefully read through the exposed pages. "These are listings of exactly how much treasure left from Potosi, headed first for Lima, then Madrid. Amazing!" he said, shaking his head. "They give the amount, the ship names and sailing dates, everything."

Matt gestured at an elaborate faded map behind the glass. "Local lore has it that Potosi produced so much treasure that it would have built a bridge of silver and gold from here to Madrid."

Tom nodded. "I believe it. The gold and silver from the New World made Spain the richest country in Europe in the sixteenth and seventeenth centuries. This is where Philip II got the money to pay for the Spanish Armada."

Tom surveyed the dim interior of the Mint again, enjoying the silence and letting the musty smells seep into his soul. "This place is wonderful. Just look at these coins. Hundreds of them. The fact that they're pure gold makes them valuable enough. They're so old and in such wonderful condition, they must be priceless." He looked around the room. "Not much security around here."

"Yeah," said Matt. "The Bolivians are used to doing everything on a shoestring. Good thing they shot Butch and Sundance way back when."

Tom tapped the thick glass on one of the coin cases. "Too bad more Americans don't come down here. This is great history."

Matt laughed. "Potosi isn't exactly on the way to anywhere. If you want to come here, you're going to have to make a special trip."

"Yeah, but the coins themselves would make the trip worthwhile. These are relics of the Spanish Main, the *reales*, the doubloons that Sir Francis Drake and Henry Morgan and all those pirates fought over. Guys like you, Matt."

"Ah, Tom, you flatter me."

***

The two men arrived back at the airport in time for a sandwich before Ambassador Brent and Colonel Adams returned. During the climb-out from Potosi, Ambassador Brent stuck his head in the cockpit to get a better look at the city. "Potosi is my favorite city in all Bolivia. Believe it or not, that dusty little place had a significant impact in European history."

Tom nodded. "I have seen pictures of Potosi in old Spanish books and history lessons, but I hadn't made the connection. There are lots of cities named Potosi scattered around Latin America."

Brent's smile lit up his gray eyes. "There's even a Potosi, Texas, near Abilene. Most Americans know nothing about this one at all. It was a magnificent city in the 1600s and 1700s. There were nearly two-hundred-thousand people living there at one time with dozens of churches, great plazas, and luxurious homes. Potosi's economy collapsed in the early 1800s, but boomed again in the early 1900s." Brent paused to survey the vast open space surrounding Potosi.

Tom adjusted the trim on the aircraft as he made a small course correction to the northwest.

"I've spent a lot of time trying to reinvigorate the region surrounding Potosi," Brent said, "trying to help the locals and to help our own programs. When the mines shut down in 1986 by government decree, most of the miners had to leave to find work elsewhere. Some of them still hang around the cities to beg. Worse, many of them moved

42

to the *Chapare* region east of Cochabamba to work in the coca fields or in the coca industry."

"You're kidding. You mean the *narcotrafficante* worker force is displaced miners?"

"To a large extent." The Ambassador shook his head, sadness apparent in his voice.

"But getting back to my original point, the President was forced to fire the miners in order to cut the public-sector payroll." Brent leaned forward. "If we could only jumpstart the local economy, we'd attract those displaced workers back to where they prefer to be and hurt the narco business at the same time."

Tom sat silent for a minute as the idea that had been flitting across his mind coalesced. "Sir, have you ever been to Alaska?"

Brent shook his head.

"Well, I've done a lot of flying up there. If nothing else, this flight has shown me that Bolivia has huge sections of inaccessible territory. In Alaska, airplanes have made a major difference, really opened up the country to development. I read a Bolivian Air Force report that said it was trying to get its air network going again, to fly into the boondocks where the civil airliners won't go. Maybe we could jumpstart our programs by way of helping the Air Force in its nation-building efforts."

Brent tapped his perfect teeth with a forefinger. "Intriguing idea, Tom. I'll have to look at this some more. On the surface, I like it. The Air Force has been very good in its support of our programs so far. Perhaps if we reward it, the other services will see the advantage of working with us."

"Exactly, sir. The FAB already has an infrastructure. We could improve it by getting better airplanes, some training programs, and decent logistics support. We can help the country grow."

"Yes, of course," Brent said, pursing his lips. "I like this idea more all the time." He elbowed Adams in the ribs. "Dick, why didn't you think of this? You're the transport pilot here."

Brent looked out the windscreen at the forbidding mountains, "We could use the transports ourselves for logistics, as necessary. In the meantime, the FAB could be helping the people in the frontier." He clapped his hands. "Tom, great thinking. Work on the details. If the Bolivians are interested, we'll present the plan on my next trip to Washington." Patting him on the shoulder, the Ambassador returned to his seat.

The flight back to La Paz turned out to be much more than simply reversing course. With almost completely unlimited visibility, a totally new vista greeted Tom's eyes as he watched the majesty of Illimani unfold. The great tan expanse of the arid altiplano was staggering, the scope of the shimmering Lake Titicaca enormous. Crossing the last jagged ridge of mountains prior to descent into the airport, Tom was surprised to be suddenly over downtown La Paz. Amazing. Everything was described with superlatives here—stupendous, magnificent, highest, even poorest. Never had he seen anything quite like it.

Another tight fighter landing pattern and featherlike touchdown; Tom taxied to the ramp and shut down the engines. As the Ambassador and Schmidt headed to their waiting convoy, an olive-complected man of medium height approached the aircraft. Despite the civilian clothes, Tom knew this slender man with impeccable posture was military.

"Sir, I'm Master Sergeant Arturo Galvani," the man said with a salute. "I work for Colonel Adams in the Defense Attaché Office. *Bienvenido a Bolivia.*"

"Nice to meet you, Arturo," said Tom, returning the salute then extending his hand. He had a feeling this guy could save his butt if he ever needed his butt saved. "Colonel Adams told me he had another blue-suiter squirreled away in the attaché shop. Good to know you're around."

"Sir, I called the FAB headquarters for you this morning. General Camacho will be in Argentina for the next two days. But he said he could see you this afternoon. I called your wife and got your uniform." He handed Tom a sheaf of legal-sized folders with "Confidential" stamped in red block letters. "Here's a dossier on the General to read before the meeting. And here's another on the other key FAB officers, including all the generals." He grinned at Tom. "And, of course, I included all the info on fighter pilots that we have—all the fighter wing commanders and squadron commanders down through flight commanders. Mario Torrez said you were a demon for details."

44

Tom laughed. "Why am I not surprised that you know Mario Torrez?"

'Mario was one of my instructors at admin school. We were at Randolph together just before I came here. He called two weeks ago and told me to make myself available if you needed me. He loves living in your house, by the way, Colonel. Says it's like living in a palace. He told me to say thanks again."

***

Motoring down the airport highway to the headquarters of the *Fuerza Aérea Boliviana* in Colonel Adams's staff car gave Tom a chance to study General Fernando Camacho's dossier. First in his class at the Bolivian Air Force Academy, *El Colegio Militar de Aviación*, attended flight training in the United States, basic and advanced fighter school in Argentina, former fighter squadron commander, wing commander, and commander of the Bolivian War College. All the tickets punched. Married. Two grown kids attending college in the States. The glossy eight-by-ten photo on the inside cover revealed a distinguished, almost Hollywood-handsome man. Should be an interesting guy.

The staff car pulled to a stop in front of a dirty white building that looked like any other multistory building along the crowded street except for the Bolivian flag flying in front and two armed airmen guarding the open front doors, men who looked all of sixteen years old.

Tom and Colonel Adams were met by General Camacho's *ayudante*, Captain Luis Valdez, who escorted them through the narrow halls to the fourth-floor office. Tom settled into an armchair and began to leaf through the latest version of the FAB magazine, which was liberally sprinkled with pictures of General Camacho delivering speeches and reviewing his troops. It also included an in-depth article on Grupo 71, the FAB transport wing. He was engrossed in memorizing faces and names when the door opened and Valdez signaled for them to come in. Adams led Tom into the spacious office, saluted, and introduced Tom.

Tom crisply saluted. "*Señor, Teniente Coronel Tomás Callahan. A sus órdenes, mi general.*" Camacho looked surprised but returned the salute and motioned the visiting Americans into chairs. Valdez was already rushing off to get the coffee when Tom stopped him. "Captain Valdez," he said, in Spanish, "could I please have some *mate de coca* instead of coffee?"

"You like our coca tea, Colonel?" asked Camacho, smile wrinkles forming around his dark eyes.

"General, right now, it's the only thing keeping me alive." By this time, Tom knew that Bolivians were proud of the medicinal qualities of their unique tea and consumed it in quantities that put British tea drinkers to shame.

Tom settled back in his chair and patiently endured Adams's stuttering attempts at a Spanish conversation. Classic Spanish colonial furniture, which suited the dignified Camacho's rank and personal style, filled the room. Tom studied the impressive eight-foot square antique map of Bolivia showing the country's original boundaries. The writing was in old Spanish, and the frame of dark, carved wood was unable to tone down the lavish color and gilt favored by the unknown cartographers of the era. A massive carved Andean condor with a three-foot wingspan dominated the area behind Camacho's antique desk, clashing with the personal computer, fax machine, and two sleek touch-tone telephones.

When Adams's conversation finally ground to a halt, the talk turned to flying stories. According to his dossier, the General was immensely proud of his USAF wings and enjoyed telling stories of his rookie flying days. When he had graduated from the *Colegio Militar de Aviación*, thirty in his year group had gone on to pilot training. Camacho had been first in his class, so he and the next five graduates had been sent to Moody Field, Georgia to fly the T-6 Texan. The other twenty-four had received the standard FAB training. Now, all twenty-four were dead, every one killed in aviation accidents. Of the six USAF trained officers, five were still actively flying, and one was medically retired. Understandably, Camacho was an outspoken advocate of the USAF.

"Tell me, Colonel Callahan, what type of aircraft do you fly?"

46

"Sir, until now, I've only flown fighters and trainers, but here I'll be flying the C-12 with Colonel Adams."

"Really?" Camacho arched his eyebrows in surprise. "We've never had a USAF fighter pilot here. Did you fly fighters in the Gulf War?"

"Yes, sir. I was attached to the 33rd Tactical Fighter Wing flying F-15Cs out of Saudi Arabia for nearly five months."

The general nodded. "The C model is the air superiority version," he said with pride, enjoying the chance to show off his professional knowledge. "Did you come in contact with Iraqi fighters?"

Tom hesitated. "Yes, General. We came close on several occasions. Of the thirty-five Iraqi aircraft shot down, my unit accounted for fifteen."

' And you? Did you account for any?" asked General Camacho, sounding like his dossier: a bright, hard-nosed officer who always wants answers. Very much a commander.

Tom met his eyes. "Yes, sir. I shot down two MIG 29s."

Camacho smiled broadly. "A combat veteran! This is superb!" He slapped his desk in delight, startling Adams who had been staring out the window unable to follow the Spanish conversation. "I would be grateful if you would speak to our War College about some of your experiences."

Tom bowed slightly. *"A sus órdenes, mi general,"* and quickly changed the subject. "General, I just had a talk with Ambassador Brent. We were discussing the fact that additional FAB transport aircraft would really be helpful here in Bolivia."

Camacho gave him a quizzical look. "Certainly. The planes we have now are tired and need major overhauls which we can't afford."

"What if we could get more transports for you—more modern C-130s for example, along with spare parts and training?"

Camacho laughed. "Using what for money, Colonel? Your good looks? You are indeed a handsome fellow, but I know your budget. Your predecessor used to remind me at every opportunity. You don't have enough money to buy us a used Cessna, much less C-130s."

Tom leaned forward. "What I'd like from you now, General, is an agreement in principle. Would the FAB be interested in expanding its transport fleet? If so, assuming we get legal approval from Washington, the United States government would provide additional funds for newer aircraft. These aircraft would be used for the logistics support of the joint counternarcotics efforts here as well as to expand your standard transport around Bolivia. Is that satisfactory?"

Camacho stared at Tom. "*Dios Mío!* You don't waste any time, do you?" He leaned back in his chair. "I don't know if you can pull this off, young man, but I like your style." He made a temple with his fingers as he thought for a long moment. "I agree in principle but I have to discuss it with the Minister of Defense. I'll do that tonight." Camacho paused, clearly thinking about his next move. "In the meantime, how do you like your office accommodation in the embassy?"

Tom hesitated.

Camacho stood, motioned for the American officers to follow, and led them around the corner to a spacious and airy office next to his own. "Your predecessor used to complain about how small and inconvenient his office was. I would like to offer you the use of this office for the time you are in my country."

Tom had no idea what to say. "Thank you, General. This is quite an honor. However, I'll have to check with the MILGROUP commander and the Ambassador. I'm not sure of the embassy policy."

Camacho gave a casual wave of his hand, dismissing the problem. "Valdez, get the American Ambassador on the phone." Five minutes later, the general had the astonished Brent's blessings and thanks.

"Well, then, Colonel, you can move in any time. Perhaps next week you can speak to our War College about the Gulf War." Camacho added, "I have flown the MiG 29 myself." Noting Tom's surprise, he continued, "Three years ago when I was the commandant of the War College, we visited Cuba as our graduation trip. I flew with the chief Cuban Air Force test pilot. It's quite a machine."

"Yes, General, the Fulcrum is a wonderful aircraft. I flew one at an air show." Tom didn't mention that his flight had been a 'Welcome Back from Saudi' birthday present from Colleen: a thirty-minute flight in the MiG 29 at the California International Air Show in Salinas,

48

which cost a thousand dollars a minute of flying time, or that Colleen also had a flight in the sleek Russian jet.

Camacho escorted the Americans to the front entrance, talking flying all the way.

In the car on the way back to the embassy, Adams demanded, "What was all that about MiGs? Did he really say he had been to Cuba? And why did he take us to that big office?" As Tom related the conversations, carefully omitting his Saudi experiences, Adams's pale blue eyes turned hard.

Chapter Five

Presidential Palace,
Plaza de la Revolución, Havana

Kurt Wallerein could tell that Fidel Castro had pulled out all the stops for this visit. Rather than being wined and dined, Castro was shrewdly playing to the biases of his conservative guest by showing Wallerein the seamy side of the Cuban revolution. Wallerein had witnessed firsthand the economic and social problems Cuba was facing due to the abandonment of the ex-Soviets. He felt the increasing isolation Fidel was dealing with as a result of maintaining the cause of socialism in a hostile hemisphere.

And, Wallerein conceded to himself, the strategy was working. It was good to be among committed socialists again such as these *fidelistas*. But it was painful to see the price Cuba and the Cuban people were paying for the honor of carrying on the revolution; the ancient American cars now pulled by donkeys because the *Yanqui* trade embargo made spare parts impossible to obtain; the underemployed workers; the pervasive poverty.

What might have been a pleasant drive through the countryside for someone else showed Wallerein long stretches of road with shacks here and there standing empty without even a stray animal in sight. Flatbed sugar trucks passed, packed with people desperate for public transportation.

Havana's stately broad avenues were devoid of traffic. The mix of architecture was staggering—Spanish colonial, French palaces, soaring Art Deco, and collapsing tenements. Most buildings had molting plaster and peeling paint. The crumbling masterpieces were another testament to the effects of the economic sanctions of the hated *norteamericanos*. Yet these spirited Cubans had a world-class medical system and ready markets for their biomedical technology. Cuba wasn't just a country of farmers; it was full of sophisticated, educated people, ready to serve as the model for the rebirth of socialism. All it needed was a push. And Wallerein's dream was to provide that push.

Discretion forced the men to maintain a low profile; even in the closed Cuban society, problems with secrecy existed. For the West to know that the infamous German terrorist had visited Havana would not do. They dined together in Castro's apartments overlooking the immense Plaza de la Revolución. After the food was cleared away, Castro dismissed everyone save Ambassador Hernando Cortez, who remained as interpreter.

"Kurt, what we need to do is compound problems for the West, especially the Yanquis. Create chaos in selected regions in order to restore the old order." He poured himself another inch of rum. "We have to act, now! Socialism must regain the initiative soon or be snuffed out forever."

Wallerein's mind raced as he calculated how much to reveal. "Comrade, I have a network of people all over Europe and the Middle East. We can help each other."

Fidel acknowledged Wallerein with a tilt of his glass. "And I've got a network of people throughout Latin America. I'm willing to make them available to you."

Wallerein's expression did not betray the immense relief he felt. Although he had recently inherited many top people from the Eastern Bloc as the communist world had imploded, he had far fewer than the international press gave him credit. He owed his recent fame to the quality of the people he recruited.

No spy agency in history was more successful than the *Hauptverwaltung Aufklärung* (HVA), the little-known section of the former East German *Ministerium für Staatssicherheit* (Stasi) that specialized in foreign spying operations. Its specialty had been inserting moles in key positions throughout NATO, especially West Germany, and, in certain select cases, into the United States. In 1956, the HVA had inserted one hundred agents into West Germany disguised as political refugees. Many ended up in positions of power and influence. One of them, Günter Guillaume, was among Chancellor Willy Brandt's closest advisors, who passed all sorts of high level secrets back to the HVA. Soon after Guillaume was discovered in 1974, Brandt's government collapsed.

The HVA ran a terrorist training camp near the village of Briesen, near Berlin, complete with tennis courts and a commissary stocked with western foods and liquors. Over the years, Wallerein met with many HVA senior officials there. When the HVA was officially disbanded on May 23, 1990, many of the senior leaders were arrested and tried for espionage. Some committed suicide. Others saw what was coming and defected to one of the few remaining socialist states, bringing files of contacts and agents as bargaining chips. Wallerein had enlisted the best of this group, and subsequently inherited their networks.

And while Castro counted only a few hundred operatives scattered throughout Latin America, they were intensely loyal and dedicated. Their effect could be leveraged somewhat by the fact that democracy was still superficial in most of the region. Together, the two leaders could muster a small, but potent force. The main problem was economic—money.

Leaning forward, he lowered his voice. "What I propose to do is to link my groups with yours to reignite the revolution."

Castro sipped his rum, a smile playing on his ample lips, while Wallerein sketched out the rest of his plan. "I will arrange the initial funding through my contacts in the Middle East. We go after control of the drug cartels in Peru and Colombia. There are only seven major ones, after all, and we know who they are." He couldn't repress a slight smile. "If you remember, when I was working with the KGB and the Czechs in the late '60s, I helped arrange some of the first training programs for the initial cartels in Medellín."

Wallerein reminisced for a moment before he continued. "First, we eliminate any opposition and take control of the individual cartels. Then we link them together. Your people feed the drugs to my groups, we'll distribute them. First in America and Europe, eventually Asia. The system will quickly become self-financing. The money flows back into more revolution. Ultimately, we will own the countries themselves, picking them off one-by-one."

"And then springboard into the rest of Latin America?"

Wallerein nodded as he paused to take another sip of strong Cuban coffee, "You can flood the countries with Cuban-trained doctors, teachers, and soldiers to bring the revolution back to the people. Finance the unions and other progressives. You know all the key players. Who better to do this than you?"

A smile lit Castro's face as he acknowledged the compliment.

Wallerein continued, "I want to export terrorism to the United States on a large scale to keep everybody off balance. The Americans are the key; they have been immune far too long."

Surprised, Fidel's first reaction was caution. "The gringos could use these terrorist attacks as an excuse to attack Cuba."

Wallerein nodded. "That's why my people are needed. The best way to hurt the Americans is to use nonaligned freedom fighters. We are shadowy, scattered all over so there is no single place for the Americans to strike back. At the same time, Cuba is a sovereign state, which will afford us some advantages in the international community. We must be careful at first. As we become more successful, we can become bolder, more open."

"If we proceed," said Castro, "I think we should include Bolivia. It's a large producer of cocaine, and there's virtually no structure to the industry. Better yet, no opposition to speak of, so we can get a quick payback."

"I thought you might say that," replied Wallerein, nodding. "It will be a fitting tribute to the memory of Che Guevara. It happens that one of my best operatives is there as well. She's in a particularly good position to be of assistance."

Castro thought that over. "What exactly did you have in mind for the Yanquis?"

"A good dose of some sophisticated biological weapons."

Seeing the startled look on Castro's face, Wallerein hurried to explain. "Chemical and biological agents are more terrifying to civilians than nuclear weapons. I want to immobilize the American people with fear. Biological weapons are the best solution. Very effective and psychologically devastating."

Castro shook his head. "I've had first-hand experience with conventional warfare—bullets and bombs. I'm not sure about spreading deadly germs, even to blood enemies." He paused. "Plus, this new American president is an unknown factor. He might overreact."

Wallerein huffed, "The American president is a boy with soft hands and no balls."

Pensive, Castro took out one of Havana's finest cigars and placed it unlit into his mouth.

Wallerein watched patiently as Castro stalled. Because of the Americans, Cuba was bankrupt. The revolution was endangered. Thus, Castro himself was endangered. Sooner or later, he was going to realize this.

"The Yanquis have sophisticated research agencies that can identify any virus and where it came from," Castro said.

Wallerein nodded and smiled. "We'll use one of their own viruses."

"How can you do that?"

Wallerein waited.

Castro's eyes widened as the penny dropped. "You have a scientist inside their government!" He pounded the table in delight.

Wallerein thought it wise to nod modestly. "If we use something from their own stocks, they will turn inwards to find a scapegoat. Their government is always looking for reasons to control its people. Look at the persecution of the so-called militia groups, for example."

Castro settled back and regarded him with more respect. "All right, Kurt. I agree." He met Wallerein's eyes. "But only if you personally take charge of the operation."

Wallerein, jolted, began to argue, then reined himself in. He had never been to the United States to see his life-long enemy up close. He had spent most of the past ten years hidden in his sanctuary outside Tripoli. He built his organization long-distance using trusted lieutenants, venturing out of Libya only for furtive high-level meetings that could not be avoided. Wallerein remembered the tension of being in the field, the rush of adrenaline during an operation. He was tired of hiding in the desert.

Kidnappings and assassinations were for lieutenants. Biological warfare was suitable for him.

He reached across the table, took a cigar from a surprised Castro's pocket and settled back into his chair. "I agree."

Chapter Six

Conference room, U.S. Embassy, La Paz, Bolivia

The temporary conference room of the Embassy was a small one, made smaller by the massive oval mahogany table that jammed the main door and forced everyone to enter single-file through the side door that opened only part way.

At Matt Schmidt's insistence, he and Tom Callahan were the first to arrive. As he stepped to his seat, Tom shook his head at the array of organization nametags scattered around the table. No matter how long he was in the government, somebody always had a new acronym. It never ended.

Tom watched as the Country Team filed in, pecking order already established, and waited for the Ambassador to motion them to be seated. Tom knew that a typical embassy Country Team was made up of the Chief of Mission—usually an ambassador, the Deputy Chief of Mission (DCM), and heads of each major department. In Bolivia that translated into twelve units, all with their abbreviated names spelled out on placards carefully placed on the table in strict order of protocol. The MILGROUP was accorded the last seats for Matt Schmidt, in his capacity as acting MILGROUP commander, and then Tom.

"Ladies and gentlemen," said Ambassador Brent, "I'd like to introduce the newest member of our embassy staff, Lieutenant Colonel Tom Callahan." Heads bobbed and murmurs of greeting floated around the table. Brent gave Tom a thumbs up. "Colonel Callahan has already made his presence felt with the Bolivian Air Force. He's been adopted by General Camacho and given an office in the FAB Headquarters. That should significantly help our access to the FAB." He grinned as he looked around the table. "Not to mention that yesterday's flight to Potosi was the best flying I've ever experienced in the C-12. Now I won't have to fear for my life every time I get into that damned plane."

Brent waited for the expected chuckles to die down then asked each of the other principals to give a thumbnail sketch of his or her organization and mission to help orient Tom.

The DCM, Patricia Pointer, elegantly coiffed and dressed in a severe tweed suit, gave Tom a cold stare of appraisal, then started her deposition in brisk, precise Spanish. "As DCM, I am in charge of the day-to-day operations of the embassy. I have also been appointed as counternarcotics coordinator for Bolivia. All operations are run through my office. All message traffic and written correspondence dealing with counternarcotics matters are cleared by me personally. When the ambassador is not in Bolivia, I am the *chargé d'affaires* and, as such, am acting ambassador. Is that clear?"

"*Sí, gracias, señorita.*" Tom had been warned that Pointer had never married and was very sensitive about being called *señora* rather than *señorita*. He had no trouble at all understanding why she had stayed single.

The next man, George Rodgers, glanced at Pointer, then in a voice that rasped—probably from too many cigarettes, deliberately spoke in English. "Tom, I'm the DEA Country Attaché. All DEA assets in-country work directly for me. We are Department of Justice rather than Department of State. Most of my agents are out in the field. Our primary group, the Snowcap team, is located at our base camp in the Chapare region of Bolivia, near the city of Cochabamba. By virtue of an intergovernmental agreement, all DEA agents have arrest authority here in Bolivia just as they do in the States."

A pudgy man, dressed in an expensive suit and Harvard tie, spoke last. "I am Nicholas Barton III. I shall endeavor to explain to you the functions of the Narcotics Assistance Section, or NAS, in as few words as possible...."

Tom smiled inwardly. Schmidt had warned him that Barton never said or wrote anything in as few words as possible.

Barton droned on. "NAS is here to provide operational support to the operations-oriented DEA. We constructed and operate the base camp in *Chimoré* village in the Chapare province, from which the DEA Snowcap teams lead the Bolivian National Police patrols.

"We've also sequestered the U.S. Army Special Forces trainers at Chimoré to keep them out of mischief. NAS operates the U.S. government-owned UH-1H helicopters that are flown by the Bolivian Air Force as part of the 'Special Force for the Fight Against Drug Trafficking,' commonly referred to as the Task Force. The Bolivian Air Force contribution to the Task Force is the aforementioned helicopter unit that goes by the name of the *Diablos Rojos*, which of course translates to Red Devils...."

Out of the corner of his eye, Tom could see George Rogers doodle on his notepad while the man next to him leafed through a thick report.

Oblivious, Barton continued... "The Red Devils were formed originally by NAS with six aircraft. We are now up to sixteen. The MILGROUP is to provide support at the direction of NAS to accelerate this expansion—"

As Barton paused for breath, Schmidt jumped in, "Tom, the original instructor who set up the transition course to qualify Bolivian helicopter pilots in Hueys was the U.S. Army attaché here, a lieutenant colonel. All the follow-on instructor pilots for this unit are U.S. Army warrant officers. Many of the Bolivian pilots were sent to the U.S. Army flight training facility at Ft. Rucker, Alabama by the MILGROUP on our own initiative. The Defense Department has had a bigger hand in this campaign than just executing support directives from NAS."

Barton's fleshy face reddened. "These are State-funded and controlled programs, not military programs, Schmidt!"

"Gentlemen, gentlemen, back in your corners!" commanded the Ambassador as the two men exchanged bilious looks. "Let's not forget that we're all on the same side here. Continue with the briefings, please."

***

Walking down the stairs back to the MILGROUP afterwards, Tom faked Barton's Harvard accent, "Matthew, my dear boy, I gather you don't see eye to eye with Nicholas Barton III."

Schmidt snorted. "He's a pompous Ivy League asshole. Thinks nobody else around here knows anything. And he's especially threatened by the presence of military types around these damned counternarcotics programs of his. He forgets that it took a presidential decree, a direct order from the President to the Secretary of Defense, to make us do this stuff, for God's sake!"

Tom's briefings in the Pentagon had confirmed this completely. Even General Walters wasn't particularly happy about the programs, but orders were orders.

"These people from State don't know beans about operations. They think they do but they don't. And arrogant! Jeez, people like Barton wrote the book on arrogance." Matt grinned briefly, then turned serious again. "The Foreign Service Officers I've met don't much like military types. They think we're semi-literate cretins because we can't decline nouns in Latin or Greek. But they know we can get things done. And it scares them to think that we'll actually do something while they sit on their ever-widening asses drinking single malt scotch and talking about it."

"I take it that you are not overly fond of the State Department policies here?"

Matt looked Tom in the eyes. "I don't have any time for these silly games The MILGROUP is here to help, but we're here to do things right, too. Part of that process is to resist when State, DEA, or NAS wants to do something we know is stupid."

He shook his head. "They just aren't willing to admit that we might actually have operational expertise. Hell, between the three officers in the MILGROUP, we have almost fifty years of military experience, including lots of combat time. Probably triple that counting our enlisted men. And those draft dodgers in the country team couldn't care less."

The men picked a path through the maze of tables, chairs, beat-up bookcases and file cabinets in the crowded MILGROUP area and came upon a smiling José Hernandez. *"Buenos días, Tomás.* How'd you like your first country team meeting?"

Tom rolled his eyes. "I got the real fire hose treatment—maximum information in minimum time. But Matt's lively little exchange with Nick Barton got the blood flowing again."

"*Dios mío!*" said José, raised his hands, his handsome face contorted in mock horror. "Don't let Barton hear you call him 'Nick'— My name is Nicholas Barton III," he said, mimicking Barton's accent pretty well for a native Latino. "Our good friend Nick is from a very old and very prominent Boston family."

"Barton has an exaggerated opinion of his family and of himself," said Matt. "According to him, anything west of the Charles River is uncouth and uncultured." Apparently, this was a sore point for the California surfer boy. "The rest of us barbarians should be grateful to his family and the rest of the Mayflower descendents. Call him Nick and boom—instant explosion."

"Yeah, Matt does it to him about three times a week!" said José.

Matt shrugged. "I get tired of hearing him pontificate, especially about how great his family is. Who cares?"

"Well," said José, "he's richer than Methuselah."

Tom and Matt looked quizzically at each other. Then Matt laughed. "Tom, you'll have to excuse our Puerto Rican friend here. He sometimes has a problem with our gringo culture. José, you've combined two idiomatic expressions: it's 'older than Methuselah' or 'richer than Croesus'."

José looked at Tom. "This *inculto*—barbarian—is from California. His idea of class is a guided tour of Universal City Studios. And he talks to me about culture?"

Matt accepted the insult with a bow and brought the conversation back to the meeting. "About the only positive thing to come out of that gaggle upstairs was that you've pissed off Adams big time."

"How do you figure?"

"First of all, he's a crummy pilot. Everyone knows that. Second, Adams has been here two years and still has to call over to the FAB headquarters for permission to visit. And when he goes over there, they don't tell him anything. Or if they do, he can't understand it. Now you show up and in two days wow the Ambassador with your flying, come up with a great plan to open up the back country, and get adopted by

60

the Air Force commander who gives you an office and free access to every FAB unit in the country. Adams sat there in that meeting just seething. Watch him, my friend. He's nearly as mean as Pointer."

Chapter Seven

Calacoto, La Paz

Tom Callahan clutched at his seat restraints as Colleen drove their big Range Rover through the twisting, narrow cobblestone streets that spiraled down the hill towards the Calacoto section of the La Paz suburbs. It was the season of the poinsettias and along the river tall flowers threw their vibrant colors against a terrain otherwise so rocky and barren it might have been lunar. Houses, mostly dull mud shacks without windows or real doors, hunched against the hills along their route.

The Callahans arrived at the small embassy commissary, met the Schmidts, and prowled the aisles to stock the shelves of their walk-in bodega. Matt and Olga introduced Tom and Colleen to everybody they knew, which seemed to Tom to be everybody in the Embassy.

"Excuse me, Commander Schmidt." the commissary assistant interrupted. "There's a phone call for you."

Matt spoke into the phone for several minutes, then waved Tom over.

"It's the consulate. They need a medevac. That's your department, pal, far too complicated for an old sailor like me. Go for it."

Tom took the phone. "Lieutenant Colonel Callahan. May I help you?"

"John Taylor here. I'm the duty-dog this weekend. We have a problem and need your help. An American citizen, a journalist, has been injured in the mountains west of the town of Apolo. The

Ambassador wants to organize some sort of a rescue. Can you take over from here?"

Damn. Where was Apolo? "Okay, John. I'll go see Colonel Adams, then head up to the Embassy."

"Thank you, Colonel," said Taylor. "We haven't a clue up here on how to organize something like this."

Neither do I, pal. Tom slowly wandered back to the group. Not down here, anyway. Hope Adams knows who to talk to.

"I have to go in to the embassy," Tom apologized to Colleen and explained the situation. "Sorry to wreck your plans for us but it's pretty important."

Colleen walked Tom out to the car. "Tommy, don't worry about me. The Schmidts will haul me around."

"Darlin', I'm sorry."

"Relax, lover boy. You need to go find that poor bloke."

"I just wish I knew how to go about it," Tom confessed. "It's tough enough in the States with all our rescue guys, but Bolivia's a whole different ballgame."

Colleen kissed him lightly on the lips. "Well, if it can be done, you'll be the one to do it."

***

Tom was ushered into Colonel Adam's spacious house to find him in his study reading the morning paper and enjoying a Bloody Mary. Tom explained the problem. Adams folded his paper and frowned. "This kind of mission has never been done in Bolivia before. The FAB has no capability for this sort of thing, no concept of complex mission planning."

He paused and lit a cigarette, got up and paced the room, smoke partially obscuring his red-rimmed eyes. "Furthermore, I just can't see the FAB doing anything to help us. And why was this jerk up in those mountains anyway? Another media asshole trying to make us look bad down here. Screw him! He's no friend of ours."

Tom said, "Colonel, I need to get in touch with the FAB. Please either call them yourself or give me the numbers."

Adam took another drag on his cigarette and crushed it out in an ashtray. "I'll do it for the Ambassador. But you are wasting your time, young man."

***

Armed with the attaché's list of the names and home phone numbers of Bolivian Air Force key players, Tom headed up the hill to La Paz. At the Embassy, he found the Bolivian National Police sergeant and his security staff huddled around the HF radio. "*Buenos días, sargento.* What's the latest from Apolo?"

"*Buenos días, mi coronel.* The gringo journalist has broken both legs. His two companions left him four days ago and hiked out to find help."

Tom whistled softly. "If it took four days to hike out of there, those mountains must be some kind of rugged."

"Yes, sir. They called us on the FAB High Frequency radio from Apolo, asking for assistance. We lost contact because Apolo's in a valley and HF reception is never very good from there."

Tom gathered all available details, thanked them for their help, and headed for the DEA situation room to find maps to actually locate Apolo and orient his thinking. Apolo was beyond the range of a Huey launched from the nearest FAB base at Trinidad. The mountains around Apolo were higher than a Huey's authorized service ceiling. That, combined with hot climate and rough terrain, was why nobody had ever tried to fly choppers up there before. After hours of solitary brainstorming and more fact finding, he called the NAS duty section to arrange for the use of the Hueys.

The deputy chief of NAS said, "Mr. Barton is down in Chimoré village, therefore out of touch. Incommunicado as it were."

"But we need the choppers tomorrow," said Tom.

"Sorry, but I cannot authorize anything of the sort."

"Listen, pal, the choppers are flying whether you want them to or not. You either get off your ass and make this happen or I will."

The receiver went dead.

He slammed down the phone. Bloody bureaucrats! He took a deep breath. Hold on, Tommy boy, you're losing your temper again. Whenever you do, you do something spectacularly stupid.

He forced himself to count to twenty very slowly, then dialed Ambassador Brent's three-digit private home number. "Sir, this is Tom Callahan."

'Yes, Tom. Thank you for calling. Did John Taylor speak with you about the injured journalist?"

"Yes, sir. I'm at the embassy now, putting together a plan. I'll need your permission to proceed. I've tried to make it as simple as possible but it's still going to be tough." He sketched out the bare essentials.

"Sounds complicated to me, Tom, but go ahead."

"The problem, sir, is that Nicholas Barton is in Chimoré and his deputy won't authorize use of the Hueys."

'I'll take care of that. You just do what you think necessary. Use my name when and where you have to. And, Tom…, if you pull this off, it could be our big break and a real shot in the arm for the Bolivian Air Force. Good luck!"

Next Tom called General Camacho at home to request FAB aircraft support and the technical assistance of his aide, Captain Luis Valdez, a Task Force veteran instructor pilot.

Valdez arrived at the Embassy simultaneously with Schmidt. He produced an aerial chart of the Apolo region. "*Mi coronel*, this is the runway—short, dirt, and uphill," he said, pointing out the location of the airfield and the hills surrounding the village. "The biggest FAB airplane that we can get in there is a Fokker 27 twin-engine turboprop."

"Have you been in there before, Luis?" Tom asked.

"*Sí, mi coronel*, many times," Valdez replied, brown face showing a tinge of embarrassment. "Before I got married I had a girlfriend near there. I used to fly up on weekends."

Tom laughed. "Well then, we're going to have to make sure *Señora* Valdez knows that this trip is strictly chaperoned."

The completed plan called for three Task Force UH-1H Hueys to be flown from Trinidad to Apolo the next morning. There they would be refueled with Jet-A flown in from La Paz on a FAB Fokker 27. The DEA CASA 212 transport would be available in the afternoon to bring in more fuel in case the first search was unsuccessful. After talking with the FAB and dispatching Valdez to contact the people at Apolo through the FAB HF radio network, Tom coordinated with the DEA flying operations section and the Task Force to finalize the next day's operation.

***

Tom sat in the jump seat of the Fokker 27 as it made its slow sweeping approach over the jungle-clad mountains into the short landing strip at Apolo. After a bumpy landing, the pilots taxied back up the dirt runway to the lone wooden building that served as a terminal. Tom could see a knot of FAB personnel waiting in the mid-morning sunshine.

Captain Valdez tapped Tom on the shoulder and pointed. "*Mi coronel*, that is Captain Jorge Gomez, a classmate of mine from the Academy. A good man, but cocky. He is commanding the FAB helicopters."

Stairs were brought up to the aircraft. Tom disembarked first, followed by Matt Schmidt, José Hernandez, and Valdez. Captain Gomez, a stocky young man who looked like he could be Valdez' cousin, stepped forward and saluted. *"Capitain Gomez, señor. Bienvenido a Apolo, mi coronel."*

Gomez motioned to the group. Two large civilians ambled up. "Colonel Callahan, these are the injured man's companions. May I present Peter Hudnutt and Luis Garcia?"

Greetings were exchanged. As the FAB ground crews off-loaded fifty-five-gallon drums of aviation fuel from the Fokker, Gomez led the group down to an area near the helicopters where a tent had been erected to serve as a temporary operations center.

Gomez had already worked out his plan: load Nelson's companions on board the Hueys, fly to the general area on the map where Nelson had fallen, and let the companions guide them in on visual cues.

Tom was skeptical. Land features looked very different from the air than from the ground, and the guides, once airborne, would probably become quickly disoriented. Not to mention that he had already learned that maps of that area were grossly inaccurate. Conscious of his advisory-only role, Tom silently vowed to let Gomez organize the expedition his way.

The three-ship formation lifted off and headed generally west, with Gomez in the lead chopper. Tom rode with him, acting as another spotter, José flew in the last aircraft, while Matt remained behind to coordinate for the next sortie, should one be needed. The terrain rose immediately, even steeper than Tom had expected; mountains and jungle were a nightmare combination. No wonder Nelson's companions took nearly four days to hike out.

The FAB aircrews worked well together. Radios chattered as the pilots struggled to keep each other informed. Tom watched the altimeter spiral up through thirteen thousand feet, passing the authorized service ceiling for the aircraft as the search took them into the higher valleys. Skimming the sharp ridges and treetops, the crews searched in vain for any sign of Porter Nelson.

Tom was impressed at the skill of the pilots even as he despaired at the obvious lack of search-and-rescue training. These guys were great sticks, even better than the folks in the embassy knew. Here they sat on the edge of a stall because of the altitude and all they were thinking about was completing the mission. Just keep us in the air, he prayed. None would survive a hike out of there dressed the way they all were.

Near the Bolivia-Peru border

Porter Nelson sat under an ancient mahogany tree in what he had come to think of as his primary observation post, manned from dawn to dark. His five-day old beard was itchy, his bandages stiff with blood. He leaned back against the trunk so he could look up and down the steep valley. The white-water river at the bottom of the steep slope threw off a haze of mist that caught the early afternoon sun, colors dancing. The ever-changing sound of water crashing against the rocks was hypnotic. Porter could see streams plunging from cliffs on opposite sides of the valley, forming two waterfalls. *A lovely scene, a splendid* campsite. *Except*, he thought, *I might die here*. He had grown to loathe the valley. He loathed the trees. He loathed the dirt the trees grew in. He never wanted to sleep anywhere again other than in a king-sized bed with thousand count Egyptian cotton sheets. His broken legs stretched out in front of him. His exposed flesh was swollen from the fractures and multiple insect bites, nasty bugs like none he had ever seen. *I must look like shit, and I smell like a cadaver. I can almost see the waves of stink rolling off my body. Pretty damn pungent. At least these blow flies think so.*

Where the hell are those guys? Shit! Five days already! Or has it been only four? Damn! Can't remember. What happened to them? Did they even make it to Apolo? Were they ambushed? Did they fall? Or just go after their gold?

Porter liked Bolivia, liked the people, maybe even especially the people. He just didn't want to die in Bolivia. And the thought of being eaten was horrifying. Everything that could go wrong had pretty much gone wrong, starting with the cold, nightly monsoons. When it wasn't raining, it was hot with humidity off the scale. The word sultry popped into his mind, unbidden. Sultry, as in hot, humid, and oppressive. But sultry also meant passionate. Big-busted women in smoky bars in black-and-white movies. He laughed. "Porter, old pal," he said aloud, "you've been alone here too long."

Alone because Santiago, that son-of-a-bitch, had taken the mules and most of the supplies. Having no food was bad enough, but losing his rifle was worse. Now he was unarmed except for a machete. If a jaguar happened across him, he would be up the proverbial creek. All he had were a few odds and ends left behind in Santiago's rush to escape: a nearly empty bottle of Amoxicillin to keep the fever at bay, the machete, and his trusty Soviet Army issue signal mirror, a momento of three months spent with a Spetznaz unit in Afghanistan. Right now, his main survival task centered on staying hydrated and keeping his legs elevated. Despite the excruciating pain that shot through his body with every movement, once a day he crawled from his sentinel tree across the steep, rocky access down to the river to fill his two remaining canteens.

Hudnutt and Garcia had also left him a bottle of Chilean pisco brandy to help ease the pain. Nelson resisted the urge to drink it all at once. Getting blotto could be suicidal. He allowed himself only one drink every twelve hours, one at "breakfast" and another as night closed in.

The nights enveloped him in total darkness. He had seen black nights before in the mountains of Borneo and Afghanistan. But there he had been with others, physically fit, and chasing his stories. Normally, he was not a man who could simply sit still. He had to move—to do something.

The sun was high in the sky—what little of it Porter could see through the trees and the sides of the steep valley. The temperature soared and the humidity was nearly suffocating, hard to breathe. A bath would be worth the risk. He stank so bad that every big cat in northern Bolivia had to be homing in on him.

Porter rolled onto his stomach and crawled downhill towards the swirling current, canteen straps clenched in his teeth. Pain lanced through his battered body as he dragged his lacerated legs across the sharp gravel. He paused to rest where the pitch of the beach steepened. The cool spray in his face lured him on. He mentally went through the descent, then maneuvered himself between two boulders. Almost there.

His hand slipped on a wet rock. He surged forward, bashed his head and bulleted into the shallow water. The current caught him and spun him around. He banged into a rock, and almost blacked out from the agony. He spun in the current and wedged between boulders. Torrents of water cascaded over Porter's face and filled his nose and mouth. The heavy flume pinned him down. Waves seemed to press the very life out of him. His lungs might burst. He thrashed against the force of the water. Frantic, he rolled over with his empty canteens beneath him. The buoyancy popped him free.

The unrelenting current carried him further downstream. Gasping for breath, he rolled onto his back and clutched at a canteen strap. Using it as a lasso, he whipped it at the passing rocks, again and again. It caught and stuck in a narrow opening, snapped him around the rocks into a shallow eddy pool, nearly yanking his shoulder apart. Porter fought through the blinding pain and forced his battered legs down until he felt bottom. Screaming in agony, he used his feet to push him onto land. He labored through the gravel until his entire body was away from the water. Blackness sucked him under.

***

A faint rush of water. Gradually, the volume increased as he regained consciousness. He tried to move. The blast of pain from all directions propelled him back to consciousness. He could taste blood on his lips. Fire in his broken legs. New cuts and bruises. His injured shoulder revolted, and he cried out in pain. The ooze on his face was drying blood from yet more slashes in his scalp. His head seemed about to burst. He tried to move but could not seem to roll over or sit up. A panic surged through him, more terrifying than the cold water that had nearly crushed him into the rocks.

Dazed, Nelson was slow to hear a low humming noise. He looked around, unsure what the sound was and where it was coming from. It grew louder. Whop-whop-whop. His heart leapt. A helicopter! But where?

Frantic now, he clawed at the ground, desperate to get back to the camp site and his signal fire. An olive-drab military helicopter flashed overhead, perpendicular to the valley. He screamed and flailed his arms. But the chopper stayed its course until it disappeared behind the ridge.

"Please God! Let them come back! Make them come back!" Silence.

Apolo Airfield, Bolivia

Nearly two hours after takeoff, fuel state low, the Red Devil choppers returned to Apolo. As the mechanics refueled the aircraft, Tom motioned Captain Gomez aside for a private chat.

"I am impressed by your leadership, Gomez. But what you're doing won't work."

"But, Colonel, we will find him!"

"Not the way you're going about it, Captain. Listen up." Tom gave him a quick and dirty ten-minute lecture on search and rescue techniques.

Gomez nodded, chastened. He thought for a few moments, then said, "Sir, I would be pleased if you would give that same lecture to my troops."

Gomez called his crews together in the ops tent. "Men, I have asked Colonel Callahan to lend his expertise to our operation." With a wave of his hand, Gomez gave Tom the floor. "Sir, if you would."

This time Tom's briefing was more detailed. "In summary, gentlemen, slow down. Keep your eyes outside. This guy is an experienced outdoorsman in a survival situation. There should be a signal fire. He has two broken legs so he hasn't gone anywhere. He fell down a cliff into a valley with twin waterfalls. Look for water."

As Tom climbed back into the lead Huey, Schmidt shouted over the engine noise. "Weather's coming in fast, Tom. Better get that guy back soon!"

***

Today was Porter's last day, one way or another. He had missed the helicopter fly-by. Why would it come back? *God*, he thought, *it just had to!* The fire was ready to go, sodden wood and all. He would be ready this time.

He had to be. He knew something about helicopter operations from his days in Afghanistan. Search and rescue guys rarely backtracked. But maybe, just maybe, this would be such a time. Woozy as he was, he knew he couldn't survive much longer.

Shit, who am I kidding? I'm done for. His eye caught sight of the half-empty bottle of pisco. Why not? The phrase dead-drunk popped into his mind. *Why the hell not? Why waste good pisco? I'm going to die anyway.* He crawled towards the bottle. He held the smooth glass in his hand. The temptation was strong. *No! Not yet. I can always drink this tomorrow. Just one more day, Porter, old bean. Stay with it one more day. You can always get drunk tomorrow.*

Then he heard it. A machine! It's gotta be the goddamn chopper!

He dropped the bottle and rolled himself towards the fire. Matches! *Shit! Santiago stole the matches! Jesus, how stupid can I be? Gotta get my lighter!* He scuttled on his stomach towards his pack, desperate. He tore at the pockets, frantic. His hand closed on glass. His signal mirror! God bless the Russian Army!

Tom could see huge thunderclouds building over the mountains in the heat of the afternoon. The lead Huey bounced and shook through the turbulent air. He tightened his shoulder straps, leaned forward, and craned his neck to see between the pilots as they flew through the valleys.

He checked his watch. Nothing except dark-green jungle and the occasional river had flashed under the choppers for over an hour. He cross-checked the fuel gauges. Fifteen minutes left—max. With the weather coming in, this was probably the last sortie of the day. Tom stared through the cockpit windscreen. The chopper rolled in on another river.

There! A flash off to the right. Tom pounded Gomez' shoulder and pointed. The helicopter banked sharply and seemed to pause in mid-air as the pilot heeled it over to come around to the new heading. Long seconds passed.

"I have it, sir!" said Gomez, excited. "Something flashing!"

"Signal mirror, Captain. Look, there are the twin waterfalls!"

They closed in. "I have a visual on our man!" said Gomez. He maneuvered the aircraft and paused about fifty meters away, hovering above the rocky terrain. "I can't land here, sir—overhangs."

Tom threw off his shoulder straps, hooked up the safety harness and leaned out the door.

"I'll go down."

The crew chief swung the winch perpendicular to the side of the aircraft. Tom snapped himself onto the lowering device and gave a thumbs-up. He descended, twisting in the rotor downwash, protecting his eyes.

Dismounting and shielding his eyes from the blowing dirt and sand, Tom waved the chopper off. He trotted over to the injured man and shouted over the high-pitched whine of the engine, "Mr. Nelson,

I'm Tom Callahan. Ambassador Brent sends his regards. We're here to take you home."

Nelson clutched at Tom's hand. "What the…? American? Here?"

Tom laughed. "Lieutenant Colonel Thomas Patrick Callahan, United States Air Force, at your service. You look like you've had a tough week, *amigo*."

Checking over Nelson's damaged legs, he made some adjustments to the crude wooden splints.

Nelson said, "Don't know why you're in Bolivia. Don't care. But I will never complain about paying taxes again."

"No charge, Porter. Always ready to help. We have a medic back in Apolo. And you look like you could use some food."

"Starving. I could eat a plate of roasted goat sphincters. And a beer."

"We might be able to find you a beer, my friend. After the medic, though."

Tom signaled to the helicopter pilot. He eased the Huey over the camp and let down the heavy penetrator device. "You'll have to go alone. The terrain here is too steep and rugged to land the Huey. Sorry but this is going to hurt."

Nelson waved it off. "Don't worry," he yelled. "Just get me the hell out of here!" Tom let the penetrator touch the earth to ground any electrical charge, then dragged Nelson to the hoist. He unfolded the seat, fastened the injured man on with the safety strap, and gave a thumbs-up to the aircrew. He moved away from the rotor wash and watched as Nelson was hoisted aloft and wrestled into the helicopter.

The crew chief leaned out and gave Tom a thumbs up.

"Yeah, man!" Tom shouted and danced a little jig. He could see the pilots laugh as they moved back to pick him up.

Again they lowered the penetrator and soon Tom reached the door of the helicopter. He swung himself inside, unsnapped, hugged the crew chief, and clapped the pilots on the shoulder. Nelson lay huddled on the helicopter stretcher, face pale.

As the aircraft banked away toward the airfield, Tom pulled open a small cooler. He shouted over the engine noise, "It's not goat sphincters and beer, but maybe this will help." He handed the journalist a peanut butter sandwich and a Gatorade.

Chapter Eight

Nicholas Barton III stormed into the MILGROUP offices. "Callahan, just what the hell do you think you're doing with my helicopters?"

Tom looked up from putting the finishing touches on his report. "Why, good morning, Nicholas. What can I do for you?"

Barton's voice rose and echoed off the walls of Tom's tiny office, "Keep your bloody hands off my helicopters!"

Schmidt stepped in. "Calm down, Nicholas. Everything was cleared by the Ambassador. Tom talked to your deputy. You were out of the loop because you were in Chimoré."

"I leave town and you assholes try to take over my section! You could have compromised our big operation next week."

"Enough of that crap, Barton," Schmidt said in an icy tone. "If you have any problems, you can take your complaints to the Ambassador. But leave my people alone, understand?"

Tom stood. "Nicholas, look at this more positively. Just think of it as a feint. Nobody would expect us to be launching an operation right after something like this. The choppers over flew an area where they had never operated before. Now a whole new section of the country knows about the Red Devils. The narcos know we can expand our operating territory whenever we need to."

Barton's face went beet red. "I'll get you for this, Callahan!" and stormed out of the MILGROUP.

Tom watched Barton's broad backside as it lumbered down the hall. "Matt, I think our NAS friend is a tiny bit peeved."

Thirty minutes later, the department heads assembled in the embassy conference room for their Monday morning country team meeting. Matt and Tom were greeted with back-slapping congratulations from the DEA and USIS chiefs, silence from Adams, and smoldering hostility from Barton.

"Great job, Tom!" said George Rodgers, cigar clenched between his stained teeth as usual, leaning over the table to shake hands. "Really tremendous."

"Couldn't have done it without DEA support, George. We needed the extra gas your guys flew in."

USIS Chief Clarence Johnson said, "American journalists the world over will get a kick out of this, Tom. Now maybe they'll be a bit easier on embassy staffs." The beefy black man smiled. "Not bloody likely, but a pleasant thought. Anyway, congratulations. Well done."

All conversation ceased as Ambassador Brent entered, trailed by Patricia Pointer. He slid into his leather captain's chair at the center of the long walnut table and took a long look around the room. Beaming, he said, "I'm sure you all have heard the news, but I want to officially offer my congratulations to the MILGROUP who engineered a brilliant rescue yesterday and saved an American journalist from certain death." Brent raised an eyebrow in Tom's direction. "Mr. Nelson also said something about a picnic. Getting drunk? Colonel, do you know anything about that? Picnic baskets and booze?"

"Actually, Mr. Ambassador," Tom deadpanned, "There are many historical precedents. For example, in Europe, St. Bernard rescue dogs carry small barrels of rum. Perhaps Mr. Nelson was referring to being drunk with happiness."

"I'm sure that's it!" replied the Ambassador, still beaming. "Tom, now that you've experienced your trial by fire, what were your impressions of the Red Devils?"

Tom stalled and looked down at his notes, then back up to meet the Ambassador's probing eyes. "Well, sir, initially, I thought everything was great. But I got to spend some time with those guys this past weekend. There are some serious issues that need to be corrected."

The Ambassador stiffened and his smile faded. "Such as?"

"Mr. Ambassador," said Tom, taking the plunge, "the original reason the Red Devils were placed in Cochabamba was because the FAB's only helicopter unit was there. Cochabamba is about eighty-three hundred feet above sea level in a valley surrounded by fourteen-thousand-foot mountains. To get in and out of the city, the Hueys have to fly through narrow passes well in excess of their authorized service ceiling. Those high-altitude flights have resulted in an average of one compressor stall per month at about three hundred fifty thousand dollars a pop—not to mention two bent tail booms caused by hard landings."

Barton waved a well-manicured hand, dismissing Tom's argument. "We're under our funding ceiling. Things are just fine the way they are."

"Nicholas, this isn't a budget exercise," Tom responded, surprised. "These are real people we're talking about."

"You've been out on a helicopter once, so now you're an expert on helicopter operations, Callahan?" Patricia Pointer asked.

"Patricia, have you ever talked with an aircrew member?"

Pointer flinched as if he had slapped her. "Of course not. They just drive us around."

Tom bit his tongue and forced himself to count to ten. "Patricia, the nice flat safe terrain between Trinidad, Santa Cruz, and Chimoré where most of the embassy staff flies is not where the Red Devils normally operate. That kind of flying leads people here to mistake these machines for flying taxicabs. On the contrary, these guys are operational. They fly in combat conditions all the time." He shook his head. "But that's a different discussion. The real concern I have now is those compressor stalls."

"Okay, Tom," said the USIS chief. "Could you please explain 'compressor stall' in a way an old reporter can understand?"

"Certainly, Clarence. Inside a jet engine, compressor blades push the incoming air through, compressing it until it reaches the combustion chamber. A compressor stall is an interruption in the air flow for some reason—in this case, because of exceeding altitude capability of the engine. The interruption of airflow is sort of like a hiccup, except it can result in either damage to the compressor blades or cause the engine to quit, or both. It can get hairy pretty quickly."

The reporter regarded Tom for a few long seconds. "Have you ever experienced a compressor stall?"

Tom nodded. "A couple of times, as a matter of fact. While I was an exchange pilot in Australia, I had one at low altitude in a single engine Mirage coming off a gunnery pass. The engine basically tore itself apart, and I had to eject." Tom turned to face Barton. "These helicopter guys don't have ejection seats, Nicholas. Somebody could die." He paused to let that sink in before addressing the Ambassador. "Sir, a crash is inevitable if the Red Devils stay in Cochabamba...."

Barton's fist crashed down on the walnut table. "Callahan, I won't sit here and let you talk about the Task Force. It is not your program—it's not for you to decide."

"Nicholas," Brent said, "all the programs here are U.S. government, not from any particular agency." He paused and drummed his fingers on the table. "But you're right—it's not Tom's decision. Nor is it for any one individual alone to decide. I have the responsibility for the decision. I need input from everybody. That's why this is an appropriate forum for Tom to bring up the discussion."

George Rogers leaned forward. "Where do you want to put the helicopters, Tom?"

"I don't know yet—haven't had time to study it." Tom shrugged. "Probably Santa Cruz or Trinidad. Both are less than a thousand feet above sea level and are even closer to our area of operations than Cochabamba."

Tapping his gold pen against his teeth, the Ambassador thought for a moment. "Colonel Callahan's brought up some interesting ideas. The prudent thing is to study them. I want you two," he pointed at Barton and Tom, "to research the issues and make recommendations for basing the Red Devils. We created the unit, and we owe it to them to keep their interests in mind, especially after that rescue."

Tom agreed. Barton muttered something under his breath.

"Before we adjourn," said the Ambassador, "I need to inform you that I just received an unexpected call from Southern Command headquarters. The new Commander-in-Chief of SOUTHCOM, General

Thornton, will be stopping in on his way back from Argentina on Friday for several hours of briefings. This will be his first visit here. Everyone knows the enormous importance of General Thornton and SOUTHCOM to our programs. You are expected to be ready to brief the General on any subject he wants to know about. With any luck, he'll finally announce his selection for our new MILGROUP commander. If so, Matt, you'll be free of those shackles."

"Fine with me, Mr. Ambassador." A smile split his freckled face. "Maybe I'll be able to get out with the troops where I belong."

"That's it, people. Let's get back to work." The Ambassador stood, then turned to Callahan. "Oh, Tom, I'm having the Japanese ambassador and some others over tonight for dinner. Informal, nothing special, just a few friends. I'd like you and Colleen to join us. Consider it an opportunity to practice your Japanese."

***

Back in the relative safety of the MILGROUP, Matt relaxed in his chair and kicked his feet up on his desk. "Congratulations, Tom, you were great! You have now displaced me as the person most hated by Nick and Patricia. I thought nobody'd ever be able to do that. And you haven't even been here a week yet. Can't wait to see what you come up with next."

Tom chewed on his lip and sat down across from Matt. "That didn't go well, did it?"

"Listen, pal, Nicholas Barton is the quintessential Washington brain-dead bureaucrat. He's only interested in furthering his career in any way he can."

"Even over the bodies of some aviators?" Tom shook his head.

"Yep! Such are the ways of our brethren in Washington. Admit a mistake? Not a chance. Nick is a headquarters weenie out in the field to get some command time so his resumé will look good for the next promotion board. You know—an asshole."

"The thing is, Matt, all of us including Barton will be gone in a year or two. These flyers will be here for the rest of their careers—or lives. They have to live with our decisions."

"Look, Tom," said Matt, no longer smiling. "Make no mistake about it. What you did in there was exactly right. You're just going to have to accept that Barton and Pointer hate you now. So, big deal. Let's just hope this new MILGROUP commander, whoever he is, has the courage to stand up to those peckerheads."

Chapter Nine

Headquarters, U.S. Army South (USARSO) Fort Clayton, Panama

The formation of sweating soldiers rounded the last corner of the expansive parade ground, guidons flying, the Airborne cadence carrying through the early morning still air across the huge quadrangle. Colonel Billie D. Steele, U.S. Army, zigged around the formation, shouting and cursing to ensure that the men were in perfect formation as they ran past the knot of photographers assembled in front of the USARSO Headquarters building. General Jefferson E. Thornton, III, U.S. Army, Commander-in-Chief (CINC), U.S. Southern Command, led the run. The carefully orchestrated photo op was one more step in Thornton's career.

Colonel Steele, Thornton's executive officer, darted in and out of the tight formation. Even on a military base, a place renowned for outstanding physical specimens, Steele's powerful build stood out like a tank in a Volkswagen showroom. His muscular frame was topped by a bullet head, bristling with close-cropped hair. His acne-scarred face contorted as he screamed in the ears of soldiers unfortunate enough to attract his attention.

Steele knew that Thornton needed the appearance of perfection. A man in a hurry, the General had blown into Panama six weeks ago after the surprise retirement of the previous CINC. Well-connected in Washington, he knew everyone who was anyone and the location of all their skeletons, real and imagined. He could make things happen or he could—and would—withhold resources and kill the pet projects of those who crossed him. Steele's job was to see that Thornton's projects and plans were executed promptly with no deviations tolerated.

After halting the formation and smiling professionally for the requisite photographs, Thornton's people kept the troops at a discreet distance while the slender, elegant General and the bulky Steele walked together across the quadrangle to cool down from the run. They ignored the commanding general of USARSO, a mere brigadier, and his staff. Sweat streamed down their bodies in the heat of the Panamanian morning. Both stood and watched for several minutes as a Liberian-flagged freighter steamed past in the channel of the Panama Canal less than five hundred yards away. The freighter appeared to be sailing down the highway on the other side of the USARSO perimeter fence.

The agitated swipes of the General's towel alerted Steele to the General's bad mood.

Thornton turned and said, "That son-of-a-bitch Brent is not cooperating with me in Bolivia. I need to get control of all the counternarcotics programs in-theater ASAP before our new weak-kneed president cuts off all our money. I want my people in place and running those programs *yesterday*."

"Yes, sir," Steele said. "I understand. Now that we don't have no more forces in the Balkans, those programs are the only game in town,"

"I'm a war-fighting CINC, damn it! One of only five the Department of Defense has in the whole world. I've got combat troops under my command, for Christ's sake." Thornton swung his towel. "Our South American programs are on Washington's front burner. This is *the* place to be right now. I don't give a damn what the asshole ambassadors think. I don't have time for those limp-wristed State Department morons to make up their minds."

He stretched his arms over his head and wiped his carefully shaven face. "I've decided that I need to put my own man in Bolivia." He turned and drilled his cold eyes into Steele. "So, I want you to go down there, Billie."

Steele groaned inwardly. He didn't want the job. He wanted to be where the action was, with Thornton.

"Sir, you want me to go to Bolivia to chase narcos?"

"Damn it, Billie, you've missed the point. The narcos are unimportant. What is important is getting control of the programs. Money, people, programs. They all fall into place when you're pulling the right levers." Thornton wiped the sweat from his forehead. "Power. That's what life's all about. Hell, the counternarcotics programs are all doomed to failure. Those idiots in Washington have no earthly idea of what's going on down here. But they're still pumping real money and people into our theater of operations."

Thornton glanced at Steele's face and laughed. "Cheer up, Billie. The one-star list comes out in a few weeks. You'll be on it—it's already fixed. You'll only be in Bolivia five, six months max. I'm not planning on being here very long. You know that. I've got bigger plans than SOUTHCOM, but I had to come here for the four-star billet and visibility. Now I'm a CINC. If I work it right, in eighteen months, I'll move over to be Supreme Allied Commander-Europe, a real power position. From there, who knows? And you'll be with me, with a command billet of your own under your belt. First, though, we have to do this."

He thumped Steele's chest. "Remember, you'll be my man in Bolivia, the CINC's representative—don't underestimate the clout of that position. You go down south and get your hands around the throat of the Ambassador and his deputy, that witch. I don't know where she came from—and don't care. All I know is that somehow she convinced Brent to put her in charge of the counternarcotics program. She doesn't know beans about tactics, logistics, or anything. A typical arrogant, anti-military Ivy League know-it-all, and she's smothering the program with paperwork, covering her pretty ass. Probably trying to be an ambassador herself."

Thornton took a swig of water from Steele's bottle, rinsed his mouth and spat. "She'll be your second target, though. Start off with the MILGROUP. That'll be easy. None of the officers there are worth a damn. That's why those weenies are in MILGROUPs in the first place."

Thornton clapped Steele on the back. "Just kick some ass, Billie-boy! You're good at that!"

Steele sighed. He liked being able to throw around the General's four stars in Panama. His peers despised him, but it didn't matter. He didn't need them. He needed only Thornton. Thornton had a coterie of hand-picked officers such as Steele on his staff, unscrupulous men, willing to do Thornton's bidding because they knew he would take care of them. Steele was tied to the CINC tighter than any marriage could bind him.

"*A sus órdenes, mi general*," Steele smiled, and made a show of clicking his heels. "I can use the chance to polish up my West Texas Spanish."

The Residence
Sopocachi

"Pretty good party," said Tom Callahan to his colleague, José Hernandez. "Fancy getting together at the Residence to play volleyball with diplomats from Eastern Europe! Times sure have changed!"

The lush grounds of the U.S. Ambassador's Residence were decorated with flags of the United States and the countries of the former Warsaw Pact. Tables were spread with food, decorations, and flowers. There was a long line at each of the two bars set up at opposite sides of the grounds. Diplomats of former Warsaw Pact embassies and their families took advantage of the relaxation of political tensions to get to know the American contingent in the second annual "US versus Them" volleyball tournament.

Hernandez' eyes followed the lively volley. "The worst thing is that the commies are cleaning our clocks! They must play volleyball every day from age three. Look at that old guy spike. Jeez!" Yet another Russian spiked a shot down the throats of the American team, composed mostly of young, muscular Marines from the embassy guard detail.

"Look over there, Tom. Pointer's with that new Cuban diplomat, Cortez. I saw his picture in the paper this morning."

Tom saw Pointer, attired in a flowered print dress and matching stiletto heels that Colleen would never wear, standing close to the Cuban, engaged in an animated conversation. "And?"

"Seems like she always hangs out at these social events with Soviet Bloc types or Marxists."

"So she's a commie groupie. You've been reading too many spy novels, amigo. This is the real world."

José shook his head. "Pointer is left-leaning, even by State Department standards, Tom. Have you ever listened to her after she's had a few drinks? She's a mean drunk. She thinks she's so fine, so much smarter than the rest of us."

"José, being intellectually arrogant is not a political statement or a crime. If it were, we'd have to shoot half the people in the State Department. She's just working the crowd. Maybe she's trying to get some good intelligence to send to Washington."

"If she is, she's keeping it to herself. I've asked the spooks in the embassy. She never sends any intel. I don't trust her one little tiny bit. And neither does Matt."

Tom said, "And speak of the devil, look what the tide washed up."

Matt Schmidt stepped into the weak afternoon sunlight, carrying a small bundle in his arms, grinning like had just won an Olympic medal. "Boys, I'd like you to meet my first-born son."

He laughed at the sight of his two now speechless friends. "I had a phone call yesterday afternoon from some Bolivian Navy friends," he said. "They'd heard of a three-day-old baby whose mother had just died, leaving no known father or relatives. We went to look at him and just fell in love. Olga is over the moon."

"He's beautiful," said José, spellbound, staring into the baby's olive-shaped, bottomless black eyes. "*Felicidades, Mateo!* Could I hold him, please? I need the practice."

Matt carefully transferred the tiny bundle to José's arms. "I wanted to name him Zachary after my father. But Olga warned me that her family would never be able to pronounce it properly, so we settled on Paul."

José laughed. "I hope you realize that the Garcias will always call him Pablo."

Tom asked, "Why did you decide to adopt rather than to keep trying to have your own?"

"Hey, Tom, this boy is my own, as of last night. I was raised in a family of eight kids—two were adopted. It's the greatest thing going. And, at our ages, Olga and I don't have any more time to waste."

"So, what do you have to do now?" asked José.

Matt reached for the baby. "The laws here about adoption are pretty strict for foreigners. Some Bolivians are sensitive about Bolivian babies leaving the country. We're lucky that Olga's a Latina. Ambassador Brent told Patricia Pointer to help us. Despite our differences, she's been surprisingly effective. We'll get some legal rights this week from the Children's Courts. But have to wait at least six months before we get the final adoption decree. Then he's ours, no matter where the Navy sends us next."

"This calls for champagne!" Tom said with forced enthusiasm. "Be right back." As he headed to the bar under a red, white, and blue canopy in the trees, Tom passed the newly arrived Cuban diplomat leaving the Residence grounds. Draped on his arm was Patricia Pointer, carrying a long-stemmed red rose.

Chapter Ten

U.S. Embassy, La Paz

General Thornton's arrival had thrown the Embassy into a tizzy. He had been briefed, wined and dined, and briefed again by nearly the entire State Department staff.

Tom Callahan sat cooling his heels in the Embassy multi-purpose room with his MILGROUP colleagues, waiting for their fifteen minutes of fame. Thanks to Patricia Pointer's published schedule, the MILGROUP presentation was dead last. In keeping with the lifestyle in Bolivia, the briefings had begun late and run past General Thornton's scheduled departure. Now Thornton was sequestered in the Ambassador's office, meeting privately with Brent, Patricia Pointer, George Rodgers, and Nicholas Barton III. It looked like the MILGROUP briefing would not happen.

Matt Schmidt, looking tired and drawn from his first four nights of feeding young Paul, slumped over the conference table. José read over the briefing again as Tom leafed through a stack of FAB publications.

Suddenly General Thornton appeared at the door accompanied by a large, stocky Army colonel. José blurted out a quick "ten-hut!" The officers scrambled to their feet.

General Thornton looked them over, then simply said, "Gentlemen, as of this moment, Colonel Steele is your commander."

Steele closed the door behind the departing General and turned to the astonished MILGROUP officers. "What the hell is going on here?" he barked. "You look like a bunch of State Department weenies, not military officers! Things are going to change now that I'm in charge here. Starting tomorrow morning." He swung his gaze from one officer to the next. "I want the entire MILGROUP in the Embassy at 0700 to brief me on the current situation. Then I'll lay down the new way of life you girls are going to live. That's zero-seven hundred, ladies, in uniform." He spun and hurried after Thornton.

The three friends stood at stunned attention.

Matt broke the silence. "Maybe I submitted those extension papers in a bit too soon."

"*Dios mío!* What an asshole," said José.

"Where in the world did this guy come from?" asked Tom. "I thought officers like that died out after the Franco-Prussian War."

José shrugged. "All I know is that he's new to Panama. He showed up in Thornton's entourage. I'll get on the horn to some buddies up there and see what I can find out about him."

"In the meantime, I've got a small problem," Tom said. "I've got a takeoff in three hours to take the Ambassador up to Cobija for a of couple days. Obviously, I can't make that meeting tomorrow."

"No problem, Tom," Matt said. "Even a Neanderthal like Steele knows ambassadors outrank colonels. I'll let him know where you are."

Tom grinned. "Have fun."

"We'll be good little scouts, and he'll come around," José ventured, unconvinced.

"Horsefeathers!" Matt snapped. "I'd rather hug a grizzly than kiss up to that sonofabitch."

"Relax, Matt," Tom said. "Steele will calm down or he'll self destruct down here. No way the Ambassador will let him wreck things."

"Not so fast, Tom," Matt said. "Brent pissed off SOUTHCOM big time when he had the last MILGROUP commander fired. He can't do it again, even if Steele is an asshole. He depends too much on SOUTHCOM's goodwill to work our programs. And Steele must be one of Thornton's boys or he wouldn't be here."

He shook his head, "until we can somehow de-fang this Prussian wanna-be, we're stuck with him." He slumped into his chair. "Looks like the end of paradise for us."

88

U.S. Embassy, La Paz,
0700 Hours

Colonel Billie D. Steele strode into the embassy multi-purpose room. Dressed in his tailored Class A uniform with its five rows of ribbons, he knew he cut an imposing figure. His mind raced through his carefully prepared and rehearsed text. Steele had learned many things from General Thornton; how to force his will into the teeny minds of underlings was at the top of the list. Separating the officers from the support of the enlisted men was his first priority. Steele looked forward to this meeting. Kicking butt was his specialty. Now it was show time.

"Gentlemen, the MILGROUP commander!" barked the sergeant closest to the door. All snapped to attention.

Steele turned and slowly surveyed the room, staring at the frozen faces, trying to force the power of his personality into each mind as he had witnessed Thornton do so many times.

"At ease," he snarled. The men went to parade rest. Deliberately not giving permission to be seated, Steele walked slowly back and forth in front of the men. "As of 1600 hours yesterday, you now have adult leadership in this MILGROUP. You people have been out of the military far too long. Things are going to change around here. General Thornton selected me as the most qualified man in the entire United States military establishment to straighten out the mess in this unit and in this embassy. You will perform or you will be replaced! Is that understood?"

The Army members of the MILGROUP, far more used to this type of haranguing than members of the other services, responded with a chorus of, "Yes, Sir!"

Steele continued to pace the narrow room. "I'm here to provide you with the best Oh-6 leadership in the U.S. Army! You people won't have the privilege of working for me for long. I intend to be on the next promotion list of general officers and out of this dump. But until I do, you are mine. Do not ever forget that!"

Snapping out the order to be seated, Steele instructed Schmidt to begin the briefing. As Matt began, Steele's eyes darted around the room, taking inventory of the staff's faces, one at a time. He interrupted, "Where's the Air Force guy—what's his name?"

"Sir, Lieutenant Colonel Callahan flew the Ambassador to Santa Cruz yesterday," Matt Schmidt replied.

"What do you mean, flew to Santa Cruz?" Steele's eyes narrowed. "Didn't I give orders for everyone to be present for duty here this morning? Since when are orders optional?"

"Sir, he was scheduled to fly the Ambassador to Cobija and Santa Cruz. You left the room yesterday before we could speak to you."

Steele swore and pitched his yellow note pad across the room, nearly hitting a sergeant in the head. "Who gave him permission to miss this meeting? Who countermanded my orders?"

Matt replied in an even tone, "Colonel, I told him—"

"I should have known it would be you, Schmidt. That's just the kind of thing I've been led to believe you'd do—try to screw your commander."

Red-faced, Matt began, "Colonel, I—"

"Shut up, Schmidt! Now I know why this unit is so screwed up. It was the officers all along. These men will benefit from my leadership now, Schmidt. You're through as acting commander, mister. You're not fit to command a rowboat, much less a group of men like these."

Matt jumped to his feet. "Just a minute, Colonel—"

"Sit down and shut up!" Steele's veins bulged on the side of his massive neck. "One more word from you and you're outta here! Permanently, mister. Are you ready for that?"

Schmidt stopped abruptly. Steele saw the stricken look on his face and knew he had beaten him. Officers were so damned predictable. Threaten their careers and they folded like lawn chairs. Schmidt was no better. Steele glowered around the room, daring others to challenge him as Schmidt sank down. The briefings continued through the rest of the morning.

Four hours later, Steele slipped into the Ambassador's office, to search for anything that Thornton could use. Instead, he found the DCM, Patricia Pointer, sitting at the desk. She looked up with a start.

"Oh, excuse me, ma'am. Thought maybe the Ambassador would be in," he lied.

"No, he's off to the countryside for three days." Then she added in a low, bitter tone, "He's not particularly adept at letting us know his plans in advance."

Steele gave her a tight smile. "I'm used to serving masters like that, Patricia. Don't let them get to you. Often, they treat the worst those who they're threatened by."

She looked up, as if seeing him for the first time. *Bingo!* Steele thought, with rising excitement. *Stay with it, boy. But be careful. She's a smart 'un.*

She slowly appraised Steele again, hazel eyes sweeping him from head to foot, then motioned him to a chair.

Steele sat down and encouraged her to speak openly of her opinions of the Embassy. He also found out that Patricia Pointer had spent an undergraduate year studying abroad at the *Freie Universtät Berlin*, spoke German, Spanish, and French fluently, and was Phi Beta Kappa, whatever that meant. He hadn't taken her for a sorority type.

After about twenty minutes she concluded with, "Our beloved Ambassador has very strong likes and dislikes. For example, he loves your Commander Matt Schmidt and Golden Boy Callahan."

He snorted. "Well, he's dead wrong there. Schmidt's a limp-dick and Callahan's a wimpy fly boy, out playing with his toy airplane instead of working for a living. They're both in for a rough time if they think they can hide behind the Ambassador. Hell, I just threatened to ship Schmidt home, and he wilted like a two-day-old salad."

Pointer laughed. "Well, you sure found his weak spot fast enough, Colonel. Schmidt's particularly vulnerable right now."

"Why is that, ma'am?"

"He and his wife just got a Bolivian baby. They have to stay here for another six months to complete the adoption or they'll lose him. Mrs. Schmidt is busy building a new utopia for their precious little darling. I suspect that if anything happened to the baby, Olga would be a basket case." She smiled again. Steele felt a stab of excitement. "Normally, Matt Schmidt could be counted on to go nose-to-nose with any authority figure. But you've discovered his Achilles heel. Congratulations."

Steele filed away that little tidbit. He'd have to watch Schmidt. "Well, Patricia, as the ranking DoD officer in-country, my word is law for those little pricks. I'm on top here and I can get what I want. If anybody can handle those two prima donnas, it's Brass Balls Billie."

He watched her carefully for a reaction. Nothing. He smiled inwardly. This job was going to be easier and a hell of a lot more fun than Thornton meant it to be. What a favor, after all.

***

Forty-eight hours later, Steele sat back in his executive leather chair, gazing out of his Embassy office at the rooftops of La Paz, reflecting on the time since he had met Patricia Pointer. After their conversation in the Embassy, she had swept him away as he had never been before. Smart, sexy, and as tough as the diamonds she loved to wear. An intriguing puzzle, quite unlike the airheads he normally dallied with. American women were spoiled, headstrong, and spirited like unbroken mares.

Early in his career with Thornton, the General had counseled Steele on the need to have a wife in order to be successful in the Army. Steele had gone wife-hunting and had managed to find the near impossible: a mild-mannered, lonely heiress from West Texas with just enough family oil money to propel Steele from lower to upper middle class. Their gray, passionless relationship had served them both well. He had the requisite wife to trot out when social occasions demanded, and she had a fast-track Army officer whose job conveniently took him away from her ranch for long periods of time, a story that played well in conservative Midland and Odessa. Natalie Steele had been content to remain in the background, comfortably settling into her social role as rancher and Army wife. She was reluctant to leave Texas for the high altitudes of La Paz. They had agreed to meet in two months in Rio as a public face-saving tactic satisfactory to both.

Steele knew that having an affair here in the small embassy population was not smart, even for a man who delighted in breaking the rules. But he couldn't stop himself from accepting Pointer's invitation to her house for lunch. Over drinks and imported oysters, conversation had rapidly turned to double entendres. By late-afternoon, he had found himself in her ornate bedroom.

Steele was a great, coarse bull of a man, not given to subtleties, especially in bed. Surprising him, this suited the sophisticated Pointer. Now, seated in his comfortable yet efficient office, looking quite the professional, he gently massaged his neck and shoulders and smiled at the flashbacks the bruises evoked. This morning, he had even foregone his usual early morning run for a soak bath in his apartment hot tub. He and Pointer were the same; they could satisfy each other's needs. He wondered if she were thinking of him at that moment. He would have to be very discreet, but he was ready to do anything to keep this new life episode alive.

USAF C-12D 30499
25,000 feet above the jungle east of La Paz

Approaching La Paz from the east in clear weather was a visual experience of a lifetime. Over the course of the ninety-minute flight from Santa Cruz, Tom Callahan watched the flat, cultivated tropical plains surrounding the city slowly give way to the tropical terrain and rivers curving off towards the Bolivian city of Trinidad and the border with Brazil to the north. Off the left wing to the south, the hills gently rose and gradually became rugged, snow-covered peaks, utterly devoid of vegetation. The mountain range eventually split, leaving just enough room for the Cochabamba Valley, with its crazy patchwork of farms clustered along the narrow river that wound its way downhill. Illimani, at 21,122 feet, loomed straight ahead, snow-covered and brooding. The Cordillera stretched off to the horizon both north and south, with jagged, white-topped mountains waiting patiently to snag unwary aviators.

But today, Tom's view was spoiled by a line of huge cumulonimbus clouds building up along the eastern edge of the Cordillera, towering overhead, and blocking out the mountains. Colored like an ugly bruise, they threatened violent weather.

As pilot-in-command of this flight, Tom flew from the left seat. He found more pleasure in the seven-passenger Beechcraft C-12 than he had expected. The sturdy, maneuverable, and quiet plane was just fast enough not to be boring. He particularly enjoyed flying through the mountains into the short dirt strips that were common in Bolivia, something he had never before done in a USAF airplane.

Adjusting the weather radar, he searched the clouds ahead for signs of embedded thunderstorms. As they entered the solid overcast, Adams said, "We're cleared down to eighteen thousand feet. Let's go. Standing by with the descent checklist."

Tom glanced over his instruments. "We're still forty miles out. I'll stay up here for a bit longer."

"Let's go down now," said Adams, jabbing a finger at Tom. "Why wait until we're right over the field and have to do all that fighter pilot shit, screaming down and bouncing the Ambassador around? You're right on course. Lots of lateral clearance. I strongly recommend that we begin our descent now, mister."

"Sir," responded Tom, "the controller said 'at pilot's discretion'. There's no radar coverage. We're in the weather. I don't know exactly where the mountains are—"

"Damn it, I'm a colonel and I said we're going down! *Now!*"

"I'm pilot-in-command," Tom said. "We're going to stay up here at twenty-three thousand until I can see. I'll be damned if I'm going to fly into a mountain."

Adams slammed the checklist to the floor and gave Tom a murderous look. Tom stared back at him until Adams dropped his eyes. Tom remembered a story General Walters had told him about his father. Sean Callahan, then the youngest full colonel in the Air Force, had remained a colonel for six years after he jumped on some asshole who thought he was God because he wore a star. Must be genetic, this aversion to assholes.

They flew on through the clouds in heavy silence. Tom busied himself with preparations for the approach and landing, Adams sat sullen, with arms crossed, staring out the windscreen. Suddenly, the clouds parted. Through the ragged opening, less than two thousand feet directly below, were the rugged glaciers adorning the crest of Illimani.

Adams's head snapped back as a solid wall of granite and ice appeared immediately in front of the aircraft. Though the instruments indicated exactly on course, the aircraft was at least one mile south putting them directly over the peak instead.

If Tom had allowed himself to be coerced into a premature descent, the spunky little C-12 would now be just rapidly cooling wreckage on the side of the mountain, one more offering to its hulking mass.

Adams went white and refused to look at Tom. He sat very still while Tom flew the approach, landed, and taxied to the parking area. There was no room in Tom's world for flying prima donnas. They were clearly going to have some words, "*mano a mano*" about in-flight procedures.

He ran through the checklist items alone, then announced over the interphone, "Engine shutdown—complete."

He took a deep breath and unstrapped. The Ambassador popped his head in the small cockpit. "Tom, would you mind coming with me in my limousine? I'd like you to introduce me to the commander of the FAB transport unit. I can express my personal gratitude to him for help in the rescue of Porter Nelson."

"Good idea, sir. He'd like that."

"Dick," Ambassador Brent said, "you can catch a ride to the embassy with the other staff car. I'll see you at tomorrow morning's staff meeting."

After the Ambassador turned away, Adams whispered to Tom. "Goddamn you, Callahan."

***

Arriving late that afternoon to the MILGROUP, the somber mood hit Tom in the face. No more good-natured banter and repartee. None of the enlisted men would meet his eyes. *Odd,* he thought. Tom put down his flight bag and straightened his uniform. Sticking his head inside the door to Steele's office, Callahan knocked lightly. "Colonel, you wanted to see me?"

Steele roared, "Is that the way you report to a superior officer, mister? Get in here!"

Surprised, Tom walked in and saluted. "Lieutenant Colonel Callahan, reporting as ordered, sir."

Without returning the salute, Steele ground out his question. "What makes you think you can disregard orders and absent yourself from duty while the rest of us work for a living?"

Annoyed, but determined to keep his voice neutral, Tom said, "Sorry, Colonel. I thought you knew—"

"Don't give me that shit, Callahan. I want to know exactly what you were doing out there. You were swanning about the countryside, doing a job the Army does with a warrant officer, weren't you?"

Face hot, Tom counted slowly to ten. "Sir, I flew the Ambassador to Santa Cruz and visited our FAB operations."

"Bullshit, Callahan. You were depriving this unit of the services of a field-grade officer. I can't for the life of me figure how you made it to lieutenant colonel."

Working himself up into a rage, red faced and spitting with fury, Steele rounded his desk and stood toe-to-toe with Tom. "Callahan, you're supposed to be a professional military officer, even if you are only in the Air 'Farce'; and you're supposed to do your duty, not flit about the countryside like some kind of flying Boy Scout."

Tom Callahan locked eyes with Steele, which seemed to drive the colonel into near madness.

"Callahan, you obviously don't have the slightest concept of duty to country. I'm not surprised, either. I've known people like you before. Bad blood. You probably come from a long line of shanty Irish. Dumb and lazy."

Tom shoved his face within an inch of Steele's. "Colonel," he began in a slow, steady voice, "you may be the MILGROUP commander, but you will never speak to me like that about my family."

"What!" roared Steele, "How dare you! I'll have your ass for this!"

Tom leaned closer and whispered, "My family has been professional soldiers in the service of the United States since the Civil War. My great-grandfather, grandfather and father all graduated from the United States Military Academy at West Point. All were general officers. You are out of bounds here, sir. I will not tolerate it from you or anybody else! Is that very clear, Colonel Steele?"

Astonished, Steele dropped his eyes and stepped back. Tom saluted, spun on his heel, and strode out.

Chapter Eleven

MILGROUP offices

The MILGROUP admin sergeant knocked, then came to attention in the doorway to Colonel Steele's office. "Sir, the DCM would like to see you upstairs."

"Later!" Steele slammed the door, narrowly missing the sergeant's face. A minute later his desk telephone lit up. "What is it?" he roared into the phone.

"Sir, it's the DCM," apologized the sergeant. "She says she really needs to speak with you. Now."

Steele threw his appointment book at the wall. He forced himself to take several deep breaths. Only the lure of seeing Patricia again pulled him out of his tantrum.

Patricia Pointer gave him a radiant smile as he entered her spacious and well-lit office.

"Thank you for coming here so quickly, Billie. I know you're busy." She moved out from behind her desk, took his hand, and guided him to a comfortable chair. She sat next to him, so close that he could taste her flowery perfume. He glanced around, seeing her office for the first time, walls lined with books, and so neat despite the enormous amount of paper that flowed through it every day. The only personal touches were silver-framed photos of her toy poodles on her desk. He hated them, detested all yapping excuses for dogs, especially ones that jumped up and slobbered all over him. He was a hunter. The only dogs worth a damn were big dogs bred for hunting or ranching. But he would never say so to Patricia.

"I need your help, Billie, with George Rodgers and Nicholas Barton." She sketched the situation in a couple of minutes. "You are a strong, forceful man. The kind these men respect." She handed him a sheaf of papers.

He pondered the papers for a moment, conscious of those searching hazel eyes on him. He glanced up from his reading. "Why are you showing me coca paste interdiction reports?"

Pointer leaned forward and slid her hand over his knee. "We haven't had many successes recently. We need time to get the kinks out of our interdiction programs. I need someone like you. You can help me buy the time with the other members of the narcotics team. With a little more time, we can get these programs moving in the right direction, you and I. You can provide me with some of your operational expertise, and I can provide State Department cover for you. We make a big splash, get our professional kudos, and move on. We both win."

Exactly what Thornton sent him here to do. Unbelievable! "This is going to cost you, Patricia," he said, thinking out loud. "Rodgers and Barton aren't going to go down easy. They'll want something in return." He thought some more. "We'll need Adams. He's a department head, too. Not to mention DoD. He'll be important to these guys."

She flashed him a radiant smile and caressed his leg. "You can handle Adams, Billie. He's spineless. He needs a powerful man to control him. If he sees you with me, he'll join us."

Steele knew he was being stroked, literally and figuratively. And it was working. His body responded as he remembered her soft, creamy flesh just inches away beneath that taut silk blouse. He forced his attention back to the papers.

"And for your information, Mister MILGROUP Commander," she continued, "Adams is so angry at your man Callahan he can't even think. One of my people was at the airport when the C-12 landed. Ambassador Brent asked Callahan to go with him to visit the FAB transport wing and poor Richard had to ride back with the motor pool vehicle. He was furious."

"Callahan, huh?" Anger surged through him. Here was a golden opportunity to separate the two Air Force officers in the embassy. Step one: isolate Callahan.

He leaned closer to her. "Whatever you say, Patricia." Whether he was going along because of his orders from Thornton or for the way she smiled at him, he didn't know. "But first we need to capture Adams."

A few minutes later, Steele watched Patricia in action as Colonel Adams entered her office.

"Thank you for coming, Richard," she said. "I know you're tired from your trip, but we have a problem with our latest counternarcotics activity report. I have already consulted Colonel Steele. He thought perhaps you could give us the benefit of your advice."

"Why don't you ask Callahan?" Adams asked, bitter. "Everybody else around here is going to him for advice these days."

Patricia smiled, "Yes, Callahan has been rather fortunate recently. Beginner's luck, perhaps?"

"Callahan's trying to make me look like an ass," Adams said. "The Ambassador has bought Callahan's act. He thinks that punk kid is some kind of genius or something. Like the sun shines out of his butt."

"I know what you mean. Annoying, isn't it?"

"Hell, that damn kid is bulletproof down here. The Bolivians love him. He's the flavor of the month with the Ambassador. Can't do anything wrong—Brent won't make a move with the Bolivian military without first consulting him."

"I'm not consulting Callahan, Richard, I'm asking you. I don't want a boy's advice. I need the benefit of your experience. Please."

Adams looked up with a shy smile. "What can I do for you, Patricia?"

***

The next afternoon, Pointer assembled in her office the small group of men that made up the embassy's "narcotics core," chiefs of the agencies directly involved in counternarcotics operations. Today's meeting also included Adams and Steele.

"I'm sorry to ruin your afternoons, gentlemen, but we have a problem that needs our attention today."

Steele smiled. "No problem, Patricia. Always happy to work with you, anytime."

"What's up, Patricia?" inquired DEA chief George Rodgers. He gave Steele a withering glance. This was cutting into his golf time.

"It's the quarterly counternarcotics report I have to send to State tomorrow. The statistics just won't wash. Our trends are going the wrong direction."

Nicholas Barton III scowled. "What do you mean, the wrong direction? Statistics are statistics, patently neutral."

"We have been running more patrols and operations and having less success, even with our increase in funding. We need better results in our reports to SecState," she said without a flicker of emotion.

The atmosphere in the room went silent.

A frown wrinkled Rodgers' craggy face. "Patricia, you have DEA's stats in your hands. That's all there is to it."

"And NAS's as well," added Barton.

Steele, taking his cue from Pointer, jumped in. "You guys are not paying attention to the DCM. This is serious shit. We've collectively solicited funds and equipment from the U.S. government. This embassy has, your agencies have, and each of you individually have gone on record working the system for funds. We've got to produce positive results now before the dweebs in Congress cut our nuts off."

He turned to Patricia and gave a slight bow. "My apologies, Patricia. Just a figure of speech."

She nodded. "I've heard the phrase before, Billie. But it does convey a sense of urgency, doesn't it, gentlemen?"

Steele took the hint. "You men work for agencies that get funded directly by Congress, just like I do. Your budget has always been directly tied to number of arrests, amount of paste destroyed, and labs captured. Your individual promotions depend on those statistics. You just can't walk away and leave the DCM holding the bag."

Steele pushed himself out of his chair and paced the office room, continuing his speech, carefully prepared by the newly-formed triumvirate: Pointer, Steele, and Adams. Like a television news commentator, Steele could be a convincing and persuasive talking head, if properly scripted. As he spoke, Adams made approving noises on the sidelines. George Rodgers held up his beefy hand.

"Okay, okay, Billie, I get the picture." Turning to Pointer, he said, "I'm not happy about this, but I agree with your reasoning. We're doing the right things down here but simply need more time to make things gel in the field. I'll look at our definition of 'labs destroyed'. We keep stumbling over the same labs twice or even three times. Maybe I can figure a way to throw all the numbers in together. That'll add some substance. After all, a lab's a lab. And I might be able to conjure up some more coca paste seizures."

"What about your MILGROUP people, Steele?" asked Barton. "They see a lot of these reports, too."

' Don't worry about them. I'll deploy them in the field to make sure they're so busy they won't have time to pee, much less think."

Steele and Pointer spent the better part of the next two days finalizing the report and its inflated statistics until it read smoothly and supported Pointer's earlier position papers. Soon the other members of the narcotics core committee became ardent supporters, creative in their manipulation of the data. With a suitably straight face, Pointer presented the report to the all-too-trusting Ambassador. The report went out in the late afternoon message traffic, the inflated figures now the official position of the embassy country team.

Turned on by mentally manipulating co-workers and their statistics, Steele and Pointer promptly retired to the DCM's spacious house to celebrate. Barely pausing in the kitchen to grab a bottle of wine, they headed upstairs.

Steele sat in her bed, happy and naked. Joining him with matching attitude and attire was his hostess, boss, and partner. "Here's to us and our dear friends in the narcotics core committee!" he said, raising his champagne glass to hers. "Long may they serve us so well."

"I'm going to miss this while you're in Panama, Colonel," she said, snuggling up. "Can't you delay your trip until next week?"

"Sorry, sweetheart. Gotta go back tomorrow and do army-type stuff. I won't be gone long." Steele smiled. He knew Thornton planned to leak the news of his promotion to brigadier general, probably Friday morning. He could hardly wait.

"Since you're running off and leaving me alone, at least you could bring me back a present."

"Sure, Sweetheart, anything."

"Okay, how about talking to Thornton about getting the intelligence people at SOUTHCOM to pass me, or us, information on counternarcotics operations in Peru and Colombia? Right now that's compartmentalized and they won't tell me about anything other than Bolivia."

"Why should SOUTHCOM give you that operational intel?"

She ran her hand over his chest with provocative slowness. "Because, Billie, that way we can plan our operations in Bolivia better, to tie into the regional operations. We could learn from the other counternarcotics teams if we only knew what they were doing. Also, that intelligence would help us deny refuge to narcos being attacked in the other countries. You know, give them no place to go."

"I don't know," he said, alarm bells sounding. Things were moving too fast. "But I'll speak to the General about it if it comes up."

"Well, maybe I can think of something to help you make it come up," she said as she slowly disappeared under the sheet.

"Yeah," he said smiling up at the ceiling, "maybe you can."

***

Steele sat back in his first-class seat and took a sip of his beer as he watched the broad expanse of Lake Titicaca slide under the airliner's wings on his way to Panama City via Lima. He was approaching the highpoint of his career, to which he had devoted nearly every waking moment for the last twenty-six years. He chuckled, thinking back to the West Texas judge who had given him the choice of enlisting in the Army or going to jail for the savage beating he'd inflicted on a drifter. Neither the judge nor Steele had figured he'd end up as a general. He'd gone to Vietnam a scared young punk and had come back with several rows of combat decorations and on a path to a commission.

Steele shifted uncomfortably in his seat as he recalled how his unit was overrun and wiped out. He had panicked and run. The next day when the U.S. Army had again secured the area Steele crawled out of hiding. The investigation board had very precise views of what happens in battle, so Steele deliberately used phrases and wordings that would match their preconceptions. He played to their own standards of conduct. His convincing story of how he had fought until overcome by exhaustion met with their approval and reward system.

Steele watched the gray fields slip by as his plane made its approach into Lima. As they taxied to the terminal, the sight of the Peruvian Air Force's Russian-made aircraft lined up at the combined civilian-military airport brought him back to his one nagging problem in Bolivia: how to deal with Callahan. Normal intimidation had not worked. Knowing his own reputation as a hard ass was now on the line, Steele had discreetly examined Callahan's seemingly perfect career in hopes of discovering a potentially fatal flaw. Can't mention it to Thornton—he'd think I can't handle some jerk-off flyboy. Steele smiled as he helped himself to another beer. *I'll fix that guy.*

During the descent into Panama, he saw the blue Pacific emerge from the gray rain clouds that seemed to live in the Panamanian skies during the monsoon season. The airliner touched down smoothly on the wet tarmac at General Omar Torrijos International Airport, throwing up a rooster-tail of spray and using the runway's entire length to slow down and turn off. Steele's excitement mounted as the aircraft taxied to the terminal. He knew that Thornton would send his chief of staff to whisk him off to VIP quarters at Fort Clayton. No doubt, at breakfast with the CINC tomorrow or Friday, he'd get the good news about his first star directly from his mentor.

First off the plane, excited as a schoolboy, he hurried to immigration and customs. Walking briskly through the automatic double doors separating customs from the reception area, he was surprised to see only a motor pool staff sergeant driver waiting for him.

"Where the hell is the chief of staff?"

"I'm sorry, Colonel," said the nervous young sergeant. He backed up a step, "Sir, all the officers are in a meeting up at the headquarters. I'm sorry to have to tell you…, well…"

"Spit it out, sergeant!"

"Sir, General Thornton had a heart attack this morning. He's dead."

Chapter Twelve

Headquarters, U.S. Southern Command
Quarry Heights, Panama
Friday, 0830

Two days after the death of General Thornton, Colonel Billie D. Steele sat cooling his heels in the outer office of the SOUTHCOM J-3 (Operations), Brigadier General Tony Mason. Steele leafed through a dog-eared copy of Armor magazine, barely able to contain his anxiety about the BG list, a list that he knew Mason, now the ranking Army general at SOUTHCOM, would have by this morning.

Steele had spent little time with the J-3 during his time in Panama but had watched the other staff colonels run SOUTHCOM operations according to Thornton's directives, effectively preempting Mason's command authority. Now that the acting CINC, Rear Admiral Brothers, no admirer of Thornton's, was in the saddle, the colonels were scattering. Steele's only hope of protection was to be on that list.

Christ, what the hell was taking so long? Mason was deliberately making him wait—the bastard. Probably reading a comic book while I'm out here sweatin' bullets.

Decades later, Mason buzzed his secretary to pass in Colonel Steele. "Morning, Tony," Steele said with a casual wave as he breezed into the office.

General Tony Mason sat at his walnut desk, incongruous in the otherwise spartan office, decorated only by photos of military scenes in the SOUTHCOM Area of Responsibility (AOR). He made no move to rise or offer his hand.

"Colonel," replied Mason, icily. "I don't believe I've ever given you permission to address me by my first name. You will refrain from doing so in the future."

Steele pulled himself up. "Yes, sir."

Mason stared at Steele for a long moment, then motioned to a chair. Steele sat. Mason continued to read a file containing the morning message traffic from all over the AOR. At length, he closed it and set it in front of him.

"Steele, I've just reviewed some of our messages with your office. It seems that every request J-3 has made during your brief tenure in Bolivia has been ignored. Why exactly is that, Colonel?"

Steele didn't answer at once, trying to dodge the problem he had created by reporting only to Thornton. Palms sweating, he said, "Um, well, sir, ah, the unit has been a little slow to respond during the change-over. I'll get right on those lazy butts and get you some answers."

Mason's cold gray eyes bored into Steele. "You do that, Steele. What did you want to see me about?"

"Sir, I just wanted to stop in to say howdy. I'll get on the horn to Bolivia ASAP and try to get your people whatever they need." Steele wiped his sweaty hands on his trouser legs. Come on, you bastard, thought Steele. You know why I'm here. Tell me.

"Thank you," Mason commented dryly. The conversation was over.

Steele reluctantly stood, saluted, and turned to leave. As he was nearly through the door, General Mason added, "Oh, Steele. I just heard about the BG list. Better luck next year."

It took all of his training and self-control to keep walking as if he had heard nothing. Closing the door behind him, he forced a nod to the secretary, and marched out to his waiting staff car. *No! It couldn't be true! The son-of-a-bitch was lying.*

Steele raced his staff car over to the (J-1) Personnel section at Fort Amador. Waiting for the lieutenant colonel personnel weenie to find the time to see him didn't improve Steele's disposition. Now, actually sitting in the little peckerhead's office, staring at the folder on his desk, Steele was filled with foreboding.

The prim little man said, "Colonel Steele, you know that list is still not released officially."

'Balls!" Steele exploded. Peckerhead flushed. "You know damned well that everybody in the Army will know who's on that list by noon. Tell me *now!*"

"All right, Colonel," Peckerhead said, adjusting his Army issue black-rimmed glasses. He handed Steele a sheet of paper.

Steele frantically searched list over and over. The name "Steele, Billie D." was nowhere to be found.

Barely restraining himself from throttling the personnel puke, Steele stumbled out of the building and into his car. He beat on the steering wheel and screamed. He panted, blood pounded in his ears. Somebody must have red-lined his name after Thornton died. It could only have been the Army Chief of Staff. He and Thornton had clashed for two decades.

Thornton's political clout had died with him.

Steele forced himself to collect his wits and sort through the wreckage of his plans. He picked up the car phone and called a couple of colonels he had worked with at Quarry Heights. Both said they were too busy. Running out of options, Steele headed to the Officer's Club to try to find someone who would talk with him.

Making his way through the lunch buffet line, Steele spotted two familiar Army colonels, Steve Chiabotti and Tom Simmons. "Hi, gents," Steele said, forcing a smile. "Mind if I join you?"

"Hey, asshole," said Chiabotti. "What are you doing in Panama?" Thinking he was joking, Steele chuckled and started to pull out a chair.

"Don't you get it, you stupid shit?" Simmons said, jerking the chair from Steele's hand. "We don't want you here anymore. Nobody here wants you around, scumbag."

"Thornton's goon. That's all you ever were," said Chiabotti. "You're too dumb to make it in the real Army, you ass-kissing prick. All balls and no brains."

"Get out of here!" Simmons said. "Retire before somebody court-martials you for some of the things you did for Thornton."

Later, stalking around his VIP quarters, slugging from a bottle of whiskey, Steele lost it. He threw the near empty bottle at the full-length mirror, shattering both, and spraying shards of wet glass over the carpet. With his mentor gone, Steele's "friends" seemed to melt away like ice cubes in Panama's tropical heat. Everyone at Quarry Heights hated Thornton's group. Thornton had trampled on reputations, egos, and pet projects to get what he wanted. Secure in his ability to protect them, his staff had done the same. Now Thornton was safe from the revenge of the living, while his ex-staffers were not.

This isn't the way it's supposed to go! I'm supposed to get my star and go back to Fort Hood as Deputy Division Commander. Yes, sir, General Thornton, sir, you son-of-a-bitch! Why couldn't you have died next week? Steele gave a savage kick to a foot stool and watched it bang against the wall. Steele had no intention of rolling over. I'll show them. No brains, huh? I'm one hell of a lot smarter than they think. They don't know what they've started here. Nobody screws with ole' Billie D. Nobody!

He turned to get another bottle of whiskey, stumbled over the footstool and collapsed on the floor.

Chapter Thirteen

Lupe's Bar, Panama City

The afternoon sun bore down on the beach, slipping in and out of the heavy clouds. The sultry, ninety-five-degree air was at the standard Panama ninety percent humidity. Only a light breeze stirred. At low tide the deserted beach was covered with stinking seaweed.

Colonel Billie D. Steele sat at the corner patio table he had reserved at Lupe's Bar, sipping a Red Stripe beer. He had chosen Lupe's because he knew he could converse without being disturbed by the crush of happy-hour drunks. He had his plan worked out. Now he needed some assistants.

A fishing boat chugged along the shore and he let his gaze follow it, enjoying the tension, the anticipation. Seated across from Steele, also drinking a beer, was Master Sergeant Don Payne, who had been both Steele's best and worst assistant under Thornton. The illegitimate son of a career army enlisted man and a Mexican cocktail waitress, the swarthy Payne had been raised in a barrio in San Antonio. Lean and of medium height, his handsome features were marred by a cruel mouth. With his street-perfect Spanish, he could blend into any group of Hispanics. A born organizer, Payne could be an excellent NCO. He was also prone to violent acts. His sadistic streak had caused several difficult problems in the past. In Vietnam, Payne fit in well—combat had taken the edge off of his need to hurt. He had even been decorated for bravery. Especially adept at interrogations, his motto had been 'Payne's the name; pain's the game.'

The peacetime army that followed the war proved entirely different. The amoral Payne had not adapted well. In Germany, Steele had overheard two officers discussing how to court martial Payne. He had immediately recruited the man, just as Thornton had recruited him, then worked hard to keep him in line. Payne's special talents were too valuable to lose. Now they could come in handy.

"So, Don, what do you think? I say we take it to these snobby State Department pricks from their fancy East Coast schools. We can beat these guys and make us a bundle at the same time. I figure less than four—maybe five months and we can retire to someplace like Rio."

Payne sipped his beer. "Sounds good to me, Colonel. You've always steered me true in the past. There sure ain't much future for me around here now that the General's dead." His dark glasses glinted in the late afternoon light. "I like the idea of screwing with the system."

"Okay," Steele said, hiding his elation. He could celebrate later. "Based on your combat experience and native Spanish, I'll make an official request to your unit here in Panama for you to come down to Bolivia on extended temporary duty to be my operations sergeant." An idea struck him. "I'll offer to pay your TDY per diem out of MILGROUP funds. Ha! That should get their attention." He grinned. Steele was pleased with that. Thornton would be proud. Maybe he had learned more from watching the general than he thought.

"I want you to start growing a moustache, Don. It'll help you look more like a Colombian when you get out in the field. All our intelligence information shows that things are starting to heat up in Colombia and Peru, so it seems logical that Colombians will show up more often in Bolivia. When you get to La Paz next week, I'll have the intel we need to get started. With my connections in the Embassy and you and your two buddies out in the boondocks, it should be a snap."

Payne took another pull on his beer. "I know they'll be interested, Colonel. They got out of the Army a couple months ago and can't find no work back home. Both speak Spanish and are Ranger qualified, too. They'll do what I tell them. If the DEA guys are as dumb as you say, we should be able to run circles around them."

Both men sat for a moment, sipping their beers.

Payne broke the silence. "How about the guys in the MILGROUP? Won't they get in our way?"

"Don't worry about the MILGROUP. I'll have them jumping through hoops all over the country so they won't get anywhere near us. Before I leave Panama, I'm going to meet with the senior Air Force puke in SOUTHCOM, get some information, and see what I can stir up. Patricia Pointer says he's a real cretin."

Steele smiled and relaxed for the first time since arriving in Panama. "Now that we've settled that, why don't we get us some women and celebrate? I need to let off some steam."

Payne's face flushed. "Colonel, I've got me this girl—"

"What's that got to do with anything? I'm *married*."

"Yes, sir. But your wife's a lady and she's back in Texas. Mine's right here and she's a regular hell-cat. She don't like me to fool around—she'd castrate me with a spoon if she caught me."

"Ah, yes. The feisty kind. The rougher, the better."

Chapter Fourteen

Outside Villa Tunari village, Bolivia

Raul Rodriguez stood along the narrow slash in the jungle that passed for a dirt road, straining to hear the drone of the Cessna 206 that was now ten minutes late. He stalked up and down the edge of the road. Clenching and unclenching his massive fists, he muttered dire threats against the lives of the pilot and all his family. In a few more minutes it would be too dark for the pilot to see the road where Rodriguez and his men had piled the plastic bags containing that night's shipment of coca paste. He could almost hear the putty-like paste rotting in the heat of the Chapare; if it spoiled, Rodriguez's bosses would lose their investment. Narcotraffickers were not known for taking their losses graciously. Even the relatively laid-back Bolivian narcos were prone to violence—not on the scale of Colombian narcos, but violent nonetheless. Rodriguez had no desire to have to explain the loss of an entire plane load of the paste needed that night in cocaine laboratories a hundred miles to the north.

"*Ay, carajo,*" he cursed. "Where is that son-of-a-whore?"

He sensed the airplane before he heard the roar of the motor. The plane swooped in, low and fast, hurtling down the narrow passage through the trees. The pilot put it down expertly and taxied rapidly to the loading point. The ground crew swarmed around the plane, their silent expertise the fruit of many such nights' labor. Another group of men erupted from the murky jungle to quickly form a human chain. While the pilot kept the engine running and his feet on the brakes, they passed the sand-bag-sized sodden plastic bags hand-to-hand into the aircraft.

Rodriguez shouted over the engine's roar. "Why so late? It's almost dark."

"UMOPAR patrol. About two miles away," the pilot shouted back. "I tried to lure them off to the north."

Rodriguez' stomach lurched. UMOPAR, the *Unidad Movil de Patrullaje Rural*, the Bolivian National Rural Police, was the main unit in the combined Bolivian-U.S. counternarcotics operations in the Chapare. Trained by the U.S. Army Special Forces at their camp in Chimoré village, they were the narcos' biggest problem. Sometimes, though, UMOPAR officers could be bribed to be in an area where no pick-ups were scheduled. Unfortunately, to Rodriquez' knowledge, no narcotrafficker had bribed the new UMOPAR commander yet to intercept only the minimum numbers necessary to keep the gringos happy.

Rodriguez whirled and shouted, *"Rapido! UMOPAR!"* The sweating laborers hustled, desperate to finish and escape. The last bag landed in the already moving airplane. Rodriguez ran alongside and slammed shut the cargo door. He dropped to the dirt to avoid the aircraft's tail section. By the time the UMOPAR patrol burst upon the makeshift airport, the fully-loaded 206 was airborne and Rodriguez and his men had disappeared into the brush.

***

Later, Rodriguez sat in the small open-air cafe and listened to the gentle night breeze blow through the palm trees. He stroked his carefully groomed moustache and smiled as he teetered back in his battered rattan chair. The damp T-shirt clung to his bulky frame.

"You look particularly pleased tonight, amigo," Hector Rivera said with a smile as he poured his friend another beer.

"Si," replied Rodriguez with a contented sigh. "My paste is moving again." He mentally crossed himself and breathed another sigh of relief. Now he might even get a day off. "We need to do something about the new UMOPAR commander, though."

"Don't worry, *amigo*. I will deal with him."

"You really think so?"

A smile crossed the dapper Rivera's face as the smaller man swirled the beer in his glass. "I know his primo. I expect this man will be more expensive than the last. We'll just pass the cost on to the gringos."

"It's not the UMOPAR patrols that I really worry about—it's when the gringo DEA goes along that causes the problem," Rodriguez said.

Rivera nodded as he brushed bread crumbs from his placemat. "Fortunately, we really only have to worry about them during the daytime."

"Si. When the sun goes down we do our best work. I still can't believe that they haven't figured out nighttime operations would really hurt us."

By dark most of the DEA agents were lounging in their camp or in the local bars and restaurants. That signaled the beginning of the work day for the *narcotraficante* community. Rodriguez and others like him gathered along roads or primitive airstrips hacked into the jungle, awaiting the arrival of the light aircraft that swarmed into the Chapare at dusk like squadrons of hungry mosquitoes.

"Remember when the DEA decided to build speed bumps across the main road to Santa Cruz so we couldn't use it for a runway?" Rodriquez asked.

The Americans had put ripples of dirt nearly two feet high across the highway in hopes of stopping Rodriquez and his compadres. Typical gringo arrogance. The bumps were so big that the Bolivian trucks high-centered, bringing commercial traffic to a halt on the only road linking Bolivia's second and third largest cities. In reality, four or five-inch humps would have been more than enough to shear the nose gear torque link of the Cessnas.

Both men laughed. Rodriquez said, "You were magnificent. It was a stroke of genius getting the truck drivers' union organized to protest."

Rivera waved away the praise. "How could I not, as a patriotic Bolivian citizen?"

Rodriquez studied his friend again. "Now, thanks to you Hector, the authorities are too afraid of the union to try it again." He sipped his beer. "Tell me, *amigo*, are you still sending *campesinos* to the gringos to sell false information?"

Rivera nodded, pursing his thin lips. "Si. My *primo* goes in tomorrow to tell of a big lab upriver. Very convincing, my primo. He'll charge the gringos a fortune for the information. Then he'll take a DEA patrol on a wild goose chase." He chuckled. "With any luck, the patrol will be completely lost and take a long time trying to find their way back to Chimoré."

"Hector, you're a genius," Rodriquez said. "Only you could turn spying into a profit center." They laughed again.

Chimoré Base Camp, Monday

The FAB helicopter swooped down towards the landing zone as if under fire from enemy troops. Hauling up on the collective, the pilot brought the aircraft to a hover a foot above the ground, then lightly touched down. Immediately, ground crew swarmed around the chopper, ducking to avoid the swirling rotor blades.

Lieutenant Colonel Tom Callahan dismounted, then turned to extend his hand to Ambassador Brent. Loosely surrounded by ten heavily armed UMOPAR troops, the party of visitors meandered down the main road of the camp, past the VIP quarters to the Special Forces hooch for the requisite lunch of Meal, Ready-to-Eat (MRE). Ambassador Brent always insisted on having the visitors to the base camp eat what the troops ate; the higher the rank of the visitor, the more important he felt it was to have him or her touch, smell, and taste what was actually happening in the field. Too many Washington bigwigs and staffers thought they could get all relevant information from reports. Brent believed differently. He tried to escort as many of the high-ranking visitors as possible out into the field, especially on "*Chapare Safaris*," the overnight treks out to the UMOPAR camp right in the narcos' front yard.

Gratefully settling down in the cool of the fans, Brent turned to the sweating Deputy Assistant Secretary of Defense (Latin America) Bradford Ward. "Brad, any comments?"

"Well, I'm certainly astonished at the extent of the coca growing in the area. It's so blatant!"

"Blatant and legal," said Brent wryly. "It's traditional in the Bolivian culture to grow coca. Of course, it's not traditional to grow it here in the Chapare. All this is relatively new cultivation, within the past fifteen years or so. The coca growers' unions and their hack politicians conveniently overlook that small detail."

"Mr. Ward," Captain Eduardo Ramirez, leader of the Special Forces "A" team in Chimoré, spoke up for the first time. He pointed through the window at the hill overlooking the camp. "Look up there on that hill, sir. See the light green patch?" Ward nodded. "That's coca—looks like a regular tea bush." Ward's mouth dropped in disbelief. "And when you drive out of the Chapare to Cochabamba this afternoon, you're going to see probably a hundred families spreading coca leaves out to dry in front of their houses right on the road. And they'll smile and wave at you, even knowing you're with us."

Ward looked to the Ambassador for confirmation. After seeing Brent's amused expression, Ward shook his head and said, "Simply amazing. Coca growing within sight of our camp. I would have never believed it if I hadn't seen it. Thank you, Captain, for pointing it out. And I can hardly wait for this drive to Cochabamba!"

Brent stirred some Tabasco sauce into his MRE in a determined attempt to elicit some flavor, then looked at Tom Callahan. "Well, Tom, what do you think of your first Chapare Safari?"

"Very interesting, Mr. Ambassador. What strikes me most is not just how much coca they're growing, but just how much damage the narcos are doing to the environment. I had heard talk in the embassy about the destruction, but I had no idea it was this pronounced. The amount of slash-and-burn clearing alone here is staggering," said Tom. "Sir, could you please pass the Tabasco?"

Brent tossed the small bottle to Callahan and said, "The slash-and-burn is only a small part of the total damage, Tom. There are entire stretches of rivers sterilized from the waste precursor chemicals. And where there aren't any rivers, they just use any small pond or lake nearby. The long-term effects here will match anything we have in the States, up to and probably including nuclear waste problems. There are hundreds of potential Love Canals here just waiting to be found. And Peru is a disaster."

"From the air," Tom said, "you can tell the Chapare used to be a magnificent place, lush green semi-tropical jungle stretching for mile after mile. But now the smog is terrible. I think we need to let people back home know we're losing here on two fronts: drugs and the environment."

"Good point, Tom," Brent said. "People in the States conveniently don't associate cocaine with the thugs and criminals producing it, much less the manner in which it's produced. They'll raise an enormous hue and cry about styrofoam plates or disposable diapers, yet overlook the very real environmental damage done in the production of illegal drugs."

Ward thought for a minute. "Maybe the DoD should help get out the word, send some publicists down here to take pictures. I could get some of the National Guard units to deploy some folks."

"The problem with that, Brad, is that the government propaganda machine is not trusted by the very people we need to reach." The Ambassador drank from his water bottle. "The fact that narcos today knowingly commit ecological havoc should be publicized for the scandal it most certainly is. What we need is to get more journalists down to Bolivia to expose it. Like the guy whose life young Colonel Callahan here saved, and who wrote that great newspaper article."

"You're right," Ward agreed. "Which reminds me. Tom, I enjoyed the article in the *Washington Post* about that rescue. It was an excellent piece written by someone who is clearly an admirer of yours. Well done, sir."

Tom could feel his ears turning red. Brent smiled at his embarrassment and asked, "By the way, Tom, heard anything from Mr. Nelson recently?"

"Sir, Porter's doing fine. I just got a letter from him, as a matter of fact."

"Good, glad to hear that. Let's keep Nelson in the loop. I want you to contact him again. Maybe he could be persuaded to write another article about Bolivia."

"Yes, Tom," Ward concurred. "How can we get Mr. Nelson some good information? He's been down here and knows what it's like. He might spread the word to some of his more open-minded colleagues."

"Sir, the new Air Staff Bolivian desk officer, Major Angela Davidson, could do it. She's a classmate of mine. One of my favorite people, in fact." Tom stood. "I'll call her now and she can make arrangements between Nelson and your office."

Angela Davidson was one of Tom's oldest friends and he was thrilled to be working with her again. One of the first women pilots in the USAF Special Operations world, she led team insertions and low-level parachute drops during Desert Storm. Angela had been a comer in the USAF until she nearly died during the birth of her first child. The feisty Davidson had turned up on the Air Staff the week the previous Bolivian desk officer had been granted a humanitarian transfer to Idaho to care for a dying parent. Tom knew that if any way existed to make things happen in Washington for the Bolivian programs, Angela would find it.

Captain Ramirez escorted Tom to the SF comm center. "Who's the DEA guy out there by the hooch, Eduardo?"

"James Kelly, sir."

"The one you've been telling José about, the guy who hangs out with your troops trying to learn good operations stuff?"

Ramirez nodded. "Keeps getting his ass in a crack with his boss because he's pro-military, Colonel."

Tom picked up the field telephone and started dialing. "Keep him in the fold, Eduardo. We need all the friends we can get."

The phone was answered on the second ring. "Air Staff, Major Davidson."

"Hi, Sweetcakes."

A short pause. "Tommy, you cut that out."

"Are you sure it's Tom? Not another of your legion of admirers?"

"Only you would be so crass as to refer to a distinguished Major of the United States Air Force as Sweetcakes." She laughed. "Where are you? You sound all scratchy."

"I'm calling from the Special Forces hooch in Chimoré. I'm with the Ambassador and Undersecretary Ward. We decided it was time for you to get to work. Here's your first task as Bolivian desk officer. Remember the name Porter Nelson?"

"The journalist?"

"He's been in Georgetown University Hospital since he got back to the States. He needed surgery, but he's recovering okay. We need you to go over to see him tomorrow before he gets released. Stop by Mr. Ward's office. They'll have some info for you to take to Porter."

"Yes sir, Tommy, sir."

"Just get the lead out, Angela."

J-5, Political-Military Affairs
Quarry Heights, Panama
Thursday, 0900

Colonel Billie D. Steele entered the small brick building that housed J-5 and headed down the stairs for the next step in his plan. In SOUTHCOM, security assistance programs were placed under J-5, making Brigadier General Gerald Myers, USAF, the functional manager of all MILGROUP personnel in Central and South America and Steele's official boss. Steele thought Myers, a long-time tanker pilot in the Strategic Air Command, was primarily an ass-kissing staff weenie with command pilot wings. He was serving his first assignment as a brigadier general in political-military affairs, an area completely new for him. Everyone in Panama knew he coveted a second star and wanted no screw-ups that could be linked to him.

Myers' secretary, a pudgy middle-aged Latina, looked up as Steele entered the office. "Good morning, sir," she said without recognition.

"*Buenos días, señora,*" he replied with a slight bow. "I'm Colonel Steele, MILGROUP commander from Bolivia. I'm here to meet the General."

"Do you have an appointment? The General is quite busy."

Steele took a deep breath. This bitch was going to be a pain in the ass. "No, señora," he said, trying hard to be charming. "*Pero, mi jefe es su jefe*—but my boss is your boss." He noticed an eight-by-ten picture of an Army private on her desk, a young man who could only be her son. "Is this your boy?" She nodded. "Good looking kid."

"He just graduated from the advanced infantry school," she said, beaming through her too heavy make-up. "He's going to Germany next week."

119

"Well," Steele said with a smile, "speaking as an armor officer, infantry's gain is armor's loss. That's a tough school that he just finished. You should be proud of him, *Señora*. He looks like a good troop."

She glanced at the picture, then back to Steele. "Please excuse me, Colonel. I'll check with the General if he can see you." She stabbed the intercom button. "General, Colonel Steele's here from Bolivia. He would like to see you. Your next appointment's not for another thirty minutes," she added with a wink at Steele.

Steele smiled and gave another small bow.

"Send him in," said Myers through the intercom. Steele thought he detected a note of resignation in his voice. Or was it suspicion?

The lavish wood-paneled office provided a contrast to General Mason's austere box. Just like the Air Force to bask in luxury. He rendered a smart, military salute. "Colonel Steele reporting, sir!"

Myers, a handsome man with dark wavy hair with just a touch of gray, returned the salute and offered Steele a chair and a cup of coffee.

"Nice of you to stop by, Colonel. I'd like your opinion on what I can do to improve our programs in Bolivia."

"Well, sir. Things are going pretty well. We're just overworked and understaffed, like everybody else." Steele smiled knowingly at Myers at the universal complaint of military commanders. He then initiated a lengthy technical discussion designed to dazzle this particular Air Force general.

Twenty minutes later, Myers looked up from his notes. "Billie, I think we can work on those problems for you. Thanks for bringing them to me directly, especially your ideas and solutions. I appreciate that." He sipped his coffee. "Anything else I can do for you?"

Steele hid his smile at the open invitation and hesitated as if considering the idea for the first time. "Well, General, we could use the combined intelligence brief for SOUTHCOM's entire AOR."

Myers' face hardened. "Why do you need that?"

Steele kept his face guileless. Myers might be an idiot but would be ruthless in protecting his career. "Sir, the DCM thinks we could use it."

"Patricia Pointer, the DCM? She struck me as a pretty tough nut."

120

"Me too, General, at first. But she has a good brain and wants to help. She feels that getting this intel would enhance our planning capabilities." Steele locked eyes with Myers. "General, my job is to make you look good. I can't do my job unless I know what's happening."

Myers preened but still looked doubtful. "And the DCM? How do we keep this intel from falling into the wrong hands?"

"Don't worry, sir," Steele said, repressing a smile. "I've been handling her pretty well."

Myers studied him. "As you may be aware, Colonel, things are not going well for us in Ecuador and Peru right now. We sure as hell don't need any more problems in our AOR."

Yeah, thought Steele. *You mean you don't need any more problems on your watch, you bureaucratic prick.*

"I'll look into it," Myers said after a moment. "But don't you dare cross the line into operational stuff. That is outside your legal purview and would get us all hung. Understood, Colonel?"

Steele nodded, carefully repressing his elation. Myers was reverting to form, covering his ass. "Yes, sir. Thank you, General."

After a long pause, Myers said, "Now, speaking as the ranking USAF officer in this theater, how's your Air Force section chief working out?"

Gotta do this just right. "General," he said carefully, "as you gotta know by now, it's real hard to tell the good guys from the bad guys in Bolivia sometimes. Many military officers are involved in drug smuggling. Young Callahan is right in the FAB headquarters or out flying with the FAB nearly every day. He has lots of friends in the FAB. I hope he can tell the clean ones from the dirty ones. I know I can't. And neither can the professional spooks in the Embassy. There's the problem. I just hope he knows where to draw the line."

General Myers frowned. "Well, Billie. You keep an eye on him and if you need some help reining him in, just let me know. I've seen youngsters overseas go native before. It wouldn't be the first time a GI forgot which country he was working for."

"Thank you, General. I'll keep that in mind."

Steele stood, popped to attention, saluted, and exited the office. Outside, he allowed himself a broad smile. His plan was on track.

Chapter Fifteen

**Callahan's Residence,
Calacoto 2330 Hours**

The strident ringing of the telephone crashed through Tom Callahan's sleep. He groped about in the dark. "Callahan."

"We need some aircraft for an operation tomorrow," a man said. "The DCM says for you to arrange it." The carefully neutral voice on the phone belonged to a DEA agent that Tom Callahan barely knew.

Tom sat upright in bed. "How many and what type?" he asked, now wide awake.

"Two C-130s."

"C-130s? Are you sure? George Rodgers and I decided they shouldn't be used in any future operation. They're unsafe."

"Well, it's been undecided then," said the smug voice. "The DCM says to get moving, we need those planes this morning."

"Can you spare any more details, like maybe takeoff times?" Tom asked, thoroughly irritated.

"Have them show up at El Alto airport at 0700 tomorrow morning, ready to go."

"You mean I have less than eight hours to get two airplanes cranked up—plus crews? In Bolivia? You're kidding!"

"That's right. Make it happen."

"Oh, I can make it happen all right, even if it means driving all over town myself collecting crewmembers. Remember, most of these guys can't afford phones. But first, I get to call the Air Force commander and wake him up to get the authorization for the flights."

"The DCM is your authority. Use it."

"The DCM's orders may be enough authority for you and me, pal, but Patricia Pointer doesn't run the FAB. Those crewmembers aren't going to do diddily squat without General Camacho's okay. My next question is why you waited until now to call me."

The voice mocked, "I thought you military types are supposed to live and breathe operational security."

"Security, my ass," Tom said. A thought hit him. "You planning wizards just forgot about the airlift until now, didn't you?" The prolonged pause let Tom know he was right on target.

"Just get the airplanes ready, Colonel." The telephone disconnected with a loud click.

Tom sat in the dark holding the now dead receiver, trying to decide if he was more angry at the stupidity of the embassy staff or at the unnecessary danger for the DEA and UMOPAR troops resulting from this decision.

"Who was that, Tommy?" Colleen mumbled.

"Some idiot at the embassy."

"C'mere, Tiger."

"Colleen, I've gotta go."

"Come *here*," she said more forcefully, tugging on his arm.

As he settled back into the bed, Colleen snuggled up closer. "What's the problem?"

"I think I just got double-crossed by George Rodgers. We talked about using FAB C-130s in his larger raids. Colleen, those aircraft are unsafe! Last week, I finally got him to agree that we shouldn't use them again. Now, I get a call ordering me to whistle up two for a 0700 show tomorrow morning. It's crazy!" He paused. "And what's even worse is that they even forgot to work out their airlift requirements until now—gives me the willies just thinking about how incomplete the rest of their planning must be. This is what José and Matt have been saying all along—these guys don't know what they're doing. People are going to start dying soon unless we can get somebody to listen to us."

"So what are you going to do?"

"Well, first I've gotta call General Camacho, then start working out how to assemble two complete crews."

124

She gently stroked the hairs on his chest. "Do you have to go right now, lover boy?"

"Colleen, do you always get turned on when there's a time crunch?"

"You never complained during graduate school," she said, affecting a pout.

He grinned down at her. "Why do you think I've encouraged you to stay in school all this time? Just love those finals weeks!"

"Well, you better take advantage of me now, flyboy—I'm almost out of grad school." She slid her hand lower across his stomach.

' Oh, no," he said as he reluctantly slid out from under her touch. "I'm planning on you going to law school, then maybe medical school." He kissed her softly. "Now you just roll over and go to sleep. I'll go get those planes lined up and the next thing you'll know, I'll be crawling back in there with you. Then we can pretend I'm late to some other appointment."

UH-1H 'Huey'
Tail Number FAB 72
Near San Ramon, Bolivia

Special Agent James Kelly of the U.S. Drug Enforcement Agency checked his weapons for the twentieth time in five minutes as he stood in the door and watched the green of the jungle flash underneath the fast-moving helicopter. Even the continuous, loud whop-whop of the Huey's rotor blades and the early morning air, already hot, rushing through the crowded crew compartment could not distract him from the fear that twisted his guts. His street skills wouldn't help him here. This was a real jungle, not a concrete one like Chicago. But Kelly reveled in the action. This must be what it was like in 'Nam, riding helicopters into the boonies to make an attack.

He tried to keep oriented to the terrain. To maximize operational security, Kelly had waited until the two helicopter crews were assembled at the aircraft before he designated the targets and the route of flight. While more DEA and UMOPAR troops captured the narcotraficante-controlled town of San Ramon and the cartel radio station, Kelly and his two choppers planned to surround and snag a group of cartel bosses—*jefes*—known to be meeting at a heavily guarded ranch outside the town.

The pilot turned to Kelly, pointed towards a distant clearing and gestured at his watch—right on schedule. Kelly nodded and moved next to the door. He identified the main house and outbuildings. Tiny figures in the yard evolved into humans as the choppers closed. The humans scattered as the helicopters' intended target became obvious. Kelly pounded his fist on the door frame. He had the targets in the bag!

Kelly's lead ship swooped towards the main building, number two cut off escape. The lead aircrew dodged sporadic ground fire and flared the aircraft a foot from the ground. Kelly leapt off the skid. His men boiled out of the chopper, personal gear slapping at their bodies as they ran.

They crashed through the main building. The second team surrounded the area. The UMOPAR troops rounded up the bad guys into a group. Only two brief scuffles broke out.

Kelly's police instincts screamed. He grabbed his UMOPAR lieutenant. "Something's wrong. This is too easy." Some of the faces were sullen, some smirking; but nobody fought or protested too much.

"Shit, these guys are just punks. They aren't the *jefes!*"

Kelly and the lieutenant dashed through the buildings and found a radio receiver on a desk. Words of warning from the drug cartel headquarters in San Ramon poured out loud and clear. "Those bastards knew we were coming! None of our guys captured the radio station!"

They raced back to the assembled group. The UMOPAR lieutenant singled out one of the smirking prisoners. He slammed him against the wall. "Tell me where the *jefes* went!"

The prisoner spit in the lieutenant's face.

The lieutenant grabbed the man by the throat, whipped out his combat knife, and jabbed him in the groin. "Tell me, *pendejo*, or I'll feed you your own *cojones!*"

The man danced on his toes. "They're gone," he managed, eyes popping.

"Where?" the lieutenant spat out, his face only centimeters away. The lieutenant pressed the knife deeper. The sweating victim tried to stand taller. "Now!"

"In c-cars, south, five minutes, no more. P-please!"

Released, the prisoner slumped to the ground, clutched his groin.

Kelly dashed back outside and shouted for his first squad. He gave the "land now" signal to the lead chopper, which still hovered overhead, its M-60 machine gun trained on the area. He gestured to the second team to stay put and dashed for the bird with his men streaming close behind.

Clambering aboard, he pointed to the south and screamed, "*Vámonos!*" As the pilot lifted off and accelerated, Kelly grabbed a headset to call the agent-in-charge of the operation in San Ramon.

"Smokey, Smokey, this is Little Bird, over."

The radio crackled to life. "Go ahead, Little Bird." Kelly could hear sporadic shots of gunfire popping in the background of the transmission.

"We are at the target. All the suspects have departed the scene to the south in automobiles. Am pursuing in lead helicopter. Request you send elements to block the main road before the western cut-off. Over."

A pause. "Negative, negative Little Bird. Proceed to San Ramon. We need you here."

"Smokey, I can catch those guys! They left less than ten minutes ago! They can't be far. Over." That dumbshit couldn't mean that! Jesus, this was why they were here.

"Negative, Little Bird. Leave one team there and get your ass back here ASAP. Acknowledge, Kelly!"

Kelly bit his lip in frustration, swallowing the scathing words he wanted to scream out. "Wilco. We'll be in San Ramon in fifteen minutes." Kelly slammed the console. "Weak dick!" he screamed into the dead microphone. He couldn't believe that he had to abandon this chase, the major reason for the attack on San Ramon in the first place. Another leak in security. Shit! Nothing can be kept secret in this damned country. Things must be really screwed up in San Ramon right now—he's desperate. Well, this is the last time I'm gonna call that asshole for instructions during an op. Next time out, we're having radio problems.

Callahan's Residence
Calacoto

Tom Callahan selected a compact disc from his extensive collection. Tonight's dinner concert would be performed by John Williams, a contemporary Australian guitarist who had studied under the great Spanish classical guitarist, Andres Segovia. The Callahans thought Williams' unique background matched some of their own musical and cultural interests.

Tom settled back into his chair and smiled at his wife. "This is better than going out to a restaurant any time. I get to pick out the music and the wine, and nobody minds if I smooch with my date. What a deal!"

The cook, Teresa, brought out the steaming piles of food—fresh grilled trout from Lake Titicaca, steamed fresh vegetables, and Tom's favorite, *arroz con queso*, rice with melted Bolivian white cheese, and placed them in the center of the dining room table. She left the Callahans admiring the feast and shuffled back with the heated dinner plates. Tom was a fanatic about eating food hot; it cooled rapidly in the altitude of La Paz.

"How'd it go today, luv?" Colleen asked.

Tom took some time to consider his answer. "We had an operation today. It was a disaster. Patricia Pointer is trying to blame the operators rather than her planners. And is she ever anti-military. Won't listen to a thing we say unless some State weenie agrees with us."

Colleen didn't seem surprised. "How about our favorite colonel?"

"She seems to get along with Steele okay, but the love doesn't trickle down very far. Personally, I can handle it, but I don't like the stress it puts on the troops."

"Why do you think she's never married? She's attractive enough and bright. Are you men as put off by her as the women in the embassy are?"

128

"She has a few too many hard edges on her to suit me—you know I like my women to have a little muscle on them." He reached under the table and gently squeezed her thigh.

"Why, you cheeky bugger!" She slapped lightly at his hand.

Tom laughed. "How goes the dissertation? Get anything done today?"

Colleen said, "I refined my computer model some this afternoon and ran it again. Seems to be shaping up."

Tom knew better than to take those casual words at face value. His wife was as fiercely proud of her profession as he was of his own. And just as good at it, too. Maybe better. Life in La Paz agreed with Colleen. Tom thought that she had never looked happier. For the thousandth time, he wished his father could have met Colleen.

Outside, the night burst into flames as Mother Nature put on one of her patented La Paz light shows along the eastern slopes of the mountains. Lightning blazed and the crashes of thunder came so loud they sounded like rolling artillery barrages. Tom looked out the window. "Man, I'm glad I'm on the ground tonight. This is not a good time to be flying."

Colleen sipped her wine. "How was your flight to Trinidad? Olga says that it's a wonderful place to visit."

"Not now," said Tom. "The locals are a wee bit uptight at the present moment. There's been another outbreak of Bolivian hemorrhagic fever in the Beni region."

"I saw that in today's paper. I got the gist of the article, but then it went all technical and I couldn't follow it."

"Remember the hantavirus we have back in Arizona and New Mexico?"

Colleen nodded. "It's quite nasty."

"Right. In the States it kills roughly half its victims. My mom said that there were about forty cases in New Mexico last year. Nineteen people died, a couple of them up close to her in Taos. The virus here is a cousin, called the Machupo virus. And victims don't have a chance." He took a bite of the delicious chicken. "There haven't been any cases for several years. But now two Machupo outbreaks in two separate villages within days."

"This sounds pretty horrible."

"Fortunately, we have a National Guard medical team nearby. Pointer had me fly a couple of the doctors up to Trinidad this morning." He chose not to dwell on the details of the grisly disease.

"Some of the victims were children?"

Tom nodded. Both were silent.

"Honey," Colleen said. "We need to talk about the adoption."

Tom's stomach immediately rebelled. He slid his chair back from the table and tossed his napkin down. He began pacing alongside the table. "Colleen, we don't have to do everything Matt and Olga do."

"That's not a fair thing to say and you know it."

"Look, Sweetheart, I think adoption is a great option for some people. I'm just not sure that I want to do it. I'm not convinced that we can't have our own. I want a baby that's part you and part me."

"Honey," she said "we've been trying for nearly five years. We've had every test in the book and the clock is still ticking. We can keep trying, but meanwhile, we'll have a real baby to care for and love."

Tom sat and fumbled with his wine glass. "Why do we have to decide anything now, Colleen?"

"We don't have to decide yet, Tommy. Just come to the orphanage and look at the children with me. Please?"

He sighed. "Okay. I'll go, but only if you come with me. And no commitment."

El Alto Airport, Saturday, 0830

Inside the terminal building, Colonel Billie D. Steele, U.S. Army, impatiently pushed through the slow-moving crowd. He showed his diplomatic passport and was waved through immigration which enabled him to get to the baggage claim area first and stand around shivering as he waited for the incredibly slow luggage handlers. God, he hated Bolivia! The altitude always made him feel light-headed and slightly nauseous. He promised himself to get out of La Paz more often, preferably to the tropics in Santa Cruz, certainly at least down to Cochabamba.

Intent on passing through the airport as quickly as possible to the lower altitude of La Paz and his apartment, he did not notice the woman until she sidled up next to him and whispered a throaty, "Hello, soldier. Can I give you a lift?"

Aha, this was what he had missed in Panama. "Patricia, you give me a lift just seeing you." He kissed her on both cheeks, Bolivian style. "As a matter of fact, you give me a rise, too."

"Okay, I give you a lift and a rise. Now can I offer you a ride?"

"Oh, talk dirty to me, woman!"

She took his arm. He grabbed his suitcase and they meandered through the crowd to the parking lot, looking like a well-to-do married couple, him dressed in his suit and her in her fashionable, ankle-length, fur-lined coat. "The Ambassador is out of town so I borrowed his official car," she explained as they settled in. The big Cadillac had sound-proofing and a shade to isolate the passenger compartment from the front seat. Pointer closed the shade and produced a bottle of champagne and two glasses.

They snuggled and toasted his return.

"I was sorry to hear about your General Thornton, Billie. I knew he was important to you."

Steele sighed. "Yeah, he was." Forcing himself to brighten up, he changed the subject. "I talked to Jerry Meyers, the J-5 at SOUTHCOM. He's a real Air Force idiot—so afraid of making a mistake he won't even fart. But I smiled at him, said 'yessir' a lot, and fed him some of the ideas you mentioned. He'll do anything we suggest, I think."

"Good. I'm really looking forward to working with you on operations and planning. You can teach me so much."

"Thanks, Sweetheart. It's nice to come home to some kind words."

"Words aren't the only things you're coming home to, Billie. I'll see to that."

Pointer slowly undid her belt and pulled her overcoat away from her bare shoulders.

"Patricia, did we forget to wear our clothes again today?" he asked, delighted. "Oh, silly me." She giggled as she slid out of the coat, completely nude except for her knee-high leather boots. "I wanted to be the first to welcome you back, Billie D."

Chapter Sixteen

Tripoli, Libya

Running an international terrorist organization was much the same as running a global corporation. As Chairman and CEO, Kurt Wallerein had to attend to the administrative details of a corporate structure, which included all the span of control problems of a sprawling business, plus a few added security ones. His staff was small, chosen for their loyalty. Those less than competent were eliminated during the course of their often, short-lived careers in an environment as savage as any Darwinian survival model. His former second-in-command was the latest casualty.

Driven by the need to recruit Spanish-speaking operatives, Wallerein had decided to have his deputy attempt contact with the Basque ETA separatist movement. With Spain too dangerous for the Basques to surface, the meeting was scheduled for Marseille.

Wallerein loathed the French as only a German could. He was convinced they'd sell their grandmothers for a glass of wine. Yet he was careful not to flagrantly violate French law. After all, despite almost two decades of blundering about, it was the *Direction de la Surveillance du Territoire* (DST) that had kidnapped Carlos the Jackal from the Sudan and had him rotting away in a Paris prison. The damned DST had crashed the Marseille meeting and killed or arrested everyone.

Perhaps after this operation in the United States, Wallerein would lead another team into France and take out the capital. The phrase *'Is Paris Burning?'* would take on a different kind of meaning in the new millennium.

With a sigh, Wallerein surveyed the reports and papers stacked neatly on his desk. He flicked on his computer and checked his e-mail. Everything destined for him was routed through several servers in different countries. Nothing critical was ever sent to him directly. He still harbored suspicion about the security of the cyberworld. Delicate or incriminating messages were delivered in person. A bit cumbersome but secure, which was why he was still alive and active when most professional revolutionaries of his generation were dead or in prison.

A guard appeared with Wallerein's lunch, fruit with yogurt, which he invariably took alone. As he finished, his chief-of-staff arrived, bearing the usual thick sheaf of reports, faxes, and phone messages. Wallerein studied the first and most important: a signal delivered by hand that morning from South America. Perfect.

A council of war was scheduled for this afternoon in Wallerein's conference room. At precisely one o'clock, Wallerein strode in and took his place at the head of the long mahogany table. Ambassador Hernando Cortez, Colonel Carlos Lopez of the Cuban *Dirección General de Inteligencia* (DGI), and several of Wallerein's staff, the core of his operational planning group, sat expectantly. Operational planning was Wallerein's specialty. Fidel wanted him to use his own resources to keep the Cuban participation to a minimum. Fine. Wallerein preferred it this way.

After they had exchanged greetings and settled down, Wallerein handed his chief of staff several closely-typed sheets. "Here are plans to step up violence in the Andean region. Send funds to our people in Lima. They are to blow up power transmission lines and assassinate more village leaders, effective immediately."

Hernando Cortez seemed surprised. "But comrade, these are standard actions, nothing original. I thought we were going to carry the revolution to the Yanquis and their puppets."

Wallerein responded calmly. "Exactly. They are standard Sendero Luminoso tactics. We will use the Sendero to confuse our enemies. The Sendero will deny the new bombings. Nobody will believe them and all attention will be focused there."

Nobody on the planet was Maoist these days except for the Sendero. The attack on the Japanese embassy years before had merely confirmed world opinion that these backwards Andean peasants were locked in a serious time warp that Wallerein planned to turn to his advantage. "In a few weeks, we will launch a new program."

Wallerein turned towards Lopez. "Ecuador is different. The Americans have just been secretly granted a free hand there. They're planning to move in about fifty new DEA agents and two aircraft. The first aircraft arrives from Peru to the new American base in Loja in six days."

He stood and pointed at the huge wall map that dominated the room. The small town was less than a hundred kilometers from the disputed border with Peru. "I want you to shoot it down on its arrival. I'll have a Stinger missile delivered to Havana in two days. One left over from Afghanistan. That will confuse the Americans and frighten the Ecuadorians as well."

He motioned to a swath of the lower area of the country. "Simultaneously, I will have my people launch limited attacks on western Ecuadorian military bases here, here and here. That will effectively isolate this entire region, from Guayaquil south to the border."

"Can you do that? What about the Ecuadorian response?"

"The Ecuadorian forces will be busy conducting a classified operation with the Americans, code named "Condor" east of the mountains. There can be no response," Wallerein said.

Cortez looked up, a huge smile on his face. "Ecuador will think that Peru made the attacks. It could start another war down there!"

"Precisely."

"The whole region will be in an uproar," said Cortez. "Peruvians accusing Ecuador, the Ecuadorians accusing Peru. The politics in the area will be aflame!" He pounded the table in delight. "And neither side will ever trust the Yanquis again. Brilliant!"

Wallerein knew that he had just shocked the Cuban. He had his sources, which he was careful to keep to himself. Colonel Lopez would, of course, confirm this information through the DGI system and pass along to Fidel the quality of Wallerein's intelligence. Fidel had to be reminded that he was partners with a serious player.

After working through more details with the team, he walked along the cold concrete corridors to his office. Waiting for him was a large, gray-haired man who stood when he entered.

"Welcome back, comrade." Wallerein said with genuine warmth to Doctor Nikolai Yazov. "Excellent work on that hemorrhagic fever epidemic in Bolivia. What was the final death count?"

"Twenty-seven." Yazov sat down and settled into the leather chair. "As you remember, we decided to use the aerosol instead of the mice as vectors for the virus. The wind proved to be a bit less predictable than I thought. As an obvious foreigner in those tiny Indian villages, it was difficult for me to be inconspicuous. So I erred on the side of caution and only sprayed at night."

Wallerein nodded his approval. He tried to imagine what it would take to wander around in the pitch-black of a tropical night in a peasant village concealing cans of gut-wrenching death. This man was no ordinary research scientist. A treasure for The Cause.

"Just as we anticipated, a team of American military doctors from one of their deployments was sent to the villages," he said. "Next week, we will begin to have stories published in various South American newspapers linking the Bolivian fevers with the Americans."

Wallerein was pleased at the involvement of the American army doctors. It had been an easy thing to arrange. Details were easy when you had the right people in the right places. The Americans were far too trusting.

"Excellent."

Wallerein slid a folder across the desk. "Now for Phase two. This is some additional information from one of your professional colleagues."

Yazov carefully studied the contents. "This man is quite knowledgeable, even brilliant. I read several of these papers on my trip. He's been in the field, not just another academic. Even been to Bolivia, as I recall."

Wallerein studied the Russian carefully. The arcane, technical information in the folder seemed to intrigue his colleague. "We're going to meet him next month in Maryland."

A smile spread across the Russian's recently sunburned face. "I look forward to the opportunity to discuss his secret research. The genetic engineering of the Bolivian Machupo virus that he's working on is fascinating. It's perfect for our requirements." Yazov looked over the top of his glasses. "How obliging of the Americans to do our work for us."

"And the laboratory? Can you set up what we need in America?"

"I already compiled the list of equipment needed and faxed orders to supply houses in the States. It's all readily available." He eyed Wallerein. "Relax, comrade. Anyone with a PhD could do this."

Wallerein cocked an eyebrow. "That's not what the CIA Director told the American Congress last week." He handed over a copy of the *Washington Post*. "He said it was nearly impossible for a non-nation state to culture a virus and deliver it in the quantities that we propose."

Yazov glanced at the headlines and shrugged. "That the CIA would lie to their Congress is hardly a new concept. The premise for this entire operation is that a few hundred kilos of the right virus, properly applied, can kill hundreds of thousands of people. I have done this before on a limited scale in India." Yazov took a long breath. "*Tovarishch*, I have been working my whole life for this opportunity. It will not escape me this time."

Wallerein exhaled slowly and felt his confidence surge. He was not the only revolutionary in the room. This man was as dedicated as he was. Ruthless. Brilliant. And one of the world's experts on biological weapons. Together they were a great team. Wallerein sipped a glass of mineral water and mentally reviewed his plan. It was a good plan. Parts of it were brilliant. Simple, direct, and designed to cause maximum harm to the Americans and their government. The results would change the political world.

Chapter Seventeen

C-12D, Tail Number 30499

Colonel Billie D. Steele watched the snow-clad mountains surrounding La Paz drop away into the tropical plains that extended under the aircraft all the way to Santa Cruz. He was anxious to get out in the field. Across from him sat the newly arrived Master Sergeant Don Payne who was reading the details of today's itinerary.

Much had happened since the meeting in Lupe's Bar. Steele made his official request for Payne's services in Bolivia. His unit had been only too glad to see him go, the longer the better. Payne's assessment of his first two recruits, Carlos Vaca and Miguel Montoya, had been right on target. Both men had spent just enough time on civvie street to discover that the money they saved wasn't going to last forever, that their jobs would never satisfy their need for action and that the local police were no friendlier to them than the military police had been. They immediately agreed to meet Payne in Bolivia without any need for lengthy explanations. He told them to travel light and sent them each tickets to fly directly from Miami to Santa Cruz, paying from the slush fund that Steele set up. Everyone would rendezvous today at a small hotel on the fringe of the city.

"Okay, Don. One last time." Steele sat with his back to the pilots, keeping his voice low enough that the engine noise in the cockpit would prevent Callahan and Adams from overhearing. "While I go to see General Calleja, you go in-brief your compadres. We'll all meet at the hotel at 1630 to work out the details. Be ready to work tonight. You'll probably move out to Villa Tunare or Trinidad in a couple days. Stress to your troops that this is a short-term operation, to stay away from the booze and women. There'll be plenty of time and money for both later. Questions?"

"No, sir. Don't worry about the men. I'll keep them in line." Payne's smug smile annoyed Steele. Payne had insisted on bringing down his civilian girlfriend, Rosa Molina, to be the new MILGROUP administrator. Steele reluctantly agreed to have her transferred to Bolivia on temporary duty, provided Molina's cover story would keep her in the MILGROUP offices in La Paz.

"I've been able to get pretty good intel from the dweebs in the Embassy. The DCM has been pretty cooperative," Steele continued, with a straight face.

"Yes sir, seems like you picked up some good 'pointers' from the General." They both laughed.

"Old Thornton was a master at getting what he wanted. So now when I have a problem I just ask myself, 'Billie boy, what would Thornton do here?' Helps me think."

Steele settled back to go over his notes once again. This meeting would be crucial to his plan. If he failed, he would end up in jail. Or dead. If he succeeded, it would launch his program. It boiled down to this meeting with this particular Bolivian army general. Game time.

Steele arrived at the headquarters building for the Military District of Santa Cruz five minutes early, dressed in an immaculate Class A uniform. The Bolivian commander, General Armando Calleja let him cool his heels in the ornate outer office, decorated with pictures of all Bolivia's one hundred sixty-plus past presidents, the vast majority of whom were Bolivian Army generals.

From his intelligence briefings at the embassy, enhanced by classified material from SOUTHCOM, Steele knew Calleja hated Americans and the pressure on the Bolivian Army to participate more actively in the combined Bolivian-U.S. counternarcotics operations. Calleja had reluctantly gone along with the intergovernmental Annex III agreement which established a training base for the Bolivian Army at Manchego, just to the east of Santa Cruz. There, Green Berets worked with a Bolivian infantry battalion, training in the art of drug interdiction. Steele also knew Calleja had already made a substantial

138

amount of money from kickbacks from the Bolivian companies involved in the design, construction, and operation of the base.

Precisely fifteen minutes late, the general's ayudante showed up and escorted Steele into the General's office. General Calleja was gracious, dignified, and slightly reserved. The first few minutes of conversation over the obligatory coffee that was always too strong, and always upset Steele's stomach, were the usual preliminaries between military officers around the world, including previous assignments and formal professional schools.

"General, I suppose you wonder why I'm here," Steele said as lightly as possible. He had prepared himself well for this meeting in the style of his late mentor, even practiced his lines in his living room mirror to get the correct effect.

Calleja nodded and smiled. "I presume it is because of the camp at Manchego."

"No, sir. I want to talk to you about smuggling coca paste. I know that you're involved and I want to discuss it with you. Alone."

Calleja leapt to his feet, face purple, and pounded his desk. "How dare you accuse me, a general, a superior officer, of such a crime? This is an outrage!"

Steele did not flinch. He had anticipated exactly this response. He stood and looked Calleja directly in the eyes. "Mi general, please excuse my bluntness. I, too, am a soldier, not a diplomat—"

"You're a lying dog, that's what you are!" shouted Calleja.

"I am not here on behalf of the embassy," Steele continued. He didn't like being called a liar, even though he was an expert. "I'm here on my own behalf. However, that doesn't alter the facts. I know that you are involved in drug production and transportation, and I know how you do it."

He produced a blue folder embossed with the embassy crest. Opening the folder, he pulled out a thin sheaf of typed papers. "For example, you are connected with the Rodriguez family. You provide Bolivian Army transportation documents, Army facilities, and probably some of your trusted staff." He held the folder out to Calleja. "Please, sir, look at this list if you doubt the data."

Calleja hesitated, then reached for the folder. He sat down and slowly read the document, which read like an operations order. His thin aristocratic face blanched as he studied the list detailing his activities. He looked up briefly with a murderous look, then returned to the beginning, obviously stalling for time. His left eye twitched again, and his face drained of color. Bemused, Steele imagined how he'd like to play poker with this man.

"Mi general, I used information from several sources to put this list together. Nobody else in the embassy knows about it." He took a drink of the now cold coffee. "Remember, I'm an Army officer, too, and I understand the way you think. I've attended some of the same schools and read the same manuals that you have. I knew where to look for trends, and when I saw them, I knew that the commander would have to have planned and authorized these activities." Steele stopped, reminding himself to go slowly. Calleja was a proud, not to mention angry, general officer. "We are similar in many ways, you and I."

That statement hung in the air for thirty seconds as each man studied the other. "Mi general, I come to you openly as a fellow Army officer. I no longer have any love for the United States. I have been unfairly denied promotion. My personal honor has been insulted by the government and the Army. I want to strike back." Steele's anger flared again. He took a deep breath to regain control. "I know that you are no friend of the United States. I know that you are a professional military officer near the end of his career, just as I am."

Calleja was senior for a one star; he would never attain his second. His older brother, Jorge, had been a revolutionary in the late 1960s with many of the politicians now in power in the government. Jorge fought in the field with Che Guevara in those heady days of Cuban messianic fervor. After a massive manhunt, Bolivian Army Rangers, trained by the U.S. Army, captured Che and most of his men. Both Che and Jorge Calleja were executed in the field, without trials.

Young Armando spent the next year in exile in Cuba until he could quietly slip back into Bolivia, along with the man who was now the Bolivian Minister of Aviation. His army career was a testament to the Byzantine world of Bolivian politics, where family ties often counted more than any other factor. The rank of brigadier general was his pay-back from the Party for the death of Jorge.

"We share many things, mi general. We have the same objectives here. I offer you my services to help you in your efforts."

Calleja thought a minute, staring directly at Steele. Then he brightened and said, "Colonel, we have not had the opportunity to show you our headquarters facilities. Please, I will show you myself."

Steele's mind was racing, trying to decipher Calleja's intentions. Had he surrendered? Or did he have something else in mind? His already upset stomach churned a few moments. No, too many people knew where he was. Calleja wasn't dumb enough to kill the commander of the United States' military mission in Bolivia, at least not on his own base. Steele remembered Thornton's own personal maxim in such spots. "Always fall back on your strengths." Steele decided to act the part of the professional visiting military dignitary.

As they made the standard VIP tour of the facilities, he dug back into his memory to recall matters discussed in the Army's professional education program and thanked his stars that Thornton had insisted that he attend those courses in residence, just as Calleja had done. He listened to Calleja's commentary, asking professional questions and making approving noises where appropriate.

By the end of the tour in front of the base gymnasium, Steele was sweaty from the tension and the unaccustomed heat and humidity of Santa Cruz. The General pointed to an enclosed racquetball court. "This is my pride and joy. All those mandatory PT classes at your Command and General Staff College course turned me into a fanatic. I had this built for my officers so I would have someone to play. Care for a game?"

Steele was particularly good at racquetball, a sport he found useful in many ways. He loved the competition, the chance to crush an opponent's ego. Moreover, he had received many tutorials from the fitness-conscious Thornton in the confines of a racquetball court. "Certainly, mi general. I don't get enough exercise in La Paz—still can't cope with the altitude very well."

The men entered the base gym. The attendant scurried to find Steele a set of gym clothes. In the locker room, Steele began to disrobe.

He noticed Calleja's furtive glances in his direction. Of course—he's checking for a wire! Steele hid a smile. No wonder Calleja wanted out of his office.

After proposing a best-of-three set, Calleja went on the attack. His aggressive play and carefully placed shots marked him as a true student of the game.

Steele started slowly, rusty from lack of exercise. Soon he played like a madman, crashing into the walls as he allowed the General to run him around the court with his expertly placed shots. Steele took just enough of his serves to allow the General the satisfaction of making some difficult returns. Calleja put Steele away with a dramatic final surge, winning two of the three games.

Calleja beamed. "A magnificent set, my friend!"

"You ran my legs off, sir!" said Steele as sweat ran down his face. "Don't think I want to play you again—you play too smart."

"Come, my friend. After such a match we both need a swim in my pool." Calleja led the way through the changing room where they slipped on suits and then into the deserted pool area. After a few minutes in the cool water, Calleja asked, "What exactly do you have in mind?"

Steele said, "We can help in many ways. I think you are having problems with organization. Your system is entirely too casual. My men and I can help tighten it up. Things need to be made more efficient, more military!" Again, Steele cautioned himself to go slowly. "Your training needs to be more intense. And product distribution is far too hit-or-miss." He paused again. "My men are experts at many things, sir, including convincing people to cooperate."

Calleja pursed his lips. He regarded Steele a long moment then shrugged and leaned forward. "You have caught me at an unfortunate time."

"Why is that?"

"An important shipment was seized this very morning. It has precipitated an unexpected problem with regard to my credit with the other families."

"A cash-flow problem, mi general?" Steele knew the drug trade was highly credit-intensive; debts had to be paid off in order to keep the system functioning. Failure to repay narco-debts was an extremely risky situation that frequently resulted in serious bodily injury.

"Precisely."

"Perhaps, mi general, you would allow me to help solve this problem as an opportunity to demonstrate my seriousness and good intentions?"

Calleja smiled slowly and nodded. "If you would do this for me, it would be a great favor."

Delighted, Steele listened to the general's terms of surrender. He had, in one afternoon, accomplished what a whole embassy full of overpaid State Department faggots could not: willing and smooth international cooperation.

***

When Steele entered the small suite at the Santa Rosa Hotel, the newcomers rose to attention out of habit, causing him to smile inwardly. They looked like real soldiers. Flat-bellied, steely-eyed killers. And those dark complexions would let them blend in perfectly down here. Great!

Satisfied with Payne's recruiting efforts, Steele said, "Men, we're in business. The General has agreed that we should be part of his organization." He smiled. "And that's what we'll do—for a time." Payne and the two ex-enlisted men exchanged glances, anticipating action. "But first, he laid down a test. Something that will prove our efficiency and skills, not to mention give us some good practice." He turned to Payne. "Are these men read in on the situation here, Master Sergeant?"

"Yessir, I told them we'd probably be workin' tonight."

"Apparently, there are a couple individuals that have caused the good General some problems recently," said Steele. "He wants them eliminated ASAP. So we do it for free as a gesture of our good will."

"No problem, Colonel," said Payne. "We're ready to move out right now. I got us the car like you said, and issued the weapons. I smuggled a few with me on the C-141 from Panama, but we're gonna need some others."

143

Steele nodded. "Good. Getting more weapons and explosives will be next on our list." He pulled a set of drawings from his briefcase. "Here are the names and addresses of the targets and some maps of Santa Cruz that the General gave me. I drove by the houses and made a couple sketches." He thought for a minute, jotting down notes all the while. "This'll have to do. I'm having dinner with the General in La Paz two days from now. We need to have accomplished the mission by then. Might as well do it tonight. No screw ups. Terminate with extreme prejudice. You know the drill. They get dead, very dead, very messy. Make it look like Colombians, meaning if the families are there, take them out, too. Then go through their home offices—there are some business records the good general wants back."

Turning to Vaca and Montoya, Steele said, "Remember the mission, what you're here for. Keep your noses and dicks clean. If things go right, we'll be out of Bolivia in three or four months with enough dough to buy booze and women for two lifetimes. Screw it up and we all die." He paused to let his words sink in. "This is the major league, gentlemen. We gotta go all the way, no holds barred. The more violence we use, the more the finger will point to the Colombians. I'll collect intel and work the disinformation program up in the Embassy. You guys will get your instructions from Master Sergeant Payne. Follow them to the letter. Remember, DEA and UMOPAR have to play by the rules, we don't. We are going to use all the rules against them. We are going to be efficient and ruthless."

The men spent another two hours working out details, poring over maps and discussing reports generated within the MILGROUP and embassy. Checking his watch, Steele stood and said, "I've got to get back to the airport. Any questions?" There were none. Payne wasn't terribly bright, but he was efficient. "Okay, let's move out. Good hunting."

Chapter Eighteen

Devon's Restaurant, Washington, D.C.

Porter Nelson settled back and luxuriated in the Corinthian leather seat of his newly-discovered favorite Washington restaurant, sipped a superb Cabernet, and watched as his dinner companions read through his notes. "Are you sure of all this, Porter?"

Porter nodded. "Hey, I was surprised by it, too, Robbie. I just wanted you to have a look to see if you could either shoot me down or add some ideas. I don't want to go off the deep end out of ignorance."

Robert Robinson looked back to Nelson's notes. "This indicates quite a working relationship between the KGB, the Stasi, the Czechs and the Cubans in South America."

John McCord said, "That shouldn't be a surprise to anybody. All that we're missing are links with the Bulgarians."

Nelson had asked two of his professional associates for their evaluation of several new leads. They sat in a pleasant restaurant favored by Nelson's journalist friends, located in a plush, multi-level mall hidden behind a well-preserved, historic brownstone facade. Robinson had worked in CIA field operations for nearly twenty years before being medically retired. He was now a security consultant to several international corporations. Nelson met him in Afghanistan, where they had shared a few bottles and swapped many lies. McCord, a long-time friend, had been a journalist for years, specializing in economics and intelligence.

"Porter, just how did you get on this track?" asked Robinson. The quiet Robinson was a natural foil to Nelson's nervous energy. He was the quintessential CIA spook, always digging, always analyzing.

"It was pretty convoluted, actually," Nelson said. "I wrote that article about my rescue for the *Post* while I was still in the hospital. Then Tom Callahan asked me to do an article on ecological damage done by the drug trade. I found that nobody north of the equator knew anything worthwhile about Bolivia so I started doing some proper research on drugs which led me into a review of overall U.S. policy in Latin America since World War I."

Both Robinson and McCord groaned.

Nelson laughed. "Hey, I had a lot of time on my hands in that hospital." He laughed again. "Anyhow, one of the books I read was an in-depth analysis of the birth and rapid growth of drug cartels in South America. It piqued my interest, probably because of my experiences in Bolivia. The author lives just across the Potomac in Virginia—in Fairfax, actually, so I went to see him. Fascinating guy."

McCord frowned as he sipped a vintage port, a legacy of his years in England. "Is this the guy who thinks the communists funded and trained the original cartels during the '60s? One of those conspiracy theory nuts, always trying to prove that international events are being orchestrated by some group like the gnomes of Zurich or the Zionists or by Robbie's buddies over at the CIA?"

"I know him, Porter," Robinson said, taking a bite of his steak, "I met him at a symposium in New York last year. Interesting theories."

Porter shook his head. "I'm not sure they're theories anymore, Robbie." Turning to McCord, he said, "No, John, he's not one of those Oliver Stone types, finding conspiracies in every crisis. But, yes, I thought this guy was a little cracked too, until I saw some of his source documents."

"Any good?" McCord asked, skeptic eyebrow cocked. "I'd heard they were pretty thin."

"Well, some are dated, especially the stuff he used in the book," Nelson conceded. "And he relies on the testimony of some questionable characters a bit too much for my liking. But he has some new information now, stuff that has surfaced since the fall of the Berlin Wall. It's especially good and pretty current on Cuba, pointing in a direction that's hard to ignore. Anyhow, that got me started, and I uncovered a few more tidbits on my own. What you have in your hand now is part of it. My stuff almost always points to Cuba and Fidel Castro."

Robinson carefully looked through Nelson's notes. "So you think Castro fingered General Ochoa Sanchez and had him executed to deflect attention from himself on charges of drug running?"

"No question," Nelson said. "I think it's pretty clear now that Castro has been involved in drugs for years right up to his cigar. Originally, he started out as an enthusiastic commie, trying to help Soviet surrogates—mainly East Germans and Czechs—set up the cartels in Colombia and Peru. Eventually, he caught on to how much money he could generate—mostly for the Castro family. He used Ochoa as his agent so he could keep his distance. Ochoa had to deal with all the creeps the cartels sent to Cuba to do business."

"Then he had Ochoa executed? Why?" McCord asked with a glance at Robbie.

"Well, I think he started having problems with Ochoa when the general came back from the fighting in Angola. Such a popular guy, his troops just adored him. In fact, evidence indicates that Ochoa was funneling quite a bit of the drug profits right into the Army—sort of a welfare fund for his troops. Castro doesn't like potential rivals—the record certainly shows that! He's killed off enough of them. So when our Congress threatened to launch some investigations about Cuban involvement in drug smuggling, Castro took the opportunity to knock off his rival, all the while sounding very pious about trying to stamp out drugs."

McCord took another sip of port as he considered the implications. "So you think there is a connection with the drug trade and Cubans-as-Soviet-moneymen in Latin America?"

Nelson nodded emphatically. "Absolutely. Especially in Bolivia. It wasn't an accident that Che Guevera happened to go there. And there are lots of connections between the Cubans and certain high-ranking Bolivian officers. But I'm thin on really hard information. I'd hoped you could help me."

Robinson sat back and chewed his lower lip. "Back to these source documents you think so highly of, Mr. Investigative Reporter. Right now might be the best time in history to search them out. Since the fall of the Berlin Wall, secret files from the East Germans and even the Russians have been pretty easy to get into. To really investigate this right, you need to go to Moscow and look through the Party files. Probably to Prague as well, maybe even Berlin."

Nelson's pulse quickened. "Can you help me get in there, to get access to those files?"

"Let me make some phone calls. I still have a couple of friends left in the Agency. What the hell, maybe I'll even go with you."

U.S. Army Medical Research Institute for Infectious Diseases Research and Development Command (USAMRIID), Ft. Detrick, Maryland

Engrossed in his computer model, Christopher Lansky, PhD., did not even hear the mailroom clerk as he entered the office and deposited Lansky's morning mail in his in-basket, sitting slightly askew, as usual, on the corner of his walnut desk. A "lab rat," sporting the stereotypical white lab coat and perpetually mussed hair, Lansky was the newly-designated Director of Research for USAMRIID, complete with deadlines, reports, and Congressional oversight.

The alarm on his wristwatch went off, startling Lansky and breaking into his thoughts. He glanced at his watch in surprise and swore softly at the loss of his morning. Annoyed, he punched off the alarm, hit the computer SAVE key, and logged off. He leaned back in his leather chair and swiveled around.

Lansky's blood froze when he saw the European-looking manila envelope, slicker and less bulky than the American version, sitting there on his desk like a hand grenade. His body trembled and his stomach rebelled. In a flash, his nightmares of the past ten years returned as all delusions vanished.

Christopher Lansky had been one of the enlightened of his generation of American college students. An academic scholarship to Swarthmore College in Philadelphia had been his ticket out of rural Maryland. At the height of the Vietnam War, Swarthmore, a *very* liberal arts college, sometimes called "Joseph Stalin U" because of the Marxist predilections of its faculty, seethed with anti-war activists.

Many of the professors were brilliant, articulate, and enraged with the Establishment. They never missed an opportunity to damn every level of the government in the United States as evil, corrupt, and unworthy.

Lansky found the politics fascinating. At the urging of his academic advisor, he spent his junior year at the *Freie Universität Berlin*.

Oh, the ideas. The drugs. The women, all dedicated to progressive thought and free love. What a life for an idealistic young man! Lansky reveled in it, consumed with the passions roiling the Berlin academic world, attending class whenever convenient, demonstrating whenever possible.

He became a true believer in the cause of socialism. Following his passions, he announced to his circle of intimate friends his intention to join the Communist Party. One of those friends was a recruiter for the Ministry of State Security looking for idealistic young people. Over several weeks, he convinced Lansky that he could do more by remaining anonymous and working with the Stasi.

His mission was to return to the United States, to pursue a successful career in his field of microbiology, and to become a member of the Establishment.

It had been ever so easy to fool the Army. He simply "became one" with the company policy. He was coached by his contacts in Berlin never to deny his activist past but to show that he had outgrown all those young passions. Hell, the current U.S. President had demonstrated in the streets while at university, as had half of his youngish appointees. To have been a student radical was something of a badge of honor in this administration.

Now Lansky was quite the dedicated professional, brilliant in his field, and he had quickly climbed the career ladder in the civil service. He sent a steady stream of classified reports back to East Germany, knowing they were grist for the Soviet bioweapons effort.

He didn't know how many others like him the HVA had woven throughout the American government and industry. But there certainly were more. Some he had read about in the papers. He identified with people like Jonathan Pollard, an American Jew who had spied for Israel out of a sense of patriotism, an adherence to higher principles. He

149

despised John Walker and Aldrich Ames and their ilk who spied for money.

But gradually the great utopian vision of worldwide socialism vanished as reality set in with marriage and a family. He watched it decay during his trips to Germany for the Army. All the dreams collapsed under the weight of the lies, all the lies, the impossibility of it all. College was so long ago. A lifetime ago. Since then space flight had become routine. Computers had changed the world. And he was stuck in a revolutionary time-warp of his own making.

Then the contacts abruptly ceased, victims of the convulsions that ripped through the Eastern Bloc. Lansky read about the riots in East Berlin, attacks on the Ministry Headquarters and fantasized about his file being destroyed in the chaos.

With no contacts for so long, he'd convinced himself that he had somehow escaped his past. But now, here was this ominous envelope on his desk that announced he would be contacted tomorrow with a meeting place.

Lansky covered his face with his hands and sobbed. He would never be free again.

The buzz of the phone startled him.

"Dr. Lansky, the colonel is on the line. He says you're late and to please come to the conference room immediately. The reporters are here."

When Lansky entered the conference room, Colonel Sid Hoffritz, Chief of the Institute's Public Affairs Office, was finishing his briefing on the history of the Institute. Four reporters from local papers sat around the table with briefing guides and working papers spread out over the polished mahogany conference table.

Irv Cohen of the *Baltimore Sun* smiled as he shook hands. "The Colonel says you're from this area."

"Yes," Lansky said with a smile, "I'm a homegrown boy from right here in Frederick. I did my doctorate at Johns Hopkins and my wife's from Towson."

"The Colonel also says you are one of the world's experts on hemorrhagic fevers."

"I don't know about that, but I spent six long months tramping around the tropical areas of Bolivia."

"Doctor Lansky," asked Steve Smitherman, *Leesburg Tribune*, "the Colonel explained that the Army's requested a major expansion of Fort Detrick. That's good news to our readers, of course, because of the economic impact on the local area, but can you explain why bigger facilities here are necessary in these days of a shrinking military and base closures?"

"Certainly," said Lansky, taking a deep breath. "When Desert Shield was being cranked up, the U.S. military was convinced that Saddam Hussein would use biological weapons. We had almost half a million troops in the Gulf—most were not inoculated properly. DoD had to contract out to the Michigan Department of Public Health, the only American facility that has approval from the Food and Drug Administration to make vaccines and antitoxins. Now DoD is trying to build a proper-sized facility here."

"Why?" asked Smitherman. "I see this bio-stuff all the time in grocery store novels but except for the anthrax in the mail, I haven't seen much evidence of a credible threat."

"Oh, the threat is real, all right. Those same novels point out that biological weapons are the poor man's nukes. Or phrased more accurately, a poor country's nukes."

Smitherman glanced over his notes. "Okay, Doctor, assuming you were a Saddam Hussein with one of these toxins, how would you deliver it?"

"Aerosol delivery is the best way to disperse toxins," responded Lansky. "Unlike chemicals, biological toxins need to be breathed to be effective. Basically, there are two ways to disperse the toxins—line source and point source. Just put an aerosol generator on a boat or a crop sprayer airplane and allow the wind to disperse the toxin along a line.

"Point sources are the classic explosives—grenades, mortar, and artillery rounds."

"Or Scud missiles?" asked the reporter from the Post.

"Or Scud missiles," Lansky nodded. "The explosions kill a lot of the toxin, though. You're down in the one to five percent efficiency range with explosives, as opposed to the forty to sixty percent range of line sources." The reporters scribbled in their notepads.

"How would a country use biological weapons?" Smitherman asked.

"The weapons can be employed strategically, tactically, or even covertly," Lansky said. "The toxin doesn't have to kill to be effective. Remember how frightened people were over the anthrax scare? Some toxins act immediately, some require an incubation period, so people can be infected for days and not even know it—the 'walking dead,' moving around, spreading the disease. Massive casualties from exposure to biological toxins are possible, even likely—we're talking tens of thousands of people, if the conditions are right."

Irv Cohen asked, "Do you foresee problems in the proliferation of biological weapons?"

Lansky nodded. "In the past twenty years, while the world was preoccupied with nukes, there has been a biological revolution. Rapid production procedures, gene splicing in particular, make it unnecessary to stockpile large supplies of toxins. Very nice for terrorists—difficult to detect with overhead imagery, or even on-site inspectors."

"Unlike a nuclear program," Cohen pointed out.

"Exactly. Inspectors looking for biolabs face the same kind of problems that DEA inspectors face looking for cocaine labs in South America—the labs are small, portable, easy to hide. And look at the poor success rate we have in the drug arena."

"Then you think we'll be fighting germ warfare in the future?"

Lansky held up both hands. "Those questions are for people like you to debate. I'm only a scientist." He stood and motioned to the door. "Instead of just talking, let's go to the lab and I'll show you where I work. Ever since I was a little kid, I've lived in the world of laboratories and professional journals. My wife says I have my own little version of the world—and she's right. All I ask is to be allowed to work in my lab during the day and to go home to my wife and daughters at night. That's my idea of heaven."

152

Outside Potosi, Bolivia

"More *chicha*, Renan?" asked Jaime Suarez of his cousin who nodded. Jaime poured more of the pale, straw colored fermented corn beer into Renan's gourd cup. The men were huddled against the cold on the earthen floor of Jaime's adobe hut in a small mountain village near the mining town of Potosi

Renan took a sip of the frothy beer. "I have decided to go to the Chapare, and I want you to go with me."

Jaime took his time to respond. Both men were full-blooded Quechua Indians, born and raised in the Andes around Potosi. Their stature, at a wiry five feet three inches with barrel chests for the extra lung capacity needed to survive at altitude, combined with brown skin, black eyes, and a thatch of thick black hair, set them apart from most Bolivians of mixed blood. Jaime respected his cousin who had actually been to Cochabamba, over three hundred miles away, an unbelievable distance. "I've never been anywhere except Potosi. Tell me again about the Chapare."

"We'll get work in the coca fields," Renan said, sounding confident of his information. "They need people in the Chapare who can work hard, and nobody can work harder than Potosi miners! It's hot and it rains all the time, which makes it tough for mountaineers like us. But there are plants growing everywhere, and we won't have to spend much on food. After a few months, we'll come back to Potosi with enough money to buy a pig and a cow. Even two cows! And decent houses for our families."

Jaime thought about his village. Everywhere was the grinding poverty of the Bolivian highlands, adobe huts clustered together, no running water, no electricity, no heat other than from the cow-chip cooking fire. Proud people with little to eat, little to do other than survive, and little hope for the future. Jaime refused to give up hope. He would die in order to save his family. How could working in the Chapare be any worse than death? And anyway, it was just for a few months.

"Jaime, there's no work here in Potosi. Do you want your baby to grow up poor like we did? Work at shit jobs all his life, barely staying alive?"

Jaime didn't want to leave his wife, Clorinda, or their little baby, but Renan was right—there was no work to be had in all of the Potosi region. The small private silver mine where the cousins had spent the past four years working twelve-hour days had finally closed. Almost all of the mines were closed now. Ever since the president closed the government-owned mines years ago and fired thousands of miners, things had been hard. For Jaime to believe that Potosi had once been the largest city in the western hemisphere was difficult. What once used to be the source of legendary wealth was now one of the poorest cities in the poorest country in South America.

Jaime wasn't interested in history or missed opportunities. He simply wanted to feed his family. Mind made up, he decided to go, even though it meant leaving the cool, familiar mountains for the sweltering lowlands. He reached out and shook his cousin's hand.

***

Days later, Jaime, stooping under the weight of a hundred-pound bag of coca leaves, joined the line of laborers shifting the *cargas* from the plaza to the waiting trucks. Both Jaime and Renan had found work quickly. Coca buyers always needed extra unskilled labor and recognized the work ethic of the miners. Bolivian miners were renowned for their ability to endure, to work under inhuman conditions. The mine workers' union was also known as the most difficult and reactionary of all the Bolivian unions. Their anti-government demonstrations often ended with explosions of dynamite sticks, or blasting caps, routine tools of the miner's trade.

Sweat poured off the men as they scurried back and forth from the trucks like so many two-legged ants bent double from their over-sized loads. Jaime focused on getting as many bags as possible so he could move on to the next job for the next coca buyer, whatever it might be. The work available was exactly the kind he had expected to get—brutal physical labor. Nightfall frequently found both Jaime and Renan collapsed on the floor of their crude hut, exhausted and dehydrated, but determined to go on.

Neither of the Suarez cousins had been able to save quite as much as they planned. The food plants that grew wild in the Chapare no longer grew in areas near their hut because they had been destroyed by the cultivation of land for coca, coca, and more coca. The men had neither the time nor the energy to spend walking the distances now necessary to find wild food, so they had to buy provisions in town. Still, they were managing to send some money back to their families, with the cooperation of other mountaineers returning to the uplands. They had found many other families from the areas surrounding Potosi; people displaced from their traditional homelands by economic forces beyond their comprehension. All day long they strained and sweated; at night they dreamed of returning to families and homes.

Chapter Nineteen

MILGROUP Commander's residence
Illimani Building Apartments,
Sopocachi, La Paz

Colonel Billie D. Steele sat with a beer in his hand, watching through the picture window as the colors of the sunset played over the face of Illimani.

Master Sergeant Don Payne said, "This is a real nice place you got yourself, Colonel."

Steele grunted, then grinned, pleased at the evaluation of his luxury apartment penthouse. "Yeah, I'm practicing the life of the idle rich so I'll be good at it when we leave here."

They both laughed and toasted each other with their beers. Things were going well.

"Don, tell me about the op. General Calleja and friends were quite impressed. Word on the street is that the 'Colombians' were very efficient."

Payne pulled out some index cards and referred to his hand-written notes. "The surveillance showed that one house would be easy, one difficult. So we took out the easy one first for practice. All the family members were home, so we popped them. We had plenty of time to ransack the house, looking for the papers." He took a sheaf of papers from his battered briefcase and handed them to Steele. "The General's IOU is on top, so he should be a happy camper now. He was down for over two hundred thousand dollars. No wonder he wanted this guy done."

Steele whistled softly. This was a bigger game than he had hoped. "What else did you find?"

Payne's grin broadened into a greedy smile. "This guy was obviously the accountant and treasurer for the cartel. We found boxes of cash in the back room. Nearly four hundred grand, mostly in twenties and fifties."

Seeing Steele's hard look, Payne fished out another piece of paper. "Okay, Colonel, exactly three hundred ninety-six thousand, four hundred and fifty dollars. Here's the breakout." Steele studied the paper as Payne continued, "All the money's in the hotel. We need to know what you want us to do with it. We can't keep hauling it around the countryside every time we move base."

Steele nodded. "Early next week I want you to drive to Cochabamba via the Santa Cruz-Cochabamba highway. Take your time and get to know the road—it isn't very good. It goes right through the Chapare. Look around Villa Tunari and Chimoré, but don't spend a lot of time. And make sure you're not seen by any DEA agents. Check into the Cochabamba Hotel and call me here. There is a cartel bank in Cochabamba where we can safely deposit the money for the time being. When you're squared away in Cochabamba, I'll have another mission ready for you." Steele smiled again. "Now tell me about the other hit."

"It was loud and messy, per your instructions. We got the guy. He was in the sack with his wife and a girlfriend. Pity we couldn't have hit that house quietly. It would have been fun to play with the women for a while."

Steele made an impatient gesture with his hands. "There'll be plenty of time for that. Good job, Don. Tell the men that for me." Payne nodded and Steele mentally shifted gears. "Okay, when you get back to Santa Cruz, call this number." He handed Payne a slip of paper. "Identify yourself as Carlos. Do whatever they tell you to. It's your hook-up with the cartel. They should take you to their headquarters to show you how they do things. Don't get into any long-winded discussions, just look and listen. The three of you should talk among yourselves and work out some sort of a 'straw-man' program for training and operations. You know—objectives, safety, patrolling, maybe even some formal lesson plans. Then call me here and we'll talk about how we're going to beat these guys into shape. We'll even schedule a graduation field training exercise, an operation that will get everybody's attention. I have just the place."

Steele pulled out a map. "Our Ambassador's favorite spot in all of Bolivia is in Potosi. He talks about it at every opportunity. And how those Ambassadors can talk! They're worse than generals!"

Payne chuckled dutifully.

"Anyhow, Don, there's supposed to be this old colonial mint, the *Casa de la* something down there, just chock full of rare old gold coins. According to Brent, they're priceless. Better still, apparently nothing much goes on in Potosi, and security isn't all that great."

"Sounds just like what we're lookin' for—maximum payoff, minimum risk."

"Exactly," said Steele, pleased with Payne's attitude. "I want you to wander down there and do a recon. Be unobtrusive. Stay overnight and see what the town is like after dark."

Payne nodded. "Roger that, Colonel. Should be fun."

Steele continued, "I'll take the C-12 down next week and get an aerial view of routes of ingress and egress. We'll meet back here and work out the details. In the meantime, get back to the Chapare and get those guys into shape for this raid." He held up his beer in a mock toast. "My friend, we are going to rock the Bolivians' world."

MILGROUP
U.S. Embassy, La Paz

Steele sat at his desk, trying hard to concentrate on the DEA intelligence reports that Patricia had given him. Or rather, traded him for the intel he received from Quarry Heights that covered the whole of the SOUTHCOM Area of Responsibility. Patricia didn't give anything away. His mind kept returning to last night with Pointer in her luxurious house. Only in private could he act out the passion that sprang up every time he saw her. Even casual conversation in the embassy was dangerous for him—he was sure that someone would detect his growing infatuation with the DCM. All this emotion was unnerving to a man proud of his independence and strong will. Worse, it was distracting him from his primary mission, something he couldn't allow.

Out of the corner of his eye he saw Lieutenant Colonel José Hernandez stride up to the doorway, hesitate, then knock three times. He entered, shutting the door behind him. "Colonel, I've got some bad news."

Steele glared. "Speak, I don't have all day."

Drawing a deep breath, Hernandez said, "The shipment of ammunition and grenades for the Chimoré base camp left the warehouse here in La Paz about two hours ago. Without guards."

"What do you mean, without guards?" The op order, written by Hernandez himself, specified two UMOPAR troops and a Special Forces sergeant accompany the shipment, critical to future operations in the Chapare, all the way to Cochabamba.

"Sir, I just got word from the SF team house here in La Paz that the sergeant assigned to guard the load released it to the Bolivian driver. It was so late in the day that he didn't want to make the trip to Cochabamba in the dark."

"Didn't want to drive in the dark?" Steele's jaw dropped. He slammed a huge fist onto the desk. "Am I hearing right? A sergeant in the United States Army Special Forces was too scared to carry out his duty because it was *dark*? And he sent an entire truckload of ammo and explosives off into the night, unescorted?"

Hernandez unconsciously came to attention and responded, "Yes, sir, that is correct."

Steele paused, then lurched back into his chair, breathing hard. "Tell me about this terrible, fear-inspiring road, Hernandez."

"Colonel, the major road between La Paz and Cochabamba is a winding dirt strip, often only one lane, that climbs and descends through two major mountain ridges. It takes five to six hours driving time in a fast car under the best of conditions in daylight."

Steele nodded. He'd been on roads like this in Honduras and Panama, roads with spectacular views and equally spectacular drop-offs, lit only by the moon. And the Bolivian truck drivers scared the shit out of him, passing on curves, on hills, whenever they damned well pleased. The Russian army attaché, a Spetsnaz major, had been creamed by a truck passing on a hill just the previous month, killing his daughter and seriously injuring his wife. Since this road was the major connection between La Paz and the lower section of the country, there would be lots of big motor coaches and trucks driving at night without headlights, ready to run you right off the road.

An idea formed in Steele's mind. "Lots of accidents, I assume?"

"Sir, almost every curve in the road has flower-covered crosses marking where somebody went over the edge. Lots of vehicles just don't make the turns. They sometimes plummet a thousand feet or more."

"So," Steele slowly drew circles on his desk with a stubby finger, "there are lots of deserted sections along the way where nasty things could happen to our truck. Presumably this is why our man decided to chicken out."

"Sir," said Hernandez, "I've already ordered the other SF troops out to find him. They think they know where he is. We should know something here pretty quick."

Steele continued, "You get me all the particulars. I want to know exactly how much of what is on board. I want to know which company the driver works for, his name, what kind of truck, exactly when it left, and anything else you can find. And I want it yesterday!"

"Yes, sir." Hernandez turned to leave.

"And one more thing," Steele said, jabbing his finger at Hernandez. "You get that asshole sergeant out of here. I want him on the next thing smokin', the very next airplane out of my country. You write a detailed list of charges: dereliction of duty, disobeying orders, and anything else you can think of for me to send to his commander in Panama." Steele squinted. "I'll bet he's got a honey here in La Paz, don't he?" Watching Hernandez's face, he said, "I thought so. Not the first time a soldier has done something dumb because of a woman." His smile was grim. "Well, you make that letter nice and tight. The Army's trying to cut back on personnel. We'll just give them a chance to cut back this particular soldier. Dismissed!"

As Hernandez shut the door behind him, Steele allowed his smile to expand. He'd been raised on the *carpe diem* mentality of the armor corps, meaning you made your own luck, and you made it happen now.

160

Here was an opportunity to solve his operational problems that he couldn't have invented if he'd schemed for a decade. Payne was complaining that he couldn't make his training program for his Bolivian recruits realistic due to lack of ammunition, and here was an entire truckload! Steele laughed outright as he picked up his phone and requested the embassy operator put him through to the Hotel Cochabamba.

Chapter Twenty

Ida Lee Recreation Park
Leesburg, Virginia

The threatening thunderstorms building off to the southwest increased Christopher Lansky's sense of dread as he crossed the Potomac River headed south on Highway 15 from Frederick, Maryland. Stomach churning, Lansky barely managed to control himself as he alternatively sobbed and raged at the memory of the menacing voice on the phone directing this meeting. He could almost feel the noose around his neck.

Ignoring the comfortable and well-manicured farms on the Virginia side of the river, he approached Leesburg and turned right at the long curving drive into the park and forced himself to pay attention. As per instructions, he parked his car by the recreation center, walked across the grass to the pavilion, and sat at the picnic table to wait.

Five minutes later, a plain white Chrysler van pulled up from behind the library building and parked along the road near the pavilion. The sliding door opened and Lansky watched two men get out. A stocky middle-aged man carried a leather briefcase as the two walked towards the picnic table. They sat opposite Lansky and deliberately placed the briefcase on the table.

The stocky man said, "I have looked forward to this meeting for a long time, Herr Doktor." He gave a slight bow of his head. "Allow me to introduce myself. I am Kurt Wallerein. This is my colleague, Doktor Nikolai Yazov."

"It is a pleasure meeting you again, Doctor Lansky," said Yazov. "What do you mean, 'again'?"

"We met when you were part of the UNSCOM inspection visit to our Biopreparat facilities in Obolensk. I didn't know then that you were one of us." He smiled as if savoring the irony. "I might have actually told you the truth about our experiments."

Lansky's heart skipped a beat. Biopreparat. Yazov. Of course. The former First Deputy Director who was largely responsible for a major push by the Russians to develop a "perfect bug" for biological warfare against NATO forces. When that failed, he had disappeared along with hundreds of other Russian scientists, deserting a sinking Russia like so many of their experimental rats.

"What do you want from me?" Lansky blurted.

Wallerein acted as if he hadn't heard. "Your dossier is most impressive, Herr Doktor. Many awards, commendations. Published articles. Most impressive."

"What do you want?" Lansky screamed.

"Tell me about your research with Bolivian hemorrhagic fever."

"I can't tell you about that. It's classified."

Wallerein opened his briefcase and extracted an envelope. "We were concerned that your revolutionary fervor might have faded since we last heard from you. Perhaps this might refresh your memory."

Lansky opened the envelope and extracted several typed sheets. The closely typed pages contained a list—a compilation of the several hundred documents and reports that he had sent to the East German Stasi. They had him again.

Wallerein's eyes went hard. "I think the question of classification has been decided by your past reports, Herr Doktor. Now, once again, tell us about your research with the Bolivian virus."

Lansky's mind raced, and a sinking feeling hit him. What the hell was going on? He shrugged, trying desperately to appear unconcerned. "Nothing dramatic really. It's another rodent borne virus, much like the hantavirus virus found in the American Southwest. Passed by inhalation of aerosols of rodent excreta or secreta or by eating contaminated food. Patients develop fever, headaches, fatigue, vomiting, diarrhea, abdominal pain. The blood fails to clot. Victims may bleed from the nose and mouth, and internal organs."

Wallerein nodded slowly. "You will deliver a sample of your Bolivian hemorrhagic fever virus to me by tomorrow afternoon."

"But why? You can get that in Bolivia easily enough."

Wallerein's smiled broadened. "We prefer your altered strain. The genetic engineering you are conducting is quite fascinating."

Lansky was aghast. Not twenty people in the government knew of the research he was conducting to make the Machupo virus a viable bioweapon. God, could this man have someone else inside USAMRIID?

"It's impossible!" he protested. "Security's too tight."

"You will deliver on time or this list of documents you provided us—with your name attached—will be sent to the Pentagon, your boss, and perhaps, your local newspaper."

"No," said Lansky, weakly, quivering from fright. "I can't do this anymore." He tried to sit up straighter. "I won't."

Wallerein's eyes turned ice-cold. He took another envelope from his open briefcase and handed it to Lansky. With trembling hands, the terrified Lansky opened the second envelope. He took out pictures of his family, recent ones showing his young daughters in their schoolyard, his wife walking the dog, his brothers at their store in Rockville, his parents sitting on their front porch drinking ice tea in the evening, as well as his wife's parents and sisters at a wedding. Then it dawned on him that this was his whole family, everybody in the world that he loved and who loved him. There was no way out.

"You are not taking this seriously enough, Herr Doktor," said Wallerein, eyes boring through Lansky. "If you do as you are told, I will not harm these people. This is not a choice of whether to cooperate or not. This is a choice of whether you and your family live until next week or not. Very simple."

Wallerein paused. "You will deliver the container. Understood?"

Lansky sat, stunned. This was worse than anything he had imagined. He was terrified of Wallerein—terrified of what Wallerein could do to his family, terrified physically to be seated next to someone who was obviously a world-class killer, and now, terrified beyond belief at the implications of this demand for biological toxins. His PhD brain was so overwhelmed by what it considered "unprocessable data" that it threatened to shut down completely; as it was, it could only manage to send feeble impulses to his body to execute a slow, almost indistinguishable nod.

"No tricks, Herr Doktor. My Russian colleague here is quite knowledgeable in these matters. The container will be secure and safe to transport. Any accident to my men will result in 'accidents' to your dear ones. Is that clear?"

Potosi, Bolivia

"Okay men, time to move out," said Master Sergeant Don Payne. The seven men, three Americans and four Bolivians, checked their equipment one last time, per the U.S. Army manuals Payne was trying to drill into their heads. He had to keep reminding himself that, before his arrival, these people had never seen some of this equipment and never had any formal weapons and explosives training. Not a by-the-book man on many things, Payne was a stickler for safety rules. He had seen too many people injured or killed in training and in combat for not keeping safety and common sense in mind. He had no intention of getting maimed because some bozo couldn't remember to think.

Payne and his former Army pals had accomplished a lot in the short time they had been in Bolivia. They had been accepted into the Rodriguez organization, watched its operations for a few days, and were now in the process of altering its slip-shod approach to business. Payne had no formal training in management theory, but he certainly understood efficiency. He was the product of some of the U.S. Army's toughest training schools and had been a platoon sergeant in an infantry unit until an unfortunate run-in with the Military Police. Payne suffered no delusions of turning this group of rag-tag recruits into Rangers skilled in stealth, infiltration, raids and ambushes, but he could teach rudimentary forms of those skills. After all, most of his recruits were thugs and bullies used to sneaking up on people and doing them in the back. What was standard for bullies was called good tactics by soldiers the world over.

To offset the weaknesses of his people, Payne added the use of terror. He found a happy training tool: by day he worked with his new troops; by night, he led selected members in an ambush of uncooperative and troublesome people. His men learned to be aggressive and brutal. The opposition within the narcocommunity in the Chapare quickly crumbled. The loosely organized Bolivians were no match for his ruthless methods and superior training. Soon he would be ready for his assault on the UMOPAR and DEA.

Tonight's operation was to be a major step along that path, carefully chosen as a sort of graduation exercise for these particular Bolivians. Led by Payne and his ex-Ranger pal, Carlos Montoya, it should be a walk in the park against the Bolivian National Police. The Police, and for that matter the Bolivian Army, were poorly trained and armed. Police officers had little live-fire training and often went to work with no ammunition for their obsolete and poorly maintained weapons.

It had been trivial to set up an ambush for the ammunition truck outside Cochabamba. A bullet to the brain of the defenseless driver and Payne's ordnance problem was solved. He now had several tons of ammunition and explosives.

The target tonight was the loosely guarded Casa de la Moneda in the ancient city of Potosi—tough enough to be a confidence builder for these, his best recruits to date. But not too tough. The chief redeeming features were the lax National Police guards and the gold coins.

Payne had scouted the city, the Casa, entryways, and exits. The plan was as simple as he could make it—infiltrate, get the gold, and escape. Payne refined Steele's original plan to include killing the guards. In his opinion, the killings were necessary to make the national papers and terrorize the authorities. The extra noise of the shootings would also scare the bejeesus out of the locals. News of the operation would filter down the ranks and into the countryside, making Payne's job in the Chapare that much easier.

The men slowly maneuvered through the narrow alleys, each following a predetermined path that they had rehearsed a dozen times, avoiding any spots of light that punctuated the main streets. One Bolivian split off from the main group and circled around to the back entrance.

Payne stopped at the last corner and peered around while the remainder of his team crouched behind a fruit cart. He had an easy direct line of sight across the plaza to the high metal gates surrounding the Casa. Five guards appeared backlit against the subdued light of the Casa, plus the one he knew was in the back of the building, probably asleep in the guard shack.

Payne motioned to his number one Bolivian. The man carefully eased himself around until he had a full view. "Three of them outside, two in the guard shack," he whispered.

Payne nodded and took a final look. He gestured for two men to come forward. He gave a few quiet orders, then waved them forward. When they reached their assigned positions, they stopped and waited for the signal.

Payne checked his watch. Ten more seconds. He sighted down on his target again. Just like a shooting gallery. He squeezed off a three-round burst at the first guard who was dead before he hit the ground. The others were dead nanoseconds later, ambushed by their own countrymen.

Montoya and his Bolivian shadows raced across the Plaza and through the open gates, checked the guards, then scrambled down the ramp into the building.

Ransacking the museum was quick and efficient. The Bolivians methodically smashed the glass in the cases while Payne and Montoya loaded handfuls of precious coins into their small canvas satchels.

"*Vamanos!*" Payne shouted. The team dashed up the stairs to the ground floor and out the back. The last of Payne's Bolivians tossed a satchel charge through the open doorway as he escaped. The explosion rocked the entire block, cracking the Casa's thick, ancient walls. The blast demolished everything on the ground floor and lit a massive fire, which destroyed the rest of the magnificent historical building.

Chapter Twenty-One

MILGROUP Commander's Apartment, Sopocachi

"*Inculto!*" screamed Brigadier General Armando Calleja, face nearly purple with fury as he stormed into Steele's apartment. "How could you do this? The Casa de la Moneda was a jewel, a genuine Bolivian marvel, a piece of our history. Now it's gone forever."

"Mi general," said Steele, trying to calm the outraged man, "You knew we were going to stage a raid for training—"

"But not in Potosi! Bolivians were killed in this raid. You should have checked with me!"

"You're right, sir. I should have asked for your approval of the target. I did not consider the historical value." He stood at attention. "I assume responsibility for the decision. I apologize, sir." He glanced at Payne, who took the hint and popped to attention as well.

"Mi general, my apologies as well, sir. We was only thinking of a suitable challenge to the troops. We shoulda thought to ask you, sir."

Steele said, "What's done is done, General. Actually, sir, the Spanish raped that area for their own benefit, not to benefit the country of Bolivia. Potosi could be looked at as another blight on your country left by outside imperialists.

"From a tactical position, sir, we've now focused attention on Potosi for a while—we've gotten the Chapare off the front pages. The dead guards were National Police, not soldiers. That will make the Police look pretty bad, not the Army."

Still unconvinced, Calleja paced the room. "You should not have proceeded without consulting me."

"*Si, señor,*" Steele agreed again. Anything to cool the man down.

Calleja stopped. "You must do something else. An attack on some American force—the DEA or somebody. American blood must follow Bolivian blood. And soon." This was not a request.

Steele nodded. "As it happens, mi general, Master Sergeant Payne and I thought the same thing. We have just the target." He spent several more minutes giving the general the outline of his next operation.

Calleja nodded and smiled for the first time.

"In the meantime, sir, we also have the extra benefit of the gold coins we liberated." Steele nodded slightly at Payne who quickly unzipped a heavy canvas bag. He poured onto the table a golden stream of dozens of irregularly shaped coins.

"The ambassador told me they're worth millions. He knows what he's talking about." Steele laughed. "All the financial wizards say you should have some of your personal portfolio in gold. Here it is, General. We can trickle these coins onto the world market for years."

Steele watched as Calleja let the coins slip through his fingers again and again, seduced by the texture of the gold. Steele thanked his departed *patrón* General Thornton for lessons about how to exploit the foibles of his fellow man. Steele's idea to take over the Rodriguez cartel was advancing rapidly. The hijacking of the truckload of ammunition and explosives had enabled him to accelerate the timetable. Payne had established several new leaf processing facilities and another lab. To staff it posed a problem until Steele told him to strip the other sections of the Rodriguez work force in Villa Tunare. Resistance to this re-organization surfaced briefly, but Payne and his men had broken a few heads and even shot one particularly vehement resister.

Steele smiled at this new version of the "draft." He needed workers to expand production; conscription was essential. Payne would also advertise for volunteers, who would be whisked away to work camps in the jungle. If these two methods didn't work, Steele would just come up with another solution—probably start raiding other cartels for workers. Payne'd have to pop a few more labor leaders pretty soon. *Gotta watch that Payne, though,* he thought. *Don't want him to go out of control like he did that last time in Germany. No room for error here.*

Thanks to the recent rise in extreme violence in Peru, Ecuador, and Colombia, Bolivia was still largely off the radar in Washington, though DEA and NAS intelligence reports to Washington had started to reflect a growing number of drug-related killings in Bolivia. Steele deflected these summaries as long as possible, but now detailed a slight rise in his own accounts to SOUTHCOM, lest he arouse suspicion. He labeled the Casa attack as the work of violent robbers, á la Butch and Sundance.

Ambassador Brent had been broken-hearted to learn of the ransacking and destruction of the Casa de la Moneda. He reluctantly asked the State Department to re-classify the security status of Bolivia and had beefed up the Marine guards around the embassy. Steele searched for ways to make these changes work for him. He and Payne settled on a dramatic show of force to deflect more attention from the counternarcotics operations.

Now they had Calleja firmly aboard. Still watching the mesmerized general slowly fingering the gold coins, Steele's thoughts turned back to Callahan. He was the only one in the MILGROUP smart enough to see what Steele had in mind. He'd get him, Steele vowed, before he was through here. Didn't know exactly how, but Callahan was going down hard.

U.S. Marine Corps Detachment House La Paz

Master Sergeant Don Payne, disguised as a *campesino* in a greasy Bolivian felt hat and traditional clothing, sat in the back seat as ex-private Miguel Vaca drove the ancient yellow Volkswagen van slowly along the cobblestone street to U.S. Embassy Marine guard detachment. Payne and the other three occupants were studiously casual while assessing the position and number of the police guards in front of the center house. Rounding the corner, Vaca slowly reversed, headed back and stopped just opposite the two green guard shacks that straddled the front gate. The van's side door slid open, releasing loud Andean music into the early afternoon air. Payne and Montoya stumbled out of the vehicle, joking loudly, holding rolled blankets in their hands as they stood talking through the open door to the driver and front-seat passenger.

***

Corporal John Scott, USMC, precisely groomed as only a proud young Marine can be, descended down the main staircase and entered the large dining room of the Marine House.

A chorus of hoots and laughter greeted him. "Wa-hoo, look at the stud!"

"As if we didn't know where you're going!"

"Yeah, give a guy corporal's stripes, and look what happens! All that extra pay goes to his head, and he goes nuts. Gotta get married to get help to spend it all!"

Scott stared hard at his friends clustered around the dining table chowing down their dinner and said, "And you Marines need to remember just who is the corporal and who are the lower-than-whale-shit-on-the-bottom-of-the-ocean privates!" He gave them the finger, then added, "Hey, c'mon guys. Cut me some slack. I'm just going to visit Maria."

"Yeah, right!" Private David Scher said, drawing out the word and elbowing his companion with an exaggerated motion.

"Sure, Dave," said Private Steve Morley, with a wink. "It's just a visit. Just because he took the first bath he's had in three weeks is pure coincidence."

"Going home to meet the parents! Whooee, this man is as good as hitched."

"Holy smoke!" said Scott. "I forgot the present for her mom." He turned and dashed up the stairs, followed by the good-natured taunts and laughter of the other Marines.

***

Outside the gate, Payne and Montoya finally finished their loud good-byes, turned and ambled past the guards. Pivoting around slowly, Payne dropped to one knee as both men pointed their rolls of cloth at the guard shacks.

Flames and noise erupted as two Uzi automatics sprayed death at the three Bolivian policemen. Payne fired two quick bursts and disintegrated the gate lock. Inserting fresh magazines into the weapons and discarding the blankets in one simultaneous, well-practiced maneuver, they charged inside the Marine compound, followed closely by another thug carrying a small satchel. Crashing through the flimsy door into the house, the gunmen pumped bullets down opposite corridors. The slugs slammed into two surprised marines. The third attacker threw the satchel up the staircase towards the living quarters. The three then spun around and dashed back to their van, firing as they ran. Leaping into the vehicle, Vaca raced the ancient car down the street, skidding around the first corner as the sound of a loud explosion tore the air.

C-12D, Tail Number 30499
Approaching Santa Cruz 12 o'clock noon

The weather was some of the worst Tom had experienced in his four months in Bolivia. Thunderstorms towered in all quadrants like enormous explosions waiting to smash unwary aviators. He shuddered at the violence lurking inside those deceptively beautiful clouds—the pounding hailstones, the sudden ice that could turn the most advanced technological marvel into a flying Popsicle, the updrafts and downdrafts that could rip off his wings like a child tormenting a fly.

Tom glanced over his shoulder. Colleen gave him a dazzling smile and a hearty thumbs-up. She had flown with Tom many times and relished visits to other parts of the beautiful countryside. The Ambassador concentrated on a history book. Mrs. Adams, a sour-faced woman and a distinct non-flyer, studiously ignored Tom's inquiring glance. Both Bolivian bodyguards sat with barf bags in their laps.

The Ambassador and the two Air Force officers were en route to an FAB formal function at its Air Force Academy located in the tropical city of Santa Cruz. The invitations offered transportation by the FAB, but Ambassador Brent had opted for the C-12 in order to return early the next morning. Tom smiled to himself. The Ambassador must be regretting coming at all. Brent did not travel well, and rough rides typically upset his delicate stomach.

Torrential rain slammed into the windscreen and the small cabin echoed with noise. The plane lurched through a sudden updraft, then a massive downdraft. Books and papers flew though the cabin. Everyone tightened their seat belts, then clutched at their arm rests.

Tom checked his weather radar. Thunderstorms. The silent screams of reds and yellows marked the extent of the cells across the scope. The storms on the scope had not even moved in the past few minutes. Shit! The radar was broken.

Ambassador Brent shouted, "Tom, what's the weather like in Santa Cruz?"

"Right now, Mr. Ambassador, I'm more concerned about the weather right here."

Ferocious blasts of air slammed the aircraft again and again. Tom tightened his shoulder straps. He dug into his flight bag and pulled on his Royal Australian Air Force issue white leather "magic flying gloves" that he only wore when things got tense in the cockpit. Over his shoulder he saw Colleen's eyes widen. Now she knew this was serious.

Tom spoke to Colonel Adams on intercom. "Colonel, tell Approach we're descending. We need to get out of this."

"Santa Cruz Approach, Spar Niner Niner departing flight level two five zero for lower."

Tom directed Adams to begin the descent checklist, and reviewed the Non-Directional Beacon (NDB) instrument approach into Viru Viru International Airport.

"Spar Niner Niner, cleared to five thousand and for the NDB approach runway three four. Winds are out of the north at four zero knots."

Tom turned up the volume on the cabin speaker system. "Hang in there, folks. The winds up here are about eighty knots but only forty knots on the ground. Once we start down, we'll get out of these clouds, rain, and all these bumps. We'll be on the ground in about ten minutes."

They descended through heavy cloud deck, bouncing and wallowing down to the initial approach altitude of five thousand feet.

Tom began the approach; they broke out of the clouds passing through three thousand. The rain stopped. Blessed silence. Muted cheers arose from the rear of the aircraft.

"Tell Approach I'm going visual."

"Approach, Spar Niner Niner going visual."

"Roger Spar, contact tower on one one eight point six."

"Viru Viru Tower, Spar Niner Niner with you. Request straight in."

"Spar Niner Niner, cleared straight in. Negative traffic."

The buffeting diminished. The airport appeared through the haze just off the nose. More cheers.

"Tower, Spar Niner Niner has the runway in sight."

"Spar, cleared to land runway three four right. Winds are three four zero at four zero knots"

Tom maneuvered the still wobbly aircraft onto an extended final. Below, he could see long rows of tropical trees, planted perpendicular to the runway, bent over nearly double. He planted the aircraft on the runway. The passengers burst into loud applause. The normally staid Ambassador Brent even gave a two-fingered whistle. Tom took his time to taxi to the parking area in front of the Third Air Brigade headquarters at El Trompillo, the military side of the airport.

No ground crew emerged from base operations to guide him to the parking area. Tom taxied as close to the building as he thought wise and shut down. He led the passengers, heads ducked, coats flapping, through the gusty wind and rain showers, across the tarmac into the headquarters building. No duty officer. Instead Tom found himself staring into the surprised faces of most of the generals in the FAB.

General Camacho stepped forward. "*Buenos días, Tómas.* I'm very surprised to see you this stormy morning."

Tom gestured at the Ambassador and the group. "Sir, we're here for the graduation ceremony. Is there a problem?"

Camacho laughed. "The problem, my young friend, is that the entire Bolivian Air Force is grounded because of the weather. The ceremony is cancelled." Camacho turned to his staff. "Please note, *mis amigos*, that while our beloved air force is unable to fly, these *norteamericano* aviators have braved the weather and flown in here with their ambassador and their wives."

Camacho gave Tom a surreptitious wink. Tom knew that Camacho was immensely proud of his USAF wings as were three others of his staff. Several other generals were ardent supporters of Fidel Castro and his regime in Havana. Camacho must be thrilled at this accidental example of the abilities of the USAF. Not even the most fanatical fidelista could deny what he had just witnessed.

Camacho turned to Ambassador Brent. "*Señor Embajador*, I am very embarrassed that we have inconvenienced you. Perhaps we can make some small amends by inviting you and your staff to lunch?"

***

General Camacho, a fine host, had outdone himself as he wined and dined the Ambassador whose programs meant so much to the FAB. Ambassador Brent and the Callahans sat the head table. The rest of the American delegation who had arrived the day before, were scattered about the large dining room. Colonel Adams disappeared. The restaurant, Los Patos, served only roast duck along with the arroz con queso and vegetables common to the region, as well as bottles of excellent Bolivian red wines.

As the party began to break up, Tom noticed a worried-looking embassy security officer enter the room, head straight to the Ambassador, and whisper into Brent's ear. Brent blanched. He covered his face with his hand for a moment. When he looked up, his face was drawn and pale. He motioned to Tom and Colleen. "We have to return to La Paz at once. The Marine House has just been bombed. Three Marines were murdered."

"*Damn!*" Tom swore and felt a white-hot rage. Colleen buried her face in Tom's shoulder and sobbed—she knew all of the Marines, many had been to their house. He stroked her hair. With a huge effort, Tom managed to blot out his anger. "I'll get Adams, Mr. Ambassador."

He cradled Colleen's tear-streaked face in his hands. "Not now, Sweetheart. We have to hold it together. We'll grieve later. I need you to round up the others and get them to the cars. We'll fly out as soon as we get to the plane."

She nodded, wiped her eyes with his handkerchief, and strode away.

Tom spotted Adams teetering unsteadily on a corner bar stool, glass of amber liquid in hand, staring out the picture window.

"Damn it, Colonel!" Tom said. "We have to fly back to La Paz ASAP and you're drunk!"

"I'm fine. Let's go fly," slurred the colonel. He staggered towards the Ambassador, stumbled and slumped against the wall.

Tom hauled the limp man to his feet. "Colonel, you are in no condition to walk, much less fly. Damn it! You are a disgrace to yourself and the Air Force. Now you're smashed just when we need you the most!" He shook the dazed colonel.

Brent approached the two men. "Tom, we need to get moving."

"Sir, I'm sorry. Colonel Adams can't fly."

"But, Tom, I must get back!" The Ambassador's eyes flashed. "We have dead and wounded Marines to look after! Can't you put Adams in the copilot seat and you do all the flying? He wouldn't touch anything."

Hell, Adams just sat there in the best of times, Tom thought. He looked around. "Wait a second. I'll be right back." He headed directly for General Camacho.

"Mi general, I need to get back to La Paz right now. I have passengers and the Ambassador. I need Valdez to fly as my copilot."

"Of course, Tom. Anything else?"

Tom shook his head. "This is our problem, sir. Thank you."

Camacho motioned his aide over. "Go with Colonel Callahan. Do what he says. I'll see you in La Paz tomorrow."

Tom and Valdez returned to the Ambassador's side. "Sir, Captain Valdez is qualified as an instructor in the FAB C-12. It's not legal by USAF regulations for him to fly with me, but it's the best we can do. Let's go."

Again, the storm battered the small plane as Tom flew the standard departure out of Viru Viru. The air inside the aircraft smelled nearly poisonous as Adams puked his guts out. Everybody wore oxygen masks. The smell of one sick person in an aircraft often made others sick—even Tom felt queasy.

After level off, Tom turned over the controls to Captain Valdez and attempted to establish HF radio contact directly with the American bases in Panama. No luck. He tried a general broadcast. "Any station, any station, this is Spar Niner Niner."

After a pause, a scratchy voice came back, "Spar Niner Niner, this is Antigua Air Station. Can we be of any assistance?"

"That's affirmative, Antigua. I need a phone patch to Southern Command in Panama. How copy?"

"Copy you five-by-five Spar. Unable a phone patch to Panama. But we can get you into the States."

"Roger, I copy, Antigua. I need a number at the Air Staff in the Pentagon." Tom recited Angela Davidson's office number.

After what seemed like an hour, the radio crackled. "Spar Niner Niner, I have a Major Davidson on the line. Go ahead, sir."

"Angela, this is Tom."

"Tommy, where the hell are you? You sound like you're in outer space!"

"Angela, just listen. I'm in the C-12 flying from Santa Cruz to La Paz with the Ambassador. I need you to get word to Lieutenant General Walters that the Marine House in La Paz was bombed a couple of hours ago. Three, I repeat, three Marines were killed. Do you copy?"

"Roger that, Tommy. Three Marines killed."

"The Ambassador needs to be in La Paz to lead the investigation. No suspects have been identified yet. No organizations have claimed responsibility. Get the word out and make sure people in the Pentagon have the right story."

"Wilco, sir. I'll get right on it."

Chapter Twenty-Two

Conference Room,
U.S. Embassy, La Paz

"As you saw from the crime scene video, Mr. Ambassador," said the Regional Security Officer, "the entire entryway to the Marine House was destroyed by the blast.

All the windows in the house were shattered. Flying glass is what killed one Marine and severely lacerated another. Two more were killed by the Uzis. An additional two were knocked out by pieces of falling ceiling and also cut badly by the glass. Fortunately, the others were out playing basketball or on duty at the Embassy.

"In summary, Mr. Ambassador, we have three Marines killed, two critically injured, and one seriously injured. It was bad, but it could have been much worse."

"I don't see how it could have been much worse," muttered Ambassador Brent, face still drawn and pale. All the blood and gore shook him badly. "Who did this?" he demanded.

"Sir, we are sorting through the wreckage of the house now. We have two FBI agents down here working with the Bolivian Police on bomb threats and bombing investigations. Also, the Naval Investigative Service is sending down some people. And the Bolivian Police are quite interested in helping."

"So," Tom said, "what you're saying is that you don't know anything."

The RSO shook his head. "Sir, it's too early to tell. It could be any of several urban terrorist groups, the Zárate Willka, or the Renewal and

Change Movement—anybody. Nobody has yet claimed responsibility."

The political officer added, "We have all our contacts out looking for leads, Mr. Ambassador, in all the usual places. DEA has agreed to shift its informants from active drug cases to helping us solve this crime. It doesn't look like the work of the group that threw the bomb at the Mormon mission in Sucre last Christmas. Nor does it look like a Shining Path assassination spillover into Bolivia."

Ambassador Brent stared blankly at the wall, then turned to face the group. "Gentlemen, it appears that Bolivia is starting to catch up with the rest of the world in the violence department."

Tom said, "Mr. Ambassador, Gunny Chafin is responsible for writing formal letters to the families. If you'd like, I can draft additional letters for your signature."

"Would that be useful?"

"Sir, nothing you or anybody else can do will bring those Marines back. At least you can make the families know that their young men were appreciated. When my father was shot down, President Nixon sent us a letter. My mother still has it. I think it helped comfort her." He didn't add that it hadn't helped him a bit.

Tom left the meeting to call SOUTHCOM J-5 on the MILGROUP STU III classified phone. He shook his head, weary to the bone. He was lucky he had managed the HF phone patch from the aircraft directly into the Air Staff in the Pentagon. Major Angela Davidson had passed on word of the bombing to the appropriate offices around the Pentagon.

Frustrated by the Bolivian phone system in his attempts to get through to Panama, still holding the phone, Tom sat back in his chair, only to be confronted by the new MILGROUP administrator, Rosa Molina. Her black stiletto heels clicked as she stalked across his office.

Molina thrust some papers at Tom. "Colonel, I'm disapproving your request to send the MAC station manager to Rio next week."

"Rosa, it's not my request. The USAF and Military Airlift Command want him to attend a meeting for all station managers in South America. The USAF is paying for him to go, not the MILGROUP. All you have to do is process his orders."

179

As the only operational USAF officer in the embassy, Tom supervised the MAC station manager who loaded and unloaded all the MAC aircraft that transited Bolivia. The Station Manager, a retired U.S. Army staff sergeant and a Bolivian national, was a very hard worker. He was also something of a wheeler-dealer and had somehow crossed the literal-minded Molina.

"It's a boondoggle, and I'll be damned if I'm going to do it. That butthead don't deserve a good deal like this!"

Tom slammed down the phone. "Now wait just one minute—"

A head popped in the door. "Excuse me, Colonel," said Master Sergeant Don Payne. "I overheard the conversation. If you don't mind, sir, I think I should talk to Rosa about this." He dragged the protesting Molina away to the outer office.

Tom exhaled audibly, swallowed his temper, and returned to the frustrating task of trying to call Panama. Most long-distance calls from La Paz had to be booked with an operator, sometimes requiring an entire day or more to get through.

Finally successful, Tom was talking with the J-5 desk officer when Rosa returned with more papers. Waiting patiently until Tom looked up, still talking, she smiled and motioned to the papers. "Sorry, Colonel, I didn't realize the meeting was so important." Handing him a pen, she said, "Please sign these blank orders and these shipping documents and I'll fill them in for you later."

Marine House,
Miraflores, La Paz

Special Agent Henry Griffen sifted through the debris of the house, hoping to find some clue that would enable him to make sense of the crime. One of the FBI's best bomb investigators and one of the very few Spanish-speaking agents in the field, Griffen had grown up poor and black in New York City's Spanish Harlem, narrowly avoiding the temptations of street life, until he had enlisted in the Army to side-step the inevitable draft. Given a choice of career fields, city-boy Griffen had chosen ordnance more from a desire to avoid the infantry than any particular interest in demolitions. He found that he actually enjoyed the discipline of the Army and did well. He had become a highly trained bomb-expert. He left the Army two years later and used his G.I. Bill benefits to attend NYU. Degree in hand, he joined the Bureau.

Griffen and his stocky partner, Al Schwartz, also from New York City, were the first investigators on the scene, minutes after the blast. The rescue crews from the police department and curious bystanders hadn't disturbed too much of the evidence. The house was cordoned off, allowing the two agents to work without distraction.

Reconstructing the attack was fairly straightforward. Spent shell casings marked where the gunmen had shot and killed the guards. Griffen walked from the sidewalk up to the gate and imagined himself shooting at the locks. Passing through the gate, he went through the front door and into the house. Satisfied, he retraced the most direct escape route. There it was—a clear imprint in the soil, made by a running man. He crouched down and motioned to his partner.

"Hey, Al, take a look at this."

They looked at the imprint, then back to the door of the house and to the gate.

"It's where it should be," said the shorter man. "And it's got a fine layer of plaster dust from the explosion, so the print was there before the bomb went off."

"I checked with the staff," Griffen said. "The gardener raked this area smooth just before the bombing—he was working in the back yard when the bomb exploded."

"So this came from one of the bombers." Schwartz grinned. "Looks like a running shoe, big one, too." Placing his own shoe carefully alongside the impression, he said, "About size thirteen, I'd say."

"Yeah," Griffen replied. "Let's get a plaster impression." Squatting back on his haunches, he said, "Al, how many Bolivians have you seen wearing size thirteen Nikes?"

Near Frederick, Maryland

Kurt Wallerein strode through the lab, carefully inspecting equipment and a program he was struggling to understand. He stopped next to what he had just learned was a Mark IV biosafety hood, located next to a large freezer cooled with cylinders of liquid nitrogen. The stainless-steel appliances glistened, computers churned out reams of charts and color graphs, and the two Cuban technicians scurried back and forth. Things were going well, better than expected.

Wallerein paid close attention to Nikolai Yazov's explanation. He understood most of it, thanks to his recent intensive study program. Yazov was a maniac for details. What Wallerein heard from the Russian was that the virus would do what they planned.

"The virus is exactly what we needed," Yazov said. "My predecessor at Biopreparat defected to Britain in 1989. He told the British that the Soviet Union had created a "perfect bug," one that resisted all current antibiotics—that was incurable. This is better. Incredibly lethal—with a ninety percent mortality rate, although I need more tests for that. It's so hot that it kills within hours, it is difficult to transmit human to human, and because of its structure, it shouldn't mutate so it will stay hard to transmit." He sat next to Wallerein. "When Europeans brought smallpox and other diseases to the New World, the American Indians died by the millions because they had no natural immunity. Today nobody on the planet is immune to this new virus. We're all Indians now."

Wallerein nodded. "We must minimize secondary infections. An epidemic is counterproductive to our goals. We want to terrorize, not destroy, humanity."

Yazov handed Wallerein a thick computer print-out. "My team has run multiple simulations to predict dispersal patterns. You can see the effects of one planeload of virus spread on a clear, sunny day. And some permutations based on differing weather and wind conditions."

Wallerein studied the charts. They were dense mathematical models based on best estimates of weather and sunlight conditions. Ironically, sunlight was lethal to this delicate tropical virus. Interesting. That in itself should help minimize its spread.

He looked up. "After the outbreak in the United States, Latinos—and many in other countries—will link the Americans to the epidemics in Bolivia."

"They are two separate strains," Yazov warned.

"The distinction will be lost on peasants," Wallerein said, dismissing the differences. "Our disinformation will 'prove' that they were merely mutations of the same strain. And, remember that the American outbreak will be caused by the American engineered virus. Something they can't deny. At any rate, distrust of the Americans is at an all-time high now in Latin America. Our new stories will show that the outbreak in the United States was an accidental release of toxins from Fort Detrick. A military exercise gone awry."

Yazov nodded. "An excellent idea, comrade. That will confuse the authorities. Delay the reactions."

Wallerein looked around the lab one last time. Only a few more days. "Since most of the government leaders will be dead, as well as many of their experts on viruses, we'll have an opportunity to strike again and again before the Americans can react."

Near Villa Tunari

Jaime Suarez smoothed the last sheet of the black plastic lining into the pit and climbed out, hoping to disappear into the group of men gathered around. He had heard of these maceration pits and been warned away by his *Potosiño* friends. The first step in the processing of coca leaf into cocaine began with filling a plastic-lined pit or *pozo* with coca leaves, adding a solution containing sulfuric acid, and having men laboriously stomp the leaves into a paste, much like grapes were stomped to make wine. Unlike grape stompers, coca stompers worked all day or night with their feet and legs in acid, while breathing the noxious fumes—*narcotraficantes* did not obey OSHA safety directives. Suarez knew what acid could do to exposed body parts and mucous membranes; a miner, he was well experienced with chemicals. Many of the altiplano *campesinos* did not know about chemicals and, desperate for the work that lured them far away from their native highlands, volunteered to be stompers. Jaime wanted to be as far away from those pits as possible, and to take his cousin with him.

Paste production had increased dramatically in the preceding weeks as more pits were dug at secluded spots along the rivers. Jaime's gang moved the paste in bulk to primitive but efficient new laboratories built in the Chapare jungle. Rather than merely turning leaf into paste, then shipping it to Colombia or Peru for further processing as in the past, the Rodriguez cartel was now vertically integrated, finally involved in the cocaine business from leaf to finished product to wholesale distribution.

More perishable paste meant more shipments; more shipments required more airplanes. The Rodriguez cartel now added extra airplanes through the simple expedient of approaching pilots in Trinidad and Santa Cruz and offering large salaries with exclusive work arrangements. If the pilots refused, they were beaten the first time, shot the second and their aircraft stolen.

Both Jaime and cousin Renan had been "recruited" by the press gang techniques now employed in parts of the Chapare, initiated by the Colombian and Mexican associates of the newer Rodriguez cartel. Jaime Suarez was not even sure where his cousin was. Something had gone seriously wrong with their dream.

Chapter Twenty-Three

Kantutani Highway,
Sopocachi, La Paz 2130 Hours

Colleen Callahan was anxious to get home. Ever since the Marine House was bombed, the MILGROUP had been under a 2200 hours curfew. Though technically not a member of the MILGROUP, Colleen thought the circumstances warranted the curfew, official or not, and considered it prudent to comply. To save time, she drove her favorite route, the lightly trafficked Kantutani.

Her mind was on the adoption process and the Callahan family. It was clear to her that it was the concept of adoption that Tom was having trouble with, not an actual baby. If she could find a healthy baby and put him in Tom's arms, that should do it. He was a big softy and would just melt. That afternoon, she spoke with General Camacho's wife, Adriana, who was an enthusiastic supporter of Colleen's plans. If Colleen had her pegged right, Adriana now had the wife of every commander in the FAB out scouring the countryside for adoptable babies.

Entering the dark street leading down into the Kantutani, Colleen passed only one car. Sailing down the road, her mind working through her problems, she noticed a roadblock up ahead under a streetlight, two cars placed nose-to-nose across the road, manned by National Policemen carrying flashlights and shotguns.

Strange. There were never roadblocks around here before.

She slowed the big car, reluctantly downshifting. The car ahead of her passed through the assembled vehicles, which were then closed together, almost as if the roadblock were exclusively for her. Just paranoia....

The hairs on the back of her neck stood up. Her instincts screamed "Caution." Something wasn't right.

She slowed about four car lengths away from the men. Oh God! What had she been taught about roadblocks? With a precipitous drop on one side and a stone wall on the other, there was no room to crash through the rear end of either of the police cars. And not a prayer of plowing through the two heavy engines in the middle.

A policeman stepped out of the shadows.

There! That copper was wearing Nikes, not boots. And his hair was too bloody long for a Bolivian policeman.

Adrenalin surging, Colleen slammed the Rover into reverse and stomped on the accelerator. Tires screaming, she shot backwards out of the cone of the overhead light. She yanked up on the emergency brake and spun the wheel hard to the left.

The nose of the car swung around through 180 degrees. Releasing the brake, she shifted into first and floored the gas pedal.

Heading up the hill, she aimed directly at the car she had passed less than a minute ago. Blaring the horn and flicking her headlights at the oncoming car, Colleen willed the big Rover to accelerate.

Popping sounds. The front window of the other car exploded. It veered crazily off to one side as she shot past. More bullets. Her rear window shattered. One bullet thumped into the dashboard. She glanced at her rearview mirror. Her heart stopped as she saw the two phony police cars separate and turn up the hill in pursuit.

She prayed for a plan. She swept around the mountainside, shifting up through the gears. She used the whole road to maximize the big car's performance. Sharp curves forced her to slow down—she used the gearbox rather than the brakes to avoid the tell-tale lights. In the rearview mirror, she saw the lead car gaining. One man leaned out of the passenger window, trying for a clear shot.

Cresting the top of the last hill before the city, Colleen had an inspiration. The embassy! It had armed guards day and night.

She skidded around the curve in a sweeping turn and headed up Avenida Sanchez Lima. She snapped the wheel to one side and then back again to dodge another on-coming car, then another. The one-way traffic coming at her was too heavy. She was cut off from the most direct route to the embassy.

Hurtling down the street towards the Prado, Colleen glanced at the mirror. Only one car visible now, very close. Close enough to fire again. At the bottom of the hill, she swerved left, narrowly avoiding a bus. Racing up the Prado, she was again forced from her side of the road into the opposite lane. She knifed through the traffic with horn blaring and big engine racing. The Rover crashed over the center median, scattering pedestrians like ten pins. More shots cracked. She whipped the wheel hard over, squirted between a taxi and another bus, and up a side street towards the embassy.

Her eyes caught movement to her right. Another bus—too close to avoid completely. She jammed the accelerator. The Rover surged ahead but the bus clipped the rear fender. Colleen bounced off a parked car, spun up on the sidewalk and back into the street, engine roaring.

She skidded around the last curve to the embassy, tires smoking, and slammed into the corner streetlight, caving in the right side of the vehicle. Leaning crazily against the post, the big car's engine gasped and died. Colleen flung open the door and leapt out. She lowered her head and charged like a fullback across the street, between the two stunned Bolivian guards posted at the embassy's front entrance. She dashed up the stairs and crashed through the last door separating her from the safety of the United States Marine security detail.

Chapter Twenty-Four

Ambassador's Office,
U.S. Embassy, La Paz
Next day

"Tom, are you sure Colleen's okay now?" Ambassador Brent asked.

"Sir, she's still a little shaken but probably more angry than anything else. She's a pretty feisty lady. What bothers me is why anyone would try so hard to shoot her."

"We're wondering about that ourselves, Colonel," said Special Agent Griffen. "To your knowledge has she been involved in any group or with any people who could be considered controversial?"

"Nope," Tom said firmly, shaking his head. "Absolutely not."

"Why was she out in the first place?" Patricia Pointer accused. "Driving down that back street wasn't so smart, was it?"

Tom sighed. What sort of abusive childhood had the DCM endured to make her turn out so insecure and confrontational? "Colleen was trying to comply with a curfew. The Kantutani is hardly a back street. We have never had an incident on the Kantutani, nor has the embassy ever suggested that Americans not use the road. She was doing a perfectly normal thing."

"She had no business being out in the first place!"

"And why is that, Patricia?" Tom demanded. "The embassy hasn't issued any warnings, or made any statements that conditions here are unsafe. Is it because Colleen is 'only' a spouse, a poor defenseless woman, and therefore she can't possibly be doing anything worthwhile outside the home?"

"In case you haven't noticed, Colonel, I am a woman as well," Pointer sniffed. "It's hard to imagine I would not champion women's causes."

"Wrong," said Tom, aware that he was losing his temper. "Your 'support' to the other women in this embassy has been non-existent!"

Pointer glared back at Tom as an uneasy silence fell on the Country Team.

Nobody spoke up in Pointer's behalf.

Ambassador Brent ended the stalemate. "Mr. Griffen, why do you think Colleen was attacked?"

"Sir, we can't tell if the bad guys were singling her out or if they were striking randomly at an American citizen. It could have been a robbery attempt, a kidnapping for ransom, or a planned execution. All we know is that we had an incident." He looked directly at the DCM. "It would have been much worse except that Colleen handled herself superbly and got away, leaving two very dead bad guys squashed by the bus."

"Any clues as to their identities?" asked Tom, determined to stay calm.

"No, except they are both Latino. We're operating under the assumption that they are Bolivian, though they certainly were not Bolivian policemen. We should find out in a day or two if they were known criminals or terrorists."

Ambassador Brent dismissed the group, but motioned for Special Agent Griffen to stay seated. Pointer hesitated at the door.

"Thank you, Patricia, go ahead. I need to speak with Mr. Griffen for just a moment. Please start the staff meeting without me. I'll be down shortly."

Making sure the door was closed before he spoke, Brent turned to the big black man. "Well, Henry, any word on our other problem?"

Griffen shook his head. "No, sir. I've gone through all the obvious places. Whoever is leaking classified material from this embassy is very good. He knows the system and is quite clever. Al Schwartz is

189

upstairs now going through some of the classified records again. Maybe we can establish a link between when the material arrived here and when it showed up in one of our counterintelligence traps in the States."

Brent seethed. "Well, I don't mind telling you that this situation distresses me no end. Someone in my embassy." In his previous assignment in Washington, Brent had become convinced that State had a high-level mole somewhere, probably in Europe. His sketchy analysis, which even Brent conceded was mostly intuition, was rejected by State as too conjectural. Now the leaks were happening in his own embassy. Again, nothing concrete, just a compromised operation here and a couple of injudicious comments overheard at one or two of the many diplomatic functions he attended. Because of his previous and inadvertent cry of "wolf," he felt he had to go outside his own agency. On his last trip to Washington, he had visited FBI headquarters to get assistance from its counterintelligence branch, thus bypassing State's own security force. The current FBI Deputy Director, Jacob Borenstein, and Brent had attended the National War College in Washington together some years before. Two of only a handful of civilians in the overwhelmingly military school, they became close friends and stayed in touch. Borenstein agreed that the circumstances warranted scrutiny and had dispatched Griffen and Schwartz to Bolivia using the cover of training assistance for the Bolivian police. Since their arrival, the evidence of a leak had become compelling.

"Yes, sir," said Griffen. "I understand. Hurts the trust factor, doesn't it?"

"Damn right! The worst part is that I can't shake the feeling that the failure of the San Ramon raid and most of this recent violence—like this attempt on Colleen—is part of it."

"Sir, I wouldn't be surprised. I've seen lots worse things done to cover a trail. We got lucky here. Mrs. Callahan was brilliant. Ninety-eight people out of a hundred would have been killed in that ambush."

"She's an extraordinary woman."

"One hell of a lady," said Griffen. "When Al and I got to the embassy to interview her, she was as cool as if nothing unusual had happened, more concerned about her husband's reaction than the wrecked car." He laughed. "And you should have seen the Marines surrounding her. Like a bunch of very angry, very well-armed big brothers! Talk about protective! Hell, I even had to show my ID to talk with her—and I work with those guys every day!"

"I understand the Marines are quite fond of her. She's an agreeable and attractive woman. Quite outspoken as well," Brent added, wryly. "She doesn't think our counternarcotics policies here are properly directed."

Griffen said, "You don't think she might be gaining access to information, either through her husband or some other means? Most everybody seems to respect her."

"She's a resourceful woman and certainly intelligent, but she's not the leak," Brent said. He paused. "But feel free to check her out if you need to. If there is anything that I can do to help, including calling your boss for more manpower, please let me know." He stood and offered his hand. "Now, if you'll excuse me, I've got to deal with these news attacks on the United States in the leftist press. It's like somebody turned back the clock down here in Bolivia."

U.S. MILGROUP,
U.S. Embassy, La Paz

"Colonel Callahan, could I speak with you, sir?" asked Captain Eduardo Ramirez, U.S. Army Special Forces.

"Good morning, Eduardo," Tom said as he motioned the young officer to a chair next to José Hernandez. "What's up?"

"A couple of things, Colonel. When I got here three months ago, the security situation in the Chapare was pretty calm. Now we have beatings, murders, and hijackings. Not to mention the Marine House bombing and the attack at Potosi. I'm almost afraid to let my men leave the base camp. And the camp's not all that secure, either."

José nodded. "He's right, Tom. When the UMOPAR set the base up, they strung concertina wire where it was convenient, not where it was necessary. It's laughable. In places, the wire has been trampled into the ground—a fence doesn't even exist. Intruders don't have to go through the gate, they can just find a hole."

191

Ramirez nodded. "Sir, SOUTHCOM and 7th Special Forces Group ordered us to beef up security at the base camp. At a bare minimum, to get more concertina wire. We have to keep people out. We can't just shoot them."

"Sounds reasonable to me, Eduardo. What's the problem? Just do it."

"Colonel, the problem is that the bureaucracies of DEA and NAS are battling out who should pay for the upgrades and won't let us do anything until the issue is resolved by the accountants. In the meantime, my troops sit, exposed and vulnerable. I don't like it, sir." He took a deep breath. "I just had a meeting with Mr. Barton. I told him that we needed security upgrades to the camp. I showed him some detailed plans—"

"Let me guess. He blew you off."

"Exactly. Told me he wouldn't pay for any improvements until DEA ponies up an equal share. And that it was non-negotiable."

Tom shook his head and wondered what percentage of GS-14s was as dogmatic as Barton. "Well, Eduardo, the solution is fairly simple. We've got some concertina wire left over from the Potosi deployment just sitting in our warehouse at El Alto. You get your truck up to the airport and tell the MAC Station Manager that I said to load the wire for you. Take it to Chimoré and string it. When the system catches up with the situation and your stuff arrives, we'll either swap or you take mine down and return it. Okay with you?"

"Sir, that's great by me. But Mr. Barton will explode. Technically I work for him down here—"

"Well, technically doesn't cut it, Captain. I don't give a damn who you 'technically' work for. You're still in the Army. That means you're entitled to MILGROUP support. You've got a problem, and we can fix it. The paperwork and the bureaucracy can deal with the results."

Before a much-relieved Ramirez could answer, Nicholas Barton stormed into the MILGROUP and turned on Ramirez. "You little prick! I had a hunch you'd slink down here. I told—"

Tom interrupted. "Nicholas, Captain Ramirez may live on your base, but he is in Bolivia under the command of the MILGROUP.

We're responsible for his safety and the safety of his men. He has a legitimate problem. We've solved it. No big deal."

Barton slammed the desk with a meaty hand. "This is an internal matter that doesn't concern you!"

"No, Nicholas, it concerns me very much. I'm concerned about the way things should be, not about the way things are. I'm not going to let a bureaucratic snafu endanger the lives of these men."

"I forbid you to interfere! You don't have the authority."

Tom stood and said in an even voice, "Listen, Nick old buddy, while Colonel Steele is on leave in Brazil and Matt is in the field, I'm acting MILGROUP commander. Those men will not be endangered because you can't get off your ass!"

Face flushed with fury, Barton nearly shouted, "Callahan, stay the hell away from my base!"

"Fine, Nick. You want to play your little bureaucratic games with us? Let's go on upstairs and have a chat with the Ambassador. He might be interested to hear your philosophy regarding security!"

Barton pulled himself up short at the reminder of the Ambassador. "I swear I'll get you for this!" With a snarl, he stalked out.

Ramirez let out a long breath. "Thank you, Colonel. I'm sorry I had to put you on the spot like that."

"Captain, write this down: commanders get paid to look out for their people."

"Don't thank us yet," José said and laughed. "You'd better get moving and get up to the airport before our good friend, Nicholas Barton, the 'Turd' burns down the warehouse to keep you from getting that wire!"

After Ramirez left, José closed the door and sat down facing his friend. "Tom, I spent a long time talking with our boy Ramirez yesterday. He and his warrant officer are quite concerned about these new developments in the Chapare. They don't see all this violence as random like the intel weenies do. It's much more deliberate, more orchestrated against our guys and un-cooperative *campesinos*."

"Almost like a military operation?"

"Yeah," Hernandez said, giving Tom a quizzical look. "How'd you know?"

Tom grinned. "What do you think I do when I'm out in the field?" He pulled open a notebook and shoved it across his desk to José. "The new batch of NAS guys in Trinidad has a couple retired SF troops. The SEAL Team leader and I talked with them and the troops they replaced. They've noticed a pattern, much more precise and exact than in the past. Very American Army-like, with time schedules, objectives, all that stuff. It's all in there."

"Looks that way," said Hernandez, leafing through Tom's notes.

"The most professional druggies are Colombians, José. Does that mean we've got Colombians in Bolivia now? Any indications from your guys?"

Hernandez shook his head, "Not yet. DEA insists that there is only the occasional Colombian buyer passing through, no shooters. My people agree."

Leaning forward, Tom said, "Put on your 'big picture' glasses and think about this. First, in the past four months we've seen a dramatic increase in violence in Peru, Colombia, Ecuador, and Bolivia. Is that a coincidence? Do you seriously think the cartels have started working together?"

"Impossible, Tom. The Colombians are slaughtering each other as we speak. No way they'd get it together to work with Peruvians. Even if it made business sense."

"Exactly. Second, DEA operations in several countries have been compromised recently, one after the other. Not just in Bolivia. Third, the operations the bad guys are launching throughout the region are remarkably more sophisticated and violent than in the recent past. With an added emphasis on revolutionary politics, as well."

"And yet that's not the way the intel folks at Headquarters see it," said José.

"Right. I think that perhaps they're focusing too much on the individual pieces of this puzzle and not enough on the entire region. Especially on the political side of all this. This is not business as usual, writ large."

"For the bad guys to do these operations so well would take some good insider intelligence." José hesitated. "That means a leak in our system somewhere."

"Wouldn't be the first time, pal."

The two men looked at each other for a moment.

"I'm going to have Matt Schmidt move up from Puerto Villarroel to Santa Cruz to look around a bit." Tom paused, thinking hard. "I don't know who to trust."

DCM's House Calacoto

"Ummm, that was nice," murmured Patricia Pointer. "Welcome back to Bolivia, Billie D."

Steele stretched in Pointer's oversized bed. His trip to Brazil was more successful than he had expected. His wife had been ill from the long trip from the States and confined to bed for five of the seven days, which suited Steele fine. Taking advantage of his diplomatic status, which exempted him from customs inspection, he brought with him a suitcase full of cash to deposit in the Bank of Brazil. He made contact with well-connected friends of Calleja to discuss extending the reach of the cartel into Brazil. He made a big deal about potential profits and had been exceedingly generous to several of the Brazilians. Steele was confident that greed assured these men would do anything he asked in the future.

"Thanks, Sweetheart. Anything happen while I was away?"

Pointer snapped out of her languorous mood and sat upright. "Of course, I forgot to tell you about the little incident involving our friend Callahan's wife." As she related the event, Steele's confidence slipped. His blood ran cold to learn that the bodies of two dead gunmen had been recovered.

"Billie, Billie, you're not listening to me," pouted Pointer, shaking his arm. "I said isn't it incredible that she got away like that?"

"Yeah," he said trying to appear interested and calm, thankful for the darkness. "I wonder what's going to happen to those bodies? Will they identify them?"

"Oh, probably not," Patricia said. "No doubt they're two Bolivian college student radicals out to bag a gringa. Or common robbers. It's no wonder she got attacked, the way she flounces around dressed the way she does. She's been asking for it."

"So the bodies are still in the morgue?"

"Of course. They'll be there until they're identified or they have to be buried, which is soon, I would imagine. They were in pretty bad shape." She lay back and snuggled up to Steele. "I really don't like that bitch. It gives me the creeps to be around her. Reminds me of the sorority types who gave me so much trouble when I was in school." Pointer paused. Mistaking Steele's silence for attention, she continued, "All my life I was different from the other girls. At boarding school they wore fancy clothes, told each other how pretty they were, and went to parties. I wore mostly black and stayed in my room to read poetry and philosophy. And it was worse in college. Hardly anybody was interested in serious things like class oppression—it was boys, clothes, parties, and more boys."

A growl from Steele. "Babe, we're just going to have to do something about those two."

Chapter Twenty-Five

Leipzig, Germany

Porter Nelson pushed away from the metal desk and took a sip of cold coffee. Yuck! He'd been living on the stuff for six days now and it was getting old. He and Robbie Robinson had spent this trip to Leipzig reading classified government reports in the recently refurbished, but still dreary, basement of the annex to the *Deutsche Buecherei*, a closely guarded centralized collection and storage facility, formerly used by the East German government. Porter marveled at Robinson's ability to gain access to these particular Stasi files. Amazing what good contacts, coupled with a modicum of bluster and liberal doses of bribes could accomplish. Also amazing that these files still existed.

On November 9, 1989, a boisterous crowd of nearly a million Germans surged across the Berlin Wall. In the weeks that followed, unrestricted travel allowed West Germans to stream into the fallen communist portion of their country. On January 15, 1990, the world watched live on international television as a furious mob swarmed through the Stasi headquarters complex on the *Normannenstrasse* in a run-down working class district of East Berlin known as *Stasigrad*. The crowds smashed windows, trashed offices, and scattered documents all through the complex. Rumored to have been masterminded by the West German secret service, the *Bundesnachrichtendienst* (BND), the assault ensured that many classified files were saved from destruction by the Stasi itself. The recovered files proved that East Germans were the most spied-upon society in Europe. The government spied on the citizens and the citizens spied on each other for the government, often children on parents, spouse on spouse.

The problem Nelson and his friends faced now was the sheer volume of material. The East Germans had, in typical German fashion, classified everything, right down to some 8,600 graduate dissertations. Deep in the Stasi archives in this one building, stacked in neatly bound folders on rows and rows of shelves, were hundreds of thousands of reports, photocopies, and transcripts which detailed the planned movements and activities of selected international revolutionaries such as Carlos the Jackal and Kurt Wallerein. Porter concluded that the East Germans were more than efficient, they were positively anal about writing things down.

He looked over at Robinson, also surrounded by files and immersed in reading. Both were studying the records of HVA foreign operations, trying to find something concrete that would tie Castro and his Cubans to narcotrafficking in the region. It was slow going for Nelson; his German was excellent, learned from his maternal grandparents who had been forced to flee Germany in the 1930s. But he was not accustomed to the arcane, formal bureaucratic prose in these damned reports.

At college, he minored in Russian and was proud of his accent and vocabulary which had earned him a series of exclusive interviews with President Yeltsin. Porter was especially proficient at military jargon and swearing, something perfected in Russian foxholes covering the Afghan War. Early on in this six-day reading marathon, he switched to the Russian translations of the sometimes lengthy messages, translations routinely made for the KGB officers assigned to the Eastern Bloc intelligence services.

Robinson's German was nearly perfect, his Russian just a shade less so, and his years with the CIA had made him expert in deciphering the obfuscations in bureaucratic mumbo-jumbo.

Porter yawned and stretched again. Plodding through the files was a tedious business because of the German penchant for compartmentalization and obsession with security. Some topics would be available up to 1961, others through 1981, others not at all. Despite those gaps, the files still seemed relatively unreconstructed by those who would revise history by selectively destroying or falsifying records. Rules forbade the copying of any information held in the files. He had to memorize anything he thought valuable. His reporter memory for details served him well as he furiously entered data into his laptop every evening.

Porter sighed, stretched his arms above his head, and glanced at the wall clock. This was their last afternoon in the dimly-lit basement. John McCord was to meet them in Berlin tonight with the results of his own investigations in Moscow. Porter sighed again and reached for another report, this one stamped *Streng Geheim!*—Very Secret.

He read the Russian, then casually flipped through the German. Something was different.

He looked through the batch in his inbox pile and found another marked "Very Secret." Again, something different.

Why? His mind came to life. It was a familiar sensation—one he always felt whenever the critical clue to a particularly complicated puzzle slid within his grasp. Masking his excitement, he casually handed the two folders to Robinson.

"Robbie, look at these. Notice anything?"

Robinson looked at the classification stamp in surprise. "Where did you get these? These reports are for East German decision makers. Really high-up decision makers, too. Foreigners aren't supposed to see them."

Porter shrugged. "They came back from the archives with my last request form." He laughed as he waved two more classified files. "Nice to know that even Germans screw up occasionally."

Robinson took his time with each of the folders, carefully reading through each original document, then cross-checking with the Russian translation. He looked up at Porter. "There are subtle differences in each of these between the German and the Russian versions." He looked back through the files, checking himself again. "Like there was something in the original report the Germans didn't want the Russians to know."

Porter nodded, mulling over that statement. Something was hidden in the differences.

Click.

"Their sources," said the investigative reporter.

Robinson thought that over. "Okay. Assuming there is something the Germans want to keep hidden, the question is why?"

"I think the question should be what, Robbie," said Porter, excited now. "This is human intelligence. Maybe the Stasi, or more likely, the HVA, had human sources independent of the KGB, sources worth protecting." Porter's mind raced with the possibilities. "Let's try to identify the sources. Assume that the source is as important as the message."

Robinson nodded thoughtfully then glanced back through the files. "It seems that each of these altered reports has to do with internal discussions within the American government."

"That's why this is so important, Robbie."

***

Five hours later, Porter Nelson drove the rented Mercedes through the German countryside back towards Berlin. He maneuvered through traffic on the former eastern side towards the hotel. Keeping with the spirit of the mission, Porter and his friends were staying at the Radisson SAS, formerly the Palast Hotel, the home of record of terrorists during the 70s and 80s.

The hotel bar was crowded with businesspeople trying to land contracts for the re-building of the former East Germany. Porter's heart sank—where was John McCord? They needed him to help put this all together. Porter elbowed his way across the room and spotted McCord at a side table.

"Where have you been?" McCord asked. He shook hands with his friends, motioned to the waiter for more drinks and started talking. His story spilled out quickly. The trip to Moscow. The interminable waiting. The endless run-around with mindless bureaucrats. Then a chance meeting with a KGB general, a contact-of-a-contact. "Then one thing led to another." McCord paused. "Have I got something for you! An HVA lieutenant colonel here in Berlin who will talk with us, as a favor to the general. Tonight."

"On the record?" asked Porter, not daring to hope.

He shook his head. "Probably not. But he'll speak off the record for background. Confirm stuff we have. You know the drill."

Porter glanced at Robinson. Out-of-work former KGB officers were now almost routinely featured in the western media as they testified to Congress about U.S. prisoners of war interrogations in Siberia or offered their services and secrets to Hollywood and Washington mythmakers for big bucks. The KGB was still functioning in Russia, under a new name, of course, but retaining much of its previous power and authority. As was the case for the intelligence services and secret police in most other East European countries where the governments were still made up of ex-communists.

The situation for the veterans of the HVA was something else entirely. The current German government had tried HVA spymasters like Generals Harry Schutt and Markus Wolfe for treason and announced plans to prosecute others, down to the border guard level. Predictably, this drove most of the former HVA officers underground or out of the country. An HVA officer who would augment what they had found in those files was a big deal.

They finished their drinks, then headed back out, wending their way eastward through the former Soviet sector of Berlin. The dingy towers of high-rise apartment blocks loomed in the distance through gaps in the dull, monotonous buildings. There were very few cars or trucks on the roads and precious little activity in the crummy shops along the way.

McCord checked the address again and stopped the car in front of a corner apartment building. Not a particularly impressive-looking structure, it was surrounded by a brick wall topped with rusting barbed wire. Not a tree in sight for blocks. The annex in Leipzig was dreary but it was positively up-scale compared to this workers' paradise. The building was still under repair; men worked on it under dim, shielded lights, busy shoveling. Porter grimaced. This was the product of a system that tried to take over the world yet couldn't even keep its own streets and public buildings in decent condition.

They parked in the semidarkness, walked under the broken archway and down the dimly lit corridors, footsteps echoing off the grimy parquet floor and hard stucco walls. The smell of grease, dirt, and sweat hung in the humid night air.

"John, do you always arrange meetings in caves?" Porter griped. "Why not a sensible office building? And in the daylight? I'm expecting a vampire or something to leap out of the shadows."

McCord grinned. "Nothing like a little atmosphere to set the stage." He found the right apartment and rapped on the door. They eased in and were offered seats around the only table in the tiny room. McCord produced a bottle of schnapps and they drank the obligatory social toast.

Porter looked closely at the man who took the chair across from him. Grim looking bastard. Thin, salt-and-pepper hair. Expensive clothes that had seen better days.

"Thank you for your time, sir. Do you mind if I ask why you agreed to meet with us?"

"My former general in Moscow asked me. It is a favor to him."

Porter nodded, still suspicious of a set-up. "I know the transition to democracy has been difficult for you."

The colonel gave Porter a look of contempt. "Difficult? My former colleagues are driving taxis, trying to live on pensions that haven't been paid for months." He swept his hand in an arc, indicating the grimy apartment. "I live here, enveloped in luxury."

Embarrassed, Porter went to work. Part of being a good investigative reporter was to ask the right people the right questions. If his hunch was correct, this could be the guy to confirm it. Porter took a deep breath and stared the colonel square in the eye. "The HVA recruited Americans as agents."

The colonel's bushy eyebrows twitched but he said nothing. Porter decided to try a shot in the dark. "They're still active."

The colonel's face remained impassive. He drummed his bony fingers on the battered tabletop while he scanned Porter's face. The reporter remained deadpan, but it was difficult.

"We had such a program," the German finally said. He sighed heavily as if resigning himself to the next step. "Not even our friends in the KGB knew of it. During the Vietnam war, we focused mainly on exclusive college campuses, looking for disaffected and idealistic young people, recruiting some to help us."

"Especially those studying at foreign universities," guessed Porter, heart beating faster.

The colonel nodded, surprised. "I was a case officer. My contact was a student at the Sorbonne. Later, we helped him get an internship in the Defense Department. Now he's a member of the Senior Executive Service in the Pentagon." He took a sip of schnapps. "In my department, we had several such contacts in your government. The best was codenamed *Rote Rose*—Red Rose, because she loved flowers. Highly placed in the State Department."

"Where is she now?"

He shrugged. "I don't know. Lost track when the Wall came down."

Porter held his emotions in check. This was bigger than he had ever anticipated. Or ever dreamed possible. Yesterday he would have blown this guy off, thinking that this information was too good, too convenient. Disinformation given just to take money from gullible American reporters. But that was before he had seen those files in Leipzig. The pieces fit. God, what a story!

"Anything else we should know?"

The colonel's bushy eyebrows knit together as he frowned. "Whispers, mostly. Recruiters are at work, looking for experienced agents. A couple of people drop out of sight here, a couple there."

"And?"

"You Americans are so damned smart, you tell me."

Porter had a flash of insight. This guy is pissed. He's mad because he spent his life working for probably the best intelligence organization in the world. Now he's sitting in this dump, eating beans, and he's lost his prestige, his dreams. Everything.

He shook his head. "We Americans don't have a clue. This is the HVA's field of expertise, not ours. You people were the best."

The colonel stared for a long moment at Porter. "All Spanish speakers. Shooters, not clerks."

Porter felt his pulse jump. An operation was being put together with Spanish speakers. Clearly not for the Basque ETA—no profit in that. South America then.

The colonel continued, "Recruiting is not that hard these days. I have even been approached myself, several times."

"Why haven't you gone with them?"

His gaunt face flushed. "I worked for my country. I am not a mercenary."

Mercenary. Porter thought that over. Mercenary terrorists being recruited. That could be only one guy these days. "Wallerein. Is he active in South America?"

The colonel smiled again, this time for real. "Very good, young man. He even visited Bulgaria recently."

As they stood to leave, the colonel smiled, apparently confident that he had surprised the Americans. "Tell your friends at the CIA that they could learn much from us."

Ninety minutes later they were back in the bar at the Radisson.

"This has turned out to be a very interesting trip," Porter Nelson said, more to his rum-and-Coke than to his companions.

"Interesting, nothing," Robbie Robinson exclaimed. "This is absolutely incredible! I've never seen anything like it."

"Yeah," said Porter, "but we didn't find what I thought we would."

"We can come back to that," said Robinson. "What we have now is far more volatile, not to mention urgent. It scares the bejeezus out of me."

"Why should any of this surprise anyone?" Porter asked. "The United States was vulnerable back then. The commies exploited it, just as we did right back at them. How many moles do you think the CIA has squirreled away in Russia right now? How about Cuba? Or France, for that matter?"

"Yeah, but we're the good guys," protested McCord.

"Not according to the Russians," said Porter.

"Ever since Lenin," said Robinson, "in addition to spies, the Soviets have recruited opinion makers in the West with impeccable credentials to help explain away Soviet aggression in the name of world peace. Lenin called these people '*poleznye idioty*', or useful idiots."

"Yeah," agreed Porter, "And some of the worst of those idiots were journalists. The New York Times' Moscow correspondent in the 1930s led the pack. He deliberately falsified stories and overlooked some of the major atrocities of all time. And he even won a Pulitzer Prize, for Christ's sake."

"Seems as if the communists remembered their history," said Robinson. "They recruited Guy Meredith, Donald McLean, and Kim Philby right off the campus at Cambridge University in England during the 1930s. Those guys were superstars as Soviet moles. All went to work in sensitive posts in British intelligence. They were wonderful sources of information for years."

Nelson's spirits were sinking along with the level of his drink. "Looks like it's America's turn. I hope this fizzles out after turning a few bad apples. I'd hate to think the HVA was as successful as it looks right now. When the FBI caught Aldrich Ames passing stuff to the Russians, I thought it was bad. Then they caught that bastard Robert Hanssen right there in the FBI. But this is worse. It looks as if our whole government is riddled."

"Why hasn't the CIA come up with the stuff we just did?" McCord asked.

"What we have has been right in front of everyone," Robinson explained. "When I was with the Agency and we cracked a case, invariably the info had been sitting in somebody's computer or file cabinet for months. Finding the right clues was a matter of grinding through a whole hell of a lot of material. Or dumb luck." He chuckled. "In our case, both."

Turning to McCord, he asked, "And that just leaves the Bulgarians to deal with. John, as our resident expert, how does everything stand for your trip to Sofia?"

"Looking good. I already have it fixed. My flight leaves in the morning, and my good friend from our embassy will meet me at the airport. We should be able to start work with my contacts in the *Komitet da Darzhavna Sigurnost*, the Bulgarian equivalent of the KGB, by the afternoon. With what we already have, what I get from the KDS, and some luck, I'll be able to wrap up this whole thing by the end of the week."

Chapter Twenty-Six

MILGROUP Commander's Apartment,
La Paz

"Payne, what the hell is going on around here?" Steele's voice rose. "How could Montoya screw up a simple operation like snatching a woman?" He slammed the door as Payne crossed into the apartment. "I read the FBI report. Do you know he wore Nikes with his police uniform instead of boots? God, what an idiot!"

"Colonel, I think he couldn't get any Bolivian combat boots big enough. Hell, neither can I." Payne shrugged.

Steele motioned to a chair. He had made his point and did not want to alienate Payne. "Okay, Don," he said, "let's have a beer and talk about what we do next."

"Tell me about your trip to Brazil."

Steele shrugged, then smiled. "It went great. The money's safe in the bank. I met those friends of Calleja, who were more than cooperative. Everything is set up for us to move to Rio when we're ready. Lovely houses, lovely women, lovely weather. We're going to live like kings!"

"I still say we should just waste Callahan, Colonel. He's too smart for his own good."

"Don, we can always kill him later. In the meantime, there are worse things to do to Callahan. We tried Plan A. It didn't work. So, we move on to your Plan B. How's that coming along?"

"The shipment went out yesterday on the C-141, Colonel, complete with all the paperwork. Rosa made sure all the forms were letter perfect. I'll make the anonymous phone call to Panama tomorrow." He grinned. "You know, this scam is really easy since everybody is so trusting, just like General Thornton said." Both men knew that the American military system, for all its paperwork and thousands of forms, still relied heavily on the integrity of its members to make it work. "We're like a couple of computer hackers that have just punched through a series of passwords protecting the DoD computer network. I'm ready to create murder and mayhem on the system."

"Okay," Steele said. "That'll fix Callahan, all good and proper. So," he paused, laughing, "let's get on to your murder and mayhem. Callahan told the Ambassador that some of the troops in the field think *narcotraficante* ops are running too smoothly, too precisely to be directed by Bolivians. Even used the phrase 'too military'."

Payne's eyebrows went up at this news.

"Don't worry," Steele said. "The Ambassador talked it over with Patricia who told me. I poo-poo'ed all this as being the result of overactive imaginations, men too far from home and deprived of normal sexual outlets."

Pointer had staked her professional future on her aggressive counternarcotics programs, all based upon fixed ideas about the enemy. She could not afford to have Callahan be right and another, darker, more efficient vision of enemy narcos begin to emerge. Steele encouraged her prejudices, using phrases carefully calculated to keep her thinking Callahan and the others were not competent to make such judgments, or, more easily, deliberately trying to undermine her and her program. "I think maybe we ought to start our last big move, use our new guys you've been recruiting to stir the pot some more, and then take out Callahan like you wanted."

Payne nodded, eager now. "Just tell me when, Colonel. I'll make it look like a drug hit."

"Don't make it too quick. Let him know it was us."

Payne's eyes lit up. "Then I get his wife for me and the boys to keep for a while?"

"Deal."

61st Military Airlift Group, Howard AFB, Panama

Senior Airman Andrew Brady walked slowly through the cavernous cargo storage area, leading his German Shepherd, Tonto, trying not to fall asleep from boredom. Drug searches were one of the least favorite of Brady's tasks as an Air Force Security Policeman or "Skycop," ranking right down there with gate guard. Brady, a broad-chested powerlifter, liked action—the more, the better.

Ever since a few well-publicized fiascoes during the Vietnam War, the USAF had gone to a great deal of trouble to ensure that its aircraft were never again used to transport illegal drugs. All passengers were routinely searched and all cargo was sniffed by specially trained dogs such as Tonto. This morning, Brady's desk sergeant received an anonymous phone call that yesterday's C-141 channel mission from South America carried some "interesting" cargo. Not believing a word, the sergeant nonetheless sent Brady, just to make sure.

As the team neared the end of the aisle holding the big pallets, Tonto began to perk up. "What is it, boy? What you got there?" Brady had only seen Tonto act this way once before, alerting on a piece of carry-on luggage held by an Army sergeant first class about to board a Freedom Bird, a MAC charter flight back to the States. A bit over-excited, Brady had ripped open the bag only to find that Tonto had alerted on several sets of freshly washed underwear. Embarrassing, but better to search a few extra bags than to give drugs unhindered passage.

This time Tonto was nearly in a frenzy. Brady placed the pallet location firmly in his mind, and tugging on the excited animal's leash, shouted for the cargo NCOIC.

The sergeant came dashing around the corner of the pallets, alarmed by Tonto's barking and Brady's shouting.

"Jesus, airman, get that dog away from here! He's made his point!" As Brady moved away to tie up the big dog, the sergeant examined the pallet with interest. He found the shipping documents and called for his two assistants before beginning to rip open the protective plastic.

Twenty minutes later, Chief Master Sergeant Werner 'Mad Dog' Tower, the NCOIC of the Howard AFB Security Police detachment, arrived with two sergeants in tow. "What's up, Brady?"

"Chief, Tonto alerted on this pallet. The sergeant broke it down. Tonto is only interested in this one big box here." He pointed with his foot. "We waited until you got here before opening it."

Tower grunted, then gestured to another Skycop holding a video camera. "Get this all on film, Charlie." Tower took the papers the sergeant offered him and glanced over them. "Okay, let's break open this crate!"

The men made short work of the fasteners. Ripping out the packing material, they stopped short. Carefully, one of them lifted up a plastic bag full of loose white powder.

Chief Tower flipped through the shipping documents and stopped to examine the signatures. "Looks like somebody in Bolivia's got a lot of explaining to do!"

Chapter Twenty-seven

Tripoli, Libya Operations Room,
Wallerein compound

Eight men, the majority of Kurt Wallerein's brain trust and financial backers, sat around a huge mahogany table, a gift from Gaddafi himself. The excitement was palpable as Wallerein entered and walked directly over to the small podium to address the group. He paused as he looked out over the assemblage. He knew himself to be a dour person but he was a dancing fool next to these menacing, grim-faced men.

He hated meetings like this. He was used to working alone, or at least in command, where he made the decisions. This was like being a CEO with a Board of Directors looking over his shoulder, second-guessing him. And operational security! *Mein Gott!* He shuddered at how many people must already know about this operation. Such was the state of armed revolutionary struggle in the new millennium.

Wallerein began with the news he knew the men were waiting to hear. "Our operative from the Cuban intelligence service is in the United States now. He says he will be ready on schedule. The entire team will be in place next week." A murmur of approval rippled around the big table. He pressed a button and an electronic map was projected on the wall screen. He stepped from behind the podium and used a laser pointer. "Here is the east coast of the United States, and here," he indicated with the light, "is the city of Baltimore."

"Excuse me," asked a man with a Middle Eastern accent, "but why have you chosen Baltimore instead of a more well-known American city?"

"It is perfect for our purposes," replied Wallerein. "As you can see it lies between New York and Washington so we get the attention of the East Coast media. It is a big city in its own right. It is easy for our people to get into and out of the city." Wallerein bowed slightly. "Also, Imam, Baltimore has a sizeable and active Jewish population, one of the largest in the country."

The mullah gave a thin smile and motioned Wallerein to continue.

"Our objective is to derive maximum effect from the initial operation. We plan to release the biological agent near the Inner Harbor in three weeks. On this particular Saturday afternoon," Wallerein said, "the tall ships come in from all over the world, marking the beginning of a holiday weekend." He pressed another button and a series of majestic ships, flashed on the screen. "Here are some of last year's participants. *Meine Herren*, this is a major event that traditionally gets national television coverage." He stepped from behind the podium and paused for effect. "Symptoms of the hemorrhagic fever will begin to appear within hours of exposure. Our calculations show that between fifty and one hundred thousand people will die within two days."

A collective gasp arose. Wallerein acknowledged the surprise with a smile. "Comrades, we will show the American government that it can no longer interfere in other countries with impunity. Those days are over!

"Saddam Hussein had a chance to cripple the Americans during the Gulf War. When it came down to the decision to use his chemical and biological weapons, he lacked the resolve." Wallerein shifted his gaze from face to face, burning his own resolve into each mind. "Today, the whole world knows these weapons exist. But nobody has ever used them properly. We will be the first. The American people must see that they are no longer immune to justice for the criminal actions of their government." He looked around the room.

"And for that government itself, we have another little surprise."

Viru Viru Airport, Santa Cruz

Tom Callahan reviewed the flight plan as co-pilot Major Tony Flannigan supervised the loading of the baggage and the passengers.

Tom had requested that Flannigan, a former assistant air attaché in Brazil and a graduate of the Brazilian Air Force Staff College, be sent down from the C-12 detachment in Panama to fly as a temporary replacement for Colonel Adams who had been grounded at the request of the Ambassador. Brent had insisted on this trip to Santa Cruz and Puerto Suarez to inspect the new duty-free trade zone being proposed by the governments of Bolivia and Brazil with assistance from U.S.A.I.D.

This project was critical to the Ambassador's efforts in Bolivia. Many Bolivians claimed their lack of access to the sea kept Bolivia from developing its economy, keeping the country impoverished. Instead of wasting energy in the interminable arguments with Chile over ports lost in the War of the Pacific, Brent thought it more useful to pursue negotiations with Brazil to open up the navigable Rio Paraguai for everyone's use. Having finally convinced two semi-hostile governments to initiate talks, Brent wanted to waste no time, hence the trip.

"The Ambassador and his party are aboard, strapped in and rarin' to go, boss," said Flannigan as he dropped into his seat alongside Callahan. Flannigan pushed his sweaty reddish-blond hair back as he put on his headset and strapped in. "Did you get hold of Commander Schmidt?"

Tom shook his head. "Nope. But I left a message at his hotel in Corumbá. He should be waiting for us when we get back."

The pilots performed the engine start checklist. Prior to calling for taxi clearance, Flannigan joked, "A Callahan and a Flannigan flying together. Maybe instead of using the 'Spar' callsign, we should be using 'AerLingus Niner Niner'!"

Tom laughed as his gaze swept the ramp around the aircraft one last time. He was surprised to see Master Sergeant Don Payne standing on the ramp, a set of wheel chocks dangling from his hand, waving at the plane. When Payne's eyes met Tom's, he smiled and saluted, mouthing a mute "good-bye."

"Who's that?" asked Flannigan.

"That's Master Sergeant Don Payne, the MILGROUP operations sergeant down here on an extended TDY from Panama. Don't see much of him these days. Must have been in the neighborhood and decided to say howdy. Nice of him to help pull the chocks," Tom said, returning the salute.

Payne gave a quick thumbs-up, waving and smiling as they taxied past.

Takeoff at Viru Viru was considerably less exciting than at La Paz. With the strong headwind that always seemed to blow at Santa Cruz, takeoff roll was usually short. Tom climbed the aircraft to the east for the first checkpoint over the FAB base at Roboré. Leveling at an intermediate altitude of seventeen thousand feet to avoid incoming traffic, Tom began to go through his checklist items.

Two nearly simultaneous explosions tore through the thin skin at the rear of the C-12.

The aircraft abruptly yawed left, pitched up, and rolled left over on its back. It hung, crippled, streaming fuel as the airspeed fell. It pitched down through the vertical, rolled and stabilized completely upside down. The roll flattened into a spin. Tom saw the green blur of the jungle alternate with the blue of the tropical sky. The G forces tore at his body, throwing him to the ceiling. His face smashed against the vinyl covering. Hung in his shoulder and seat straps, he flailed about. Debris blew everywhere. Passengers screamed. Warning lights glowed fire-engine red. The altimeter spun crazily down. Tom knew the inverted spin could tear the aircraft apart.

Reach the stick! Got to reach the stick.... Break the stall.... Tom focused on touching the yoke of the aircraft. He grunted as he fought the Gs and forced his hands out slowly towards the fully forward yoke. His right fingertips caught at the black plastic. Panting, his heart pounding, he cocked his fingers and slowly pulled back.

The aircraft popped upright immediately. It transitioned to an erect spin, still gyrating wildly. Slammed back into his seat by the now reversed G forces, Tom instinctively reached for the throttles and retarded them to idle to slow the rate of descent. He immediately and abruptly stomped in full right rudder to counter the rotation of the spin. Lower the nose. Give the airplane enough airflow to start flying again.

The oscillations began to dampen out. Tom initiated smooth, steady back pressure to avoid tearing the wings off by raising the nose to stop a now screaming dive. Jungle green filled the windscreen as the plane hurtled earthward. After an eternity, Tom fought the nose up into a climb as he swapped excess airspeed for precious altitude.

All the emergency indicators were illuminated. Angry red and yellow lights glared everywhere. Tom glanced over the engine instruments. He shut down the left engine to prevent another possible explosion. All of the right engine indications seemed normal. But the horrible abuse from the wild ride after the explosion had mortally wounded the plane. The controls were mushy. No rudder control. Elevator control severely limited. The sturdy Beechcraft cables lasted long enough to survive the high-speed dive. Aileron control seemed unaffected. Tom would need every bit of aileron to counteract the roll resulting from yaw as the only working engine drove the aircraft into sideslip. In a precarious and delicate balance between engine thrust and a banked sideslip, Tom leveled off and settled the C-12 into a jagged path towards the sanctuary of the airport at Santa Cruz. Only now did the cries of the passengers and the noises of the aircraft's agony register on his consciousness.

Flannigan looked across at Tom, face bloodied by flying debris. "Wh-what happened?" he managed over the cockpit noise.

"I don't know. Sounded like an explosion," Tom shouted back, both hands on the yoke. "The aft section of the left engine is blown away and there's a hole in the cabin. I'm heading back to Santa Cruz. Go check on the passengers. Looks like the Ambassador's lost consciousness. Get him on oxygen, then get back up here ASAP."

Chapter Twenty-eight

Los Tajibos Hotel, Santa Cruz

Matt Schmidt sat back in his poolside deck chair and took his first swallow of an ice-cold *Paceña Tropical*, an excellent lager brewed in Santa Cruz. He closed his eyes. This was his first afternoon off in over a week and he was trying to relax for a couple of hours. He was scheduled to have dinner with two of the NAS agents, both retired Special Forces sergeants, who had some suspicions regarding the new tempo of narco operations in Bolivia. Matt's own gut feeling said that something was dramatically wrong just beneath the surface of life in Bolivia. His BolNav friends reported increased nighttime traffic on the rivers and rumors of headless bodies floating downstream.

Matt felt a shadow cross over his face. He opened his eyes and looked up to see Master Sergeant Don Payne smiling down at him.

"Good afternoon, sir. Hope I didn't startle you."

"No problem, Don. Have a seat." Matt gestured to an empty chair. "Buy you a beer?"

"Thank you, Commander." Payne waited while Matt gestured to the waiter to bring another glass. "Understand you got some good intel and you're up here to do a little scouting around for the MILGROUP. What's cookin'?"

"Well, I'm just sort of looking around to see what's happening in Santa Cruz. There's a whole different perspective on the world around here."

"Colonel Callahan told me you were going to be here and that I was to meet up with you. Said you might need some help."

"You saw Tom? When?"

"Less than two hours ago, at the airport. He's taking the Ambassador out to Puerto Suarez."

"Yeah, he tried to call me in Corumbá, but we missed by about thirty minutes. What did he tell you?"

"He said you officers were concerned about the new techniques used by the narcos. And the increased violence. Said it sounded like the Army was involved." Payne frowned. "I am the MILGROUP Operations NCO. You hear any new stories down in Puerto Villarroel?"

Matt grimaced. "Yeah. Lots. Headless corpses floating in the rivers. Some of those rivers are full of piranhas, so for every body found floating, there probably are several more never found. There are stories about that happening up in the Cauca Valley in Colombia, but never for a minute did I think it would happen in Bolivia. Takes a real twisted mind to do something like that. Real wackos."

Smiling, Payne said, "Commander, I think I know somebody who can help. He's a Bolivian army colonel and is pretty well plugged-in to what's going on around here. I took the liberty of scheduling us an appointment with him, sir. I can take you there now and get you back in time for dinner."

Matt groaned. Damn! There went the rest of his afternoon. Oh, well. He'd be home tomorrow. And they needed whatever information they could get. Too bad he didn't like Payne better. "Okay, Don. Get your car," he said.

***

Matt always enjoyed driving through Santa Cruz. The broad streets were laid out in a circular pattern and pulsated with colorful fruit stands and the laid-back *joie de vivre* of the tropics. The people, dressed in colorful native dress, took their time here, life was more relaxed. Santa Cruz recently passed Cochabamba as the second largest city in Bolivia, a growth spurt fueled by drug money. Payne showed a good working knowledge of the city, using the side roads that cut through the rings to leave the city.

Fifteen minutes later, they pulled up in front of a typical Bolivian housing compound, surrounded by a high brick wall broken only by a wrought-iron driveway gate. Payne beeped the horn, the gates swung open to reveal a large lawn, massive house, and several heavily armed guards. Inside, the vehicle was surrounded by six tough looking men who reminded Schmidt of thugs in a bad Hollywood movie.

"Welcome to our little party, Commander Schmidt," Payne said with elaborate politeness. "Meet Carlos. He's the other 'wacko' in the group. Hey, Carlos, the Commander thinks we're wackos. Waddaya think of that?"

Carlos laughed as he walked towards Schmidt. "Yeah, we're wacko alright. We've run circles around all you 'smart' officers for months. If we're so wacko, how come we're winning?" He yanked Schmidt out of the vehicle and threw a quick, powerful punch at Schmidt's midriff. Matt doubled over; the air exploded from his lungs. Carlos grabbed Schmidt's hair, jerked him upright, and pushed him over backwards. Two of the others bound his hands behind his back, efficiently and painfully. Carlos leaned over him, "How come we're here holding the guns and you're tied up?"

"Payne, what the hell is all this?" Matt gasped.

"This, my good Commander, is the group that's been causing you so many problems."

"What? You're running drugs? Matt struggled to his knees to look Payne in the face. "You're a disgrace to your uniform, you scumball! How the hell did you ever survive so long in the Army?"

Payne laughed again. "I have very powerful friends who need guys with my special talents. Colonel Steele and I go back a long way."

"Steele, too?" Schmidt gasped.

Payne and Carlos laughed. Payne turned to Carlos. "See what I mean? These officers are really on top of it all!" More laughter. Looking back to Schmidt, he said, "It's been a good exercise, a challenge staying ahead of you and that asshole Callahan. Really should have popped him sooner. Got him today, though."

Stunned, Matt croaked, "What? He's flying out to Puerto Suarez."

"*Was* flying to Puerto Suarez," corrected Payne. "Seems his plane had a little accident about halfway there, thanks to a small bomb I put on an engine. Such a pity. So much for him—and our good friend, the Ambassador, too. Mustn't forget him." He paced in front of Schmidt.

"We have had our problems with you assholes, though. We missed getting the Callahan woman, for example." He smirked at the speechless Schmidt. "But there will come a time. We have some big plans for her."

Payne picked up a machete lying on the table by the window and waved it at Matt. "Now, Commander, we're going to talk about what you know about our operations."

"Oh, balls, Payne. I'm not telling you anything and you know it." Matt curled inward at the crazed look on Payne's face. *God help me now.* He fought the fear that threatened to paralyze him. Was he going to die a prolonged and painful death? "When I said you were a wacko, I was wrong. You've gotta be the biggest psychotic asshole that ever lived. Nothing more than a common murderer. Slime!"

Payne's temper snapped. Purple with fury, he raised the machete above his head. He paused, fighting for control, then slowly lowered his arm.

"Oh, no, Commander. Not quite yet." Breathing hard from the exertion of self-control, he said. "I need something from you now. The rest can wait." He motioned to his men. "Untie him and bring him over to a nearby table. *Andale!*" Schmidt fought the man until a vicious blow to the head knocked him nearly senseless. Payne deliberately stretched Schmidt's arm out over the table and stepped back. He raised the machete.

The blade flashed in its downward arc.

218

Chapter Twenty-Nine

MILGROUP,
U.S. Embassy, La Paz

Lieutenant Colonel José Hernandez entered his MILGROUP office, ass dragging from the endless round of meetings that Steele was forcing him to attend while he was off only God knew where. José now had to work weekends just to get his own job done. He spent last night dealing with the fallout from the C-12 bombing. The badly shaken Ambassador was parked in the Santa Cruz hospital. The embassy was in chaos.

He threw his briefcase on the desk and collapsed into his chair. First the Marine House bombing. Then the bombing of the C-12. Now Matt Schmidt was missing. And that asshole Steele had the gall to maintain these incidents weren't related. Horsefeathers!

His phone rang. "José, it's Olga. My maid just found a delivery box on the front porch."

"What?"

"The box has my name on it, but I haven't ordered anything recently. Matt always told me never to pick up anything suspicious."

"Don't touch it," José commanded, alarm bells going off in his head. Unmarked packages were the method of choice of Latin American terrorists and the subject of nearly every embassy security briefing. "I'll call the FBI guys. We'll be right there."

He collared Henry Griffen, who was on his way out the embassy doors. The men headed down the hill to Sopacachi.

"There it is," said Olga. "I don't know where it came from. It just showed up this morning, addressed to me. I'm not expecting anything. I hope I'm not overreacting."

Special Agent Griffen said, "*Señora,* this is no bother. It may well turn out to be a box of chocolate, but these days, it's always better to be careful. Please wait for us inside."

Griffen and Al Schwartz began by carefully examining the ordinary looking box bearing the address "*Señora Olga Schmidt, Sopacachi, Que tenga un buen dia*—Have a Nice Day."

"Interesting address," José said. "It has 'Olga Schmidt', not 'Olga Garcia de Schmidt' like a Bolivian would use. Probably a *norteamericano* then."

***

After an intense external examination, the agents set up their portable X-ray machine and gingerly placed the box inside.

"Jesus, Henry," whispered Schwartz, "does that look like what I think it does?"

"Yeah, I think so." Griffen motioned Hernandez over to the scope. "Better take a look at this, José."

José's face paled at the image. "Oh, my God!"

The men removed the box and opened it. Inside, resting on a bed of crushed paper, was a human hand, dried blood crusted around the jagged edges of the wrist.

"It's Matt's hand all right," José said, his stomach churning. "See that light scar running along the thumb? He did that sailing. Told me that story a dozen times." He shuddered. "And his Academy class ring—same stone, same class number. If we take that off, we'll know for sure; it's engraved on the inside with his name."

"I'm not sure we can get the ring off now without cutting it," said Griffen. "We could take some fingerprints to fax back to FBI Headquarters, but I think we'll have to ask the wife to make a positive ID."

"Shit," said José. "Wait just a minute while I go get my wife. Olga'll need some company after we leave. This is demented."

Griffen said, "It could have been worse. It could have been his head in this box."

Tripoli, Libya

Kurt Wallerein stretched and paced across his underground office as he thought through the details of the mission. The imams were positively ecstatic about the prospect of dead American Jews. Fools! Important, yes, but fools nonetheless. Wallerein himself placed far more emphasis on the future political chaos in America, the swath of dead stretching from Baltimore to Washington. Political actions for political results. Results that he would manipulate and control.

Right now, Wallerein's objective was to buy an airplane in the United States, a task he had reserved for himself. He returned to his desk and spread open the latest issue of Trade-A-Plane, which listed most of the aircraft available for sale across the country. This special color edition was splendid, showcasing hundreds of airplanes. He leafed slowly through the pages looking for one that would suit the mission. Then he saw his plane—no—*the* plane. A beautiful rebuilt Piper Pawnee, red with white stripes.

He remembered his fourteenth summer, the best one of his youth, spent with his new best friend, Hans. They had just passed their examinations for admission to one of the finest schools in Germany. The boys spent all their waking hours at the airport where Hans' father was a mechanic. Young Kurt fell in love with airplanes, especially the crop duster owned by Hans' father, a low-winged Piper, red with white stripes. Wallerein knew he was destined to be a pilot. A Lufthansa pilot eventually, since he always thought big, but a Piper pilot for that summer. Hans and Kurt washed airplanes and did odd jobs around the airport to get rides in anything with wings. Kurt enjoyed the menial work, the first time he had ever performed hard physical labor.

Then Kurt's father swooped in on one of his infrequent visits home in between his international bank deals. He was horrified to hear that the son of a mechanic, no matter how brilliant, was to be admitted to the school where he and three generations of Wallereins had studied. Predictably, Wallerein Senior knew the directors of the bank that held the mortgage for the airport. Hans' father was fired, and the family moved away in search of work. Kurt never saw Hans again.

Kurt kept up the dream of flying for several years, soloing in gliders and eventually earning a private and commercial rating, but at university, politics had intruded. Only after he moved to Libya had he been able to indulge himself again in his passion. Colonel Gaddafi had understood and allowed Wallerein to fly in jets with his air force and had even provided him with a toy, a Pitts Special.

According to Trade-A-Plane, the red and white Pawnee was owned by a real estate salesman in Jackson, Mississippi. All Wallerein needed was an intermediary to make the deal. He dialed up the Internet and did a search for aircraft brokers. His computer whirred with quiet efficiency, and a printout emerged.

***

Larry Parnes sat at his desk, idly looking through a trade magazine listing corporate jets for sale. The aircraft brokering business was slow, far slower than the pace he was used to in a Navy ready room. He had been at his new job three weeks without so much as a nibble. Or a paycheck. Maybe he had been a trifle hasty in accepting the bonus the Navy had dangled to entice him to resign during one of its periodic personnel convulsions.

Unable to pass the Class One flying physical required for an airline job, Parnes let his wife's badgering overcome his good sense, passing on a well-paying job in the aerospace industry. Instead, they were living in Yazoo City, Mississippi where his wife's family had prospered for three generations. That prosperity was about to come to a screeching halt unless he hit his stride selling used aircraft for her second cousin. The only consolation was that this town had a decent airport where he could associate with airplane people. Not that it paid his bills.

He checked his watch. His turn as the "duty-dog," manning the phone for incoming client calls was about over. In an hour, he'd have to head home, sans any business leads, to watch his wife light the Shabbat candles. Damn.

The phone broke into his morose thoughts. "Good afternoon," he said, "Anderson's Aircraft Brokers. May I help you?"

An accented voice asked, "I am interested in acquiring an aircraft. Do you have the special issue of Trade-a-Plane?"

Parnes looked frantically around his desk, then onto the coffee table. There! "Yes, sir." He scrambled around the desk to snatch it, trying not to trip over the telephone cord.

"Turn to page 36," ordered the voice. "See the red Pawnee?"

Parnes flipped through the pages. "Yes, sir. Very nice." *Man-oh-man,* he thought.

The phone number had a Jackson prefix.

"It looks good to me as well. Unfortunately, I'm in Europe now on a business trip and can't go inspect it myself."

"Sir, if you could give me your name and number, I'd be happy to check on it for you."

"Are you a pilot?"

"Yes, sir. My name's Parnes, Larry Parnes. I flew P-3s in the Navy. And a tour as an instructor in T-34s over at Meridian."

"Excellent, Mr. Parnes. Please go there and examine the plane. Look at the logbooks. Check the condition. If it is in good order, I would like to buy it. I'll give you a phone number where you can leave a voice message. This is irregular I know, but I've been looking for just such an airplane."

"No problem, sir," said Parnes as he wrote down the name and number. "In this business, when you see what you want, you have to jump right on it."

"Quite so. Please act today then."

Parnes checked the clock. If he jumped into the company Cessna 310, he could be there in twenty minutes. He dialed the phone number of the Piper's owner, fighting to keep the visions of his first commission check under control. Lighting the candles would be a bit late tonight.

Hilton Sofia, Sofia, Bulgaria

John McCord fidgeted in the small phone booth as he waited for his call to go through to the States. When the phone rang, he snatched it from its cradle and listened as the overseas operator made the connection.

"Yeah?" croaked a sleepy voice at the other end.

"Porter, this is John McCord."

McCord heard Nelson thrashing around. Probably trying to find the damn light switch. He dropped the phone twice, then came back on the line.

"Where the hell have you been? Wha—"

"Shut up, Port! I don't have much time. Listen, I found what we wanted—it's unbelievable! Much worse than we thought. Somebody is recruiting former communist agents. I have the documentation," he said. "We can trace it back! It's going to blow the lid off!"

"Great! When are you coming home?"

"My friend's working on that. There's something else. My contact in the KDS says something big and nasty is about to go down. Maybe in the States."

"What do you mean?"

"I've got one last appointment tonight. Just fell out of the sky. Could just ice this thing once and for all."

"Just fell out of the sky? Remember what you're working on, pal. This is bad-ass stuff. The guys running that country are commie thugs, no matter what they're calling themselves these days."

McCord ran his hand through his thinning hair as he glanced around the lobby, "I don't like this either. I'm scared fartless. But I think it's worth the risk. I've called in every chit I have left in this bloody country. If I go tonight, we'll have names, places, dates. The whole enchilada, buddy."

"Listen to me, John. I don't like it. You've got what we need right now. We'll take it to the FBI and let them handle it from here. For Christ's sake, get the hell out now! Don't screw around with those guys."

"I'll be careful," said McCord. "Meanwhile, the other papers are safe and I'll get out tomorrow." He hung up abruptly, afraid that Nelson would talk him out of the appointment.

He stepped out of the cramped booth and took a surreptitious look around. His armpits were sweaty and he stank. Fear. He had never been this scared. Not even under fire from a Russian Hind helicopter in Afghanistan. Visions of hideously disfigured torture victims he had seen in Afghanistan flashed through his brain. Compared to the brutal Bulgarian KDS, the KGB was a ladies' garden club.

The best way to stay alive and make the rendezvous was to hang out in public places where lots of people could see him. Surely the days of public assassinations were gone, even in Bulgaria. He hoped.

McCord went into the dining room of the Hilton and tried to eat a late lunch. A small salad, a glass of red wine and bread. Still nervous, he played with the salad, watched the clock and commanded it to move faster.

Truth be known, he was rather pleased to be back in harness, despite the danger. Since his medical retirement two years before, he had spent too long doing too little. He'd missed the rough and tumble of the old days. Being around guys like Porter Nelson and Robbie Robinson again thrilled him. And a lifetime of rooting out stories prepared him well for this—he was doing something that only he could do here. Contacts were living, personal things.

He was both excited and disgusted. That agents of a foreign power—turncoat Americans—had penetrated his government appalled and infuriated him. Stuff like that was supposed to have ended with the end of the Cold War. This was a throw back to the Sixties. Now he might actually have the coded evidence already in the documents he had obtained in Sofia. With more to come.

He glanced down at his watch. Time to move. He pushed back his chair, threw some money on the table, and strode out the front door. Ignoring the doorman and the taxi stand, he watched the cars whiz by on the road in front of the building. He waited until three taxis had passed, then flagged the fourth. Without a word, he handed the driver a slip of paper with an address and settled back as the taxi roared out into the afternoon traffic.

The driver was a good one. He actually used his turn signal occasionally instead of his horn. McCord sat sideways so he could keep one eye forward and still look for suspicious cars behind. After ten minutes, he tapped the driver on the shoulder and told him to pull over. He paid the driver, crossed the street, and waved down another cab going the opposite direction. He handed the new driver another slip of paper and settled back. He felt rather smug as he glanced out the rear window. Pretty good field craft for a reporter.

Entering the older section of Sophia with its narrower winding roads, McCord was again struck by the contrast between the Byzantine layout of city streets in older European cities compared to American cities. Approaching the rendezvous point, McCord ordered in passable Bulgarian, "Pull over here, please." They turned into a dark, anonymous side street, one of many surrounding the enormous park. The driver pulled over to the edge of the road and waited for instructions.

A black Mercedes pulled alongside. The tinted windows rolled down. McCord's last conscious thought was that of surprise—that the assassins bothered to use silencers.

Chapter Thirty

La Paz, Bolivia

Colleen Callahan clutched at the door handle of the *trufi* to steady herself as the driver raced through the crowded narrow streets, horn blaring. *Trufis* were another unique Bolivian invention that fascinated Colleen. Usually in desperate need of repair, the driver-owned *trufis* swarmed the narrow mountain roads linking the suburbs of Sopacachi and Calacoto with La Paz proper, making set runs at half the price of regular taxis. Sharing the small cars with all levels of the social strata in Bolivia, Colleen got an excellent, if sometimes pungent, opportunity to meet Bolivians and practice her Spanish.

She got out at her stop on the Prado and strolled down the crowded pedestrian street, towering over the Bolivians as she weaved through the mass of people. She spotted the National Policeman guard posted at the door of the embassy as he spoke into his radio. Moments later, a lieutenant emerged from the door and saluted. *"Buenos días, señora."*

"Buenos días, teniente." They climbed the steps to the second-floor landing, and through the security metal detector where Gunnery Sergeant Chafin waited. "Good morning, Mrs. Callahan."

"Good morning, Mike. Lovely to see you." She laughed. "You know, Mike, you don't have to meet me every time I come to the embassy."

"It's not a problem, ma'am. After all you and the Colonel have done for me and my Marines, it's a pleasure." He opened the heavy, bulletproof door and followed her through. "Sorry to hear about the Colonel and the plane. May I escort you to the MILGROUP area?"

"No, I have an appointment with Patricia Pointer."

He punched the button on the elevator to the sixth floor. "Better you than me."

The Ambassador's secretary looked up as Colleen walked into the executive suite. "Hello, Colleen." She sighed. "I'm sorry, but Her Royal Highness has asked for you to wait. She's on a call to Washington."

Colleen nodded as she took a seat, not surprised. Pointer was the type who showed how important she was by jerking people around. If her appointment had been with Ambassador Brent, Colleen would not have minded the delay. But Ambassador Brent was gone, medevac'ed to the States by the USAF using a specially equipped C-130 aircraft stationed at Howard AFB for just this purpose. Pointer, still officially just the *chargé d'affaires* and standing-in until Brent returned, was now in charge for the indefinite future. Colleen knew that this was Pointer's big chance. If she could keep things running smoothly during her tenure, she would almost be guaranteed an ambassadorship, given the State Department's frantic search for qualified women to dress up its minority hiring record.

Thirty minutes later, Pointer buzzed her in.

"Good afternoon, Patricia," Colleen said with cold formality.

Pointer sat in the Ambassador's big leather chair, stroking its arm. Behind her, the Ambassador's favorite painting had already been replaced by another, one Colleen had never seen before. Evidently Pointer had wasted no time making her mark on the Embassy.

Pointer did not offer Colleen a seat. "Mrs. Callahan, as acting Ambassador, I'm afraid I'm going to have to withdraw your diplomatic clearance, effective immediately. I want you out of Bolivia on the next plane."

"On what grounds?" challenged Colleen, as she settled into the couch facing the desk. "I haven't done anything to discredit this embassy."

"This is for your own safety. After all, your husband is a military officer and has high visibility here. And there has been one attempt on your life already. The embassy can no longer guarantee your safety. It's all for the best. Of course, I don't expect you to understand all this. Just be a good girl and leave."

Colleen shook her head. "I've done nothing wrong. You're just trying to hurt my husband through me, though for the life of me I don't understand why. He's performed brilliantly here and saved your backside more than once." She stood and placed her two American passports, the black diplomatic one and the blue tourist one, on the desk. "I still have my Australian passport. I'm not leaving La Paz."

Colleen turned and walked towards the door. As her hand was on the doorknob, Pointer asked, "And what about your friend, Olga Schmidt?"

Surprised, Colleen turned. "What about Olga? She's done nothing wrong, either."

Patricia made an elaborate gesture towards her desk calendar. "I understand she has another hearing with the Children's Court before the adoption can be finalized. Might be difficult now that the proposed father is missing, probably dead."

Colleen's knees went weak. "Let me make sure I've got this right. Because of a personality conflict you have with Tom and me—or maybe another reason I don't know about—you're prepared to derail the adoption of an innocent orphaned baby by a responsible, competent, and loving woman who has never done you any harm?" She shook her head. "No, Patricia, I can't believe that even you would be so cruel."

"If you don't leave Bolivia, immediately and quietly," said Pointer, "I'll speak to my friend, the Minister of Children's Affairs, and the Schmidt baby's adoption will be cancelled. She'll be left with nothing."

Colleen leaned on the walnut desk. "Just what is it that you want? Why are you so intent on hurting us? Olga is the sweetest person on earth. Now that Matt's gone, baby Paul is her entire family."

"Then go away. After you do, all the adoption paperwork will move forward unimpeded and she'll have the baby. If you don't, she won't. It's all up to you."

Colleen paused. If she left Bolivia, she and Tom would never get their own baby.

But if she stayed, Olga would lose Paul.

She had no real choice.

Colleen looked Pointer directly in the eyes. "I'll be on the plane. But if something goes wrong with that adoption, I'll be on the next one back. Tom and I have powerful friends, too." She leaned into Pointer's face, close enough to smell her sickly-sweet, tea rose perfume. "And if anything—anything—bad happens to either Olga or my husband, you just won't believe the problems you'll have!"

Colleen retrieved her passports, and secured them in her purse. Pointer's voice came out a trifle weak. "Your mother bear demonstration is very touching, Colleen."

Colleen laughed. "Just remember, *Patty*, in Australia we have lots of dangerous animals you've never heard of, all sizes and shapes. Just a friendly warning from one *girl* to another."

Dallas-Fort Worth Airport, Texas

The Mexicali flight from Monterrey touched down two minutes early, then taxied to the gate. Kurt Wallerein, as always, watched the movement of airplanes around the vast airport, fascinated by the ungainly waltz of so many beautiful airplanes, taxiing without apparent controls or restraints, magically avoiding collisions.

As he walked through the gate and down the corridor towards Immigration and Customs, Wallerein shook his head at the pathetic security. He had arrived on the morning's first flight from Mexico that was full of impatient and innocuous businessmen. His false documents were impeccable and he knew it. Well worn, with the proper immigration stamps of several other "visits" to the United States, typical of the efficiency of the forgers he had recruited from the former East German *Hauptverwaltung Aufklärung*.

The bored Immigration official flipped to the last entry in the passport, found an empty page, and thumped down the entry stamp. "Welcome to the United States, Mr. Baader. Have a pleasant stay, sir."

Wallerein was known in the United States, but not expected. The disguise that he wore was simple and effective: a three-week growth of whiskers, thick glasses, and a walking cap. At any rate, the police/counter-terrorist presence was minimal here in Dallas-Fort Worth. He walked through Customs with his carry-on baggage, changed terminals, dropped his sports jacket, hat, and glasses in a convenient restroom trashcan along the way. Now dressed in a golf

230

shirt and a Pebble Beach baseball cap, he boarded a smaller airplane bound for New Orleans. There, using another set of forged documents, he rented a luxury car from Hertz and headed east.

Outside Biloxi, he reached his first destination, a lovely four-star hotel near the ribbon of sand that passed for a beach and checked into his suite. He immediately undressed to catch a few more hours of sleep before his appointment.

At precisely four o'clock, he awoke to his alarm. A quick shower and shave, and he was back on the road.

Wallerein arrived at the small airport thirty minutes early. He walked around the empty parking ramp, sweating in the late afternoon heat and humidity. The hangar door was partly open. He went in. There sat the Pawnee, exactly as he had pictured it.

Wallerein loved the little plane the moment he saw it. Glorious red with narrow white stripes. He walked slowly around the tiny craft, memorizing its lines. It was beautiful.

He climbed up the left wing root and sat in the cockpit. It smelled new and the dashboard glistened. He settled back and let the feeling of the little plane excite him. Too bad he couldn't fly like a barnstormer, open cockpit with the wind whipping around his face. But if he did, the wind would bring death to him as it certainly would to the thousands on the ground.

The aircraft's plumbing and chemical hopper had been modified by the team's Cuban mechanics smuggled north from Miami. America was a vast country with a wonderful system of interstate highways created by a president who had been a soldier. Once inside the country's borders, it was a simple matter to drive anywhere. The team would drive north to its final destination. Wallerein, however, was going to fly the Pawnee.

From Biloxi to the Goochland County Airport west of Richmond was over eight hundred miles in a straight line that crossed five states. About the distance in a line from Berlin to Naples that crossed five countries. Add another one hundred twenty-five miles from Goochland to his final destination, which only he, Colonel Lopez, and Yazov knew at this point. Not a quick flight with a true airspeed of about one hundred thirty knots. The long flight would give him a chance to experience the country he had hated for all his adult life.

He found the packet of aeronautical charts and manuals written by the Aircraft Owners and Pilots Association and obligingly provided by the aircraft brokers. He looked curiously at the markings on the strange charts. The American system was, well, foreign to him—especially the instrument procedures. He was worried about that. He hadn't flown instruments in real weather, like back in Germany, in two decades. Especially in weather such as what he could see today in the skies over Biloxi—thunderclouds that reached for the heavens. He was seriously non-current. There simply hadn't been time—and there wasn't much time now.

He spread the instrument chart on a table, squinted at the line on the chart between Biloxi and his destination, and imagined thunderstorms, rain showers, and solid overcasts blocking his path. Perhaps he had taken on too much. After a moment, he cursed his weakness. Squaring his shoulders, he impatiently snatched up the papers. He would take the charts home tonight and study them carefully until he knew every detail. He would lead this mission from the front, where he should be.

Passenger Terminal Howard Air Force Base, Panama

"Colleen, the aircraft's on approach now. Be in the chocks in about ten minutes. And, oh, say, fifteen minutes for customs and Tom'll be here giving you a smooch and a tickle," said Lieutenant Colonel Gary Willis as he returned from the desk at base operations next door. Willis, the commander of the Howard-based 24th Tactical Air Support Squadron, and a former F-15 pilot, was a close friend of the Callahans. "Relax, Beautiful, it's in the bag. They'll be parking right in front of the terminal."

Colleen smiled and tried to muster some enthusiasm. "Thanks, Gary. I've just been worried sick that something was going to happen to Tom. I hated to leave like that. Arturo Galvani called this morning for Tom. He wouldn't tell me anything except that it was urgent."

232

Colleen had been in Panama nearly six days waiting for Tom. She had boarded the first commercial flight out of Bolivia, but had refused to go all the way back to the States. She and Tom decided to meet in Panama. The accident investigation board in Santa Cruz had quickly concluded that no pilot error was involved in the C-12 incident; instead, they commended Tom highly for his extraordinary airmanship. Four long days had crept by as Colleen waited for news from Olga about the adoption. Every passing day had made it less likely that Matt was still alive, thus more imperative to get the proper signatures and seals as quickly as possible.

The long-awaited phone call came that morning. Olga and Paul were now in Arizona, heartbroken at leaving Bolivia, but safely together. The consul in La Paz had been a marvel. He stroked all the appropriate people in the long line of the Bolivian bureaucracy, making dozens of phone calls and even visiting an office or two in order to get the papers pushed through. Fortunately, Matt had signed all the necessary forms before leaving for his last trip, so that hurdle did not come up.

Colleen had said nothing of her own heartbreak at having to leave Bolivia so quickly. She had cried all the way to Panama. Adriana Sanjines de Camacho had just located a baby boy in a private orphanage in Cochabamba; a picture of the six-month-old had arrived the day Colleen left. The picture now sat in her pocketbook. What would Tom say about the baby? Colleen made big plans for that evening—she and Tom had spent far too much time apart. Much to do and lots to talk about.

C-141B, Callsign MAC 40390

Tom Callahan sat in the jumpseat and watched as the approach to Howard took them from the Atlantic side in a series of giant, sweeping descending turns. The crew worked smoothly together, banter kept to a minimum as the pace of the approach picked up closer to the airport.

The Starlifter bounced and jiggled through the tropical uplifts as they closed in on the runway. Lush islands dotted the azure water and slipped under the aircraft nose. The city of Panama sprawled off to the right of Howard AFB, just on the other side of the bridge that now spanned the gap between North and South America and marked the entrance to the Panama Canal.

The pilot brought the aircraft smoothly down to the flare and gentle touchdown. The big aircraft taxied slowly, following the USAF "Follow Me" truck to the assigned parking place. An unmarked sedan sat conspicuously off to one side of the busy ramp, engine running. As the C-141 crew shut down its engines, the sedan pulled up alongside.

On the flight deck, Tom heard the noise level climb and felt the blast of heat and humidity as the entry door opened. The crew chief's voice came over the intercom, "Hey, AC. There's an OSI guy down here who says he needs to talk with the Colonel before anybody else gets off."

Tom climbed down from the flight deck and smiled a greeting at the sweaty man waiting for him at the bottom of the ladder. "I'm Tom Callahan," he said, offering his hand. "The crew chief says you need to talk with me."

"Are you Lieutenant Colonel Thomas Patrick Callahan, Chief of the Air Force Section in La Paz, Bolivia?" Special Agent David Charter demanded coldly, ignoring Tom's outstretched hand.

Tom nodded, surprised at his attitude. Charter flipped open his identification displaying his OSI badge. "I am Special Agent Charter, Air Force Office of Special Investigations. You are hereby under arrest for suspicion of smuggling illegal drugs into the United States."

Chapter Thirty-one

Panama City, Panama

Tom Callahan stood at the top of the steps, too stunned to reply. Finally, he blurted, "You can't be serious."

"Oh, I'm very serious, Colonel. There is quite a bit of evidence linking you with drugs shipped on C-141s to the States."

"Bullshit, Agent Charter," Tom roared, face flushed. "Pure unadulterated bullshit. You have nothing on me."

"If you would like, Colonel, I could take you directly to see what we have." He indicated the car. "Shall we go then, sir?"

"Damn right," Tom snarled as he snatched up his in-flight bag. "I want to see this so-called evidence of yours."

Tom sat alone in the back seat and watched in silence as the Panamanian driver drove by the Judge Advocate General's office and exited through the Howard Air Force Base main gate towards Panama City. He felt his blood pressure rise at the delay. He started counting to ten and felt the heat drain from his face. Stay cool, man.

"Where are we going?" Tom asked.

"You don't need to know," said Charter over his shoulder.

"Well, since we're not going to Albrook, where I figure we should have gone, and since we're nowhere near any of the other American bases, I'm pretty sure that I do need to know."

Charter turned and smiled. "Excuse me, Colonel. What I meant to say was that all will be revealed very soon. Please be patient."

Already Tom regretted his emotional outburst. He should have demanded a lawyer, then gone to see the evidence. Bloody temper!

The car pulled to a stop in front of a windowless, unmarked building with only a small Panamanian flag to identify it. Two tough-looking uniformed Panamanian Police Force soldiers, big for Panamanians, erupted from the building to meet the car.

Charter got out of the front seat and opened the rear door for Tom. "Here we are, Colonel," he said with a wicked smile. "You wanted answers."

One of the Panamanians pointed his M-16 at Tom as the other hauled him out of the car and to his feet. Inside the building, Tom was taken to a small room off the left corridor. The small room was sparsely furnished with a table and three chairs. Tom was ordered to empty his pockets onto the table. One wristwatch, wallet, and his diplomatic passport. Then the larger of the guards frisked him. Tom was thoroughly angry but knew better than to let his temper out of hand again. This was no ordinary lockup—no Miranda rights, no fingerprints, no pretense of legality.

Charter reappeared, accompanied by two Panamanian officers. He smiled at Tom and said, "Colonel Callahan, may I present Major Jorge Rojas and Lieutenant Marcelo Lopez of the Panamanian Police?"

"*Ah, Buenos días, Señor!*" said Rojas.

"*Buenos días, Mayor*," Tom replied. "Perhaps you could be so good as to explain why I am here?"

Rojas simply smiled, then turn back to Charter. "I appreciate your efforts on behalf of the people of Panama," he said, in excellent English.

"He's yours to do with as you see fit, Major," said Charter. "I'm sick and tired of having sleazebags like him slip through our military justice system just because they have a few medals." Charter glared at Tom. "I've had enough of seeing all my work end up without a conviction. This is my last case, and it's not going to happen this time, pal. The major'll take care of you."

Tom looked at the Panamanians, then flicked his eyes at the door. Rojas gestured at the three, armed Panamanian guards. "Colonel, please rid your mind of those romantic fantasies about escaping." He sat down and gestured for Tom to be seated on the opposite side of the rickety table.

"Perhaps you have heard of me?"

Tom remembered José Hernandez mentioning that several of the most vicious of Noriega's Panamanian Defense Force interrogators had slipped through the American net after the "Just Cause" invasion. One, a West Point graduate and a particular favorite of Old Pineapple Face, had an uncle who was the current Minister of Justice. The Minister managed to keep him in uniform instead of behind bars. The Rojas across the table was wearing the big Academy gold ring. Bingo.

Tom shook his head, determined not to play this asshole's game.

"Pity," Rojas replied. "Still, we should have the opportunity to get better acquainted over the next few days." He smiled. "Perhaps we could begin now. We have substantiated reports that you have been associating with known narcotraffickers. We also know about your personal use of illegal drugs."

"You must be joking!" Tom said. "The Flight Surgeon practically has to put me in the hospital to make me take an aspirin."

Rojas nodded, smiling. "We know better, Colonel. That is why we have you here."

"No, the reason you have me here is because Charter kidnapped me and turned me over to you!"

Rojas smiled again. "And your narcotrafficker friends?"

"What narcotrafficker friends? What are you talking about? I am as straight as they come."

"Is that so?" Rojas pulled a sheet of paper from a folder and read off the names of most of the FAB commanding officers.

Tom said, "Yes, I know them all."

Rojas looked up, a satisfied smile on his face. "Then you admit that you associate with these men?"

"Of course I do. It's part of my job."

"Your job, Callahan, does not include associating with criminals. All these men are reputed narcotraffickers," Rojas said, triumphant.

"What are you talking about? None of those men has ever been reported by anyone as being involved in the drug trade. Just because they're Bolivian officers doesn't make them narcos. Where in the world are you getting your information?"

"That's none of your concern."

237

"The devil it isn't my concern. You're using those off-the-wall allegations to attack my credibility, my reputation, and my honor as an officer. They are most certainly my concern. Not only are you using bad information, you are libeling those officers."

"Your honor?" Rojas sneered. "You gringos know nothing of honor."

Tom fixed him with an implacable stare. *"Yo se quien soy."* He paused, leaning forward in his chair. "Your opinion of me is of little consequence. And if you think I'm through fighting this madness, you had better think again. You aren't remotely interested in discovering the truth. A confession, any confession, will do. Well, I'm not going to play your body count game any longer. Get me a phone and the JAG right now."

"All you criminals are so self-righteous. It makes me sick!"

"That's life, Rojas."

"You call me Major!"

Tom spoke so quietly that Rojas had to lean forward. "You stopped being a major a few minutes ago when you crossed the line from investigator to inquisitor. American citizens have rights and privileges under the law, most especially under the Uniformed Code of Military Justice, whether you like it or not. Even in your country, we have rights guaranteed under the Status of Forces Agreement and the Panama Canal Treaty. Not to mention diplomatic immunity in my case."

Jabbing the air for emphasis, Tom said, "I can understand why that loony-tunes Charter acts as he does—he's nuts. But you're an officer, a graduate of West Point. You're supposed to set the proper example for others. I can't believe you're a party to this travesty."

Tom pushed back from the table, took a few paces, then turned. "You have gone too far. You are not a judge, you are not a jury. You are merely an investigator, supposed to gather the facts, not write your own morality play! I am through with you. I refuse to talk with you any more. Get me that phone, now, Mister!"

"That didn't go very well, Major," said an angry Special Agent Charter, seated in Rojas' office.

"On the contrary, David," said Rojas, as he settled back into his leather chair. "He's getting tired and his temper is showing." He sat at his desk and twirled a gold mechanical pencil slowly between his bony fingers. "We'll make a call to his wife and get her here. We'll act surprised at her appearance, then let them be together, for oh, five minutes—supervised of course, and listen. Then throw her out." He smiled. "The shock will unbalance him."

"How do you know where she is now?"

"It's my business to know such things."

Charter stared hard at Rojas, then shrugged. "Okay, Major, whatever you say."

"Don't worry, David," he said. "I know how to deal with him. I've done this before."

24th Tactical Air Support Squadron, Howard AFB, Panama

"Excuse me, Mrs. Callahan, there's a phone call for you," said the First Sergeant of the 24th TASS. "It's from Bolivia. You can take it on the secure phone in the ops officer's office."

Colleen glided into the office, still dazed by the events of the afternoon. She had watched her husband driven off by an OSI agent. Colleen breathed a prayer of thanks for the presence of Gary Willis, who had charged into Base Operations to rip the story out of a reluctant C-141 aircrew.

"Colleen Callahan," she said into the phone.

"Colleen! Thank God I've finally found you! This is Arturo Galvani. I've got to talk to the Colonel. Where is he?"

"I wish I knew, Arturo," she said shakily. "You're not going to believe it, but Tom was arrested coming off the plane."

"Damn! I knew something like this was going to happen. Tell me the details." Colleen related the events of the day, feeling sick as she spoke about it. "Listen, Colleen, I think I know what's going on here. I've been working with the MILGROUP getting their files ready for an IG inspection next month. Your husband's been set up. And I can get the proof. Can you give me a number where you'll be tonight?" She gave him Gary's home number. "Okay, give me a few hours and I'll try to get some evidence for you. Hang in there!" He disconnected.

Colleen sat back, still stunned. Why would anyone want to hurt her husband? Was Pointer part of this? She thought hard, trying to make some sense of the seemingly random episodes.

Gary Willis burst into the room. "I've found him, Colleen. Our operations section just had a call. He's in a building downtown, one of the old PDF buildings. Let's go!"

After a twenty-minute hair-raising drive through Panama City, they screeched to a halt in front of a non-descript building. Gary checked the address, then shrugged.

***

Inside, a Panamanian Police Force major blocked their path.

"I'm Lieutenant Colonel Willis. This is Mrs. Callahan. We'd like to see Lieutenant Colonel Thomas Callahan, please."

Major Rojas shook his head. "He's under arrest. You can't see him."

"Then please allow Mrs. Callahan to speak with him."

"No. Colonel Callahan is not receiving any visitors. Now, if you'll excuse me, I've got work to do." He walked away.

Willis slammed his fist on the counter. "Just hold on, Mister. You don't just go blowing me off like that! I know Colonel Callahan is being held here. I know he is entitled to at least a phone call and the right of counsel. He has had neither—I checked with the JAG. Therefore, you people are holding him against his will and denying him his rights!"

Rojas said, "You obviously don't know Panamanian law. Callahan is not able to receive visitors."

"Rojas, don't give me that crap! I'm an American commanding officer in Panama. I've had to attend so many law courses that I could write a book on international law."

Rojas' dark eyes narrowed. "Just why are you so interested in defending this man who is under arrest for smuggling drugs?" His voice took on an edge. "Unless, of course, you have an interest in his business. Perhaps we should start looking into your affairs as well."

Willis stepped back, then smiled. "Excellent, excellent! A threat. And in front of a witness, too." He leaned forward, voice hard with controlled anger. "I don't know what the hell you're up to, but I do know that if Mrs. Callahan isn't allowed to see her husband right now, I'm going to go see the Air Division Commander, the 12th Air Force Commander, the CINC, the Ambassador, and anybody else I can think of and relate this little story. I'll bring the whole world down on you! Is that clear?"

Rojas stared at Willis and Colleen, seemingly weighing his options. With a shrug, he gestured with his hand for them to follow him. He led them down the narrow hallway and into the dingy room where Tom sat, flanked by Panamanian guards.

"You have five minutes," Rojas said. "No physical contact." He spun on his heel and stalked out.

Colleen took her seat across the table from Tom. Gary stood next to her.

"You look great, Colleen," said Tom, exhausted and haggard. "But then, so does Gary."

Colleen smiled. "Wish I could say the same for you, lover."

"Yeah," conceded Tom, "I could do with a shower and a shave." He glanced at the wall clock and leaned forward in his chair. "Okay, Colleen. Why hasn't anyone from SOUTHCOM or Howard come to get me?"

"We went to see General Myers. He wouldn't even talk to us. And the JAG is tangled up with the Panamanians. They claim that they've never heard of you, that you're not here. How Gary found you is beyond me."

Tom grinned. "Gary's always been good at this kind of stuff."

"Arturo Galvani called up here to try to warn you of a frameup."

"Good for Arturo. Too bad we didn't know yesterday."

"Tommy, what can I do to help? Who should I contact?"

He glanced over at the guards. The room was certainly wired for sound. And the large mirror on the wall was something out of a "B" movie. He could almost see Rojas lurking behind the shiny surface. Switching to Japanese, he said, "Go to Washington. Start with Uncle Harvey. Angela can get you in to see him. Something bad is happening in Bolivia, I don't know exactly what, but he needs to get the word out.

Tell him somebody is framing me. Probably the same people that got Matt Schmidt. And that Myers was no help at all."

He pointed at Willis. "Tell Gary I need to get away from these guys ASAP and away from this guy, otherwise God only knows what'll happen. The OSI guy who arrested me was off his rocker, way over the edge. And I think Rojas is psycho. Gary's going to have to arrange something—it's going to take some high-powered intervention—and fast. I doubt they'll keep me here now that you've discovered their location."

They heard muffled shouts and footsteps pounding in the hall. Tom clutched at her hands. "Be very careful, Sweetheart. Go directly from here to the airport. And tell Gary to watch his six o'clock—"

Rojas and three guards burst into the room. "Get them out of here!" shouted Rojas to the guards. One guard grabbed Colleen, another grabbed Willis and hauled them out the door as the one leveled his M-16 at a fuming Tom.

**

Rojas stalked down the hall back to his office, trailed by Charter. Closing the door, Rojas leaned against the wall and laughed. "Japanese! Who would have thought?" He laughed again and shook his head. Americans were so unpredictable. That's why he so relished this game of cat-and-mouse. Another six hours or so of softening up, then the part he liked best. The physical. The screams. The inevitable capitulation, even from the strongest, most determined victims. Rojas closed his eyes in anticipation.

"Let's get the tapes translated!" Charter said, interrupting his fantasy.

Rojas looked up and shook his head. "Are you proposing that we knock on the Japanese Embassy's door and ask the consul to translate our tape of a prisoner that no one knows we have? I don't think so."

"But the Callahan woman's headed off to hatch some rescue plan!"

"David, at West Point we were taught that all operational plans go awry at some point." Rojas clapped the unhappy Charter on the

242

shoulder. "Don't worry. We'll move our operation to our other building. As for the woman, I have a team on her. She won't get far."

Chapter Thirty-Two

Frederick County Airport, Maryland

Kurt Wallerein flew over the rural field and descended into a careful turn to enter base leg at exactly the prescribed forty-five-degree angle. He knew his team was on the ground watching and he wanted his expertise to be obvious.

He was furious with himself. The long flight north had almost been a disaster. He had found out the hard way that it was one thing to be competent in a flight simulator, and quite a different thing entirely to be proficient in actual weather. Twice he had nearly died. He broke out in a sweat just remembering.

His flight plan had called for him to fly northeast in roughly a straight line, landing only at a string of small rural airports for fuel. He flew over swamps, forests, foothills, and finally mountains. Wallerein was astonished at the size, diversity, and sheer vitality of the land.

Because of the thunderstorms, he slid farther east avoiding the higher mountains. Late the first afternoon, he had arrived at Henderson-Oxford Airport, near a small town in north-central North Carolina surrounded by tall pine trees. He parked, supervised the re-fueling, then checked the weather. During his usual meticulous preflight, he found his right tire was deeply scuffed and the inner cord exposed. He needed a new tire, which seemed to take an extraordinarily long time to replace. Behind schedule, Wallerein had opted for a night hop. Should have been a piece of cake. But flying over dark forests and a low undercast during the moonless night, he lost the horizon, followed shortly by his orientation. Vertigo overwhelmed him. Only by the grace of the non-existent God did he manage to right the airplane instead of smashing into the tree-covered foothills. He staggered back to land at Henderson-Oxford, collapsing for the night at a local Holiday Inn.

The next day dawned with a broken cloud deck up to ten thousand feet. The forecast en route called for the clouds to scatter. Behind schedule and anxious to get to Maryland, Wallerein decided to press on. Within thirty minutes, the clouds closed around him, boxing him in a towering empty space, surrounded by cumulonimbus buildups in every direction. The slim needle of the VOR twitched like a live thing. In desperation, he tried to penetrate the flickering monster clouds on instruments. He was almost immediately snatched up by an embedded thunderstorm. The plane pitched down and rolled hard right. He fought the controls. Rain and hail battered the small aircraft. Miraculously, he popped out into clear air, covered with ice.

He managed to right the Piper and maintain visual contact with the ground long enough to find another airport, land, and wait out the storms.

Even now, as he taxied in, the mere memories of those events made him tremble. He fought the urge to puke. Well, the mission called for a fair weather dispersal anyhow. He wasn't about to go up in an overcast situation again in the little plane. Never again would he do something that stupid.

He spotted Colonel Carlos Lopez waving from in front of the second row of corrugated metal T-hangars. Wallerein taxied slowly past him to the open hangar, satisfied that he was safely anonymous in this rural environment. Weary, exhilarated and smelly, he climbed out, stretched and swung his arms side to side while he waited for Lopez. Where would the toilet be?

Wallerein studied the area. The T-hangar was unremarkable, except for the oversized workspace. It was in better repair perhaps than some he had seen on his trip from Mississippi. Inside, the hangar was divided into several areas by movable partitions. No windows. The room had a hard feel with nothing personal. Workbenches, an air compressor, tool kits, and Piper factory manuals huddled together in a neat little pile.

"*Bienvenido*," said Lopez as he approached the hangar. "How was your flight?"

"Fine, thank you. As the Americans say, a piece of cake." Wallerein motioned Lopez around the nose of the aircraft and they swung the airplane ninety degrees, then pushed it tail-first into the hangar. Lopez wrestled the doors shut while Wallerein retrieved his papers from the cockpit. "You have accomplished much here, Colonel. Good work."

The men walked to Lopez's white Chrysler van. "The airport manager is named Benny; a skilled mechanic who flies his own plane, also a Piper. He should not be a problem."

"Kill him right after I take off on the mission."

Lopez gave a slight bow. "As you wish."

"Has Parnes been taken care of?"

Lopez nodded. "Regrettably, Mr. Parnes had a fatal car accident yesterday."

Wallerein was satisfied. Parnes had seen his face. He would sell no more airplanes. Nor remember a foreigner in a red and white Pawnee heading north.

"And the toxin?"

"It is nearly ready. The rest of the team is at the safe house waiting for your final instructions."

Wallerein allowed himself to relax a bit. A few more days and his place in revolutionary history would be assured.

"Doctor Lansky isn't going into work at Fort Detrick anymore," said Lopez.

Surprised, Wallerein said, "Where is he?"

"I called his office this morning. They said he had phoned in sick all week."

Wallerein scowled. "The bastard's trying to hide—he's lost his courage." He felt a small surge of alarm. If the man panicked, there was no telling what he might do. He could blow the whole operation. "Pick him up. Take him to the safe house."

"Si, comrade."

Wallerein settled back into his seat and began to look around. He felt the adrenaline rush that he had always experienced before an operation. He had missed it all those years in that concrete tomb in Libya. Clausewitz wrote that war is the continuation of diplomacy by other means. Wallerein had done enough diplomacy and was more than ready for war, war on his terms. After this, he was staying in the field for good.

Near Chimoré
Chapare region

During the day, no boats stopped at the grassy landing along the river. Indeed, the landing was indiscernible among the jungle plants. But every night at dusk, there were always one or more small barges moored, bringing in raw paste or five-gallon cans of precursors and leaving loaded with bags of cocaine hydrochloride. The bags would be ferried to the cartel's airfields in the Chapare to be flown out.

The path from the landing led through dense underbrush to a processing laboratory concealed by the discreet placement of buildings under the trees and the generous use of netting to cover the rest. Much of the equipment was painted a mottled green.

The lab itself was small but very efficient. Designed in Europe, it had been smuggled in from Colón, Panama, the emergent regional clearinghouse for both drug paraphernalia and weapons. Quickly erected, the lab could process more than ten tons of finished cocaine annually. Until 1990, ten tons of cocaine was the U.S. government estimate of the total amount of cocaine produced world-wide. Several well-publicized drug busts in the States, netting more than twenty tons each, had forced the government to radically revise its figures upward.

The lab was staffed by regular cartel members plus about fifteen unskilled "volunteers." These men had signed contracts modeled on those offered to workers on offshore drilling platforms. The workers would live and work exclusively at the site for a fixed period of time and then would be returned to their homes, cash in hand. This contract, however, was compulsory and enforced by armed guards.

Renan Suarez had witnessed a friend receive a severe beating. He vowed to work his time and get out, go back to his mountains, and warn those still there. His people had endured too much in their history to enslave themselves again. When his cousin Jaime had arrived, Renan had instructed him minutely on the ins and outs of camp life. Renan was afraid that the younger man's temper and impetuousness would make Clorinda a widow. He was determined to find an escape route before that happened.

***

The storm clouds piled up in the distance and threatened yet another evening deluge. Renan scarcely paused to observe the commotion caused by a group of new arrivals. Several heavily-armed narcos stopped and unceremoniously yanked a laundry bag off of the head of a man, a red-haired gringo, then knocked him to the ground. The man struggled to rise but they kicked and punched him back down.

Renan was stunned as his cousin shouted "No!" then ran to the fallen man and threw himself across the gringo, protecting him with his own body. The infuriated narcos began to beat him while he clung to the other prisoner.

"Hold it!" ordered another man, the camp *jefe*. "Stop!" When the two ignored the order, the *jefe* pulled out his pistol and struck the larger one across the head, dropping him to his knees. Thrusting the weapon into the man's bleeding face, Jefe said, "Goddamn it, when I order you to do something, you do it! Next time, I'll kill you. Understand?"

"Next time you hit me," snarled the narco, "you'd better make sure you kill me, 'cause if you don't, I'll kill you."

"Get up, you asshole," said Jefe, disgusted. "Payne wants that guy alive. We got more important things to worry about." He motioned to Jaime. "Take the gringo to your shelter and clean him up. You wanted him, now you got him." As Jaime stood up slowly, Jefe grabbed the smaller man by the shirt. "And if he dies, you die!"

Jaime stooped down and carefully hefted the prisoner onto his back. He staggered towards the hut that he shared with Renan.

"Why did you do that?" asked a frantic Renan, in whispered Quechua. "You could have been killed!"

Jaime pulled the wounded man to a more comfortable position. "I had to." He began to clean the filth from the face of the semi-conscious man. "Do you remember two years ago when Clorinda was pregnant? When the gringos had so many soldiers in Potosi, working out at the airport?" Renan nodded. "At the end of her pregnancy, she was having much pain. Something was very wrong. We had no money. No doctor in Potosi would help us. We heard that the *norteamericanos* had a doctor out at their camp so I went there to plead for help." Jaime paused, as if gathering his thoughts. "At first, they said they were not allowed to help me. Then this man with the red hair came in. He told the gringo doctors to help me. They sent some men and a truck to bring Clorinda back to the camp. The doctors cut her open and took out the baby. If they hadn't, both Clorinda and my son would have died. I owe the lives of my family to this man."

"But there's nothing we can do," Renan said. "We can barely take care of ourselves."

"No, Renan, we must escape from this hell and take him with us. My family honor does not allow me to leave him behind to die! Help me clean his wounds and get him some water."

The two *campesinos* hovered around the disabled Matt Schmidt until he regained consciousness. They gave him coca tea and food from their meager rations.

Jaime cleaned the stump of his wrist and wrapped it with an herbal compress. As he worked, the winds that announced an approaching storm gave some relief from the oppressive heat.

Matt struggled to sit up. "I don't know why you're doing this for me, but I have been extensively trained by the United States Navy not to question people who are trying to save my life."

Renan translated Jaime's Quechua rendition of Clorinda's C-section into rough Spanish for the American.

Schmidt nodded. "Tell Jaime that I remember him now. I'm glad that his wife and baby are okay."

"We must escape tonight, *señor*, or the *narcotraficantes* will surely kill you."

"My thoughts exactly," said Schmidt. "How? How do they get in and out? I don't remember anything."

"They come by boats—everything comes down the river." Renan described the boats as best he could.

Motorized dugouts, mused Matt. "From what you say, I think I know about where we are. I've cruised this river a couple of times with the Bolivian Navy. Find those boats and hide in the rain. That's our best chance. We need to move as soon as it starts to rain."

The next thirty minutes seemed like a lifetime as they waited for the storm to break. At last, torrential rains and thunder crashed down with deafening intensity obliterating every landmark. Stooped low, Renan led and Jaime supported the weakened but determined American as they slid and slipped down the path to the river.

They groped around in the dark. A jagged slash of lightening illuminated three dugout canoes pulled up on shore and hidden in the foliage. Matt scanned them. "Yamaha thirty-five horsepower motors. Goddamn it, I bet these are the same ones I bought for the Bolivian Navy!"

He pointed at the largest, an eighteen-footer. "We'll take this one. But first, let's even things up a bit." He hobbled over to the other two boats and popped the quick-disconnect fuel lines off both motors. He threw the five-foot sections of hose into the larger boat and beckoned for Renan to help him aboard.

He directed Jaime to steady the boat and Renan to stand in the tepid rushing water behind the engine. Matt showed Renan how to pull the starter cord while he used his good hand to work the transmission and throttle.

The motor started on the third pull. Renan jumped in and they started to move into the main current. Matt carefully negotiated the twists and turns of the feeder stream leading to the main river. They motored out slowly. Matt had to balance the need to see the upcoming turns of the river while protecting his night vision from the lightning flashes that almost continuously lit the sky. He tried to hold to the middle of the crashing water as best he could, and prayed that they wouldn't meet other river traffic head-on.

Matt had gone to sea in fishing boats with his father when many of his friends were still Cub Scouts. He had been skipper of his own trawler at eighteen and fished until the day before he reported into the U.S. Naval Academy two years later. He was a better sailor than anyone the narcos had, and if his skills were taxed on a night like this, everybody else should be tied up somewhere safely waiting out the storm. Only desperate and foolhardy souls were out tonight. And they were both. Perversely, the very darkness that gave them protecting cover also made the other dangers of maneuvering a small boat on a jungle river more real.

Matt concentrated hard to avoid the floating debris and tree branches, fresh from the storm run-off. Fortunately, this stretch of the river was relatively benign, free from the swirling eddies and rapids found on other rivers.

Gradually, the storm abated and they made better time as the moon slipped in and out of the clouds. The vegetation along the banks began to take more defined shapes and insects rose in swarms to feed on the boat's occupants. The humidity and the smells of the jungle overwhelmed Matt's senses. The cries of animals punctuated the rapidly approaching dawn.

The engine sputtered and stopped. *Well, of course I chose the one motor that would quit tonight!* Matt managed to make it to the shore without floundering in the roiling current. Renan grabbed one of the trees on the bank and looped a line over a branch. The boat turned up into the fast current. Schmidt motioned Jaime aft. After repeated attempts to restart, Matt swore and banged his good hand on the engine case. Completely spent, he turned to the Suarez cousins. "Sorry guys, I can't go any further. It's too dangerous. You go on."

***

Four grueling hours later, the Suarez cousins finally collapsed exhausted in the underbrush. They had been stumbling through the jungle with their ungainly burden—the semi-delirious Schmidt. Matt did not make the Suarez's journey easy. Between periods of consciousness, he thrashed about, forcing the smaller men to hold him tightly and gag him to keep him quiet. Eventually, they reached the outskirts of the farms surrounding Villa Tunari.

Jaime was still determined to fulfill his promise. "It's too dangerous for us to approach the gringo camp now. We will hide him and wait here a few days. I'll go and bring back Clorinda to help us with the gringo. She knows much about medicines. Then we'll send word to the camp that he is here with us. He's one of their jefes. The gringos will know what to do."

Chapter thirty-three

Dupont Circle, Washington, DC

The phone's shrill ring broke through Porter's concentration, forcing him to stop working on the papers scattered around his desk.

"Nelson," he barked into the receiver.

"Port, this is Robbie."

Nelson tensed. "Any word yet?"

"Bad news," Robinson said slowly. "I just got a call from a pal of mine over at Langley. The Bulgarian cops found John McCord's body in a taxi outside Sofia this morning. They said it looked like a mafia-style hit."

Porter fell back in his chair as Robinson's message slammed into him. He remembered the fear in John's voice during their last conversation.

"John was right," said Nelson, sadly. "He thought that interview might be a set-up, but he went anyway. Never could resist another source. Did they find his documents?"

"Everything he had for us is gone, Port."

Rockville, Maryland

Lieutenant Colonel Mitch (Doc) Kershner, U.S. Army Special Forces, and current National War College student, settled back at his desk with a groan and another thick book on national security affairs. As he always did when at his desk, he looked at the picture in the far left-hand corner and saw his wife and teenage son smiling back at him. Mikey looked like a carbon-copy of his old man—an almost handsome, athletic six feet, one eighty-five, standing erect like the soldier he soon would be. Bobbie Sue's touches filtered through the house even a year after her death from cancer.

The front door slammed and loud footsteps pounded up the stairs. "Dad!" Mike shouted as he burst into the room, "There's a bunch of guys with guns over at the O'Malley's house. They've got a hostage, too!"

"Whoa, there, boy. Slow down," Kershner ordered as he stood up. He held Mike by the shoulders. "Now, explain what you saw—by the numbers, kiddo."

Mike swallowed hard. "I was cutting across the back yard, like I always do. Just as I got to the big oak tree, a van swung into the driveway. The doors of the van opened even before it stopped, and four guys carrying Uzis popped out. Then two more dragged this guy with his hands tied behind his back out of the van and into the house. It happened real fast and real smooth, like they had practiced—like soldiers. I don't think they saw me. Somehow I stayed back out of the headlights—don't know why, but I did."

Keeping his voice calm, Kershner asked, "How many men and how do you know they were Uzis?"

"Six men, no seven, including the driver. Pop, you taught me weapons. I know what an Uzi looks like!"

Kershner conceded that. Mike was a gun freak like his old man, something that would be useful to him when he signed in as a West Point cadet in a few weeks. Kershner thought hard. He had been concerned about the O'Malley house since it was rented three months before to what seemed to be a group of eight to nine men. These men didn't interact or even speak with anybody else on the street. Kershner hoped he was wrong, but it sure looked like bad news. Nothing much had happened in the neighborhood since the Kershners had moved there two years before, but Mitch figured it was just a matter of time before the drug-related crime of D.C. spilled over. He had no confidence at all in the local cops.

As he opened his desk drawer, Kershner calculated the odds of getting caught on the O'Malley property. If he were stopped by the cops at night while carrying a concealed weapon, he'd be in big trouble. If he were stopped, unarmed, by men with Uzis, he'd be dead meat. Kershner took his Beretta from the drawer and, after a moment's hesitation, reached back in the drawer and handed a Colt .45 to his son.

"Okay, Mikey, you can come as my backup. But no hero stuff. Understand?"

"Sure, Pop," Mike agreed, taking the pistol.

Kershner gripped Mike's shoulder. He hardened his voice. "No kidding, son. No heroics. In the Army, this is what's called an order."

"Yes, sir."

***

Kershner left the teenager behind a tree with a cell phone and strict instructions to call for help if shooting started. He crawled slowly and deliberately through the two yards adjoining the O'Malley property. Using the dark for maximum cover and drawing on fifteen years of Special Forces training, he moved noiselessly to the house. He found one of the cellar windows partially uncovered and cautiously peered into the room.

Mikey was right. A hostage! The man sat tied to a chair in the center of the room. A stocky man stood with his back to the window, talking to the seated man, blocking Kershner's view of the hostage's face. The other six stood or sat, listening intently. He had never seen a harder-looking group of men. When the speaker turned to say something to one of the group, Kershner got a good view of his face and that of the hostage. Sucking in his breath sharply, he studied the faces.

Kershner slowly crawled back out of the yard and looped around to the tree where he had parked his son.

"Well, Pop," Mike whispered, crouched in the darkness. "Was I right?"

"Yeah, Michael, you were right." He pulled his son by the arm. "Let's go!"

As they trotted back towards their own house, Mike asked, "What are we going to do now, Pop? Call the cops?"

"This is not a situation for the local cops," he said, shaking his head. "One of my classmates at the War College is FBI counterintelligence. He'll know who to call."

Back inside, Kershner dialed his classmate, Inspector Andrew Chin, from his study phone. "Andy, I'm telling you I had a clear view of them both. I've met the guy they have tied up. Name's Christopher Lansky. He visited my unit in Germany a few years back and I talked with him at a conference last year. He's a research wizard out at Fort Detrick and he looked like hell." Kershner paused. "As for Wallerein, I saw the picture of that son-of-a-bitch in the camp post office every day of the five years I was stationed in Germany. When I was an instructor at the SF terrorist course at Fort Benning, I read his writings. I guarantee it was Wallerein."

"Mitch, are you really sure? Because if you're right—"

"Listen, Andrew, I'm right, damn it." He took another deep breath. "And yes, I do know what it means. Wallerein is not here on vacation. He hates the United States and all it stands for. If the guy had some real resources behind him, he'd rank right up there as one of the worst criminals in history. He's a psychopath masquerading as a revolutionary. And he's in the States, right now. He's planning an operation here, Andy. With Lansky in the picture, it's gotta mean he's got some toxins."

"Okay, Mitch," Chin said. "I'll call my Deputy Director right now. Jacob Borenstein won't screw around with this. I'll get back to you with a plan. You keep the house under surveillance. For Christ's sake, get your kid away from there and don't do anything stupid like shooting Wallerein. We want him and his organization. Alive"

***

Mitch Kershner opened his front door. "They're gone," he said simply, as Chin and three other burly FBI agents slipped in.

"What do you mean they're gone?"

"I mean they got into their van and drove away about thirty minutes after I called you. Gone."

"Damn!" Chin said. "All of them?"

256

"All but one," responded Kershner. "He was down in the basement with Lansky."

Chin's oriental eyes narrowed to slits. "And how do you know that, Mitch?"

"Because, Andy, I went back and looked in the window."

"Mitch, you may be the best recon man in the world, but you're the civilian this time. This is our world. Please, let us do our job."

"Be my guest," said Kershner, with a bow and an elaborate wave.

Chin walked over and offered his hand to Mike. "Well done, son. You've put us on to something very big here."

Mike shrugged off the thanks. He glanced at his father and said, "But we didn't catch them, sir."

"Not yet," said Chin. "But we will." He looked around the comfortable home. "We'll need to set up a command post here. Round-the-clock surveillance on the house. Maybe they've just gone off for a recon. If they've left Lansky and one of their guys, they'll probably be back before the operation." Chin walked into the dining room. "Mitch, is the O'Malley house the same floor plan as this one?"

"Is this suburbia?"

"Good. That'll help our Hostage Rescue Team guys plan this thing. Do either of you know any of the neighbors in the houses either flanking or across from the O'Malley's? We're going to need some help."

Mike spoke up. "Yes, sir. I know the people across the street. The Drazevs. I play lacrosse with their son."

"Drazev? Are they Americans?"

Mike nodded. "They're originally from Bulgaria, but they're citizens. Naturalized last year, in fact."

Chin grimaced.

"Sir, the Drazevs are as proud to be in this country as anyone ever has been. They've got an American flag draped over one wall in the master bedroom, dozens of books about the States, and a picture of the President on the mantlepiece. Looks like a shrine to America. They'd do anything you asked."

Chin grinned and held up his hands in mock surrender. "Okay, Mike. Okay. I'd like you to introduce me to them."

257

Mike looked to his father and got a nod. "Yes, sir. When?"

"Right now. Please call them and ask if we can come over. Just tell them you have someone you'd like them to meet."

Chin turned to Kershner. "Mitch, we'll bring in some cars for surveillance of the area. We'll have to be ready to seal off the whole street ASAP."

"I've got some maps of the area upstairs that show all the streets and alleyways around here," Kershner said.

"Great, that'll help in the short term. Who knows where those guys went—they could have gone out for a pizza for all we know. The more time we have to plan this, the better. Wish we knew where Wallerein got these guys. They're probably professionals, meaning they do certain things in certain ways. But they could be fanatics who can be counted on to do the unpredictable."

Chapter Thirty-Four

City Morgue, La Paz

Special Agent Henry Griffen walked around the morgue, trying to visualize the crime. He hated the smell of death. This morgue stank even worse than those in the States. He shook his head. Why would anyone want to snatch bodies out of a morgue? Especially mutilated bodies like those?

"Al, tell me why anyone would go to all this trouble."

"Beats me," said Al Schwartz. "Those bodies must have been special somehow. The Bolivians still don't know who they were?"

"Nope," Griffen sighed, "but their medical records sections aren't very complete. Not even any fingerprint files."

At that, their Bolivian police companion drew himself up to his full five-foot-six and protested, "Oh, no, Señor Griffen. We have started a fingerprint file system here in La Paz. In fact, I ordered the fingerprinting of these two men when the bodies arrived."

On a hunch, Griffen said, "Let me see those prints. Maybe the reason we haven't identified these guys is because we've been looking in the wrong place. I'll fax them up to Washington. Maybe we'll get lucky." He clapped the Bolivian on the shoulder. "Good job, Antonio!"

Plaza Hotel lobby, La Paz

Arturo Galvani stood in the phone booth, waiting for the overseas operator to ring him back with his call to Arizona. Not yet sure of what was going on, he knew enough to be scared—and cautious. He left the embassy to use the hotel phone, just in case his own was bugged.

Anything seemed possible these days. Galvani couldn't trust anyone at the embassy now.

The phone's ringing startled him out of his deep thoughts. He grabbed the receiver. "Hello, Mario, is that you?"

"Yes, who's this?"

"Listen, *amigo*, this is Arturo. I need your help."

"Go ahead, 'mano," replied Senior Master Sergeant Mario Torrez.

"Callahan's in trouble, big trouble. Somebody's framing him for black market ops. The OSI arrested him in Panama and turned him over to the Panamanians. Word is that he's smuggling drugs on C-141s."

"What? Callahan smuggling drugs—not hardly! It isn't true, Arturo."

"Of course it's not true, Mario. That's why I'm calling. I think I know who's setting him up, but I need some help and I need to stay here. Got any personal leave time coming?"

"You bet, plenty. What do you need from me?"

"You'll have to do some traveling. Panama first, then probably down here. Can you do that?"

"If it's to save the colonel's butt, you bet."

Galvani breathed his relief. Torrez had friends in every Air Force base in the world. If he couldn't do this, nobody could. "Okay, I'm gonna fax you some information and what I need you to do. I'll be at this phone at 0800 and 1700 every day." Galvani then laid out his plan. Torrez was going to be a busy man for a while.

National Airport, Washington, D.C.

On its approach, the Boeing 727 made sweeping turns to match the bends in the Potomac River into National Airport. Colleen Callahan saw Georgetown University slip past, then watched the many racing shells on the river. The grandeur of Washington's buildings and monuments was lost on her as she again mulled through the events of the past few days. She heard the hydraulic actuators kick in as the wheels went down and the flaps were lowered. She smiled remembering how many times Tom talked her through the mechanics of a landing approach, on the rare occasions when he hadn't finagled himself into the cockpit.

Tom. He had looked dreadful. And was in danger. Somebody was going to pay.

After de-planing and clearing Immigration and Customs, Colleen spotted a uniformed Major Angela Davidson waiting for her in the terminal. The two women embraced. Colleen slung her carry-on bag over a shoulder as they inched towards the airport exit, winding through the crowds.

"Colleen, what's going on? I just got a short phone call from Sergeant Galvani. He told me what he found in Bolivia and told me to watch my ass." Angela grinned. "Figuratively, of course."

Taking Angela's arm and whispering as they walked to the exit, Colleen's words tumbled out. Angela only spoke to update Colleen with the facts related by Galvani as the two women attempted to put together the pieces to this puzzle.

Something Colleen caught out of the corner of her eye made her uneasy, especially since Tom's warning.

"Angela, keep talking," she whispered. "I think we're being followed. Just act like you're new here and don't know your way around. Follow me. We're going to make a few turns."

They descended into the lower area of the terminal, then meandered through two shops. Reversing, they went up the escalator. At least two men, both Latino and wearing knitted caps, continued to match their pace and direction. Colleen fought the urge to panic. Terrorists were even here in Washington! She racked her brain for options.

Through the terminal windows, she spotted a D.C. cop out in the second traffic lane, foot up on the bumper of an illegally-parked Mercedes, writing a ticket.

Colleen steered Angela around a corner, turned abruptly and walked through the terminal door, directly up to the policeman. She read his nametag. "Officer O'Hara, my name is Colleen Callahan. This is Major Angela Davidson of the Air Staff. I just arrived from Panama. We are being followed by some very dangerous people. We need to get to the Pentagon. Please help us."

O'Hara looked up from his pad. Colleen pointed towards downtown Washington as if asking directions. "The men following us are over by the Skycap stand, trying not to be obvious."

The policeman shook his head, apparently indicating that she couldn't get there from here and pointed towards the terminal building as if he were correcting her. He sneaked a look at the Skycap stand. "You mean the ones with the funky hats?"

"Yes. I'm not sure if they were on my plane or waiting here. We can't make it to the Metro station without them being right on us. And I don't know about accomplices so we're afraid to hop a cab."

"Okay, ladies," he said, looking off into the distance. "I was a military policeman for two years so I'll go along with this for the moment." He walked them slowly to his own vehicle, still looking off into the distance. "When I open the door to my patrol car, jump inside and I'll drive off before those guys can react. Make sure you stay down."

He pulled open the rear door and shoved them inside, then yanked open his door and jumped in. The suspects ran towards them. He threw the car into gear and had just merged into traffic when the rear window imploded, showering glass shards into the interior. He stomped the accelerator and raced away from the terminal, siren screaming and lights flashing. He slalomed through traffic towards the nearby Pentagon.

They blasted their way towards the hulking gray building. Angela directed O'Hara towards the River entrance. They screeched to a halt at the base of the wide granite stairs, leapt out, dashed up the stairs and crashed through the heavy glass doors. After a quick—but detailed—explanation to the Pentagon rent-a-cops, Angela led them as they ran through the surprisingly wide corridors and up the ramps to the fourth floor. It was Colleen's first visit to the Pentagon and she looked around curiously. Tom loathed this building but Colleen saw it as holding the key to freeing her husband.

***

Entering General Walters' office suite, Colleen headed for the inner door. "You can't go in there!" Walters' aide protested.

Walters looked up from the papers on his desk, annoyance at the disturbance vanished as he recognized Colleen.

"Colleen, what the—" Walters dropped the papers, jumped to his feet, and went to her.

"Hello, Harvey," she said as they embraced.

Angela snapped to attention and rendered a perfect salute. "General, Major Angela Davidson. Sorry for the intrusion, sir, but this concerns Lieutenant Colonel Tom Callahan. It's a matter of life-or-death."

"Relax, Major, I didn't think that you were here on a social call."

"Harvey," said Colleen, "there's a policeman outside who can verify what we're about to tell you."

Walters held up his hand, then instructed his aide to bring in Officer O'Hara and shut the door. He motioned the three to sit down in the leather chairs in front of his walnut desk. Leaning back on the edge of the desk, he said, "Okay, Colleen. Let's hear the rest."

As the story came tumbling out, Walters asked for clarification on only some minor points. He picked up his phone and spoke directly to the executive officer of the USAF Chief of Staff. "Let's go see the Chief," he said as he led them out of his office.

The group entered the E-ring suite of the Chief, oblivious to the many mementos and aircraft models that would have fascinated the visitors under different circumstances. The Chief ordered his door closed. Walters introduced Angela, Colleen, and the now dumbstruck policeman to General Trenton, then gave a quick run-down of their story. Trenton's features hardened as he digested Walters' words.

"Anything else?" he asked the others.

"Yes, sir," replied Angela. "The USAF master sergeant in Bolivia thinks he can get the evidence needed to prove Colonel Callahan's innocence and the existence of a new smuggling ring."

Trenton snorted. "I, for one, don't for a minute believe that young Callahan is guilty of anything. Even without this." He reached into his out-basket for a classified message marked "Eyes Only." Handing it to Walters, he said, "This just came in from Panama, Harvey. OSI sent an agent undercover to Bolivia last week to investigate the possibility of drug smuggling on USAF aircraft. I thought only the Chief of OSI, the Ambassador, and I knew about it. It turns out that somehow the MILGROUP commander was informed where and when this agent would be arriving. Now the agent's dead. The bad guys obviously have a high-level source in the embassy."

Trenton turned to Walters. "Take a C-20 from the 81st Wing over at Andrews, and go down to Panama. Straighten this mess out personally. I'll get on the horn to the Ambassador and bring in our legal folks." He thought some more. "After you fix the Callahan situation, go over to SOUTHCOM and ream Jerry Myers. Bring him back here 'for consultations'." Trenton set his jaw. "I want to know just what the hell he was thinking about, leaving one of his officers in a jam like this. I can't fire his ass since he belongs to SOUTHCOM, but I will speak to the CINC about this."

As Walters rose, Colleen blurted, "General Trenton, I'd like to go back to Panama with Harvey."

"Not a chance, Colleen. There's really nothing you can do right now."

"General, my husband is in trouble. I need to go. If I can't go with Harvey, I'll go back commercial."

Trenton thought for a moment. "All right," he said, "you can go with Harvey."

He turned back to Angela Davidson. "Major, you get back to your office and get on the horn to our sergeant in La Paz. Tell him to sit tight. Use your head, Angela, and keep in touch with me. I'll either be here or down with the Chairman of the Joint Chiefs. I have to let him know about this mess." He stood. "Okay, people, let's move."

Chapter Thirty-Five

U.S. Embassy,
La Paz

"Morning, Master Sergeant!" the Marine guard, Corporal Timothy Johansen, greeted Arturo Galvani and his companion as they entered the deserted embassy. "Always working. Don't you ever take any time off?"

"Good morning, Tim," replied Galvani as he signed himself in. "You know how it is around inspection time. This is Senior Master Sergeant Torrez. He's down here to run a quality control once-over on our books before the Inspector General team visits here next week. Have you seen Rosa Molina today? She was supposed to meet us here," he lied.

"Nobody from the MILGROUP is in today, Arturo. Rosa's off to Santa Cruz with her boyfriend. It's a Bolivian holiday, remember?"

"Damn!" Galvani said. "She was supposed to meet us. Tim, we need the combination to the MILGROUP safe, please."

"Arturo, I can't give that to you. You're not in the MILGROUP."

"Oh, come on, Tim. You know I'm working over there to help them out. You were here when I spent a weekend working with Rosa and Colonel Steele. Just give me the combo."

"I'm not sure that I should, Arturo," Johansen said.

"Look, Corporal," interrupted Torrez, "I've come a hell of a long way to help these people. I feel shitty from the altitude and I don't have time to screw around. Do you know this man?" he asked, indicating Galvani.

Johansen nodded. "Yes, Senior Master Sergeant."

"And you have my identification. We're here to prepare for this damned inspection. Please cooperate and allow us to do our job. I'll accept full responsibility."

Once in the MILGROUP offices, it took Galvani less than ten minutes to find what they were looking for. Rosa Molina had been efficient and thorough in her reorganization of the MILGROUP records. She also kept the combination of Colonel Steele's private safe in a special compartment of her own, a common practice among the admin community.

"Jesus, will you look at this!" gasped Arturo.

"Yeah," agreed Torrez, riffling through the papers. "This is a lot more serious than we thought." He clapped Galvani on the shoulder. "You were right, *amigo*. Great work, Arturo! Let's copy these and get out of here. I'll take the package to Panama on this afternoon's plane."

***

Colonel Billie D. Steele decided to walk the half-mile uphill from his apartment to the embassy. It took an extra fifteen minutes, but he needed the exercise to combat his fatigue. The stress of maintaining his front in the embassy and of fighting to control Payne and his boys was beginning to take a toll. That goddamned Payne! He was more trouble than he was worth. At least he got Montoya's body out of the morgue. And that asshole Calleja was up to something, that greedy pig. Might be about time to wrap up this little caper and get out of town. Wonder how Patricia would feel about living in Brazil.

Lost in thought, Steele absently returned the salute of the Marine guard as he arrived in the Embassy.

"Colonel, Master Sergeant Galvani is already up in the MILGROUP," said Corporal Johansen.

"What?"

"Sir, Sergeant Galvani and the other Air Force sergeant who's down here TDY to help prepare your files for the IG are up in the MILGROUP. They said they were going to go through the MILGROUP safes one more time."

Steele stood stock still as he digested this bit of information.

"Then I guess they don't need me getting in their way," he managed to croak out with a forced smile. He turned and walked back out of the embassy door, knowing he'd better come up with a plan in a big hurry.

Dupont Circle Washington, D.C.

Porter Nelson answered the doorbell still dressed in his bathrobe.

"Mr. Porter Nelson?" asked a nervous young man dressed in a European-cut business suit.

"Yes," replied Nelson, slightly suspicious.

"May I come in?"

"Who are you?"

"My name is David Crider. I'm from the U.S. Embassy in Sofia, Bulgaria. I need to talk to you!"

"Jesus! Get inside," replied Nelson, nearly yanking Crider through the door. He locked and bolted the door. "Sorry. I'm a bit jumpy since our trip to Germany." He gestured down the hall. "Would you like some coffee?"

"Yes, please," said Crider in a quiet voice.

They sat at the kitchen table, stirring their coffee.

Porter spoke first. "What exactly happened to John McCord?"

"He never made it back from his last appointment. I called the authorities. The police eventually found his body in a shot-up taxi."

Crider slowly pulled a thick envelope from his briefcase. "This is what John told me to get to you if something should happen to him."

Porter ripped open the envelope, scanned the summary sheet, and flipped through the photocopies of official documents. His elation faded as he looked back to Crider.

"Have you read this?"

Crider looked down at the floor. "Damn it, Crider! Did you read this?"

Crider met his eyes. "Yes," he said softly. "That's why I'm here. I flew directly here this morning."

"Jesus, now you're in danger, too. Why the hell did you do that?"

Crider hesitated. "John told me it was important that you get it. After they found his body, I just had to know what was important enough for him to die for." Nearly in tears, he looked at Nelson. "We were very close."

It took Porter a few seconds before he understood. "Ah, David, I'm sorry." He tried to soften his voice, "John was a valued friend. And a good man."

Crider wept silently while Porter tried to figure out what to do next. "Okay, David, are you in this with me?"

Crider wiped his eyes with his handkerchief and took a deep breath. "Absolutely."

"Here, then. Take this number." Nelson scribbled a quick note. "Call Robbie Robinson. Tell him to meet us at the visitor's entrance to the Pentagon in an hour. I'll use the phone upstairs to call a friend on the Air Staff. Maybe she'll be able to steer us to the right people."

Porter Nelson sat in Angela Davidson's Pentagon office as she, Colleen, and Robbie Robinson read the papers. "This is incredible!" Colleen exclaimed. "Sure helps explain why we're having no luck at all in South America. It's going to make more than a few faces very red over at the State Department, not to mention the CIA and DIA. How could they have missed it?"

"Easy," answered Robbie. "We almost missed it and we were looking for it."

"Yeah," agreed Porter. "But the question now, Colleen, is how we can get these papers to the right people the fastest way possible? This stuff is hot. But the State Department sure as hell doesn't want to hear about this from me. I'm just another journalist with a crackpot idea."

Colleen slowly drummed her fingers on the desk. "Perhaps this information can be used properly today."

"What do you have in mind?" asked Angela.

Standing abruptly, Colleen reached for her purse. "Ambassadors work for the President. It's the best way to get these papers where they're needed as fast as possible. Come on. First we're going to show this to General Trenton, then go for a visit."

***

Ambassador George Brent received his visitors in the library of his family house in Georgetown. His sunken eyes and slightly palsied handshake showed his nerves had not yet recovered in the ten days since the C-12 bombing. Nevertheless, Colleen knew she had to push her plan, and him, as far as she could.

She briefly explained the events of the last few weeks and how they were connected to his "accident."

"Colleen, I'm so sorry all this had to happen to you."

"Don't worry about me, George. I'm flying down to Panama with General Walters. But telling you about Tom's problem is only part of why we're here."

"Actually, Mr. Ambassador," said Angela, taking her cue from Colleen, "the real reason we've come is to show you the connections these men have made between recent events in Bolivia, narco-terrorists, and a network of moles in the U.S. government."

"Mr. Ambassador," Porter began, "the situation was far too complicated for me to figure out alone. I enlisted the help of a couple of friends, Robbie here and John McCord. John got too close to somebody in Bulgaria—we still don't know whom. He was killed, but not before he could make some positive identifications and confirmation of documents we discovered in Moscow and Berlin.

"Not that it's any big surprise to you, Mr. Ambassador, but there are lots of groups, individuals, and even governments that have one thing in common—their virulent hatred of the United States. Arnold Beichman at the Hoover Institution called this 'the radical entente.'"

"I've read some of his work. Quite intriguing." Brent nodded and perked up a little bit.

"Exactly," Porter said. "His writings form the framework for what we're going to show you. There are terrorists left over from the Cold War, cut off from their old benefactors in Eastern Europe. Groups that have been forgotten in the current frenzy of worry over Islamic fundamentalists. These groups have been reduced to free-lancing for whatever bunch of crazies will pay their bills. Businessmen or dictators, it makes no difference anymore. There are lots of folks cut there who still hate the United States and would love to wreck the current peace process. For example, the old communist-party hacks in Eastern Europe, now out of power, who want to promote chaos in order to restore the old regime—with themselves in charge, of course."

"Yes, yes, of course. But how does this lead to Bolivia?"

"Lots of the radicals of the '60s and '70s are gray-haired but still mean. If they let go of their old rhetoric it would prove their lives were a lie. So, they had to look for new ways to strike back. Traditional terrorist methods, blowing up buildings and kidnapping VIPs, simply won't work. Plus, the old funding sources, mainly the KGB and Eastern Bloc intelligence services, aren't there anymore, so they have to raise cash. Smuggling drugs helps provide them with what they need." Porter handed Ambassador Brent a sheaf of closely typed pages.

Brent's color returned as he read through the first few sheets, muttering occasionally. "This is outrageous! I can't believe this. Nothing personal, Mr. Nelson, but something like this, a narco-terrorist conspiracy plus an espionage fraud of this magnitude, is unprecedented. Impossible."

"Mr. Ambassador, I know it's hard to believe, but it's true." Nelson handed over several more sheets, then smiled at Brent. "Sir, I may not be much of a mountain climber, but I'm one hell of an investigative journalist!"

"Well," said the Ambassador, "you'll have to prove this to me."

"I'll be happy to show you our sources, but only off the record—at least for now. John McCord died getting the last of the evidence, and we're determined that whoever killed him will get hurt as hard as we can hurt them."

Brent agreed. Two hours later, Nelson finished. Twice during Porter's discourse, Brent made phone calls to close associates to verify some of the facts. Brent was flushed with outrage. "How did details of our counternarcotics operations in Bolivia end up in Europe?" He leafed through the papers again.

Something about those German documents bothered Colleen also but she couldn't connect the thoughts. She gently interrupted Brent's tirade. "George, General Trenton just told us that an OSI agent was killed last week in Bolivia. Somehow Steele found out he was coming."

Brent exploded. "That message was marked 'Eyes Only' for me." He paused and looked at the assembled group. "I've long had a suspicion that we had a leak in our embassy. The FBI has been looking into it."

"Did you mention the message to anyone?" asked Colleen.

His eyes narrowed. "I told Patricia."

Click.

Colleen reached for the papers and found what she was looking for. "Remember that German agent's code name—*Rote Rose*? That means Red Rose, George. Who surrounds herself with roses? Not to mention uses that terrible tea rose perfume?"

Ambassador Brent thought about that, then shook his head. "That's an extremely tenuous connection to Patricia. Lots of people love roses, including the President's wife."

"Oh? And how many of those rose-loving people are having an affair with Steele?"

"What?"

Colleen grinned. "The embassy guards that patrol around her house told me as I left Bolivia. They didn't like her running me out of the country. Not even Tommy knows this yet."

"Steele had access to all SOUTHCOM regional intelligence reports," Brent said. "That could explain why so many of our operations in Peru and Ecuador were compromised in the past several months, not to mention Bolivia. Patricia could have gotten the information from Steele."

Colleen nodded. "José Hernandez calls Patricia a commie groupie. Last month she was seen several times with the new Cuban ambassador. Now we have intelligence confirming a mole in the State Department. Classified information on our programs showed up in Eastern Europe." Colleen sat back into her leather chair. "Mata Hari would be ever so proud."

"This is still circumstantial."

"Fine. Let the FBI handle the investigation. They'll know what to look for. But don't you see that it all fits?"

Brent took a deep breath. "We always thought the real security leaks were from the Bolivians. I used to hammer the Bolivian president about it every time we met. I just cannot comprehend that the leak may have come from my own staff!"

Absolute silence filled the room. Colleen thought that her plan to involve the Ambassador was about to backfire until George Brent sat up straight. For the first time that evening, his voice was strong.

"Mr. Nelson, if you and Mr. Robinson would please give me a chance to right this terrible situation before you do anything else, I would be most grateful."

"Take all the time you need, Mr. Ambassador. That's why we're here. You're the best solution to everybody's problems. And," Nelson added with a smile, "considering the rescue in Bolivia, I can hardly turn you down. Anyhow, publishing it isn't nearly as important as topping these guys. And the story will be a lot better if it has a happy ending!"

"If events prove you correct—and I'm afraid that they will—the last thing you want is to publish this right now. It would be your death warrant," Brent said. He straightened his shoulders. "Before I go back to Bolivia, I need to talk with the President. I'll call him next. You gentlemen will have to come with me. Bring your notes. We'll have to turn them over to the FBI. Probably the CIA, as well. They'll need to act on this immediately." He smiled. "Mr. Robinson, you'll be back with your old firm as a consultant very soon, I expect.

"Colleen, I appreciate you bringing these gentlemen to me." He took her hand and gently kissed it. "We'll get Tom out of Panama. That I promise."

Brent turned to Angela. "Major, I will need you to get another plane to fly me to Bolivia right after I see the President. Please start working that out with General Trenton. I'll be damned if I'm going to let this travesty play out any longer! Not while I'm still the Ambassador!"

Chapter Thirty-Six

Panama City, Panama

Tom sat in the darkness of the small cell, breathing the musty air of the dank little room. He was still strapped into what looked like an electric chair and felt like a medieval torture rack. His bruises ached. Nothing broken. Yet. But those miserable bastards who worked him over under the watchful eye of Major Rojas were vicious and thorough.

The door to the small soundproof cell banged open, and a shaft of light split the room.

Major Rojas stood in the doorway. "How is our guest this fine evening? Ready to go?" He laughed. "If it gives you any satisfaction, this last move is proving more difficult for us than you." Rojas paused and there was a brief flare as he lit a small cigar. "During General Noriega's term, it was the criminals who had to run. Not us. So we're not accustomed to this sort of thing."

Tom slumped in his chair, eyes on the floor as if dejected and broken. Contemptuous, Rojas motioned the guard to undo the restraints, then leaned against the door watching.

The guard undid the body restraints. He bent down to free the legs. As the last strap came off, Tom kicked the man hard in the face, knocking him backwards. He launched himself across the room at the other guard. He slammed him into the wall and slung him towards Rojas, who was trying to draw his pistol. The stunned guard crashed into him and knocked the pistol from his hand.

Tom leaped towards Rojas and smashed a straight right to the solar plexus. The air went out in a whoosh. Tom shoved Rojas head-first into the concrete wall. Rojas groaned and collapsed in a heap.

He spun and double-punched the first guard in the face. Down he went, blood spurting from his nose. The other guard sprang with a shout. Tom lashed out a foot that smashed into his face and knocked him over. Another kick. Tom could hear the facial bones crunch. The man lay still, his face a bloody mess.

Tom snatched up Rojas' Glock and crouched with the gun pointed at the door. Nothing. No reinforcements. He could only hear the pounding of his own heart.

He crept to the door, pistol ready. He turned the handle and pulled. The door opened an inch—no sound—two inches—still nothing. He peered through the crack into a dimly lit corridor.

He edged down the hall, knelt and peeked around the corner. A man in a PPF uniform sat with his back to Tom, packing a box on top of a metal desk. Tom stood, stepped silently towards the man, and cracked him on the head with the pistol. Tom caught him and let him down slowly, quietly.

He rested for a moment. He allowed himself fifteen seconds to calm down.

Time to go.

He crept down the hall to the outer door. He turned the knob, pushed the door open to step out onto a dark staircase. And pitched forward in the dark. He crashed down the last three steps. The pistol skittered away into the darkness under the building.

Tom heard shouts and pounding feet behind him. The door flew open. He leapt to his feet and sprinted down the dark alley. A gunshot. Another. And another. Rapid footsteps behind him. A shot whizzed by.

He ducked into the first cross alley he came to and accelerated through the maze of dark passages, tripped over a pile of refuse. He rolled back on his feet without losing a stride. After training for months at the altitudes of Bolivia, he felt as if he could run forever in the humid, oxygen-rich Panamanian air. With the adrenaline surging through his body, there wasn't a man in the Panamanian police who could catch him on foot. Especially tonight.

In a matter of minutes, he had lost the pursuing police. He raced on, jinking through the crowded city, avoiding people, and picking the darkest streets until he had covered at least a mile. He turned into another deserted back street and collapsed in a patch of grass in the shadows.

Tom touched his bruises with his fingertips. As the adrenaline ebbed away, they hurt like hell. He shook it off. Now what? Could he trust the rest of the PPF? Would they turn him back to Rojas or over to the Americans? He couldn't take that chance. Rojas would expect him to bolt to an American base so those routes would be patrolled. Just get to a safe place. Call Gary Willis.

Tom rose and stole around the corner into the dim streetlights. He slipped into the thin stream of pedestrians now strolling home from their late-night festivities. As he walked, he made certain to move his head as little as possible. His eyes never stayed still, darting about like his crosscheck scan of instruments in a fighter. His damp shirt clung to his back. He ducked under a shop awning, then walked behind a small family group to avoid another policeman. Bloody police were everywhere. Looking for him?

The PPF cops pulled a car over and pulled the driver from the vehicle. Then another. They were searching all the vehicles. So much for the taxi option. That left the hard way, by foot.

He saw a phone box on a pedestal in the shadows outside a grimy gas station. He darted across the street. On reflex, he caressed the Saint Christopher medal under his shirt. "Thanks, Chris," he breathed, then punched in the numbers of his phone card and Gary's number.

The phone rang. And rang. Shit. Nobody home? Finally, someone picked up. "*Bueno.*"

"Gary, it's Tom!"

"Tom! Where the hell are you? Wait. Don't answer."

Tom was stunned. "Phone tap?"

Gary swore softly. "Who the hell knows?"

"I need help, Gary."

A slight pause. "Tom, you remember the restaurant we ate at the last time you were in Panama?"

"Sure."

"Can you get there without being nabbed?"

Tom recalled the areas of the sprawling city. Two miles, max. "I think so."

"How long do you need?"

"Maybe an hour."

"Okay, I'll meet you there in an hour and a half." Then he added, "Be careful, buddy."

"Always," said Tom.

***

Crammed into his makeshift headquarters ops center, Major Rojas listened to the telephone exchange, then put down his receiver. "We have him now."

"What do you mean?" protested Special Agent Charter. "There are hundreds of restaurants in the city! We can't cover them all."

"I have a car at each gate at Howard Air Force Base where Willis lives."

"We'll follow him!"

"Precisely." Rojas smiled. "It will probably be a seafood restaurant. Most of the Americans stationed in Bolivia develop a craving for good seafood while they are in that land-locked country. It is quite strange. And, since seafood in Panama is world-class, how can they resist?"

He turned to his computer, tapped in a few commands and glanced through the notes on the screen. "Willis has three particular favorites. We can concentrate on them."

"How do you know this?"

"The Willis family employs an *empleada* to look after their children. She is the cousin of one of my cousins."

Charter laughed. "Well done, my friend."

"David, I told you. I've done this sort of thing before."

***

Tom hung up and wiped his sweaty hands on his jeans. His nerves were on fire. He looked around. Bustling crowded shops, still busy in the late tropical night. The squat buildings and twisting narrow streets of this older section of town created a labyrinth that he had to escape.

The legacy of the atrocities of the Noriega regime lingered here and people were deeply suspicious of all authorities, Panamanian and American. Tom knew he could count on nobody here.

He took a deep breath to steady himself, then stepped away from the phone and merged into the street, teeming with people. He felt naked passing through the chaotic streets. Paranoia sharpened his senses. He slipped down a dark side street, crossed a vacant lot filled with litter and a burned-out shell of a dead Toyota, and emerged onto another main drag.

Tom managed the next three crossings without incident, then doubled back to check for a tail. He paused to study reflections in a dirty shop window. He lingered a heartbeat too long. A woman sidled up next to him. Dressed in a mini skirt that was too tight and a crop top too small for her enormous breasts, she purred, "Care to party, *guapo*?"

"*Que lastima, señorita.* I have no money."

She moved closer. "Perhaps a little free taste could change your mind?"

Tom's knowledge of the world of prostitution was nearly zero. What he did know was that loitering in the dark background was usually a pimp, often large, often armed. He had no interest in either the prostitute's services or clashing with her protector. He needed to disappear. Now.

He peeled her hands off his body. "Regretfully, *señorita*, I have an appointment. Perhaps next time."

Tom branched off the main artery and descended toward the southern shoreline, executing a meandering path as if he were out for a casual stroll. Now and again, he doubled back. He knew the topography and layout of the city. He knew precisely where to go. He threaded his way between the cars, buses, dodged around the milling pedestrians, and headed south to the beach.

Ninety minutes later, Tom skirted the edge of the street along the shoreline near the restaurant. The sea breeze carried the fetid smells of the low tide. He thought he heard the faint whop-whop-whop of a helicopter in the distance above the sound of the gentle surf. He ducked into the shadows for a few minutes and took stock. Only a few hundred yards to the restaurant, across open ground.

Gary Willis' blue Corvette pulled into the empty parking lot, and parked in the pool of light in the center. Gary hopped out of the car, dressed in his uniform. He glanced around, checked his watch, then looked around again. He leaned against the 'Vette. On his hip he held a portable radio, the ubiquitous "brick" carried by Air Force squadron commanders worldwide.

Tom crouched in the darkness and willed himself not to sprint across the street and leap into Gary's car. He drew several deep breaths, then stood and strolled towards the restaurant. He stopped and glanced around, listening before he walked directly to his friend.

Before Tom could shake hands with Gary, six figures loomed out of the darkness.

"Good evening, Colonel Willis," said Major Rojas. "We thought you two might try something like this." He smirked. "We followed you from Howard."

"So my phone was tapped."

"Of course." Rojas motioned for his armed men to move in. "We'll take Colonel Callahan off your hands now, Willis."

"Not so fast."

Rojas scowled and put his hand on his weapon. "Perhaps you'd like to join your friend in his cell?"

"Not particularly," said Willis, still leaning against his car. "Oh, I like Tom all right. Just not the company he's been keeping recently."

Willis raised the radio to his lips and said, "Execute."

Three Air Police vehicles roared out of the darkness, tires squealing. They skidded to a stop on opposing sides of the group. Ten Air Force policemen in full gear boiled out.

A Blackhawk helicopter roared in and circled, searchlights on, a door gunner standing in the side door aiming his M-60 machine gun at the vehicles and the people below.

Willis said, "Looks as if you were a teeny bit overconfident, Major." His voice hardened. "Drop your weapons, now!"

Rojas hesitated. Willis stepped forward and smashed his right fist into Rojas' face, sending him sprawling backwards. Willis stood over him. "That's for the way you treated Mrs. Callahan, *pendejo.*"

278

The other PPF policemen dropped their weapons and put their hands in the air. Willis motioned to the Skycops, who moved in and collected the weapons. "Right now, Rojas, you stupid shit, our Ambassador is on the phone to your President. I don't think your uncle, the Minister, is going to be able to fly cover for you any longer. Your days are over, asshole."

He turned to Special Agent Charter. "You're under arrest, dirtbag. You're coming with us." Another Skycop stepped forward and cuffed Charter, then loaded him into one of the cars.

Willis turned to the ranking policeman. "Chief, hold these guys until the real Panamanian police get here."

The Chief saluted. "Yes, sir. It'll be a pleasure."

"Come on, Tom," said Willis. "I'm taking you home."

"Just a second, Gary," said Tom. He grabbed Rojas by the left hand and jerked the gold West Point ring from his finger. He shoved his nose near Rojas' now bloody face. "My father had one of these. You don't deserve to wear one, you son-of-a-bitch." He turned and pitched the ring as far as he could into the surf.

Chapter Thirty-Seven

Howard Air Force Base, Panama

The white and blue USAF C-20 Gulfstream taxied to a halt directly in front of the Base Operations building. Tom waited on the breezy ramp along with the Air Division commander, Brigadier General Sam Worthington, the Air Division Judge Advocate General (JAG), Gary Willis, and SMSgt Mario Torrez.

The aircraft's door popped opened, and the brutal Panamanian sunlight hit Lieutenant General Harvey Walters as he emerged. He scrunched his eyes. "Hello, Sam," he said as he descended the steps. Walters returned the shorter man's salute then shook his old friend's hand.

Further introductions were cut short. Colleen Callahan appeared at the top of the steps, framed in the sunshine against the doorway, her long blonde hair swirling in the warm sea breeze. She wore a white cotton sheath dress that clung to her tanned skin, accentuating her curves. When she saw Tom, her strained expression broke into a dazzling smile. She bounced down the steps and launched herself into his arms. Eventually, Tom remembered the presence of the other men on the ramp and released his hold on Colleen.

She waved at Gary over Tom's shoulder. "Thank you, you wonderful man!" She threw her arms around his neck and kissed him too, knocking off his flight cap.

"Well, Colonel Willis," General Walters said with a grin, "I presume that you and Colleen are already acquainted."

"Sorry, sir," Gary apologized with a grin over Colleen's shoulder. "I think it must be my aftershave."

Brief introductions followed as the men and Colleen clustered around Walters in a war council on the tarmac. Colleen briefed the group on Porter Nelson's findings and Ambassador Brent's plans in Bolivia. Walters declined Worthington's offer of the VIP suite in Base Operations. "Thanks, Sam, but we've got too much to do right now. We need to move out. Have you been able to arrange things as we discussed on the aircraft phone?"

The diminutive Worthington nodded. "Yes, sir. Sergeant Torrez has the documentation we talked about this morning. The JAG and I've looked it over. It's just what we needed."

"Good work, Torrez. We'll need those papers very soon." Walters directed his attention back to General Worthington, "Sam, I'd like one of your staff cars. Could you also arrange to get Colleen to a hotel? Some place really fancy on the beach. These two deserve a decent reunion." He set his jaw. "But first, we have some business to finish over at Quarry Heights."

***

Gary Willis maneuvered the Air Force staff car carrying Lieutenant General Walters and Tom Callahan as it crested the steep hill leading up to the security checkpoint at the Quarry Heights main gate. They threaded through the concrete anti-terrorist obstacles placed there during the Noriega years. The Army guard saluted smartly at the three-star passenger and waved the vehicle through.

Willis steered the car under the portico of the Headquarters building and parked in the slot marked CINC. An Army guard bounded out of the building to direct them elsewhere, his protests died unspoken as he caught sight of the general's uniform epaulets through the car's window.

Walters took his time, delaying his exit. "Tom," he said finally, "I know you're pissed at Jerry Myers. I know you'd like to go in there and rip out his heart. Don't do it."

"Are you kidding, General?" erupted Gary. "If Tom doesn't go after him, I will. Myers tried to screw Tom over big-time—Tom could have been 'disappeared' real easy."

281

General Walters locked his eyes on the younger man. "I don't need your advice, Willis." He paused; his voice softened. "Gary, up until now, you've exhibited exceptional judgment, initiative and loyalty. I'm very impressed with your conduct. I intend to inform the Air Force Chief of Staff and the Commander of Air Combat Command to that effect. Please don't blow it now. I know how you feel about all this. In your position, I would probably feel the same. But this is way above your pay grade. I will handle it." He swiveled in his seat to face Tom. "That goes for both of you, maybe even especially you, Tom. Understood?"

Smoldering, Tom took a long look at Walters. "But I don't have to like it, General."

"No, you don't." Walters examined the bruised face. "You keep that temper of yours under control, son."

Admiral Brothers's aide arrived and led them into the Headquarters building, handed them security badges, and escorted them upstairs to the CINC's spacious inner office. Introductions were brief, formal; Brothers and Walters knew each other by reputation only. Tom Callahan's eyes burned large holes through General Myers.

Settling back in his leather chair, Walters wasted no time. "General Myers, I'd like to hear your version of the events surrounding the arrest of Colonel Callahan."

Nervous, Myers licked his lips and began, "General, I was briefed by the local office of the OSI that Colonel Callahan was linked with a drug smuggling ring using Air Force C-141s from Bolivia. I was assured that there was good evidence supporting that charge."

"Did you even think to follow up on that—like asking to review the evidence?" asked Walters. "Maybe even call in a JAG for some advice? Or maybe ask Callahan to explain himself? You know, have him in for a chat with his commander, give him some guidance if necessary? Or do you always let rumors guide your judgment?"

"General," Myers protested, "I was told the investigation was classified. I considered it safe to assume that OSI was proceeding in accordance with all appropriate rules and regulations."

Walters snorted. "Myers, that is a load of crap. You got a briefing from one wacko agent, not the 'local office of the OSI.' You didn't even try to confirm the OSI story, for Christ's sake. You were prepared to jettison the career of the nearest thing the USAF currently has to an ace—to cover your ass!" Walters's beefy face reddened, and his lips went tight. "Colonel Willis and Mrs. Callahan came to you for help. You wouldn't even talk with them! How am I supposed to interpret that?"

"General, I have had bad reports on Colonel Callahan's immoral conduct, as well as that of his wife."

Walters put his hand out to restrain Tom. "And from whom did you hear these reports, if I may be so bold?"

"Patricia Pointer. She told me that she and the MILGROUP commander feared for the reputation of the MILGROUP. They were concerned about reports of Callahan acting like a typical unsupervised fighter pilot away from home."

General Walters leaned forward slightly. "I will ignore the insinuations about 'typical fighter pilots' for the moment, even though I am one of the senior fighter pilots in the Air Force." He paused. "General, it may interest you to know that the source of those rumors you used as an excuse for your decisions, this indignantly moral DCM, was herself having an adulterous affair with said married MILGROUP commander. Steele, in turn, is very likely responsible for the bombing of the Marine Guard detail's house and the bombing of the C-12. And last but not least, Steele is most certainly running drugs from Bolivia to the States and to Europe."

Admiral Brothers' patrician face hardened. He met Walters' eyes and answered the unasked question with a slight nod.

"General Myers," said Walters, formal now, "I am here to inform you that the Chief of Staff of the United States Air Force requires your presence in Washington. Accordingly, you are to go straight to your quarters and pack a suitcase to include your Class A uniform. You will present yourself back here in forty-five minutes, passport in hand, ready to fly back on my C-20. You will make no phone calls from your quarters while you are there. Any calls you need to make can be made from the aircraft under my supervision. Do you understand these instructions?"

"Yes, sir." Myers' face was ashen and his shoulders slumped.

Admiral Brothers said, "My aide will accompany you, General, to your quarters to insure these orders are carried out to the letter."

As the door closed, Brothers looked at the men. "Well, I think that was rather distasteful, wasn't it?" He turned to Tom. "Colonel Callahan, I'd like to offer you my apologies and the apologies of Southern Command for what's happened to you and your family."

Tom smiled briefly. "Thank you, Admiral, but it's not necessary."

"Of course it is, and it's the least I can do," insisted Brothers, "considering it was a member of my staff who caused you so much grief." He chuckled. "Anyhow, I'm the acting CINC, I can do what I want, and I choose to apologize." He looked at the others. "Well, what should we do next? Get Steele on the phone and back up here or should we send some people down there to bring him back in irons?"

"Admiral," Walters said, "may I use your classified phone to call General Trenton? He'll have an update on all this."

After the call, Walters said, "I'm afraid there's more to all this than just one renegade colonel and his merry men in Bolivia. Sounds like Steele moved down to Cochabamba." He sketched out the parts of the new situation that he was cleared to relate.

"I'm going back to Bolivia," Tom said.

"Tom, are you crazy?" Gary blurted. "Haven't you had enough of this?"

"No way, Tom." Admiral Brothers shook his head. "I concur with Gary. You've endured enough already. You need to stay away from this business. Leave it to the pros."

"Sir, with respect, I'm the best guy, probably the only guy, who can end this madness. I know all the key players. I have contacts all over Bolivia and I can get where I need to go without anyone knowing. Now we have to deal with the Bolivia-terrorist connection. I'm the best chance we have of finding that out. Steele is our only lead, so we have to start there."

"You also have a vested interest in solving this," Walters said.

"Yes, sir. I do have a vested interest, but it's a lot more serious than just Bolivia now. Look, General, with all my heart, I'd much rather take my wife to the beach, drink a few piña coladas and forget the past few days while you let somebody else fix this mess. But there's no time. So I'm it. If you wait to assemble a team, some or all of Steele's people will get away, maybe even Steele himself. And I don't want even one of those bastards loose. We have to snuff out the situation in Bolivia and find the link to the terrorists in the States. Then the pros can do their thing."

General Walters laughed. "This is really going to disappoint Colleen, Tommy. She has big plans for you for the next couple of days."

Tom wagged a finger at his godfather. "There's no need to get crazy about this, Uncle Harvey. After all, the next flight to Bolivia doesn't leave until tomorrow morning."

Special Forces Team House
Base Camp
Chimoré

In the open clinic which the camp maintained for the locals, Sergeant First Class Hector Ibarra, the Special Forces team medic, had delivered nine babies since his arrival four months before. All had been boys. Word spread throughout the Chapare that Ibarra somehow only delivered boys. In Bolivia, as in many countries, boy babies were valued more than girl babies. Consequently, Ibarra was an immensely popular fellow with the locals. Pregnant women from all over the region traveled to the clinic so he would deliver them a baby boy.

An extra visitor arrived that day, a young mountain woman who, through an interpreter, told Ibarra of a wounded gringo in the area who needed help. Ibarra spoke to Warrant Officer Enrique Ramos who, in turn, brought the matter to Captain Ramirez at the morning team meeting.

In the midst of their meeting, Tom Callahan opened the screen door and strode into the room, followed by Lieutenant Colonel José Hernandez, Master Sergeant Sammie Hodges, and Captain Luis Valdez.

Ramirez's jaw dropped. "Colonel Callahan!"

Tom laughed as he offered his hand. "Eduardo, you don't look very happy to see me. I'm disappointed." Turning serious, Tom said, "We've got a very big problem here, and I need your help to solve it."

"But, sir," protested Ramirez, "my orders are to arrest you and hold you for DEA. Word is that you've been running drugs."

"I was arrested in Panama on some trumped-up charges, framed by Steele, Payne, and their friends." Tom paused to give Ramirez time to digest that bit of information. "I was released by the CINC and sent back here to try to round these guys up before they get away. I had José and Sammie meet me in Santa Cruz. Captain Valdez arranged to fly us down here unannounced because I had to get to you without anyone knowing."

Ramirez hesitated.

"Come on, Eduardo. Do you really think I'd come back to Bolivia, much less directly here to see you, if I were guilty? Or that the people up at SOUTHCOM would let me go? Jeez, Eduardo, you know me. You know what I stand for."

"Sir, my orders are to detain you."

"Think, man, think! Where did those orders come from—Steele?" Ramirez nodded, then added, "And Ms. Pointer."

"Oh, of course. We can't forget the famous Patricia Pointer, now can we?" Tom took pity on the young captain. "Here, Eduardo, perhaps this will help you." He handed the young captain an envelope bearing the two blue stars of a rear admiral.

Ramirez tore it open and scanned the contents. He looked up at Tom with a broad grin. He turned to his troops and said, "Okay, guys, the CINC says we're to do anything Colonel Callahan says."

Tom told the whole story of Steele's band of miscreants and its takeover of the Rodriguez cartel. The entire Special Forces team gathered around, spellbound. "The reason Steele ordered you to not improve your defensive posture is that he was trying to set you up, to divert embassy attention from smuggling to security. Steele was willing to trade the lives of you men for time to get out with more drugs and more money. He ordered the bombing of the Marine House. He had those Marines killed to divert our attention away from counternarcotics operations."

Growls of anger came from the men. Ramirez waved them silent.

Tom continued, "We have to move out now and find Payne's camp. Steele might be there. Our information says the camp's nearby. The bad guys will head to Brazil nanoseconds after they hear that we've discovered their scam. That's why we couldn't let anybody here in Bolivia know that I'm out of jail."

His gaze swept the group. "Gentlemen, right now you have a chance, probably the only chance you'll ever get in your career to make a real impact on the Army. You can help save the reputation of our military. José, Sammie, and I can't do it alone. We're going to do whatever it takes to stop these guys."

"All right!" Ramirez said, pumping his right arm. "Finally, rules of engagement that make sense."

Ibarra stepped forward. "Captain, what about the wounded gringo?"

"What wounded gringo?" asked Tom.

Ramirez replied, "Sir, a local woman just told Ibarra that there was a gringo out in the bush who needed medical attention."

"For what kinds of wounds?"

"Hard to tell, sir. I couldn't understand her very well. Apparently, the man had been beaten pretty badly by the narcos."

"Get her in here, Ibarra," Tom ordered, heart pounding, hardly daring to hope.

Three minutes later, Ibarra returned with a slender *campesina*, not quite five feet tall. Her bright eyes were the largest and blackest Tom had ever seen. She wore a simple dress and sandals. Draped over her shoulder was an *aguayo* containing a small child.

"Ask her where the gringo is, José. And what he looks like."

José repeated the question in Quechua. When she answered, he closed his eyes and crossed himself. He turned back to the Americans. "She says he's not far from here, Tom. She came to get us, to take us to the red-haired gringo who is missing a hand. It's gotta be Matt."

Tom whooped and all the men exchanged high fives. "Does she know of any processing camps?"

"Yeah, her husband used to work at one nearby. She says he'll show us."

Tom nodded. "Eduardo, get the men ready to move out. And bring the DEA guy, Kelly, along. He can do the arrests."

"Yes, sir. We'll be ready in five minutes."

The Special Forces team drove its Land Cruisers as far as they could go into the bush. The men dismounted, then spread out and followed the young *campesina* in a loose tactical formation, weapons ready.

Pausing at the edge of a small clearing, a now-sweaty Captain Eduardo Ramirez motioned to his men. As they began to encircle the clearing, a tall figure, clearly not a Bolivian *campesino*, emerged from under the palm leaves of a crude shelter.

Tom Callahan gasped. All caution forgotten, he stepped into the clearing.

Matt Schmidt heard the noise and swiveled around. "Tom!" he said, face splitting into a grin as the two men rushed to embrace. "You dirty dog. You almost gave me heart failure! Hey, I thought you fighter guys were supposed to come out of the sun, not sneak up like thieves!"

The other soldiers materialized and congratulations were given all around. Ibarra made a quick, but thorough examination of the stump of Matt's wrist and pronounced it infection free.

"I owe my life to these people," said Matt, pointing at the three Suarezes, standing shyly off to one side. Matt gave a brief account of what he remembered of his captivity and escape. "Clorinda really knows her stuff, Ibarra. I don't know exactly what she's been feeding me and putting on my arm, but it sure as hell worked. I'm almost recovered. She could teach you volumes about folk medicine."

Ramirez said, "Commander, if these *campesinos* worked at Payne's camp, they can lead us there now."

"They can, but they won't," replied Matt. "They're scared and they've already risked enough to get me this far. Jesus Christ, Eduardo, you can't ask these civilians to walk into a fire-fight!"

"But, sir," protested Ramirez, "how else are we going to find his camp? We could be looking for days!"

"I know where it is."

Ramirez pulled his local area map from a side pocket of his BDUs. He knelt on the ground and spread it out. "We're right about... here," he said, pointing some way to the west of the village. "Where is Payne then?"

Matt studied the map, then shook his head. "Sorry, no dice. If I tell you, you won't let me go along and I'm going!"

José Hernandez exploded. "Matt, are you out of your mind? You can't go, you cretin—you're wounded!"

"The hell I can't, José," Matt retorted. Then he paused and took a deep breath to calm himself. "Thanks to these heroes," pointing with his good hand at the Bolivians, "I've got another life to live with my family. I've only got one hand, but I can still be a father and a husband. For that I'm grateful and I intend to make the most of that life. But right now, we still have to take care of another problem—Payne and Steele. And I can still shoot. I'm going. You'll need every gun."

Exasperated, Hernandez looked to Callahan. "Tom, you talk some sense into him."

Tom looked at the determined set of his friend's square jaw. "You old pirate, you've never passed up a chance to sail in harm's way, have you?"

Matt grinned. "Listen, I'd crawl over broken glass on my hands and knees— Whoops!" He raised up the bandaged stump of his left arm. "I mean, my *hand* and knees, to have a chance at Payne. Come on, Tom, you know what I've got to do."

Tom shook his head. "José, do you really expect me to talk sense into this guy? He's right, though, we'll need every gun we can get. And we don't have time to screw around. Anyhow, the ornery old bugger won't tell us squat if we don't let him come along."

"Okay," Matt said, "that's settled. Now, somebody give me a gun." Warrant Ramos handed Schmidt his personal sidearm, a SigSauer P220.

"Very nice, Enrique." Matt looked at Hernandez. "This is just like yours, José. Excellent," he said. "Should come in real handy. I only hope Payne gives me a chance to repay him for his past kindnesses." He took Ramirez's map, squatted down to spread it out, and motioned the Suarez cousins over for consultation. Hernandez served as translator as the team drew Payne's camp and its defenses in the dirt.

"Matt," said José, "Payne was in Chimoré camp yesterday and drove out with Nicholas Barton. Since Barton never came back, we can assume that he's a prisoner now. Or worse."

"Damn, that means Payne has substituted Nick for me. Poor bastard. I wouldn't wish that on anyone, even Barton. Probably have him tied up in the shack here," Matt indicated the location on the drawing of the camp, "so don't fire on it unless you can see your target."

***

Two hours later, Tom crouched behind cover and watched as the American soldiers moved silently through the jungle surrounding Payne's camp. The two camp guards appeared bored, hot, and uncomfortable. Weapons carelessly out of reach, they were too busy talking to each other to hear the stealthy footsteps behind them. Hodges and Ramos moved closer. Two knife blades flashed simultaneously and one quick slice across each exposed throat ended the uneven match up. Two targets down. Soldiers, like fighter pilots, were not inclined to give their enemies an even chance.

As Hodges and Ramos lowered the two bodies silently to the ground, the rest of the A Team stalked the camp. Whispers and hand signals indicated new orders. Gradually, the men moved into position.

The Special Forces troops opened up from all sides. Automatic fire poured into the camp. The few cartel gunmen who didn't die immediately, threw down their weapons and put their hands in the air.

Payne emerged from inside the shack, holding a pistol to Nicholas Barton's ribs. Barton's rounded shoulders drooped.

"Stop shooting or I'll kill him!" Payne screamed, moving slowly toward his Land Cruiser.

Matt Schmidt and Tom Callahan stepped into the compound directly between Payne and the vehicle.

"Don't listen to him! Shoot," screamed Nicholas Barton. Payne tightened his grip, choking Barton's words into a painful gurgle.

Pistol raised, Matt called out, "Payne, you slimy bastard! There's no way in the world that you're going to get away. One more murder won't help you. Let him go."

"Not a chance, asshole. You get out of my way, or I'll blow his lungs out!" The men stood still, glaring at each other.

"Payne, for God's sake. Lower your weapon and surrender," pleaded Tom.

"No chance, Callahan! I'm getting out of here, and I'm taking this pig with me."

Barton stomped on Payne's right foot and threw himself forward. Payne instinctively yanked upright and pulled the trigger.

Barton crumpled to the ground. Payne was silhouetted clearly against the shack. Two shots rang out. Payne, blood spurting from what used to be his head, collapsed heavily on top of Barton's inert body.

Chapter Thirty-Eight

Ambassador's Office
U.S. Embassy, La Paz

"I told you how to find him, now do it!" Patricia Pointer shouted into the phone. "Do I have to do all the thinking around here?" She slammed down the receiver.

"Well, Patricia, it seems as if you have much to learn about the fine art of delegation," said George Brent, as he strolled into the office, accompanied by Special Agents Griffen and Schwartz, and a stocky woman.

"George... Mr. Ambassador, this is a surprise!"

"I should imagine so," Brent said, looking around the office that was still technically his. All his pictures and mementos were boxed up in the basement, he supposed and replaced by Pointer's. He motioned for Griffen to close the door, then sat opposite the flustered chargé.

Brent motioned towards the other guest. "This is Joan Donnelly from State's security section." The Ambassador paused and looked Pointer in the eyes.

"Patricia, I've been hearing some disturbing news about what has happened down here since my rather abrupt departure."

"Sir, I can assure you things are moving along. We have had some set-backs, and we can't seem to locate Colonel Steele, but—"

"Patricia, how long have you been having an affair with Colonel Steele?"

Pointer blanched. "I don't know what you're talking about. Who told you such a thing?"

"Actually, it was Colleen Callahan."

"Well," Pointer exploded, "of course she would say something like that! Colleen Callahan, the electro-babe! You can't actually believe her?"

"So, you deny that you are or were having an affair with Colonel Steele?"

"Absolutely. Colonel Steele is a friend and a colleague, nothing more."

"Really? I rather thought you might say that so I called ahead to Mr. Griffen here and had him do some checking. To start off, he spoke to the Bolivian guards at your house and found that Colonel Steele had stayed the night on at least ten different occasions."

"That doesn't prove anything. It's a big house, with many bedrooms."

"Oh, come now, Patricia, we're all adults."

"And what of it?" she challenged. "If I were a man, nobody would care!"

"Other than lying to me about it just now, it wouldn't matter at all," Brent said in a mild voice. "Had you told me about it before, I would have asked you to stop. Failing that, to at least be discreet. Which, to your credit you were. I honestly had no idea. But that's not the point. This wasn't just an affair."

Her eyes narrowed. "What do you mean?"

Brent motioned to Henry Griffen who said, "The Bolivian police took fingerprints of the two men killed while trying to kidnap Colleen Callahan. One of the men turned out to be an ex-U.S. Army soldier named Carlos Montoya, who had been stationed in Germany and Panama before he got out. We think the bodies were stolen to prevent their identification."

"So?" Pointer said. "What has this got to do with anything?"

"Montoya was a good friend of Master Sergeant Don Payne, whom you may remember was brought down to Bolivia by Colonel Steele to work in the MILGROUP. Once we had that lead, we showed pictures of Payne and Montoya to survivors of the Marine House bombing and got positive IDs."

"You actually expect me to believe that the Marine House was bombed by Americans? Don't be absurd!"

"That's only part of it, Patricia," Brent said. She was playing it tough, as expected. "These were men deliberately brought down to Bolivia by your friend Steele. There is a growing body of evidence tying Steele in with a local *narcotraficante* cartel and the increase in killings and violence in Bolivia. It seems that Steele is a very naughty boy."

Pointer fell back in her chair, stunned. "Well," she croaked, "I guess we should have fired Steele after the ammunition was hijacked, after all." She tapped the papers on her desk with her index finger. "I can put this all back together, Mr. Ambassador, and fix our counternarcotics program."

"That's not really why I wanted to talk to you today, Patricia." Ambassador Brent placed a long-stemmed red rose on the desk and reminded himself not to say too much. "Do the names Burgess, Philby, and McLean mean anything to you?"

"No," she replied, tearing her eyes away from the rose. "I don't recall them.

Should I?"

"They were Soviet spies, Patricia, recruited off the campus of Cambridge University during the 1930s. They went on to work in British intelligence as moles. Eventually, after doing enormous damage, they were discovered, but escaped to Moscow. Now do you remember?"

She shrugged. "What are you getting at?"

"The information you were feeding to your lover certainly made his job easier. A very convenient arrangement for all parties. Pity those poor Marines!"

"*I never* told Billie anything," Pointer said.

"Patricia, or should I say, Rote Rose? You needn't pretend any longer. We're not entirely dull. The connections between the compromised San Ramon raid, your total access to all the embassy's intelligence sources and Steele's oh-so-easy success are simply too obvious now. You and he created a terrorist network here to tie into your European terrorist connections."

She sat at attention, arms crossed. "How absurd!"

294

Ambassador Brent watched her for a few moments. "We now have documents which indicate that you've been spying for years on all manner of things. In Bolivia, you've been passing information on our counternarcotics operations and plans to your contacts, who passed them back to the narcos through the narco-terrorist network. In return, Wallerein and other terrorist friends could funnel money into their own causes. Eventually, you must have decided to take a shortcut and give the information directly to your lover, Steele."

"Total rubbish!" Her eyes flashed. "Steele is a buffoon, an idiot. He's not capable of any of this. And you can't prove that I've done anything."

Brent locked eyes with her. "My original choice for DCM here had a fatal car accident just after his nomination was announced within the State Department. You were selected to take his place on very short notice. It occurs to me that when we look back at your rather successful career, we're going to find even more coincidences like that, courtesy of your friends in the Stasi."

The Ambassador motioned to Griffen. "Henry, as this embassy is legally U.S. territory, I think you should now allow Ms. Donnelly to read Ms. Pointer her rights, then arrest her for espionage against the United States and conspiracy to commit murder. You can return to the States on my aircraft."

She jumped to her feet. "No! You can't do this!"

Donnelly slid behind the desk and spun Pointer around. "Put your hands behind your back…"

After their departure, Brent picked up his phone and dialed the number of the Embassy General Services maintenance office. "General Services? This is Ambassador Brent. Yes, Sam, I'm back, thank you. Listen, Sam— Yes, I'm fine, thank you. Sam, I want you to have my office fumigated and cleaned, immediately and thoroughly. And get rid of these damned roses!"

Cochabamba, Bolivia

"Turn here," Tom Callahan told Captain Eduardo Ramirez. The two dusty Land Cruisers slowly rolled into the deserted traffic circle in front of the Hotel Cochabamba, then split up and continued down the streets flanking the hotel.

Five men dressed in ordinary street clothes got out of each vehicle and stretched, cramped from the three-hour drive from the base camp at Chimoré. Several wore nylon backpacks. All carried zippered pouch-bags, similar to a European-style man's purse. Each of the smaller bags contained a semiautomatic pistol; the larger ones, Uzis captured in the last firefight.

The two groups split and strode towards the hotel. Three men circled around the back and confirmed the presence of a certain red Land Cruiser with embassy plates in the Hotel parking lot. Then they positioned themselves in strategic spots to watch the entrance and exit. One of the men, left arm in a colorful sling, spoke softly into a small handheld radio as he leaned against a doorway.

The other seven drifted through the Hotel entryway and into the courtyard, some dropping behind to sit on park benches, others strolled across the courtyard to positions by the swimming pool and tennis court, until all entrances and exits were covered by at least two sets of eyes.

Tom, José, and Captain Ramirez climbed the stairs leading to the suite Colonel Billie D. Steele always occupied when in Cochabamba. Tom climbed the north stairs, Hernandez and Ramirez the south ones. Crouching low, the men crept down the corridor towards the door with pistols at the ready. Hushed voices filtered through the open window. At a hand signal from Hernandez, the three got set.

José stood, kicked the door open, and burst into the room. "Freeze!"

Colonel Billie Steele and Brigadier General Calleja froze, still seated at the coffee table.

"Stand up very slowly, Steele," said José, pistol pointed squarely at Steele's heart, "and keep your hands up nice and high where we can see them. You don't want to give me an excuse to waste you."

Steele stood slowly, then laughed, "You assholes should see your faces! Whoo, am I ever terrified!"

Tom smoothly shifted position around José and lowered his pistol. "Well, General Calleja, having you here certainly answers a lot of questions."

"What is the meaning of this outrage?" Calleja shouted. "I am a Bolivian Army general, and this is my country! You gringos can't go around pointing guns at me."

Tom stared him down. "General, with all due respect, the game is up. We know about you and your Cuban connection. Now we have incontrovertible proof of your involvement in drug trafficking with Steele."

Tom went to the table and glanced through the papers. "Looks like they were going through their records." Both of his friends nodded, keeping their eyes and weapons trained on the captives. "What happened, Steele? Did you catch the bank by surprise with not enough cash on hand for you and your partner here?" Steele scowled. "Too bad. Picking a crummy bank was just another one of your many bad decisions."

Waving the papers, Tom exploded, "Why, Steele? Why did you do this?"

"Up yours, Callahan, you bloody ring knocker. You're so damn smart, you tell me."

Tom shook his head. "Never mind, Steele, we'll find out at your court-martial."

He paused. "Or maybe Patricia Pointer's trial."

Steele turned pale. "What do you mean?"

"You didn't know she was a commie spy? And now works for Kurt Wallerein? I thought you had everything under control. Guess you aren't as clever as you thought. I talked with Ambassador Brent on the drive here. He had a nice little chat with her a couple of hours ago. She's on her way back to the States under arrest for espionage and conspiracy to murder."

"What? Patricia?"

"Don't worry, Steele. Your girlfriend was thinking of you to the end. She called you a buffoon and an idiot, among other things. She's right, too." Tom watched Steele shrivel in shock. "I don't have any more time for you right now. You're small potatoes now that we have our missing piece, your partner in crime, General Armando Calleja."

"Get the hell out of my country. I have nothing to say to you."

"Oh, I think you do have something to say, General, especially since we've caught you running narcotics. That makes you a criminal. And your involvement with Kurt Wallerein's international network makes you a terrorist."

Calleja drew himself to his full height. "I am no terrorist. I am a soldier."

"The last time I checked, General," Tom said, "the government of Bolivia was not at war with the government of the United States. Yet you know of plans for a terrorist attack on American soil. That makes you a terrorist."

Calleja remained silent.

Tom said, "You don't have to talk to me, General, that is correct." Tom picked up a phone and requested the hotel operator make a call to La Paz. "But I know a few people you will have to talk with." As he waited for the connection to be made, Tom's eyes were locked on to Calleja's.

"Mi general, this is Tom Callahan."

"Yes, Tom. I've been expecting your call," replied General Fernando Camacho, FAB, recently-promoted Chief of the Bolivian Estado Mayor, or Joint Chiefs of Staff, currently the ranking officer in the Bolivian military. "Ambassador Brent is here in my office right now. I understand the problem. Where are you?"

Tom summarized the past forty-eight hours.

"We still don't know all the details of what the organization in the States plans to do, but General Calleja does. He says he doesn't have to talk with me."

"Let me speak with him," Camacho ordered.

Tom motioned to Captain Ramirez to hand the extension phone to Calleja. "General Calleja, the *norteamericanos* have told me that you are involved in narcotics trafficking with Colonel Steele. But we can come back to that later. What concerns *El Presidente* now is this other connection into international terrorism."

"You've spoken with *El Presidente*?" asked Calleja.

"Of course I have. How could I not? A Bolivian general is conspiring with Fidel Castro and a gang of international assassins to commit a crime in the United States, and I'm supposed to keep it to myself?"

"I don't believe you," Calleja replied. "*El Presidente* is a friend of Fidel's."

"Well, friend or no friend, he's still the president of Bolivia. Do you seriously think *El Presidente* would stand by and let innocent people die, you idiot? Why in the world would you expect *El Presidente* to support such an act?"

"To avenge our socialist brothers in Cuba. We are Bolivian patriots, comrades-in-arms with the nation of Fidel—"

"Dios mío, Calleja," Camacho exploded. "What did Fidel do to you during the time you spent in Cuba, remove your brain? Haven't you read a newspaper in the past five years? Don't you know that things have changed? Communism has failed and Cuba is collapsing. Fidel is a desperate man. He is reduced to consorting with old terrorists to try to stay alive."

"I'm not a terrorist," Calleja protested. "I am a general in the Bolivian Army."

"And all generals in the Bolivian Army are under my command," shot back Camacho, "in case you had forgotten, General. You could be the greatest general since Simon Bolivar and still be ruined by becoming partners with *norteamericano* criminals, especially psychopathic *narcotraficantes!*" Camacho paused briefly. "Calleja, you will do the following: you will accompany Colonel Callahan to the Second Air Brigade headquarters where an aircraft will fly you both to La Paz. In the meantime, I will speak again to *El Presidente*. I'll meet you at El Alto airport, and we will have a chat in private. Then Colonel Callahan, you, and I will fly in the President's personal airplane to the United States where you will tell the American authorities everything that you know. Those are my orders. Is that clear, General?"

Calleja hesitated. He straightened to attention. "I will come to La Paz, but I must hear those other orders from *El Presidente* himself."

"All right, General. I'll speak to *El Presidente*. And Calleja," he added, "you say that you're a Bolivian patriot. You had better think

299

very hard about the consequences to your country if you fail to cooperate and a major terrorist strike happens in the United States."

As Calleja put the phone down, Steele lunged for the pistol in his briefcase, dove to his right, and got off one shot directly at Tom's head before two answering shots rang out.

Chapter Thirty-Nine

Washington, D.C.

Kurt Wallerein was both repelled and fascinated by the enormous vitality he saw and felt along the Mall that stretched from the Lincoln Memorial to the U.S. Capitol Building. Joggers and cyclists threaded through the pedestrians meandering along the gravel paths, picnickers spread out their lunches among those taking naps or reading books in the open air. People of all ages played soccer and softball on the Mall's grassy infields, while children darted around chasing pigeons. Open-sided commercial wagons were parked end-to-end along the boulevards as venders crowded in to hawk souvenirs and food to the throngs of workers and tourists who surged into this area every day. The muted roar of the persistent traffic underscored the whole scene.

Wallerein and Doctor Nikolai Yazov strolled the length of the enormous Mall, trying to get the feel for the area they were about to destroy.

They stopped and stood for a moment, gazing up the Mall at the Capitol. Wallerein studied the dome of the Capitol framed against the blue sky. He remembered hearing of an American novel where an airliner was crashed into the building, killing hundreds of government officials, effectively decapitating the American government. He tried to visualize an aircraft smashing the marble dome. It was an intriguing image. Maybe that writer had an idea. Perhaps not these particular government buildings, since what he wanted was massive civilian casualties. Other, bigger buildings in another major city perhaps. He'd have to think this through. He forced himself to shelve those ideas for the future. Wallerein's primary concern now was the weather. The low-pressure system currently over the Ohio Valley could bring thunderstorms, rain, and wind which would reduce the effect of the virus. He shrugged. It was more important to execute the plan as scheduled than to wait for a perfect day.

"Come, my friend," he said to the wiry Yazov. "Let's make our first visit to Washington memorable." Wallerein looked around again. "Not much longer. A quick flight tomorrow, then this city will be full of walking dead."

They continued across Maryland Avenue to the park across from the Botanical Gardens, where the Bartholdi Fountain gurgled. Wallerein sat on a bench and lit his pipe. He studied the fountain, another creation of the genius who built the Statue of Liberty, with its aquatic monsters, shells, and fish representing the elements of fire and light. Add two more elements to the picture he thought: fear and death. Victory was so close. This upcoming action would seal his place in the history of socialism and make him the undisputed leader of resistance everywhere.

They fell in with a group of tourists sporting cameras and souvenir bags and meandered with them around to the massive west face of the Capitol. They paused in front of the dome and gazed down the lush grassy Mall lined on both sides by imposing museums and governmental buildings. The richness of the architecture and the mathematically precise beauty of the city design reached out to his German heritage.

Wallerein and Yazov ambled around the Senate side of the Capitol and crossed to the Russell Building. Using forged passes that identified them as members of the congressional staff, they walked through the pathetic security. They spared only a quick glance for the high ceilings and well-lit entryways of the beautiful building as they walked down two flights of stairs to the subway. Wallerein again shook his head at the total lack of security on the Senate side. The House at least required visitors to walk through metal detectors, inadequate as that was. He had spent nearly his whole adult life circumventing security systems. Proper security was apparently too unwieldy and inconvenient for the comfort-loving Americans. The American arrogance was characteristic, a quaint legacy of bygone days when people obeyed rules, but incomprehensible in the world of the international terrorist.

On the Capitol subway, they sat with a couple from New Mexico and their two children, who were anxious about their upcoming meeting with their globe-trotting Representative. The rough, uneven brick walls of the Capitol sub-basement corridors reminded him of the catacombs under the Vatican where he had helped the Bulgarian government's hit men prepare for the shooting of the Pope in 1981. Wallerein and Yazov followed the exposed pipes and wiring leading to the heating and cooling vents and ducts. They passed hundreds of people along the way: young women dressed to the teeth, students and tourist delegations from all over the United States. Wallerein was surprised at the number of foreign tourists, especially the Japanese.

He took a moment to point out to Yazov a self-congratulatory exhibit about the design and construction of the Capitol Building on their way down the halls and out onto the enormous patio that surrounded the building. Wallerein savored one last look around before they walked to their waiting van.

Kershner Residence Rockville, Maryland

Lieutenant Colonel Mitch Kershner shook his head as he regarded his dining-room table that now supported an operations center. Coffee cups and papers littered the table as the two FBI Hostage Rescue Team (HRT) groups studied overhead photos of the neighborhood. The photos had been taken that morning from a Maryland State Police helicopter and were a godsend for the team, augmenting the detailed maps provided by the Rockville City Hall. The HRT leader, Special Agent Hugh Clark, was assigning approach routes.

A large-screen television sat on the coffee table. The picture was the front of the O'Malley place, taken from a mobile camera mounted in the upper story of the Drazev house across the street. Nothing and nobody had entered or left the house in the past thirty-six hours.

The phone rang. The group froze while Inspector Andrew Chin snatched it up. "Chin," he barked.

"Andy, this is Jacob Borenstein."

"Yes, sir." Chin motioned to the group for quiet and set up the speakerphone.

"I'm afraid this is a good news-bad news call. We've had a break—independent corroboration, from Bolivia of all places, that your 'friends' out there are for real. They've got an operation planned. And a nasty one, just like you suspected."

"Is that the good news or the bad news, sir?"

"You're right, Andy," the Deputy Director conceded, "none of this is very good. Anyhow, we'll have the source itself up from Bolivia this afternoon. We should have more for you then. In the meantime, the Director's in with the Attorney General working out how to approach this new situation. I'll get reinforcements out there quickly, including some helicopter support, and maybe some Hazmat suits. So, be careful. Dr. Lansky had access to some very nasty bugs. Keep an eye on the house, let me know when they show up, and we'll go from there."

"Yes, sir." Chin hung up and turned to address the group. "Okay, folks, that was our confirmation. In addition to saving the hostage, we need to keep two things in mind—we need to capture at least one terrorist alive. If they've planted a device already, we need to know its location so we can deactivate it." Heads nodded. "Also, we should assume that there are toxins in that house. So be careful with your explosives and your shooting. It won't do any good to get the bad guys if we start our own little biological version of Chernobyl."

"Oh, great," muttered Special Agent Clark. "How do we always end up with the crazies?"

"You think you feel bad," Chin responded with a grin, "Mitch Kershner and I are supposed to be students at the War College, rubbing elbows with the intellectual set, not out here in the trenches getting dirty with you hot shots."

The radio crackled. "A white Chrysler van is pulling around the entry into the neighborhood."

"Okay, people," said Chin, "move into position." He motioned to Kershner. "You can watch from upstairs."

On the television monitor, the white van drove into the carport. Eight men slowly got out and stretched as if cramped from a long drive.

They unloaded some bundles and headed to the door. A minute later, shots resounded, followed by several screams.

"Jesus, something's gone wrong." Chin grabbed for his radio. "Everybody move now!"

Kershner sprinted upstairs to his second-floor office window. He watched the FBI agents swarm in on the O'Malley house. Gunfire erupted, then died away.

Moments later, a Chevy van entered the alleyway behind the houses and drove towards the O'Malley house. The van hesitated, then slammed into reverse, and careened into some garbage cans. With all of the Rescue Team's attention focused on the house, Kershner was the only one in position to stop the vehicle.

He vaulted over the balcony handrail, dropped twelve feet to the ground, rolled, and jumped to his feet. The vehicle now roared down the alleyway. Kershner brought his weapon up in two hands and fired. The bullets shattered the window. The van plowed into his neighbor's fence, then righted itself and, skidding wildly, roared around the corner, spitting rocks and dirt in all directions.

Kershner cursed as he watched it speed off.

Andrew Chin and two agents came charging out of the O'Malley house. "Andy, get on your radio!" Kershner yelled. "That was Wallerein. A blue Chevy van, late model with Maryland plates."

Chin barked orders into his radio, then asked, "What happened, Mitch?"

"They drove into the alley, saw all the activity and bolted. I think I nailed the driver. Who started the shooting?"

"Lansky. He must have gotten the drop on the guard as the van pulled in. He started shooting as soon as they walked in the door. They got him, but not before he had killed two and wounded a couple of others."

Kershner shook his head. "Pretty good for a scientist. Got any of those assholes alive?"

"Only two. The others chose to fight it out with my guys. We think one of the survivors is Cuban intelligence."

Kershner swore softly. "Good luck getting a DGI guy to talk."

Chin cursed as reports came in on his radio. His agents found a blue van five blocks away that matched Kershner's description, complete with multiple bullet holes, copious amounts of spilt blood, and a corpse. But no Wallerein.

Chapter Forty

The White House
Washington, D.C.

Lieutenant Colonel Tom Callahan rose to attention as President Anthony Grafton strode into the meeting room, late from his prior meeting and already late for his next. The tall, sandy-haired President looked tired and slightly annoyed at this short notice, urgent meeting. He nodded at the men assembled around the table. Introductions were brief.

The President's still youthful face lit up with his trademark grin as he recognized the name of Tom Callahan.

"Ah, Colonel, you must be the famous young man that Ambassador Brent's so keen on. Excellent work bringing down Steele's narcotics organization." He turned to Jacob Borenstein. "May I assume since Colonel Callahan's here that this meeting is about the situation in Bolivia?"

"Only indirectly, Mr. President," Deputy Director Borenstein replied. Taking a deep breath, he plunged in. "This morning the FBI raided a house in Rockville, Maryland, occupied by a group of international terrorists. Six were killed outright, two wounded, both severely. We haven't been able to question the wounded yet, but all indications are that this cell was led by Kurt Wallerein and supported by Cuba's secret police."

"What!" The President's face drained of color. "Wallerein here in Washington? With Cubans? That's the second time in three days that his name has come up. The CIA just briefed me two weeks ago that Wallerein and his pals had been defanged. '...By the rippling fall of the communist world,' I think was their lovely phrase." He paused. "Another gem from our friends at Langley. Did you get him, Jacob?"

"No, sir. Unfortunately, Wallerein was outside the house when we went in. Colonel Kershner here saw Wallerein's van making its escape and shot it up. We think, hope actually, that some of the blood inside is Wallerein's." He handed a sheaf of papers to the President. "We've managed to identify several of them from our files. One of the wounded is a Cuban intelligence colonel, the other a former Stasi major. The dead man with Wallerein was a Russian scientist named Nikolai Yazov. This was definitely the terrorist varsity, Mr. President."

The President stared hard at Borenstein. "Why were they here in Rockville?"

Borenstein glanced at his notes, then met the President's eyes. "They were planning a massive terrorist action, involving a biological agent. They intend to attack during festivities surrounding the arrival of the tall ships into Baltimore harbor this weekend."

The President slumped back in his chair, closed his eyes and swore. Muttering curses, he leaned forward and stabbed at his intercom. "Mildred, get the Vice President over here right now. And the Chief of Staff." He took the sheaf of papers that Borenstein handed him and began to read.

Grafton looked up from the notes, "Wallerein must be one vicious son-of-a-bitch. There will be tens of thousands of spectators in the Inner Harbor." He looked at Kershner. "I hope you hurt him badly, Colonel. Maybe he'll go crawl in a hole somewhere and just die."

Vice President Hector Cardenas and the Chief of Staff arrived simultaneously.

President Grafton waved them into chairs.

"Hector, the FBI has something I need you to hear. Okay, Jacob, let them have it." Borenstein briefly recounted the situation.

The Vice President listened, his dark Latin eyes flashing. "What makes you think it's Wallerein?"

"Mr. Vice President, Colonel Kershner is a Special Forces officer and counterterrorism expert for the Army. He has taught counterterrorism both here and in Germany. He spotted Wallerein and his men out in Maryland and reported it to us through Inspector Chin here."

"Mr. Vice President," Kershner said, "I recognized Wallerein. There is no doubt in my military mind. It's him, all right."

Borenstein went on, "Mr. President, it gets worse. Wallerein had Dr. Christopher Lansky with him, bound and gagged. The terrorists had beaten him pretty badly. And the dead Russian, Yazov, was a top biological weapons expert with Biopreparat before he defected."

"Lansky? Isn't he our expert at Fort Detrick?"

"Yes, Mr. President."

The President swore again.

Borenstein said, "Sir, we had the terrorist safe house staked out, waiting for Wallerein to come back. Apparently, Dr. Lansky got loose, grabbed a gun and opened up on his captors. My men charged in to try to rescue the doctor and salvage what they could of the operation. We found some planning documents and several maps of the Baltimore/Washington area. Even aerial charts."

"What about Lansky?" asked Cardenas.

Borenstein shook his head. "Dead. I've contacted the Army at Fort Detrick. We have agents scouring the doctor's office and home right now. Apparently, Wallerein's plan involved obtaining some type of virus from Fort Detrick and using it in on the American public."

"Mr. President," General Trenton spoke up, "we have corroboration of this from a Bolivian army general brought here for questioning by Colonel Callahan."

"Mr. President," said Tom Callahan, "General Calleja was connected with the Cubans in Bolivia." He recounted everything he knew. "Calleja said they planned another attack on Washington. What the exact target was, he hadn't been told."

"You heard this report yourself, Colonel?"

"Yes, sir. General Calleja considers himself a true Bolivian patriot. He was helping the druggies in order to cause more problems for the United States in Latin America. Once the Bolivian president showed him the error of his thinking, he spilled his guts and told us everything."

"So the President of Bolivia knows about this?" Grafton scowled. "A man who spent years in Cuba and is proud of it? The one time I met this guy, he didn't seem too happy to be dealing with Yanquis. He acted like he was only signing the drug accord for the money. I would have thought he'd be glad to hear about Americans dying in the streets."

"Mr. President, with all due respect," Tom said softly, "you don't have to be an American to be appalled by mass murder."

The President looked thoughtfully at Tom. "You're right, Colonel. I apologize for that remark." Grafton turned back to Jacob Borenstein. "But Christopher Lansky, of all people—"

Borenstein gestured towards Tom and Kershner. "Sir, these men aren't cleared—"

The President waved him silent. "These men, Jacob, have already risked their lives to stop these attacks. They deserve to know what we're up against. And I don't think they're commie spies." He drew a deep breath, "Gentlemen, Christopher Lansky is—or was—the U.S. Army's top biological research scientist, an expert in deadly pathogens. He was working on a highly classified program on the Machupo virus, trying to duplicate some of the research the Russians are conducting at their Biopreparat facilities."

Tom winced. Biopreparat again. "Mr. President," Tom heard himself say, "Ambassador Brent thinks that our government is riddled with highly placed moles. I'm just a fighter pilot, but this link between Lansky and Fort Detrick, Yazov and Biopreparat, Cuba, Bolivia and Wallerein seems to defy coincidence."

The President seemed surprised. "Jacob?"

Borenstein shot a guarded look at Tom. "That thought has also occurred to our intelligence people. We're looking into it, Mr. President."

Grafton turned back to Tom and studied his face for a moment. "Just a fighter pilot, Colonel?"

Tom felt his face flush. "Sir, I spent five months in Saudi during the Gulf War. We were convinced that Saddam was planning to use some kind of biological or chemical warfare on us. According to our intel at the time, Saddam's programs were all set up by scientists from Biopreparat."

President Grafton rubbed his face, as if trying to wipe away this latest crisis. "All right, gentlemen, where do we go from here?"

The Vice President said, "Why don't you call in the Cuban ambassador, tell him what we know and that any offensive action in this country will result in an immediate counterstrike against Cuba?"

Borenstein shook his head. "We've already thought of that, sir. It won't work; there's no time. Anyhow, the ambassador doesn't know anything. If he did, he'd have taken his family on some sort of disguised vacation somewhere far away from here during the attack. Fidel's kept him in the dark."

"Well, we sure as hell don't know much, and we can't take 'vacations' either," Grafton snarled. "The target could be anywhere from the Metro to the Redskins' football game this weekend. We have to assume the worst—that Wallerein knew about Lansky's research on the Machupo II virus and now has possession of at least some of it." He turned to his chief of staff and started barking orders. "Get the Secretary of State and the CIA Director here ASAP. We'll need to see if they can squeeze some of their assets overseas to get us some information on Wallerein's plans. Then clear my calendar for the rest of the day. Tomorrow, too." The chief of staff disappeared.

"Hector, I need you to call the Bolivian president. Tell him how much we appreciate his help. Give him my apologies and assure him that I will be in touch just as soon as this mess is cleared up. Then work out some possible reactions with Cuba should the worst happen. We need to move quickly but quietly, to avoid a mass panic."

Grafton leaned forward to address the group. "Gentlemen, we appreciate what you've managed to accomplish so far. But it's not good enough. Right now I can only think about one thing: that Kurt Wallerein, probably the most dangerous man in the world, is running around the capital of our nation right now, carrying what is possibly the most lethal virus in the world. He must be stopped." Grafton's hand slammed his desk. "Jacob, do whatever it takes to get the information we need from those prisoners. And get that bastard Wallerein!"

311

Chapter Forty-One

Outside the White House

After being ushered out of the White House, Tom Callahan and Mitch Kershner sat in Kershner's Ford Explorer and threaded their way through heavy D.C. traffic under threatening skies towards Rockville.

"It strikes me that the FBI is thinking too much like the FBI and not enough like Wallerein," Mitch said. "The question should be, what is Wallerein trying to do here?"

"There's no time. They're swamped with information," Tom said, trying to think this through. "Even aerial charts..."

Click.

He sat up straight. "How would you do it if you were Wallerein?"

"One thing's for sure, he's not going to be satisfied with a canister in a building air conditioning system."

Tom tapped the command pilot wings pinned on his uniform blouse. "Once more, ground pounder, how would you do an aerosol dispersal between two cities sixty miles apart?"

Mitch's heavy-lidded eyes widened. "Spray plane."

"Bingo! A plane could cover a huge swath of territory. It's original, which seems important to our favorite terrorist. Very much his style, too. Why settle for a few hundred dead Americans from a spray inside a building when you can go for the big-time?" Tom cursed softly. "Where's the closest airport to your house?"

"About thirty miles northwest west of here."

"Hit it, pal," commanded Tom. "If this guy gets airborne, he could go anywhere on the East Coast—we'll never catch him."

Kershner instinctively checked his rear-view mirror, then floored the accelerator pedal and leaned on the horn. "Hold on, partner." He tossed Tom his cell phone. "I'll handle the Pony Express part. You call General Trenton."

As they skidded around the turn into the winding airport entryway thirty minutes later, they could see in the distance a man hobbling towards a red-and-white Piper Pawnee crop duster parked in front of the main hangar.

"Wallerein!" yelled Mitch. "God! If I just had a rifle."

"Across the field, Mitch! Cut him off."

Kershner swore and swung the wheel. The Explorer leapt off the tarmac into the field and crashed through the weeds, splashing sheets of muddy water. As they bounced across the rutted field, they could see Wallerein open the canopy and climb in. Clouds of smoke exploded from the engine. Wallerein pulled the cockpit window shut and the plane began to move.

Tom gauged the distance between them as Wallerein accelerated down the taxiway. "We'll never catch him, Mitch. Get me to the ramp over by the hangar. Maybe I can chase him in one of the other planes."

Kershner swerved and skidded the Explorer around. He gunned the engine and raced towards the ramp, careening around several crater-like pot-holes. The powerful Ford roared onto the ramp. Kershner slammed on the brakes, fighting a skid as he rounded the hangar. They came face-to-face with a startled woman crouched over a man stretched out on the tarmac.

"My husband's hurt!" she screamed as they slammed to a stop on the slick wet concrete.

Tom jumped from the car and pointed at the Piper that was just breaking ground. "Did you see that guy?"

"He's the one that hit my husband."

Mitch knelt beside the injured man. He lay still, blood running down his face, mixing with the rain. The name stitched over his pocket said "Benny". He groaned, then opened his eyes.

"Hold on, pal," said Mitch, carefully wiping away some of the blood with his handkerchief. "You've got quite a knot on your head."

Mitch turned to the woman. "Scalp wounds always bleed like the dickens. Looks worse than it is, ma'am."

"What happened, Benny?" Tom asked, trying hard to appear calm and patient.

"He tried to force me to connect some cylinders to his plane," Benny said, voice weak and slow. "I told him I couldn't, so he smashed me with his pistol."

"He's a terrorist trying to escape. The FBI caught the rest of his group. I need a plane to catch him."

Benny eyed the ribbons on Tom's uniform blouse. "Fighter pilot?"

"Yes, sir."

Benny managed a wan smile. "I was a crew chief on F-100s in 'Nam."

"Listen, Benny," Tom said, "this guy has murdered hundreds of people. An hour ago, the President told me that he's the most dangerous man in the world. We've got to stop him!"

Benny thought for a second. "Can you handle a tail dragger?" Tom nodded.

"Then take the glider tow-plane." Benny pointed to another Piper. "I flew it this morning. It's fuel injected and has a bigger engine than his. You'll have about twenty knots on him. Comm radio's broke, though."

"Thanks, Benny."

"Just get the bastard, Colonel."

Tom and Mitch sprinted across the tarmac. Tom peeled off his uniform blouse and tossed it to Mitch, then climbed up the wing root.

"There he is!" Tom pointed at Wallerein's plane, now heading east under rapidly building clouds. "Keep your eyes on him while I strap in and get this beast ready to fly."

Tom scanned the instrument panel, which was surprisingly complete. Most "ag" planes were pretty basic, not designed to fly in heavy weather. He looked out at the rapidly deteriorating conditions. He was sure as hell going to fly in the weather today. He took a deep breath and settled in.

"Call General Trenton," he said to Kershner. "Get him to send up some help. Choppers from Andrews or something. I'll be squawking emergency so the radar people can track me."

Mitch nodded, slapped Tom's shoulder and hopped off the wing.

"Clear!" Tom shouted as he twisted the manual ignition switch. The engine rumbled and coughed to life, accompanied by rolling puffs of bluish smoke.

Mitch pointed out the receding speck, low on the horizon. Tom squinted until he located Wallerein and gave a thumbs-up. He added power and swung the aircraft around to head down the taxiway.

He took off and headed east, straining his eyes ahead to pick Wallerein's plane out of the irregular undercast. There was no telling where the German would head to make good his escape.

The question was if—and it was a big if—if he caught Wallerein's plane, what then? He had precious few options: 1) Follow—or try to follow in this muck they were flying through until Wallerein either landed or crashed; 2) try to clip a piece off Wallerein's plane; 3) or simply ram the Pawnee. Option number one was the preferred plan, but the most difficult in these weather conditions; number two was bloody unlikely to happen, except by accident in this weather; number three was suicidal.

Tom leveled off at 2500 feet, skimming just below the base of the clouds. He left the power up as long as he dared to milk every possible knot from the engine. He rolled into a shallow turn to get a better view below through the striated, chaotic cloud levels. Where was Wallerein? He couldn't be far ahead....

There! A little dot below and about three miles east. *Tally-ho, you son-of-a-bitch!*

Wallerein started a turn to the left to avoid a monstrous black cumulonimbus thunder-bumper. Tom risked another quick cross-check of the instrument panel. Wallerein stayed low, trying to keep off the radar, but mostly trying to find holes in the clouds.

Tom checked his transponder, set at 7700, the emergency code. The air traffic controllers must be screaming at him on every available frequency. Two crop dusters flying east across one of the busiest air corridors in the country would make the controllers apoplectic. General

315

Trenton must have reached the FAA by now to organize a posse. Tom just had to hold on.

The sky darkened; Tom closed on Wallerein. Heavy gray storm clouds billowed high into the atmosphere. The little plane bucked and tossed in the savage winds. Tom swung into a descending turn that brought Wallerein's plane into closer focus.

Watch the rate of closure. Don't let him see you yet, Tommy boy.

Tom slipped in and out of the clouds. Vertical air currents bounced the aircraft around like the toy that it was. His head banged against the canopy. Rain peppered the aircraft. Another shudder and hard bounce. He tightened his harness and re-checked the pitot heat and defroster. A maelstrom of swirling clouds. Jesus, this was turning into a mess.

Tom couldn't tell where the sky ended and the ground began. No way a desert-trained pilot like Wallerein could fly for long in this muck.

The storm rushed at them with a fury. The clouds reached up and swallowed Wallerein's airplane.

Damn it! One sure way to get killed was to fly into a cloud that contained another airplane. Tom felt his adrenaline surge. His pulse pounded. He could feel the sweat rolling down his back. He fought his instincts and followed Wallerein into the clouds, blind.

After an eternity, they broke out in a hole that offered a ragged glimpse of the horizon. Wallerein's plane was nose down, almost inverted.

Tom watched in fascination. He hoped Wallerein had lost control and would simply auger in. To his dismay, the plane's nose popped up and the wings righted. Wallerein was pulling G so hard that vapor condensed from the air passing over his wings. The vapor stopped; back to level flight.

Damn! Tom again slid down the rejoin line, carefully closing on Wallerein's left side.

Anchored in position off the stubby wing, Tom peered over to see Wallerein's angry face glaring back. Tom pointed at him, then down to the ground.

Wallerein unfastened the Pawnee's left window and aimed a pistol directly at Tom's head.

Two bullet holes suddenly appeared in Tom's canopy, barely missing him. He pulled on the stick to get the nose up, then rolled over Wallerein's plane, sliding in behind on the opposite wing. Wonderful! Here he was in a spray plane fighting the Red Baron who had the only gun.

Tom slid back and down and took up position in a loose close trail, certain that Wallerein couldn't see him. Maintaining visual contact was hard enough in weather like this when the leader wanted you to stay with him—nearly impossible when he wanted you gone.

Tom debated sliding in to cut the horizontal stabilizer with the prop. A savage bounce and roll of both the tiny planes answered that question. Better to just stick with him and hope for the transponder to beacon in the cavalry.

Wallerein led him down through the dark sodden clouds, the rain crashing into Tom's windscreen, distorting his forward vision. The ragged cloud tops raced by with the illusion of tremendous speed. They plunged through more clouds. Back out. Rivulets of sweat trickled down his face and neck, burning his eyes.

They exploded out of the clouds, still descending. The planes were over rolling land now. Pelting rain and screaming wind hammered them. Pine trees reached up for them out of the rocky slopes.

Suddenly, the ground split and fell away into a deep ravine. Quicker than thought, Tom had the stick down and over and sliced into the ravine to follow.

God! If there are any high-power lines around here, we're both dead. Wallerein crested a small rise and the Chesapeake Bay burst out beneath them.

Through a rip in the clouds, Tom caught a glimpse of a tanker passing under the Chesapeake-Annapolis Bay Bridge off his left wing.

He winced as a flock of seagulls whizzed right under his nose. More gray clouds. Slanted clouds forced Wallerein down until they raced along less than fifty feet above the water. Wallerein turned left. Clearly lost. Trying to maneuver out of the weather and lose his pursuer.

The clouds swallowed them again. They were alone together, all visual cues lost.

No up, no down. Two creatures locked in a world of gray cotton.

The clouds thinned. Tom glimpsed a ragged patch of the Bay below. Very close. He tried to cut the separation as they skimmed the waves, visibility improving just a bit.

Holy Mother, what's that? Instinctively, Tom rolled left.

He swore again as the Bay Bridge flashed overhead. On the other side, no Red Baron. Tom rolled into enough of a turn so that he could look behind him.

On the water's surface at the base of the Bridge, a crumpled ball of twisted metal and fabric disappeared in a fireball of orange flames and black smoke.

Tom tried to circle back and make another pass but the Bridge was now shrouded in clouds. He rolled out heading away from the Bridge and felt his strained muscles relax. Wallerein was most certainly dead. Mission accomplished—or it would be when he got himself home in one piece.

A glance at the instruments confirmed his suspicions—the attitude indicator had tumbled and was completely useless. He saw the Salisbury airport approach aid frequency taped to the panel. Benny must do a lot of spraying on the Eastern Shore. Tom dialed the frequency into the VOR and listened for the identifier.

Satisfied, he smoothly added power and gently pulled back on the stick to start his climb back into the weather. Needle, ball, and airspeed, just like Harvey Walters had taught him two decades before.

The drivers on the bridge concentrated on the traffic. Nobody saw or reported the crash. Quiet returned to the Bay.

Wreckage floated on the oily water. A body surfaced face down and bobbed nearby as it swirled for a moment in the eddies around the bridge abutment, then slid into the strong current. A large private yacht appeared out of the mist, nearly striking the wreckage. The trailing wake slapped at the pieces. The body flipped over. The man choked, and gasped for breath. His eyes opened.

Chapter Forty-Two

The White House
One Week Later

"That was a lovely dinner, Mr. President," said Tom Callahan. "Thank you."

President Grafton settled back in his easy chair. He waved off the thanks. "No,

Tom, this is one dinner Madeline and I appreciate being able to give." Raising his glass, he addressed his guests. "Thank you all for coming here tonight. The country owes a debt to the members of MILGROUP-Bolivia and your friends and colleagues. That debt can never be repaid." Vice President and Mrs. Cardenas, and General and Mrs. Trenton echoed the sentiment.

"Thank you, Mr. President," said Tom. "But I would feel better if we had found Wallerein's body."

The President waved him off. "The FBI and Coast Guard have searched the Chesapeake from the bridge south to Norfolk. Nothing. And you yourself saw the plane explode, Tom. By now, Kurt Wallerein is crab food."

"Mr. President," Colleen said, "that phone call you made to the Bolivian president was all the thanks Tom and I need. When he waived the residency requirement, the adoption papers went through at warp speed, finalized before we could even get back to pick up our new son."

"Colleen," the First Lady asked, "do you ever get to hold the baby or does Tom keep him all to himself?"

Colleen laughed.

"So," the President said with a chuckle, "Tom and Colleen get a baby, José gets command of the MILGROUP. And you, Matt, are you really ready to settle down at the Naval Postgraduate School?"

Matt nodded. "That would make me mighty happy, Mr. President. Then again, I'm already pretty happy just being alive. Thank you again, sir."

"I still don't understand Steele's motivation for all those terrible things," Madeline Grafton said. "How can an American officer think like that?"

"Well, ma'am, he won't be much of a problem for a long, long time," Matt said with great satisfaction.

"Actually, Matt, he's a bit of a problem for me right now," said the President. "The Bolivian government is both embarrassed and outraged by what Steele did in Bolivia and wants to put him on trial there instead of here in the States." He paused.

"Of course, this has been complicated by his wound. You gentlemen wouldn't care to discuss that now, would you?"

Steele had been severely wounded by two rounds from José's powerful pistol. Only quick work by Sergeant Ibarra had saved Steele's life. Steele had lost his arm and faced a long, painful recovery. Many in the embassy suspected that Hernandez, a recognized small arms expert, had planned it that way.

José and Tom silently returned the President's gaze.

Tom cleared his throat. "I'm sure glad José's a better shot than Steele is."

"I agree there," Grafton said. "And we learned a relatively cheap lesson. I now appreciate the severity and timeliness of the issue of these chemical and biological weapons in the hands of terrorists. We need to address the bioweapon proliferation question more closely. Clearly I need someone to be my advisor to help sort through the issues." He looked directly at Tom. "I want you here in the White House."

Flustered, Tom said, "But sir, these are medical issues. You need a physician, not a fighter pilot."

The President smiled. "My wife is a physician. That base is covered. No, I need a military advisor whose judgment, not to mention integrity, I trust."

Tom took a deep breath and tried again. "Mr. President, you have experts and organizations already in place to advise you. I have a squadron command waiting for me."

"Fighter squadrons are commanded by lieutenant colonels," said the president. "I have advised the Air Force that I expect to see your name on the colonels list which happens to be coming out next month. I need you to help lead this administration in coming to grips with these terrible weapons. I believe it is the imperative of our time."

Confused, Tom looked to General Trenton, who nodded. Damn. "Yes, sir."

***

Colleen, feeling light-headed, excused herself and headed for the ladies' room.

Madeline Grafton followed her.

"Colleen, do you feel all right?" Madeline asked as Colleen applied a cool compress to her face.

"I'm okay now, I think," she said with a weak smile. "I've just got a touch of jet lag, or maybe the flu. Ever since my last trip to Panama, I've felt nauseated and a little dizzy."

The First Lady arched her eyebrows. "And how long has that been?"

"Almost three weeks. Tommy and I had a wonderful weekend in a fabulous beach resort." Colleen smiled at the memories of that incandescent reunion. "I've been sick ever since. Probably from the irregular hours with the new baby and too much flying. I just don't understand why I'm taking so long to shake it off."

The First Lady smiled. "Speaking as a physician, I'd like you to come upstairs to my office. My medical bag's there. I have a kit that I want to show you and a quick test to run. After that, I think we need to talk."

Thirty minutes later as the women re-entered the room, they could hear the President and his dinner guests discussing new ideas about dealing with proliferation.

"More talk about proliferation?" Colleen teased her husband. Then she smiled as she took his hand. "Well, Colonel, I think we're going to have a little proliferation issue of our own in about eight months."

***

In a hospital room in Easton, Maryland, an unconscious, unnamed man lay in a darkened room. His chart recorded multiple broken bones, massive bruises, and the effects of exposure from being immersed in the Chesapeake. Also noted was a bullet wound in his leg.

The End

Author's Notes

The Cochabamba Conspiracy is a novel, a blend of fact and fiction. None of the Military Group (MILGROUP) members exist as depicted in this manuscript—they are all composites of people I had the honor (or misfortune) to serve with during the course of my service in the U.S. Air Force.

Bolivia is a country of staggering beauty filled with wonderful people. The grinding poverty endured by so many Bolivians has been largely inflicted by decades of corrupt government and foolish wars. When the people finally get the stable leadership they deserve, Bolivia should start to fulfill its promise.

Many of the events in The Cochabamba Conspiracy actually happened. Other events have been created or altered to fit the storyline or to minimize embarrassment to the original participants.

I owe many thanks to Carolyn Ahern, PhD, MBA. More thanks go to Carol Colenda, PhD, and Linda Sonna, PhD for their expertise in psychology and unrestrained support; Wing Commander Bob Radley, RAF, Officer Commanding, Empire Test Pilot School, RAF Boscomb Down, England, for his technical evaluation; Lt. Colonel Jeff Trenton, USAF(ret); David Scher; Phaedra Greenwood and "my ladies" in our Taos writers' group; and Bill Ratliffe, PhD, Senior Research Fellow and Curator of the Latin American Collection at the Hoover Institution at Stanford University. Also, my wife, Linda, kept me "on course-on glide path" throughout the prolonged writing of this manuscript. It would not have been written without her.

To my military compadres in the U.S. Embassy-La Paz, SOUTHCOM, and the Pentagon who made my tour in Bolivia the great experience it turned out to be: Dave Hunt, Ed Lehre, Paco Alvarez, Skip Woodward, Rick Bevington, Joe Furloni, Jim Farris, Tom Betts, and Dennis Keller—Gracias.

Great care has been taken to eliminate factual errors. Any such errors are mine and mine alone.

www.ingramcontent.com/pod-product-compliance
Lightning Source LLC
Chambersburg PA
CBHW030928260626
47169CB00002B/407